Colors of the Wheel

By Randy Kraft

Copyright © 2014 by Randy Kraft

ISBN 978-0-7414-9990-5

Printed in the United States of America

Published January 2014

INFINITY PUBLISHING
1094 New DeHaven Street, Suite 100
West Conshohocken, PA 19428-2713
Toll-free (877) BUY BOOK
Local Phone (610) 941-9999
Fax (610) 941-9959
Info@buybooksontheweb.com
www.buybooksontheweb.com

My old man died in a fine big house.
My ma died in a shack.
I wonder where I'm going to die.
Being neither white nor black.

Langston Hughes

2013

And when is there time to remember, to sift, to weigh,
to estimate, to total?
Tillie Olsen

They are all present in the small courtroom, positioned like stage props against dark wood paneling, illuminated by recessed lighting. Keisha sits front and center, facing the judge's stand, flanked by her lawyers.

Keisha's adopted parents, Margo and Daniel McGraw, are seated directly behind her, in the first row, Daniel just off the side aisle, strategically placed to catch a glimpse of her face now and then. Margo's closest friend, Nina, is seated to Margo's right, with her daughters, Emma and Jennifer, who are surrogate older sisters to Keisha. A close family friend, Grace, and her daughters, Leah and Becky, sit behind them.

They have managed their schedules to be there for several days, in a courtroom in Oakland, California, not only to show their support, but because they all belong there.

They wear black or brown or similarly somber colors, no patterns or accents, with the intention to appear dignified, discreet, as if to honor the seriousness of the proceedings and, by so doing, cement their faith in Keisha's innocence.

The only person missing is Mrs. Elliott, Keisha's adopted grandmother, and Keisha is glad she is not there to witness, although her absence tears at her heart. What might she think of her granddaughter's situation? Where might she have landed on the scale of guilt to innocence? Even as she ponders the question, she knows the answer.

At the defense table, Nina's husband Barrett, Keisha's honorary uncle, serves as second chair, although he is not a litigator. He researched and hired the defense attorney, a stately white lawyer with a swath of white hair like a symphony conductor, who has an excellent reputation defending the otherwise defenseless and who has orchestrated every aspect of the hearing. Daniel pleaded with Barrett to stay close to the case, and he has taken leave from his firm to do so.

Seated further back, alone, but prominently positioned dead center, as if a bearing wall, is a well-known race-relations advocate. He has made himself available to the defense team, although not officially, and without recompense, and he sits tall in his seat, attentive, with a notebook on his lap filled with scribbles, his presence a constant reminder to the court that more is at stake than a prolonged trial of one young woman.

Others fill the room: extended family members, the supporters or the outraged, and those whom Barrett has taken to calling the groupies, in attendance daily to observe the proceedings and report via texts or tweets or blog posts. For these, the truth and the outcome mean far less than the staging of the play, a theater for personal or political agendas.

Keisha, the main attraction of this drama, sits stony still. At twenty-two years of age, she still seems a girl, with the slight build and soft shoulders of a rag doll. In contrast, however, and in defiance of her lawyer's admonition, her wild mane of hair fluffs around her head, an effect softened only by a wide multi-colored headband, so that she seems a cross between a washerwoman and an African queen. She stares straight ahead and reveals nothing of what she is feeling – neither the nearly hysterical fear that has been her companion for months, nor the disdain she clutches deep within for what is happening to her, as if what happened wasn't enough.

The proceedings have come to an end. Everyone knows what occurred that night last fall, the night of President Obama's second election. No one has refuted the findings. Today, the judge will render his decision whether Keisha goes to trial. Barrett says it should never have come to this, politics having compromised the court, but here they are, because a black girl stood her ground against a white boy and such things cannot be dismissed without proper and public consideration, no matter the facts.

As they all rise to welcome the judge, Keisha turns her head ever so slightly to peer behind her at her makeshift family: her black and white friends and dear ones. Mostly brown, she the darkest amid their color wheel. She remains expressionless, but she catches Margo's eyes and smiles through her own to convince her mother, once again, that she is not to blame. Keisha has not and cannot assign blame to anyone, beyond the boy who assaulted her, and she knows what is happening here is much more about much more than one incident.

She turns back and reclaims the poker-faced expression she has been instructed to maintain. She takes a deep but inaudible breath. Like the sand castles she built as a child when vacationing at the beach on Long Island, like the hundreds, perhaps thousands of drawings in sketchbooks now in storage boxes, and the many paintings started and scrapped at art school in her quest to fulfill her talent, her entire existence has become past tense. And, like those boxes in the basement, dreams and mysteries stored away, for the moment.

She is a product of everyone in that courtroom: all aspirations and disappointments coming to rest on this one semi-orphan. Her defense team has been determined to ensure that the hearing is not a dictate on race, but, in the end, it is, because, in the end, everything is about race.

Keisha knows this better than anyone. She is the sum total of the lives of all her caretakers and friends, the progeny of everyone in the room, and then some.

Keisha reaches for a pen and scribbles on Barrett's note pad: *How long will we wait?* She refers to the delayed presence of the judge. Barrett smiles. Out of the mouths of babes, he thinks, before he inscribes his answer: *As long as it takes.*

Grace Brown/1990

Wisely and slow, they stumble that run fast.
William Shakespeare

"Slow down, Grace."

Grace turned to see her friend Delia squeezing her oval body into the triangular wedge of the revolving door that will glide them out of Riverside Methodist Hospital. Together, with hardly a nudge, rubber edges swooshed as they pressed through the revolution to the street. Clouds blurred the diminishing daylight; they squinted nonetheless at the glare, as they do every day, at the end of the day, released from the prison of halogen lighting.

"Ate your sandwich at the desk?" Delia asked as they emerged.

"Computer class."

Delia rolled her nearly black eyes. "I have got to get to that. Been on top of my to-do list for months, but something else always knocks it out of place."

"We have to pass the proficiency exam."

"Don't I know it. This stuff confuses me to distraction, but if I don't get it, I'll end up back on bedpans. I just haven't had time for class, much less study."

Grace nodded in agreement as they walked in tandem toward the bus stop. A line-up of hospital personnel, their white, green or blue uniforms peeking out of light-weight coats or jackets, bunched together like a bouquet in preparation to board a city bus that was at that moment easing into place, aligning itself slowly to the red-painted curb before it came to a halt with a shudder.

"Oh good, no wait today," Delia said with a broad smile, and Grace was reminded that despite the daily toil and the difficulties of being a single mother, and despite the regular griping, Delia was rarely ruffled, and she appreciated the little things, which Grace found especially endearing.

They boarded the bus, craned their necks around the crowd to see what seats might be available and eased their way toward the back, slipping into the last row. In unison, they settled their bags at their feet and released the top button of their coats. Anyone watching might have assumed them to be related, or the oldest of friends, as they moved as one: women who live similar lives, in similar skin.

Air at the back of the bus was stifling, the engine beneath their seats reverberating like a weary cannon. Passengers forced to stand leaned forward and retorted like marionettes as the bus snaked around rush hour traffic and jolted to a stop every three or four blocks. Few spoke, eyes buried in newspapers, thoughts in late day reverie, the bus a rumbling tunnel from which they escaped their working selves to the private, the two personas separated as distinctly as seats on either side of the aisle.

Delia was a heavy-set, bark-brown woman with a cherubic face framed by tendrils of graying curly hair that never quite stayed put in the rubber bands meant to hold a ponytail. Her complexion was smooth and shiny, although deep smile lines crenellated the tender membrane around her eyes. As she was generally a bit disheveled, especially at the end of the workday, she appeared older than her forty-five years. Seated at the back of the bus, she might have been perceived to be a maid instead of an experienced nurse.

In contrast, Grace was tall, slim and light brown, like a stick of cinnamon. Her long narrow legs, wiry arms, and tapered neck were reminiscent of a Modigliani model, with deep-set, light brown eyes that surreptitiously took in everything in her midst. Dark, thick, wavy hair crept behind tiny unadorned ears that matched her pearly-white teeth, although these rarely showed, because Grace's smile, like her eyes, was restrained, the smile of an understated woman who neither questioned her choices nor celebrated easily.

Grace glanced at her wristwatch.

"Planning to run tonight?" Delia asked.

"I'd like to, but may be too late. Close-out went long today."

"Takes longer every day. Between insurance and Medicaid, starting to feel like a desk clerk. Hardly nursing anymore."

Grace nodded, but she was only half-listening. She sympathized with everyone's complaints, however there was little to be done. At that moment, she was more concerned with whether she might run. The children needed feeding, there was ironing to do, but oh, how her muscles burned. Her joints ached. Sometimes she felt as if she might break.

Grace returned her attention to her friend. "New?" she asked, fingering the edge of a purple scarf wrapped into a bow around Delia's thick neck.

Delia beamed as if she had inhaled pure gold. "Josiah gave it to me."

"How sweet."

"Just like that, not my birthday or anything. Just because he wanted to, he said."

"And he spends his money on his mother, that's so dear. Tell me again, what is he doing after school?"

"He's a messenger. Runs around all afternoon on his bike, delivering who knows what, papers and documents I guess. They pay him hourly as much as they pay me, can you imagine? And tips sometimes too."

Grace smiled, sharing her friend's satisfaction.

"And his grades are holding up. That was the deal. I told him, got to keep the grades up, because this is the boy who might make it to college."

Delia frequently boasted about Josiah, the youngest of her five sons, and she wore his gift proudly, not only because it was fashionable, but because her son knew that his mother's favorite color was purple and this pleased Delia more than the gift itself. He was a late-life baby and she hoped he would be the one to get at least a partial scholarship to the state university. Two of her sons were taken by the military and two by the pariahs of the streets, so Josiah was her last hope.

Grace had similar hopes for her children, who were younger, thus a longer vista ahead, perhaps a better future. And, by virtue of a white father, they had lighter skin and finer features, and this alone might afford them greater success, Grace believed, although she never said aloud.

"The last one is the prize," Delia murmured.

Grace leaned toward Delia and whispered into her ear. "Your reward."

"Yes, indeed. Our reward."

They sat in silence for a time, savoring thoughts of their children, until Delia rose to disembark. She lived on the fringe of Northland, the neighborhood they both inhabited on the north side of Columbus, Ohio. Grace would ride another three stops, but that was her signal to prepare for departure.

"Tomorrow?" Delia asked, but quickly answered her own question, remembering that because their schedules were staggered, they would not overlap again until the following week. "No, Monday, right, see you then. Have a good weekend."

"Be well," Grace said as Delia lifted herself and her belongings to depart.

I need to run tonight, Grace thought, knowing that this would be her last chance for a few days. Fridays she cleaned the apartment while the older children were at school and in the afternoon took all three to the neighborhood library for the weekly reading. The junior librarian, an elfish older woman with eagle eyes, performed a dramatic presentation of books tied to the season, a holiday, or the birthday of a famous person whom she thought children should know, like Beethoven or Benjamin Franklin. She acted out all the parts, waving her hands about as she recited, and held up the book every two pages, ink-stained thumbs pressed on opposite corners to display the illustrations. The children leaned in to peer at the pictures and study the detail, although it was the performance they relished.

Saturday there would be an apple fair at church and her son's soccer game. Sunday, after morning mass, they might visit the zoo or the science center, or stroll the shopping streets downtown, admiring colorful autumn window displays.

Monday after work would be her first opportunity to run again, too many days between if she didn't run tonight.

Two or three times a week, that's the best she could do, but it was an imperative. Running was her metronome – keeping the pace of her body in sync with her spirit. Without running, Grace feared she would not only lose her rhythm, she might fall flat.

Her mother, Eleanor, often said that Grace was born to run. She ran first as a toddler in the park playground, from bush to tree, swing to slide, and as a girl on the hard pavement in the schoolyard. She mastered speed and style while playing a game called Dodgeball, a barbaric sport favored on school playgrounds. Far more than dodging, Grace moved fiercely, her long legs charging forward and back, side to side, her feet sliding over concrete as if on ice. She jumped up and dropped down on to the tips of her toes like a dancer. Rope-a-dope, the words of the great Mohammed Ali, might have described this scrawny girl, who moved with the agility of a boxer, a perpetually moving target, her breath heavy, her body pumping adrenaline, buoyed by a sense of potency she found nowhere else. She stopped only now and then to catch the ball, when she was able, and became one of the best of players. However, it was never about winning for Grace. She has never had a competitive spirit; rather a determination to stand her ground, without the hurt or humility of the hit.

"Who invented such a game?" Eleanor cried when Grace returned home once too often with dark bruises on her arm, a steely blue amorphous shape visible even on brown skin. "If I had my way, I wouldn't let her play, although she is good at it. Hard enough to deal with the bumps and broken bones the boys bring home, don't need Grace to be getting beat up as well."

"A battlefield, that's what that game is," a neighbor replied, shouting over the whirr of laundry machines as they waited for their clothing to dry at the new coin laundromat.

Half the machines were filled with colorful children's clothes, others with towels and sheets, or uniforms – nurse and housekeeper whites, garbage collector gray overalls, the sparkling white shirts of doormen and bellmen, the occasional blue security guard uniform. These were the colors of the working class of Cincinnati, Ohio, where Grace grew up, in the aftermath of wars in Europe and Korea, and the flaring of war in Vietnam.

The campaign for civil rights had spread steadily in recent years through the South, school integration moving slowly across southern states and points north like ink spilled on a map. Day to day, moment to moment, few felt that march, certainly not workers like Eleanor and her neighbors, only in moments like these, when they were at last permitted to use a dryer machine in a public laundromat in a mid-western city.

Eleanor, named like so many Americans born into the Great Depression after the First Lady, Mrs. Roosevelt, was thirty-eight years old that year, having risen from poverty to what she might have described as a fine lifestyle: work, family, church and music. Quite sufficient for Eleanor, who always said to strive for too much was to invite the worst. Yet, a week earlier, when Martin Luther King was shot, she found herself catapulted into despair, her sons' futures in doubt, and her daughter running in circles on the playground, dodging only the first of what would surely be many hard balls to come.

Eleanor understood that her boys needed sport to stay out of back alleys and stay on track to a better future. They needed a way to vent frustration, to seize some sense of might in a world where licorice-colored men were either invisible or threatening. Girls, she believed, needed only to stay safe from the dangers that lurked around seemingly every corner. How, she wondered, does a violent playground game serve such aims?

As the neighbors chatted and folded their laundry, Janis Joplin's voice radiated through the static on a portable radio perched atop the coin machine and they all stopped to listen, riveted by her woeful guttural tone. She sang at the wake for Reverend King.

Eleanor swayed to the music, her hips swinging left to right like a pendulum, all the while pressing her fingers into the sheets, smoothing out every tiny crease and inhaling the sweet scent of clean fabric. Although they were accustomed to the stiffer feel of clothes hung on a line, when the weather was wet, neighborhood women pinched pennies together to place their laundry in the big machines, and they took pleasure in the ease of folding hot soft clothes and the sweeter scent of fabric not compromised by soot or bugs or the otherwise indefinable stale gray scents that seeped into seams and ended up embedded in their daily lives.

"That Joplin girl must have black people in her family tree," Eleanor mused.

"Don't we all?" a neighbor asked.

"Don't we all what?" another neighbor asked.

"Don't we all have black and white blood?"

"You seen this girl move? She for sure got black blood in her, for sure."

"Well, she's lighter than the brown paper bag, that's all that matters," Eleanor pronounced, a characteristic amalgam of indignation and acceptance silting her voice.

They nodded. They knew. Their mothers had passed on the stories of their blood-lines, each child being that much more hybrid than the last, weighted by the blending of DNA, their place on the color line.

Janis was only one of the musicians to honor the reverend. Jimi Hendrix, Richie Havens, Buddy Guy and Elvin Bishop, Paul Butterfield and Joni Mitchell, among others, black and white, all came to pay tribute to the booming voice that could not be replaced, the preacher whose death set back a movement that had just hit its stride.

"I think Janis Joplin maybe has more than color in her, she's got sadness. She's felt it, deep down. You simply cannot sing that way if you don't," Eleanor murmured, and they all nodded to her expertise.

Music was Eleanor's passion: blues and country, the skinny boys from Britain, the tiny sparrow from France. She could just as well hum the notes of a Beethoven sonata as tap out the rhythm of a rollicking gospel hymn. All her life, music lifted her from the doldrums. Music and men, and in both she had perfect pitch. When the children were younger, their nightly lullabies were the same sweet and low blues standards she sang to her lovers, or a song she heard on the radio that stayed with her, like the tunes of Harold Arlen or Nat King Cole.

Her children were too old for lullabies now. They listened to Motown music on the radio and on her brother's tape player. They took solace in other ways, like Grace, who found her rhythm in running.

Eleanor imagined it must have been hard for Janis Joplin to be stuck all her life singing the music of the blues while wearing white skin. Just the opposite of little Grace, the lightest of her four children, the product of a romantic moment with a soldier home from Korea, himself a hybrid with skin so light he was surely way up the line, and she was the youngest, several years younger, the one girl, a quiet and accepting girl, who only later in life would display a hint of willfulness behind those gentle eyes when she discovered that black was not always beautiful.

Grace would not find her future much easier to navigate than the women before her. No good to be afraid, Eleanor knew, although fear is a powerful coach: keeps you on your toes and ready to run when you have to. Perhaps there was something to be said for Dodgeball.

Summer had come to an end. An autumn chill took ownership of the Ohio weather and the days were growing short. Grace checked her wristwatch as she stepped down from the bus, then pulled up the collar of her beige trench coat against a gust of air, tightened the belt, and jerked back her shoulders to straighten her spine, like a tree snapped back by the wind. She had glimpsed a reflection of herself recently and noticed a slight but perceptible slump. She would not want to appear to patients to be placid, nor would she want to age too soon like so many nurses, years older than her mere thirty-six. Appearances, Grace knew, were everything.

Her shift ran late again and she found it increasingly difficult to keep to the hours of what was already a ten-hour workday. In the sixteen years she had been a nurse, much had changed. Few nurses wore their white caps anymore, which Grace had been so proud to don when she graduated nursing school and took her first assignment in the maternity ward at Cincinnati General. The work was meaningful and the pace manageable, before cutbacks, layoffs, and the downsizing through the eighties, when hospitals morphed into corporate enterprise.

Five years ago, on as much of a whim as she had ever allowed herself, she moved with the children to Columbus, where she secured a coveted placement on the general surgery floor at Riverside Hospital. During the interview, the personnel manager repeated several times the hospital's mission to provide compassionate care, and Grace believed in their good intentions. However, patients no longer got the attention they needed and their families too often had concerns that doctors had little time to address. Grace was happy to console them during difficult moments, but that took time, and she increasingly felt the pressure of the clock, always wanting to get home to her children and, now and then, take a run.

She was aware that her colleagues snickered at her, as if jogging was reserved for the gentrified. However, from Dodgeball, Grace graduated to the high school track team. She ran the short course, sprinting easily past most of her competitors. She had hoped to train to be a marathon runner, but between nursing school, and long hours on the job, and after the children were born, all she has had time for is a five or six mile run, now and then, but run she must: the one and only time she called her own.

She stopped when she came to the corner grocery to consider dinner. She had a pot of leftover stew, compliments of her neighbor, which would warm up quickly, although it had been a while since she cooked the breakfast-dinner her children loved – scrambled eggs topped with shredded cheese. Easy. Fast. She had half-dozen eggs, and applesauce she made last weekend, so no need to stop. No time.

Time. Everyone seemed greedy for time. A metaphor for the modern age. The concrete and barbed wire dividing wall had come down in Germany and the Cold War had come to an end, but oil prices ran up and down like an elevator, and between presidential elections, everyone blamed everyone else for what pained the country. Grace believed blame was pointless. Most of the people she knew were forever challenged one way or another, trapped between the latest ideal for the so-called working class or the latest take on what ails them. Seemed to Grace every generation dealt with some sort of crisis or paradigm shift, and each imagined it worse than the generation before. Her brothers came of age during the war in Vietnam; her mother lived through World War II and her grandmother through the Great Depression. She could hardly complain about her own life, which was infinitely better by comparison. Making an honest living and pinching pennies was simply all she had ever known. Some things do not change.

The way people work, yes, that had changed, and kept changing, and while she was not resistant to change, she was well aware that too much at once was hard on the nervous system. Hardly a moment to take stock before moving on. At a staff meeting last week, the operations director informed them that soon they would type their notes into a computer, no more paper charts. Desktop computers were at every nursing station. Technology was supposed to make it all easier, they said, and Grace found it truly fascinating, but terribly time consuming. Less paper, yes, but more screen-time, more reporting. Lawyers presided over every move. She believed it was impossible to get better at what you do when you are consumed by the race to keep learning the new, as if the dodgeball was always in flight and she always fleeing the punch.

Grace turned the corner at Cook Road and picked up speed like a hummingbird focused on the nectar of a flower in full bloom. She felt the tingle of an impending run as if the same sap infusion. Once she has run, she would be a better mother. She would eagerly listen to her children's chatter at dinner, play games with them, read to them, see to their baths and prayers, and breathe a great sigh of pleasure when they were all tucked into their beds, shiny and clean like new pennies.

She charged up the wide concrete stairs to the gray row house that sat in the midst of a sea of matching buildings like a fortress, stopping at her ground-floor neighbor's apartment to pick up the children. Every evening, when Grace returned from work, Mrs. Elliott repeated exactly the same words, like a mantra.

"Little darlins they are," Mrs. Elliott crooned. As punctuation, she hugged each one to her full, low bosom as they left the apartment to greet their mother, always in age order, but in reverse, giving little Leah the first turn, then Jake, then Becky.

"Little darlins" was one of the first things Mrs. Elliott said when Grace moved in. A compact, cheerful white woman, she took Grace by the hand and walked her and the children around the neighborhood, pointing out where historical buildings once stood or streets one should avoid, before landing at the park where children played under the watchful eyes of mothers and grandmothers, the same park where Mrs. Elliott would subsequently take Grace's children for sunshine and fresh air on those afternoons she watched over them.

"Mine are all grown now," she told Grace that first day. "Grown and flown, Mr. Elliott likes to say."

"Nearby?"

"Not near enough, but I wanted them to spread their wings, and they have. My youngest, Patrice, she moved to Pittsburgh with her husband a couple of years ago. My sons are in Chicago. Salesmen, both, doing well. Sweet wives. And Margo, the oldest, she lives in New York City."

Mrs. Elliott reserved her broadest smile for Margo, a smile that revealed two teeth prominently missing as if they were never meant to be there. Above her thin nearly translucent lips, deeply dimpled, her nose was dotted with a collage of freckles that mirrored increasingly prominent age spots, as one might expect on the face of Mrs. Santa Claus.

"Margo has been promoted four times since she got there and now she's a director. Market research is what she does, not that I can tell you exactly what that is, but she works with a lot of big companies, that much I know, and sends me packages of sample products. I've got a closet full of all sorts of stuff."

"How nice."

"Yes, and her husband, Daniel, such a dear. They all come at Thanksgiving, you'll meet them then."

Mrs. Elliott's voice had the lilt of an Irish accent, which she had taken on from her husband of forty years, although her Polish roots were evident in the pungent aroma of oregano and paprika that filled the hallway outside her apartment most evenings, and a tendency to comment in her native tongue. No matter the weather, nor how much time she spent in a hot kitchen, she always looked refreshed, as if she had just stepped out of the shower, wisps of silvery hair dusting her pudgy cheeks. That first day, she wore one of the half a dozen dark-colored skirt and white blouse combinations that Grace has seen her wear every day the last five years, always perfectly pressed, and likely the same outfits she wore to work most of her life. She also wore a sweater to match the skirt, even when it was blisteringly hot, which she used to swipe her perpetually shiny brow.

Mrs. Elliott had recently retired from a forty-year career as a saleswoman in the lingerie department at Northland-Lazarus department store, where, day after day, she discreetly presented, then folded and replaced into small, shallow wooden drawers, the delicate bras and panties, slips and girdles, chosen to best serve each customer. She proved to be an excellent saleswoman and meticulous merchandiser, memorizing the styling and attributes of hundreds of products, able to convey with authority to her customers the design that matched their bodies or suited their loved ones. She remembered every purchase, every preference, memory that would retire with her and never be replaced. Her departure coincided with merchandise moving out of drawers onto hundreds of miniature hangers hung throughout the department like a pastel-colored jungle. Once relegated to home, she deployed her talent as a dressmaker to earn extra money, and keep busy, using an early-model Singer sewing machine permanently ensconced on the dining table like a centerpiece, always dusted and shiny, with a case of colorful spools of thread that looked like a wall of paint chips at the hardware store.

"Grandchildren?" Grace asked.

"Yes, the boys have children. Two each. Little darlins."

Mrs. Elliott sighed, despite the obvious pleasure of her grandchildren, and Grace suspected sadness within the sigh. She inquired no further, knowing everyone has struggles or harbors secrets, to be revealed only by choice.

"I can see your children in you," Mrs. Elliott said that day. "Those long legs and sweet personalities."

"Mostly they favor their father," Grace answered, without further explanation.

Mrs. Elliott saw what she meant, but she refrained from asking about the white man who wasn't there and was otherwise never mentioned. In turn, Grace never spoke of her former husband, and she discovered that first day at the park that Mrs. Elliott rarely queried beyond what people wished to reveal. Mrs. Elliott was not a gossip, she was a watcher, an important distinction to Grace, as it was Mrs. Elliott who became a surrogate grandmother to her children, looking after them early mornings and after school while Grace was at work. As different as possible from their dark-skinned grandmother, Eleanor, gone now, whose photograph smiled down at them from a shelf in the living room and whose wisdom echoed now and then in the sayings that Grace passed on.

Grace never forgot that first visit with Mrs. Elliott, as if a newborn duckling imprinted by an accidental matriarch. The sky that day was gray, landscape flat and colorless in the late winter doldrums, the conversation too absent of color, as if the two women were exactly the same. That was the first time Grace had ever felt on equal footing with a white person. With her husband Ray, their determination to ignore racial differences seemed only to exacerbate them.

There had been nights, early in their intimacy, a glimmer of moonlight the only illumination, Grace would lay her fingers on her husband's arm, and even her light brown skin in low light seemed so dark in contrast. Foreboding. They had violated cultural code, and she anticipated disappointments, perhaps recriminations, although she never imagined they might smolder within.

On that day, however, with Mrs. Elliott, a woman who absorbed color and texture like a painter's palette, they blended together into neutral. Two neighbors, opposites in race and shape and a quarter-century apart in age, bonded from the first and were of one mind on most things. Perhaps this came from their devotion to their Christian faith, although Mrs. Elliott was Catholic and Grace Episcopalian. In the end, Mrs. Elliott liked to say, same roots, same Lord.

"The road goes north and south, my mother always said," Grace told Mrs. Elliott on another such day at the park. "We choose which way we go."

They resided in a neighborhood settled early in the 20th century where black and white neighbors peacefully co-existed. All working class people who labored long days, earned a living wage, fretted over their children, and tried to deal with the constancy of change as cheerfully as possible. The eponymous Northland Mall, the first mall in the city, was thriving, and the high school graduated nearly a thousand students each year, many to the state university. There was a sense the city was marching into the future and more people were relocating to Columbus every day, the only mid-west city drawing newcomers, as most people migrated to communities in the warmer South or West. Grace chuckled when she read in the newspaper about these demographic shifts, because most of her family fled the South, and by choosing Columbus as her adopted home, she felt as if she were ahead of the trend.

In spite of urban development, many factories had closed, commercial streets increasingly populated by banks or insurance companies, and businesses that specialized in research and development, which portended more change, of that Grace was certain.

Mrs. Elliott raised her four children in the same modest apartment that Grace lived in, but on the ground level of the three-story building. She divvied up one bedroom to her girls, one to the boys, and she slept with her husband for nearly thirty years on a sofa bed in the living room, a thin mattress bolstered by wooden slats that Mr. Elliott cut thick enough to provide good support for their aging spines.

In her matching third floor apartment, Grace's daughters, Becky and Leah, slept in one bedroom, and she shared the other with her son Jake, their narrow beds pushed against opposite walls to carve out maximum distance. Jake had recently taken to protesting that sleeping arrangement, although he more often had the room to himself, because Grace frequently slept on the couch, reclining on two folded cotton quilts to protect her from seams and crevices, the crown of her head and the edges of her toes pressed against the sofa's thinly padded arms. With the back pillows removed, the surface was nearly equal to a twin bed, suitable for a solo sleeper, and she preferred to sleep in the living room, as if a sentry, on-guard and on-call through the night. She also felt less alone there, curling her body into a crescent and pressing her back against the upholstery as she once slept pressed to her husband.

Late at night, as silence blanketed the neighborhood, Grace slumbered to the subtle rise and fall of her children's night breathing, as sweet a lullaby as the crystal notes of her mother's voice long ago.

"Are you going to run tonight, Grace?" Mrs. Elliott asked as Grace embraced her children, all at once.

"I'd like to," Grace answered over their heads.

"You can leave them here if you like. Mr. Elliott was called out on an emergency, one of those pipes burst downtown again, so I'm just doing the mending, happy to have them here."

"Are we going to be shut down on water again?"

"No, not here, over in German Village, I think."

"Good. You are so kind, Mrs. Elliott, but I think they will be all right for a bit. Becky likes to be the little mother."

Mrs. Elliott nodded, with some consternation. "I'll keep my door ajar; no one is getting past me. Tell them to come right down if they need."

The children chattered at once as they climbed the stairs to the third floor. They hoped to impress their mother with artwork they created at school or capture her attention to a thought of consequence or a question that needed explaining, but Grace was intent on the run.

"Byc dobrym," Mrs. Elliott called to them as they climbed the stairs.

Grace smiled in response to Mrs. Elliott's other favorite Polish phrase: be good.

Every time Grace walked into her apartment, she silently sighed with satisfaction. Even that day, despite her determination to run, she took a moment to embrace the space. She would never own a place of her own, she knew, but she had made a good home for her children in this apartment and, barring the intrusion of a less kindly landlord, would remain there until they were grown, happily ensconced in spacious rooms with high ceilings, which, like the wood floors, were slightly scratched and gently sagging, as if an elderly but sturdy woman who has weathered many seasons. Several kitchen tiles had been replaced, few matched, but the oversized old stove sparkled and in the center of the kitchen was a large square oak table with spindled legs that Grace had purchased at a thrift shop, just the right size to seat them all together comfortably. At the center of the table sat a round lace doily with a crystal bowl with a snug-fitting lid, filled to the brim with sugar cubes. She took two in her tea, the one indulgence of a life-long sweet tooth. None of the kitchen table chairs matched and all were painted different colors, so each of the children chose one as their permanent place. She smiled when they were all seated there, as the shape and size of each chair matched the child, like Goldilocks' bears. She occupied the one chair with arms and that seemed fitting as well.

The living room was crowned with the ornate moldings of older buildings and although the fireplace was no longer safe to operate, the mantel suggested a grander era, and on it Grace had placed two tapered white candles in brass candlesticks, purchased at a yard sale, which she never lit, preferring their elegance untouched. A wide bay window faced west, so the late day sun, when visible beyond the more ubiquitous clouds, streamed into the apartment.

They all shared one bathroom, so her children learned to take turns or do quickly what they had to do, and often shared the space while they brushed teeth or combed hair, taking only as much time as needed, not a moment more, a good lesson for children, Grace believed, to learn to conserve both time and energy for what mattered most.

A faint scent of bleach permeated the apartment's white walls and the faded white counter tops that Grace regularly disinfected to ensure that her children grew up in a safe, sanitary environment: no bugs, no stains. White was the one color that connected her from home to work and home again, a color that might be flat and lacking in decorative value, but to Grace, the color of idealism and purity. Whiteness, cleanliness, optimism, these were all terribly important qualities for a hard-working single mother who wanted so much for her children to understand that nothing is easy, but too many people make things harder than they are meant to be.

Particularly of importance to mixed-race children, whose lives were often complicated by the question of what they were. Grace sometimes wanted to cry out to peering eyes that her children were hybrids, like a delicate tea rose blended with a dramatic climber, although they might have been better off pure bred: one race, one color. Black or white. A human hybrid lacks the elegance of a rose, more often perceived as a mutt.

She herself was such a mix of colors and races that she had no idea of the balance and no patience for the preoccupation with the color line that characterized the culture. Neither did she accept the angry rhetoric of black power that surrounded her as she came of age. Black is not so beautiful, not in this country, she knew, and brown, beautiful only in the eyes of the beholder. Still, she repeatedly prompted her children that all human beings come in different configurations, and what matters is only their commitment to the golden rule.

"Becky, honey, keep an eye on for a bit, please. Mama needs to run."

"Sure," Becky said, as she pulled Leah closer to her to peruse a book.

Becky had her grandmother's smile and her grit. Bright eyes and elegant limbs, tall and mature for her twelve years, and a quintessentially precocious first-born daughter.

"You can watch TV, maybe that new Disney show," Grace called from her bedroom, where she had quickly slipped off her nursing clothes to change into black nylon running shorts and a gray sweatshirt printed with Ohio U. across the front, and had been washed so many times the string to tighten the hood was long gone and the last bits of fiber on the cuffs ready to shred through her fingers.

"Are your jackets hung? School bags in place?" she asked as she emerged.

"Yes, Mama," the children responded in unison.

Grace gazed at her beautiful children, lined up on the couch like sparrows on a branch. Sometimes she stared at Becky as if she were someone else's child, as she looked the least like Grace, so fair she might be a white child. Jake, nine years old, seemed younger, doted on as he was by his sisters. He was the darkest in color, and the most jovial, loving nothing more than flexing his sole masculine identity. And Leah, seven, with bronze skin, nearly as tall as Jake, the quiet one, gentle as a feather.

Grace scanned the living room to make certain all was well. Because she dealt with considerable chaos at the hospital by day, she demanded as much as possible a sense of order at home. There were no knick-knacks, little to collect dust or to be swiped by the careless limb of a child, so the apartment always appeared neat and uncluttered. A few books leaned against each other on built-in shelves along either side of the bay window. Board games – Monopoly, Life, Clue, Checkers and Parcheesi – were stacked on the lower shelves, frayed edges of boxes repaired with duct tape. Library books were piled on the coffee table like a sculpture, their shiny plastic covers reflecting the light. The coffee table too seemed a sculpture, an empty relic of a huge spool of industrial wire that Grace found on the street and Mr. Elliott dragged up the stairs, sanded and painted with three coats of shellac. Dolls, mini-trucks and railroad cars, blocks and puzzles, were stuffed into baskets that nested into a corner where they could be found without searching and easily replaced. The one big closet in each bedroom, and one in the entryway, were also filled with baskets and bins holding bulky items like heavy sweaters and the extra pairs of shoes and boots Grace found now and then to hold for the children as their feet grew.

The few spots of color that dotted the apartment were in the cotton quilts that lay folded on the edge of every bed, the living room couch and the one easy chair; quilts made by distant relatives in Louisiana and Mississippi and passed down from Grace's grandmother.

"Tom & Jerry!" Jake shouted as he plopped on the couch, knocking the book to the floor and making both girls yelp at the disruption.

"No jumping on the couch!" Grace called out. "Yes, cartoons or Disney."

The children were not permitted to listen to the news and Grace watched only *Sixty Minutes* on Sundays, and that new comedy called *In Living Color*, which she considered odd. She was certain she didn't get the meaning in everything they said, but she often laughed out loud and she liked the mix of black and white characters, something so rarely seen on television.

She grabbed her house key and said to Becky one more time, "If you need Mrs. Elliott, go downstairs, her door is open, okay?"

Becky nodded absent-mindedly, her eyes already on the television.

"Come double lock the door, little man," Grace called to Jake.

"Yes, Mama," he answered, charging off the couch after her.

She listened for the locks to click in before she dashed down the stairs.

Once outside, Grace sat on the top step of the stoop and double-tied the laces on her sneakers. Shin splints pressed against her bones; her ankles felt sometimes as if they might shatter under the ballast of even her slight frame. She suspected she probably shouldn't run until she got better shoes, and made a mental note to stop at the thrift shop to see if someone had donated a gently used pair of Nike or Reebok sneakers. Nonetheless, she was determined to run, and return home renewed, gasping for breath, sweat dripping down her neck, oxygen rushing through her lungs like rapids over falls.

First she stretched. She always stretched, no time for body damage. She stood on the bottom step of the stoop and extended one leg straight out, pressing her foot onto the third step up, twisting at the waist toward her toes, flexing her toes to release the kinks, then bending at the knee for a horizontal lunge before repeating with the other leg. She squared her shoulders and stood up especially straight as she reached her arms over her head to spread her spine, then bent forward toward the ground, gracefully, like a ballerina at the bar. She leaned on each thigh one more time to pull her hamstrings to their limit.

At last she was ready to run. The sky was still grey, but as the sun hovered beyond clouds nearly touching the horizon, a silvery band of light floated above the tree line. Less than an hour's worth of daylight remained. Grace never left her children in the dark.

Because she ran only at day's end, Grace never saw her shadow, and this made her feel all the more solitary, also more commanding, as if even the sun and the moon were eclipsed by the power of the runner.

She knew well she should jog first, ease herself into the sprint, but she tended to take off like a rambunctious racehorse and kept the pace until nearly home. She headed toward one of her shorter routes, along the back of an old metal factory, down past a stretch of long cinder-block buildings with flat roofs. Weeds strangled the perimeter, and here and there a pane had been knocked out of a window, leaving a noticeably black space, like a child's smile that reveals a missing tooth. Setting sunlight reflected off the glass, casting a soft glow on an otherwise dreary landscape. Massive machinery once hummed in these buildings from early morning until the five o'clock whistle, five days a week, fifty weeks a year, now idle, rotting remnants of a rapidly evaporating manufacturing culture.

The route past the factory was straight and flat, few hills to slow her down. Not as scenic as the run through the park, but shorter distance, along empty pathways so quiet she was able to listen to her measured breathing, to the steady thud of her rubber soles on the pavement. Within moments she felt stronger. Almost mighty. No disagreeable patients or frazzled doctors to make demands of her, no pushing and shoving passengers on the bus, no children in need of attention.

A lonely train whistle blew in the distance, and Grace was reminded of her great grandmother's move long ago from Mississippi to the Mid-west. She left, like so many southern African-Americans, after the second big war, to remove her children from the segregation and persecution that was the legacy of Reconstruction. Their lives in Cleveland were neither as liberated nor as promising as expected, so when Eleanor was ready to make her own move, she chose Cincinnati, which she believed had a mid-western mindset with a southern flair. Ultimately, Grace too moved on. Thus, the sound of a train was always soothing, a reminder of the fluidity of life. The steady ebb and flow of past and future.

She had hit her stride, a smooth steady sprint. It was a lonely run on this route, not a soul in sight, but there wasn't much to fear in Northland, not if you stayed away from certain streets and certain kinds of men. Grace knew this well, five years here, shortly after her husband Ray left.

Ray was an accountant, always with the same firm, first in Philadelphia, then in Cincinnati, where they met. He seemed to be doing well, although he rarely spoke of his work, and while preoccupied, nothing in his demeanor or character might have signaled any strange predilection. He was tall and lanky, a mirror image of Grace, other than his pallor; they looked like a set of salt and pepper shakers when they walked together.

After nine years of marriage, he announced one day that he had an opportunity for a promotion at the company's St. Louis office. Ray told her not to quit her job yet, as he would go ahead for one month, and if it worked out well, he would send for her and the children. He packed up most of his clothes and a few personal items, nothing more – none of his books or records, or the guitar he purchased at a pawn shop years before and had always meant to learn to play. He left one morning with the same scratched leather valises he had acquired when he graduated from Penn State University. He hugged Becky and Jake and placed a gentle kiss on little Leah's forehead. He told Grace not to bother to see him to the train and she respected his wishes, assuming only that he didn't want to make a fuss. Ray was a man who rarely made a fuss.

She didn't hear a word from him for two weeks, which didn't surprise her, as Ray had vigilantly maintained a sharp divide between work and home. They never socialized with colleagues and she was not invited to the company picnic, nor the holiday cocktail party, which Ray claimed did not include spouses, and although she never challenged him, she knew better. She didn't mind. She had not wished to be the thorn among those roses, to jeopardize his career in any way.

The first weeks he was gone, she imagined he was busy settling in. She wasn't even sure if he had a phone at the temporary apartment he said the company arranged for him. The third week she began to worry, and by the Friday, she called the company's office in Cincinnati and asked if she might be directed to the office in St. Louis. They gave her the number and when she called and asked for Ray, the receptionist said no such person worked there. Grace assumed that because he was a newcomer, the girl didn't recognize his name, so she asked to speak with someone in Personnel. A curt voice confirmed that Ray was not only not employed at the St. Louis affiliate, he had left the company entirely, with no notice, a month earlier.

Completely shocked by what she heard, but unwilling to express either the surprise or the sudden sense of terror that swarmed over her, she thanked the Personnel assistant and hung up. She sat very still by the phone, gasping for breath, until her lungs nearly burst. She considered calling the home office again, hoping they might clarify the confusion, still believing that perhaps an error had been made; however, as she dialed, the truth came to her. Ray was gone. The dark premonition of long ago had played out.

She replaced the receiver on the handset and sat motionless, absorbing the body blow. She was on her own. A black woman with three brown children, no savings, little to call her own or provide support except her nursing credentials.

She lay in bed that night and tried to fathom her future. Their marriage had seemed to her to rise above the petty differences that define people. Had it always been a sham?

They were in love, Grace thought at the time, although, at that moment, she wondered. Unlike her mother, who adored many men, five of whom fathered a child, Grace had never been with a man before Ray. Only a few girlish crushes, no lasting romances. She was always too busy working and studying. She had no real basis for comparison. Still, they were drawn together, gravitating to each other like opposite poles on a magnet, despite the tenuous prospects for a mixed marriage.

They met at the library, she studying for the nursing assessment, he for a state-licensing exam, and from the first, they never acknowledged their differences, only the pleasure of each other's company. They both liked to read, they occasionally enjoyed a concert, they told each other about the happenings of their days and snuggled close through the night. They chose to defy convention, and construct a future together, beyond her childhood in a largely segregated Ohio and his from an immigrant upbringing in the tenements of Philadelphia.

Grace at first flouted her Pastor and sought advice on birth control, so they might save for a while and settle into married life. When the time came, conception was easy, and Grace was happy with a girl and a boy, too expensive for more, she understood, but Leah turned out to be a blessing of her own, although further burdening their finances. Grace had to take time off from work and Ray felt the predictable pressure of bills. They argued, which they rarely had, over the littlest things: a pair of socks on the floor, a lamp needed fixing. She couldn't give him the attention she used to, she was aware of that, but she thought he understood and accepted that lives change when children enter the equation. One simply adapts.

In the end, she wasn't surprised their marriage ended, only that Ray took off without a word. That he turned out to be a coward, a different sort of runner.

Although she found herself overcome with an anger she had not thought possible, Grace was not like those women who hire a lawyer and chase down their ex-husbands, demanding their due. No time or money for such things, nor would she publicly acknowledge the disgrace.

She waited a few weeks longer, harboring hope that he might surface. Perhaps she had mistaken his intentions. Perhaps he would surprise her with other plans; he never was one for sharing until he was certain of the outcome.

When the neighbors inquired, she answered blithely. "Oh, so busy starting a new job, you know? Takes time."

She told the landlord she would need another month and he acquiesced. He had been put out when he discovered that the missus of his new renter was a black woman, and although he considered revoking the lease, he decided to adopt a wait-and-see-attitude. The law was on their side, even if he had been deceived. As promised, Ray and Grace were quiet responsible tenants. The rent was always paid on time. And, when a neighbor was ill, Grace checked in to ensure they had proper care. So the landlord never minded, in the end, and when she asked for time, he had no reason to deny her.

Throughout the weeks she waited, Grace never shed a tear. Her brothers had taught her how to hold back her tears, no matter the indignity or the pain. She remembered only one significant lamentation in her entire life, when she read *Gone with the Wind*. She was fifteen years old and she cried not for Scarlett or Rhett, but because she felt the ending of the story proved only that nothing had changed and that the southern way of life, presumed broken, had only splintered, the devastation of civil war for naught.

At last, Grace sat her children down on the couch, Leah on her lap, Jake and Becky on either side, all wrapped in her arms, and informed them in as calm a voice as possible that their father had died in an accident in St. Louis. Only Becky cried, because only Becky understood the permanence of death, but in response to her tears, Leah sobbed, and Jake buried his face in Grace's body, already ashamed to be seen as weak.

Grace told her neighbors and family the same lie. She said Ray had been cremated, so there would be no funeral. She told her brothers not to come, no need.

Jake hardly slept for days when Becky described what cremation was, suggesting that Ray had been incinerated like a roast left too long in the oven, but by the time he recounted this fact to his friends, he had manufactured an image of his father as a nearly mythological superhero who had perished in the roaring fire of righteousness. By the time Leah was old enough for explanations, Ray had been erased from their memory, although she forever felt the void.

Grace clung tenaciously to the charade. She permitted friends and family members to come to her apartment with casseroles and condolences. She made a pretense of allowing herself to be comforted. She never told anyone the truth – not Delia or Mrs. Elliott or her brothers. Not even the Pastor. From the moment of his betrayal, Ray was dead to her, the status conveyed on a widow far more acceptable than a black woman abandoned by a white man. No one needed to know anything more.

These days, she was relieved that she had no husband. One less person to contend with. She appreciated her independence, despite the overwhelming sense of responsibility, although now and then, she wished there were a man there to help her sort things out, and too often her body felt cold, wanting for the warmth of touch.

Grace always kept her eyes turned downward when she ran. She knew every crack and crevice in the sidewalk, every broken curb. She had only a vague sense of the surroundings, but a familiarity of where she was based on smells and sounds and the surface beneath her feet. Only the steadiness of her footing mattered.

This early autumn evening, a thin layer of burnished leaves crunched beneath her feet. She sped up a bit and pushed her head forward, as if carried like one of those leaves on the wind. As she ran, she noticed out of the corner of her eye a boy pedaling a bike along a parallel path, his face mostly hidden by the hood of a sweatshirt pulled down so low on his forehead he might have had no face at all. A messenger bag hung off his shoulder, flopping against him as he zoomed down the path toward the factory. He suddenly disappeared, obliterated by the crumbling facade, then reappeared seconds later, on the far side of the building, cruising steadily down the lower path.

Grace was in full thrall to her run, and the boy almost out of sight, when, from the cover of a dense cluster of Sycamore trees, a car pulled out in his direction. Grace noticed only because the car sputtered a bit and invaded her vision, like a spec of dirt on a photograph. An older American car, Buick or Plymouth, the dark green paint was faded and the fender misshapen, as if a discarded old woman. Grace saw the boy lift his head to look back at the car and at that moment she recognized him: Josiah Miller, Delia's son, the same boy they had spoken of on the bus only an hour or so ago.

Grace had met Josiah a couple of times when he stopped at the hospital after school to see his mother. A quiet boy with broad shoulders and a hesitant smile, he was purposefully polite, kids always on their best behavior in front of their mother's friends. One could never be certain who they were or what sort of mischief they might be up to. Grace tried to recall what Delia was saying to her on the bus while she was preoccupied pondering whether she might run. She remembered Delia's expression of pride in her son's job as a messenger and that would explain his presence on the bike by the factory, although Grace felt instinctively that something was amiss. She had heard stories of drug dealers recruiting teenage boys as couriers, just the type of men who might drive a beat-up Buick when they did not want to be noticed.

The car moved stealthily, like a tiger stalking its prey. A dark-skinned driver wore a non-descript baseball cap turned backwards and he was hunched tightly to the wheel. The passenger, light enough to be white, had long shaggy hair, his eyes hidden behind aviator sunglasses; a cigarette dangled from his lips. She felt certain they meant Josiah harm, and he must have felt the same threat, as he sped up and took a sharp turn off the path onto the grass, down a pitted slope toward the railroad tracks. Perhaps he might make his way to the center of town where the traffic would shield him, but the sedan sped up as well, hurtling down the same slope and quickly overtaking the bicycle.

Grace felt tightness in her chest, as if the devil itself had reached in and grabbed her heart. Josiah was in danger. She stopped short and leaned against the base of a Willow tree. Gasping for breath, she took shelter under flowing limbs that bowed nearly to the ground and watched as the predators caught up with Josiah.

As the car swerved to cut him off, the bicycle's wheels spun out and keeled over. Josiah, trapped in the bike's wiry underbelly, struggled to free himself from the weight, but the driver jumped out of the car and got to him first, grabbing him by his sweatshirt to pull him to his feet.

Grace's heart pounded, faster than at the peak of the run, and so palpably she feared she might explode. She peered around her, across the rise and down to the factory, but there was no one in sight. She was alone, alone with the threat of danger to her friend's son, and she could not make herself move. She watched in horror as the taller man clutched Josiah, who squirmed in his grasp but could not escape the hold. The other man scanned the scene to be certain they were not being watched, and as his gaze turned toward Grace, she ducked further behind the tree, peeking out hesitantly a moment later to see the two men encircle Josiah. She heard the anger in their voices, but their words were muted.

Josiah screamed. "Not me!"

The larger man shook his head and growled into Josiah's face. He smacked him. Smack! Smack! He whipped his arm across Josiah's face repeatedly.

"No!" Josiah yelled, but the man hit him again and again.

Now the other man pummeled his fist into Josiah's stomach, causing his young body to droop toward the ground as if an old man. Josiah lifted his head to speak, his words stifled by a stream of blood dripping from his lips. Even from a distance, Grace knew that the boy had sustained internal injuries. She imagined the damage to his liver, his spleen; ribs likely broken, a lung perhaps punctured.

The driver continued his assault, aiming purposefully for the center of Josiah's chest. Grace knew that if the boy's aorta were torn or ruptured, his blood pressure would plummet, his very being jolted into shock. She knew too well the violations that his body had already endured and any one of these might kill him; however, she wanted to believe, because he was young, he might survive even this brutal attack.

Why, Grace wondered, did Josiah not even attempt to defend himself? Why did he allow the men to beat him with such savagery, although as she asked she knew the answer: even a fit young man was no match for two men with violence on their minds. More to the point, perhaps every black boy faced a moment when he knew he was defenseless.

Spasms rocked Grace's legs; her whole body began to shiver uncontrollably as if she were suddenly submerged in icy waters. Still, she could not move; she did not cry out. Howls were trapped in her throat, hot and bilious, as if she too had been punched repeatedly. She knew she could not save Josiah and she chose in that moment not to endanger herself or her children.

The frenzied attack continued. Grace covered her mouth with her hands but she watched, unable to turn her eyes away, as if by watching, Josiah would not be alone.

"Please," she whispered. "Please, stop. You will kill him."

Josiah collapsed to the ground in a heap. His attackers paused briefly, the passenger returning to car, slumping into his seat and lighting another cigarette. Grace saw the flame flicker momentarily. The other looked around once more, and, apparently satisfied that they had not been observed, emptied Josiah's pockets, then removed the messenger bag from his body. He pulled himself up to his full height, walked slowly to the car, as if he had only been out for a stroll, and slid behind the wheel. He slammed the door, muttered something to his accomplice, and gunned the engine. In seconds, they were gone.

Grace paused briefly to be certain they were out of sight. She pulled her body from its hiding place and ran to Josiah. The boy lay motionless. His face was barely recognizable now, whipped and bloodied. She pressed her head to his chest and listened for a heartbeat: nothing. She placed two fingers to his wrist, but no pulse.

Josiah was dead, she knew that, yet she pressed her hand against his neck, praying she was wrong; perhaps there was a pulse still lurking there. Nothing. Not a sound, not a beat. She wiped blood from his mouth with her sleeve, lifted his chin, and pushed her lips against his in a vain attempt at CPR. She blew into his mouth, desperate to reactivate his lungs, and pressed her palms to his heart before repeating the sequence. She had been well trained in emergency response, but it was too late.

Delia's son was dead. Grace watched him die. She would never forget, nor reconcile, that she stood by as his life was taken from him. Her heart was racing, her whole body shaking, spasms of terror and regret, and the encroaching chill of night.

The sky had turned dark. She looked up to see a sliver of moonlight in the distance. Her children were waiting for her, just as Delia awaited the son who would never return. Grace stood a moment by his side before trudging up the path. She stopped at a pay-phone booth and dialed the operator.

"A boy," she sputtered into the phone. "A boy has been badly hurt, by the factory."

"Who is this calling?" the emergency operator asked.

Grace held her breath for a moment. She could not involve herself. No reason to expose her children to police or thugs. No point. Josiah was gone.

"Near the metal factory," she whispered and hung up.

She turned to walk hastily down the street, stumbling over an unexpected crack in the sidewalk. She wanted to run home but she could not move any faster, and even the shorter distance back took forever. Josiah's face was embedded in every footstep.

How would she ever look Delia in the eye? How could she ever confess that she stood by as Josiah was bludgeoned to death? She chose her life over his, abandoning another child in favor of her own, betraying another mother, a friend, and betraying her oath as a nurse.

She climbed the stoop without stopping to stretch and faltered at the landing, her hands shaking so severely she was hardly able to unlock the front door. She tried to tiptoe past Mrs. Elliott's door but her feet were far too sluggish, dragging beneath her like a cripple.

"Grace, is that you?" Mrs. Elliott came to her door, wiping her wet hands on her apron. "Moj Boze. My God, what's happened?"

She rushed to Grace's side, but Grace recoiled.

"I fell. It's, it's nothing," she stammered.

"But the blood! Let me get a towel."

"No, please. I'm late. It's late. I'll clean up upstairs."

"My dear, let me help you."

"I'll be all right. I'm all right. Please, I must go to the children."

Grace was nearly shouting, her voice uncharacteristically strident, but she stood in place, as if by standing very still, she might dispel the nightmare, or perhaps Mrs. Elliott might wave her magic wand to make it all disappear.

Mrs. Elliott peered more closely at Grace. She saw that she had not fallen. There were no open wounds, no blood dripping from her limbs. She stepped toward her, slowly but with deliberation, and reached to take her hands, but Grace flinched as if she'd been slapped. Mrs. Elliott stood her ground. She knew something terrible must have happened, but allowed Grace her dignity. In time, she believed, Grace would tell her the truth, and perhaps she might offer comfort.

"It's late," Grace mumbled as she turned at last to climb the stairs.

Mrs. Elliott watched her from the landing. Grace knew that Mrs. Elliott knew that a horrific event had taken place, and there was nothing to be done. They would be conspirators of silence.

At the top of the stairs, still unable to control the quivering of her body, Grace leaned on the doorbell and Becky opened the door.

"Mama, where have you been? It's dark!" Becky admonished her.

Grace slouched against the doorway. Exhausted. Defeated. Leah and Jake looked up from the couch in surprise. The last flicker of light faded from the television screen.

"Mama?"

Becky moved closer to her mother. Grace realized the sight of blood must have been terrifying, but she had no words to soothe. She touched her lips with the tips of two fingers and rubbed a bit of blood away. The children stared, their eyes wide. Innocent.

"I fell. I'm, I'm all right," she sputtered.

Leah slipped down off the couch and inched closer to the doorway. She peered at Grace's tear-stained cheeks, her bloodstained sweatshirt, and started to cry.

"It's all right, Leah," Grace mumbled, as she made straight for the bathroom.

"Can we have pancakes for dinner, Mama?" Jake called out.

Grace silently entered the bathroom and locked the door behind her.

The children for the moment stood in place, speechless and still.

"I'll do it," Becky said at last, taking charge. She whispered to the little ones, "Let's be good helpers."

"Okay," they whispered conspiratorially.

Becky took Leah, still whimpering, by the hand to lead her into the kitchen.

"Take out the syrup, Jake. And cinnamon sugar. Leah, forks and knives, and napkins."

Grace heard Becky issuing instructions and at any other moment might have been proud, but she felt nothing. She turned on the shower full blast and while the steam filled the room, she stripped off her clothes and shoes, rolled them together into a ball, tossed them into the plastic bag in the waste basket and tied up the ends of the bag, banishing their existence. She glanced into the vanity mirror to see the barely dried crusts of coagulation spattered along the edges of her lips and in her hair, just as the mirror fogged up, obfuscating the image as she would dismiss the memory.

She stepped into the tub, bent her knees with effort like an old woman, and sat down. Hot shower water cascaded over her head and back. She buried her face on her knees and sobbed, her shoulders slumped with the weight of guilt. She sat in that position nearly ten minutes. She used a fresh white bar of soap to wash the remains of Josiah's life away. After what seemed like hours, her body red and singed and limp from the heat, she forced herself to get up.

Becky knocked on the door. "Table set, Mama," she said proudly.

"Pancakes!" Jake cried in the background.

Grace rubbed a towel over her torso so hard she further chafed her skin. She climbed out of the bathtub and stood naked at the sink, checking for remains of blood. She flushed her face repeatedly with cold water, dried it with a towel that she tossed into the hamper, and slipped into the pink terry robe that hung on a hook on the back of the door. She pulled the belt tightly around her waist and looked at herself in the mirror, wiping with her fingers through the vapor to view her image. She appeared to be the same woman; however she knew she was not the same, nor would she ever be. How easy it was to deceive. How easy to become someone else when you need to be.

She stepped out of the bathroom to join her children with the air of a woman practiced in the art of pretense. Standing over the stove, her shoulders stooped, she strained to control her trembling hands. She said not a word to the children as she stirred the batter in a large glass bowl and poured ¼ cup full into four quadrants on the hot griddle, forcing herself to pay close attention in order to flip each pancake as it bubbled to avoid burning, then slipping the browned disks onto a platter, one on top of the other, as she had a hundred times. This small gesture of nourishment had always given her pleasure, but not that night.

Becky stared at her mother, watching what was usually a pleasing ritual. She felt a frightening and unfamiliar distress, and experienced, for the first time, a desire to flee, to run away from something she couldn't understand or deal with. A sensation she would carry with her into her own future.

Jake had engaged Leah in a duel with their forks.

"Put those down!" Grace bellowed.

The children froze, rarely subject to their mother's temper. They sat up in their chairs and ate slowly, trying to swallow down every slurp of sound. Grace prepared another plateful and turned off the stove. She drooped into her chair and cupped her cheek in the palm of one hand, her elbow leaning on the table, what she had always told the children the well-mannered never do.

Becky poured more syrup for the younger siblings, as if to sweeten the setting. Jake ate all, as he knew was expected, but Leah's pancakes turned cold, and while she longed to slip into her mother's lap, she sat very still and avoided eye contact with her mother or siblings, confused and frightened, without knowing why. Soon, Becky rose to collect the plates.

"Leave them," Grace ordered, in a calmer but no less commanding voice. "Take your baths," she said. "Get ready for bed."

Grace left everything in place and fell onto the couch. She closed her eyes tightly to dispel the vision of Josiah on the ground, alone and unprotected, while she hid safely from sight.

"Mom must be sick," Becky whispered to the others, all together in the bathroom. She placed one index finger to her lips and ran the hot water into the tub. She wiped away one smidgeon of blood that clung to the edge of a tile and took a deep breath to still her distress.

When they were once again clean and sweet smelling, wrapped in their multi-colored flannel pajamas, the children returned to the living room. They stood in a line, oldest to youngest, awaiting inspection. Leah broke ranks first and climbed into Grace's lap, grabbing one of the books on the coffee table before Becky could stop her.

"Read to me, Mama," she pleaded.

"Not tonight," Grace answered, swiping her gently off her lap.

Becky motioned for her siblings to follow her into their room. She read to them half-heartedly and they listened in the same way, before slipping into their beds. They called out when ready for sleep.

"Tuck," they cried, awaiting Grace's warm hug and tender kiss good night.

"Say your prayers," she called back to them from the couch, yearning for the sound of their innocent voices.

Every night, they repeated a prayer she taught them long ago, her own version of the classic, reworded because she could not bear the thought of their death even in rhyme. The irony of the bedtime prayer that night did not escape her, and she tightly shut her eyes against tears while she listened to their recitation.

Now I lay me down to sleep,
I pray the Lord my soul to keep.
Give us hope and keep us safe.
Grant us strength for all our days.

"Strength," Grace muttered. Where will they find strength in this world? How will she protect them, even now, after all this time, in this supposedly safe place?

Margo Elliott McGraw/1996

Think you're escaping and run into yourself.
Longest way around is the shortest way home.
James Joyce

Mrs. Elliott named her daughter Margo Morgan Marion Elliott. She fancied elegant names, especially for her daughters: more contemporary and stylish than those typically given to the children of European immigrants. Her daughters would have names like the people pictured in the discarded issues of *Vogue* magazine at the department store where she worked. They would stand out from the sea of Marys and Saras, Lindas and Elizabeths.

As the birth approached, she was unable to choose between the three names she favored, so she decided to use them all, relishing the alliteration she had learned in English class. Margo Morgan Marion was the name in her mind and, once of a mind, there was no changing it. However it was Mr. Elliott who filled out the hospital's birth certificate a few hours after the birth, and when he discovered he was limited to one given and one middle name, he dropped Morgan, even though that was the name he preferred, hoping the baby would be born a son, and instead made that his pet name for her, phoning now and then long after she migrated to New York City to say, in his best imitation of himself, "Top of the mornin' to you, Morgan."

Margo was the eldest of the four Elliott children, although not the first-born. Caroline Ann, born with red hair and rosy cheeks and what seemed a hearty disposition, perished before her fifth birthday from a bad cold that turned out to be a case of polio so ferocious even an iron lung could not breathe for her. Margo was three years old at the time and soon after that barely remembered her sister, as if she had been merely a visitor. Few photos of Caroline were in the family album and her name never spoken, as if to invoke the name of a dead child might curse the others.

Within four years after Margo was born, two sons and another daughter joined the clan, and soon after, few remembered there had been a first-born. Mrs. Elliott, cheerful and patient, her eyes bright and spirit boisterous, kept her arms always open wide for a hug, infusing her children with an invisible shield that she hoped might protect them better than she had been able to protect the first. She urged them to live the American dream and delighted in every achievement, large or small. After the last of her children moved on, and after she retired, she took care of the offspring of her neighbor, Grace, and seemed to love them all the more, not only because they might have been grandchildren, but because they were fatherless, and of mixed race, thus, she believed, in need of an extra dose of kindness. Mrs. Elliott would have been the first to say that she didn't know much about most things, but she knew for certain that all human beings were able to give freely to each other was compassion, and she was a woman who held steadfast to such beliefs.

Mrs. Elliott never looked back, rather cherished every moment, commenting now and then that memory can be more curse than blessing.

Margo quickly embodied the persona of a high achieving first born. She earned straight A's in secondary school and high honors at college. She read incessantly about world history, enthralled by maps and timelines, fascinated by passages through epochs and across distant and exotic places. Byzantine and Chinese dynasties. The Medici and the Elizabethans. The politics of revolution and civil war. As she embedded herself in the stories and interpretations, she discovered that beyond logistics and networks, human beings were defined by the patterns that demarcate cultural shifts: shared values, concomitant aspirations, tribal traditions.

Heeding the counsel of her high school algebra teacher, at Ohio State University she majored in the sprouting field of industrial psychology and took several courses in statistics. She graduated with a specialty in market research and consumer decision-making, and her ultimate prowess was based only partially on skill, more so by a persistent focus on the vagaries of the decision process – the reasoning that cannot always be documented, the nuances between the lines – as one studies the past to predict the future.

Once settled in Manhattan, Margo quickly worked her way up to a high-level position in the research department of a small advertising agency that evolved, in no small measure because of her proficiency, into a multinational conglomerate. Margo, by then renowned by clients and industry colleagues for insight and foresight, and with a striking list of accomplishments compiled into an impressive resume, managed her team and her own life like a Swiss clock.

Motored by powerful natural propulsion, she unfailingly acted with purpose and tenacity, and while she has devoted her vocation to the observation and analysis of human behavior, she rarely scrutinized her own. Emotions, like qualitative analysis, she knew, were hard to read.

Quantitative data was Margo's expertise. Her interpretation of trends had been the inspiration for many new businesses and award-winning marketing campaigns. Her private life was no less important, but background rather than foreground, like billowy clouds across a blazing blue sky.

Her husband, Daniel, often said, to almost anyone in earshot, that Margo did not have a spontaneous bone in her body, and Margo never argued the point. She was insistent that every action had a reaction and everything in the end had a purpose. Even moving to New York City was the last of a carefully orchestrated set of decisions on a predetermined path. She was proudly predictable and predictability became her stock-in-trade.

"There are no coincidences, only correlations," she was quoted recently in an article for the American Marketing Association magazine on the power of marketing intelligence. "The very essence of consumer research is to comprehend and influence behavior. It is up to the research professional to explain the trend, and interpret what might be otherwise misinterpreted as spontaneous or inexplicable. Incidental behaviors might complicate the research, but nothing is a matter of chance."

A prototypical striver, goal-oriented and self-directed, Margo expected to achieve all desired outcomes, personally and professionally. However, her own commentary haunted her of late, challenging a lifetime of intentions, as she faced a goal she could not achieve: motherhood. Even Daniel, an illustrator and graphic designer, who from the first was the right brain to her left, seemed to have veered off-course.

They met only weeks after Margo arrived in the city and married two years later. Both stocky and ruddy, as if the quintessential Irish bar maid and cop, they sported nearly identical shades of chestnut brown hair and brown eyes, his straggly locks always in need of a trim, her straight mane tied neatly down her back with a ribbon. In their shared walk-in closet, one would have to look closely to know which clothing belonged to whom, their colors neutral, styles understated. She wore little make-up and no perfume; he used a scented pre-shave but no cologne. Neither wore jewelry beyond wedding rings and watches, although a tiny silver cross on a thin chain hung around Margo's neck, a gift from her mother at confirmation.

They both wore wire-rimmed glasses for reading and fancied black and white photography. They shared an interest in contemporary memoirs and British writers, a passion for foreign films, and enjoyed Saturdays wandering the cavernous marble halls of city museums, although he preferred the Metropolitan, she the Museum of Natural History. They often spent Sundays strolling the cross-town streets of Chelsea, what Daniel dubbed the walking modern art collection, slipping in and out of one avant-garde gallery after another, and flopping at the end of the day at a cozy Ninth Avenue bistro where they shared a bottle of red wine and multiple small plates for tasting. They rarely entertained, only when they had attended enough small dinner parties to require reciprocation, otherwise content to keep their own company.

Both were what they referred to as recovering Catholics, members of an extensive group of Manhattan careerists, yet they retained the straight edges and determination to be more worthy than they believed they were.

The early years of their marriage were focused on building careers and enjoying the cultural buffet of Manhattan. They each devoted four years to earning MBA degrees part-time at Columbia University – hers with a concentration in marketing and consumer psychology, his in visual communications – and often spent evenings with their noses buried in textbooks. They rarely traveled farther than a beach in winter and summer, and both donated time to professional task forces or pro bono projects. Their lives were full and satisfying, for a time.

They had spent the last five years trying to conceive a child – an agonizing process that started with two miscarriages, followed by the obligatory therapists and fertility specialists, incessant temperature taking, mind and body-altering hormone regimens, a macrobiotic diet, and two failed in vitro fertilization attempts.

The process took its toll. Without children as anchor, they found themselves like trains headed in the same direction, but along parallel rails. Emotional and physical disconnection hung between them like heavy drapery. At Daniel's insistence, they adopted a shelter mutt named Mona, an overgrown terrier with an elongated Corgi torso, which Margo walked in the morning and Daniel at night. While the dog was not especially affectionate, she served as a good buffer and perky companion, until eighteen months later, when they discovered she had a cancer too severe to treat. They kept her as comfortable as possible until time to let her go and agreed to take a breather before choosing another, their hearts terribly heavy, as if the dog had absorbed the diminishing passion for each other, its loss another painful defeat.

Neither blamed the other, the cause of their infertility elusive, but it was Margo who absorbed the humiliation with an acute, nearly unbearable sense of failure. Her life plan was incomplete. She had failed at the most natural human experience. Nevertheless, and despite Daniel's entreaties, she was resistant to the subject of adoption, as if an adopted child would be a permanent symbol of her inability to fulfill this crucial personal ambition. A flag forever at half-mast.

Daniel, on the other hand, still kept a pile of parenting books on his night stand, all dog-eared and marked with notations, and refused to relinquish his desire to be a parent. He had counseled with fellow designers to determine the best shade to tint the walls of a child's room and what sort of pattern he might stencil along the edges. He quizzed Margo's best friend Nina, and her husband Barrett, about the secrets to teaching babies to sleep through the night, although he contended he was fully prepared for long nights and planned to change diapers with panache. Daniel had every intention of being an active parent, a true partner in the process and a better father than his own, a man who had been consumed with his career and rarely in attendance. He no longer cared if the child carried his DNA, he simply wanted to be more than a couple; he wanted to be a family.

In contrast, Margo was increasingly unwilling to dwell in defeat by raising someone else's child. She argued that the bureaucratic hurdle to adopt would be too great to leap. She claimed she was no longer willing to expend the emotional or financial capital that comparable high-achievers spent to acquire healthy white babies, and she was fearful of the nightmare stories of poor black babies damaged in utero by negligent mothers. She convinced herself that if they were meant to have children, they would have had children, and tried to convince Daniel that perhaps they were better suited to a life free of such complications.

As she persuaded herself that the option of having children of her own was out of her hands, she became further convinced that adoption seemed more like the taking away of not only another person's child, but that child's destiny.

"I'm starting to feel like adoption is a form of theft," Margo confided to Nina, her confidante and fellow agency executive, whose two children were Margo and Daniel's goddaughters.

The two women had had similar conversations, many times, but Nina, known for frequent exasperation as a businesswoman, was exceedingly patient on more delicate issues. She understood that each time they discussed the subject, there might emerge a glimmer of greater clarity, a slight variant on perspective, and, perhaps, at some point, a better resolution. She also harbored an element of guilt that having children had been so easy for her and Barrett, and that too many women, like Margo, who had waited perhaps too long, or breathed in too much noxious air, or consumed too many pollutants, or a million other inexplicable reasons, seemed unable to enjoy such blessings.

"Let's face it, white babies available for adoption are born to little girls whose parents, or church, refused them abortions, or from women without resources forced to give up their kids," Margo declared.

"I suppose it can be seen that way."

"Do I want to be the caretaker of the genetics of a mother and father who toss out a child like the trash?"

"Margo..."

"I know. I'm being harsh."

They were sitting at a café on the upper level at Grand Central Station, replete with murals of French country scenes and rounded wooden café chairs around tables covered with blue-checkered tablecloths. The last of their omelets curdled on their plates and Margo listlessly shuffled the remains of salad around with a fork, as if she might discover buried treasure.

Nina watched her, waiting for the conversation to resume. Small and slight of build, like a gymnast, Nina nevertheless commanded attention because she was one of those people with an all-knowing demeanor, a guru by nature and appearance. Always elegantly dressed and coifed, Nina was more the epitome of the Manhattan businesswoman than Margo, and although they both wore slim-fitting skirts with silk blouses and tapered jackets, Margo was dressed in a simple gray ensemble, whereas Nina wore a Chanel knock-off, in a textured wool in the deep blue and plum shade of that season, that might have just stepped off the runway. Her ash-brown hair skimmed her shoulders in perfectly aligned layers and, as she had just returned from a weekend at her beach house in Sag Harbor, her naturally peachy skin was tanned, which brought out the crystal blue of her eyes. She sat erect in her seat, opposite Margo's slump, and, pictured together, the two women might have posed for a big-business recruitment poster, Nina the mentor to her colleague's recalcitrance.

A waitress wearing a bland expression and a black ruffled apron refilled their iced-tea glasses, forcing a pause in the conversation. Nina used that moment to think of suitable words of guidance, even as she silently gave thanks for two healthy children, who, despite challenges of mixed-heritage, enjoyed the blessing of attentive, affluent parents. She reached out to grasp Margo's hand.

"Have you not considered that you might be saving a life?"

"I know, I know, but lots of people want those perfect little babies. They will always be saved."

"I was thinking of the mother. How hard it must be to give up a child, whatever the circumstance. Perhaps the only comfort is knowing the child will have a better chance, don't you think?"

"I think it's never better than a nightmare to give up a child, whatever the circumstance," Margo answered in a sharp retort. "That's the one thing the whole abortion debate never mentions: even if we can end the pregnancy, the after effect is forever. Women who should not or cannot have children, shouldn't."

Nina, who was compassionate and forgiving of her closest friend, was nonetheless surprised by her severity. "Margo, that is terribly insensitive. Not like you at all. And easier said than done."

Margo, chastened, lowered her eyes and sipped her iced-tea. She pulled her hand from Nina's. "You must be so tired of this conversation."

Nina smiled and nodded affirmation, but with a kindly expression. "I just hope you can resolve this and find some peace. For you and for Daniel."

Margo nodded. "Poor Daniel. He so much wants children."

"He would be a good father."

Margo nodded. "And I might have been a good mother."

"Yes, you would, and you can be, if you choose."

Nina sat back and opened her palms, as if seeking salvation. "You know what, take mine. I mean it, take both girls, they're budding adolescents, absolutely miserable creatures, most of the time, so take them for a while. You can give them back when they're, oh I don't know, maybe twenty-five."

Margo chuckled. "Who are you kidding? You wouldn't let them go for a day."

"Okay. What about Chinese baby girls? It's awful what's happening there, plenty of adorable little girls who need homes."

"Yes, but it takes eons to get the child, and I think a baby knows from the first if it's not wanted. Do I really want a child who starts life with emotional distress?"

"Margo, every child brings some history with them, even if it's just the stress of moving down the birth canal. Truly, no one emerges unscathed."

"And what about all the cultural issues?" Margo went on, as she so often did, as if monologue rather than dialogue. "There's an aggressive movement among the African-American community to limit adoptions of black children by white couples, you know, so as not to eradicate the child's cultural history. There might be something to be said for that. I mean, it must be hard to have a different color skin than your parents, and grandparents. It is so important to know from whence you've come."

Margo paused, embarrassed suddenly that she had ignored the fact that Nina was a white woman married to a black man, whose children were lovely shades of mocha brown. She hastened to repair her remark.

"It's different for you, Nina. You know that. You're well balanced, you and Barrett. Your girls have some of each of you, they understand the blend, they know exactly where they come from. You've created your own family culture."

Nina nodded. "Yes, but you know it's not as easy as that. Kids like mine spend their whole lives choosing sides. Identity is tricky. Never simple. If I understood fully what I would have been laying on my daughters, I'm not sure I would have."

Margo smiled. "My dear, one has only to see you with Barrett to know there was no choice in the matter. And your kids reflect that."

"Yes, but..."

"But nothing. You had different circumstances. In my case, a white couple adopting a black child, that's a whole other can of worms. I can understand why people want to keep kids in their own clan, so to speak."

"So a black child is better off without a family than with a white family? I cannot accept that."

"When you say it that way..."

"It's not like you to see only the downside. What's going on in that complex brain of yours?"

"Crazy, isn't it? I have no problems making decisions, as a rule, you know that. But this, this is not a new car or another dog. I can't stop thinking about this girl I knew, a girl from the neighborhood in Columbus, who was dispatched to one of those homes for unwed mothers, remember those? She never got over giving up the baby. Went mad in fact. So maybe it's supply and demand, and I don't want to perpetuate demand for unwanted babies."

Nina shook her head vehemently. "I'm sorry, that's just crazy my friend. You are over-analyzing this. Kids get born, wanted and otherwise, and who gives a damn about rationale or process or the failings of our culture. It's the children that matter. You always say that everything happens for a reason."

Nina motioned to the waitress for the check. She reached into her purse for a credit card and when she looked up, she saw tears bubbling in Margo's eyes. "Oh honey, I'm sorry."

Margo waved her hand in dismissal and wiped her eyes with the edge of her jacket, a mannerism she had inherited from her mother, and, reminded of her mother at that moment, she longed to be a child again, waking to the sweet scent of cinnamon French toast and taking off for school with a brown bag filled with a hearty sandwich, an apple and a home-made cookie, for good health and good cheer, Mrs. Elliott used to say. In rare moments of self-pity, Margo wished she were more like her mother, or like her mother's neighbor, Grace: good women devoted to family, neither expecting nor demanding much for themselves. Mrs. Elliott would share everything with her husband for fifty years, and, when the time came, would bury him, as she had her own parents, with few regrets, because, as she frequently commented, people grow old and die, that's the natural order of things. What was implied was that children who die are an aberration, a tacit reminder of the loss of the first-born.

"And what if I had a child who died, like my sister?" Margo murmured. "I'm not my mother, I could not handle that. Nor could Daniel."

"There is always a risk, Margo, but you cannot focus on the risk."

Margo heaved a heavy sigh, without resignation, merely frustration.

"Talk to one of those adoption counselors," Nina prodded. "Maybe, as awful as it starts, it ends well. Symbiosis: a forsaken child given up to parents denied their own."

"And what about carrying on the bloodline? Isn't that the point?"

"So you preserve someone else's blood line. That has to matter, yes?"

Margo shook her head again, without certainty, trying not to obsess on the subject, but give it proper consideration. Daniel had recently had the good sense to stop asking, although she knew he was an optimist, hoping she might come around to his way of thinking.

"Just give me a little time, Daniel, I'm sorting things out," Margo told him the last time they had the conversation, one of too many to Margo's mind. She was tired of her own voice and exhausted by the recurrent torment.

"We should be sorting this out together, don't you think?" Daniel had answered.

"Yes, and we are, if you will just give me the space I need."

"Space is overrated, Margo."

She knew he was right, but try as she might, Margo was like a speeding train, stuck on the track.

"Aren't you worried about fetal alcohol syndrome?" she asked Daniel that night. "Those babies are way more likely to end up in prison. And what about crack babies?

HIV? They don't even live long enough to have lifelong health problems."

"Why only babies? Maybe we should consider older kids."

"The older the child, the more likely the emotional problems. Attachment disorders. Developmental delays. The margin of error is even greater. Zero reliability."

"We are talking about children, Margo, not statistics."

"Actually, the statistical evidence has to be evaluated. We just don't know what we're getting."

"Well, we had a dog like that, and she was happy with us."

"I cannot believe you are comparing a child to a dog!"

That was the last conversation they had, a few nights before, and Daniel since then was as sullen as a petulant teenager. Margo felt much the same.

The morning after her lunch with Nina, Margo sat in a conference room with several colleagues, all engaged in casual conversation. She was unusually quiet, disconnected to the chatter. Prince Charles and Princess Diana were in the midst of a scandalous divorce, President Clinton was facing conservative Bob Dole in the pending election, and thirty black churches had been burned in Mississippi that year; however the agency team was focused on a pitch to a new enterprise named eBay, which promised to revolutionize Internet shopping. Margo, only half-listening, was consumed with thoughts about another revolutionary event: the first cloning of a mammal, Dolly, the sheep, and she had put in a call to her fertility doctor to determine if the technology might be deployed any time soon.

"No," the doctor had answered with disdain, having no patience with what he called science run amok. The death-knell, he argued, for natural selection.

"For some of us, that apocalypse has already arrived," Margo responded.

That night, Margo stood before piles of clothing on her bed, studying them as if a display of artifacts in a museum. Every decision of late, no matter how small, seemed a terrible challenge. She was leaving the next morning for San Francisco for a presentation to an important client. As a rule, Margo farmed out such trips to members of her staff; however, now and then, her presence was required, and she also decided to go because she was desperate for a change of scene.

She enjoyed long-distance flying, particularly since she had earned the privilege of first class travel. She settled into a cushy window seat and dozed briefly, never adept at sleeping on planes, or in hotels for that matter, although there she indulged the pleasure of watching movies in the middle of the night. In the sky, she caught up on past issues of *The New Yorker*, the solemnity of air flight like a library. She watched on the private screen the movie *Mission Impossible*, which she would never have paid to see in a theater, but enjoyed the escapism for a couple of hours, and read a good chunk of John Grisham's new novel, *Runaway Jury*, perfect for airplane reading. She peered out the tiny square window with renewed marvel at the splendor of flight, watching as daylight magically sustained itself through time zones, soaring above clouds spread across the sky like filament, and the periodic glimpse of the mountainous terrain below that resembled NASA photographs of the surface of the moon.

Nothing so much mattered when suspended in that sort of netherworld, and as Margo stared at the horizon, she grazed the window with the tips of two fingers, as if she might miraculously clear the air, like steam from a mirror, to reveal her destiny. She saw nothing but clouds and infinite space. Somehow she would have to make peace with the rest of her life, and with Daniel, and she had to find a way to convince him that their future without children would have to be good enough.

In San Francisco, after a long afternoon of meetings, she treated clients and colleagues to dinner at a trendy bistro, where they consumed six bottles of a new Napa vintage. The combined effect of jetlag and wine allowed her to sleep soundly. She spent the next day finalizing plans for a research study, holding court amidst a bullpen of researchers, each occupying a padded dimly-lit cubicle with nothing but headsets and scripts and keyboards, eight hours a day. That night at the hotel she thrashed through the night, despite the plush bed and soft sheets, and finished the Grisham as the sun rose. Bleary eyed, she looked forward to the flight home, two nights away long enough.

She had a brief closing meeting that morning, arriving mid-afternoon at the airport to discover dense fog hovering like a huge, amorphous, low-lying cloud.

"Damn," Margo muttered, pacing the flat gray industrial carpet of the terminal waiting area, where strategically placed bulletin boards announced one delay after another.

Disgruntled passengers filled every pore of the airport. College students napped in corners like indigents, rolled-up hoodies their pillows. Business travelers, their ties loosened, jackets tossed to the side, eyes red with lack of sleep, toiled at laptops or consumed cocktails at airport bars, looking up only occasionally to listen to stock market talking heads on overhead screens. Margo observed the crowd as if a research project. Airport culture hadn't changed in twenty years. Those most adept at controlling their trajectories were blockaded; journeys thwarted, the prospect of the long wait rendering each of them expressionless. Not worth arguing with ticket agents or scurrying for alternate flights. They were trapped for however many hours until the fog lifted, hopefully in time to make meetings, attend events, read one last bedtime book, or, in Margo's case, return to the comfort of her own bed and put to rest once and for all thoughts of children. The time had come.

She paced back and forth, back and forth, the proverbial tiger in her cage. The fog report remained grim and the thought of sleeping in an airport hotel gruesome. Suddenly starving, she made her way to a food court where a throng surged at fast food stalls and tables were overflowing. The din settled over the space like the fog, saturated with the smell of fried and salty foods. She treated herself to a huge slice of pizza with a Diet Coke in an obscenely large cup to boost her flailing energy. She turned to scour the tables for a seat and finally inquired of a girl in her late teens or early twenties, hard to tell these days, if she might share the table where the girl sat alone reading. The girl looked up for a second, surprised, and blatantly disenchanted, but said "Sure, fine," and removed her backpack to make room before burying her eyes again in a dog-eared paperback of Oprah's first book club selection, *The Deep End of the Ocean*, which had caused a stir in the advertising community as the pinnacle of gatekeeping.

While she munched on an abundance of cheese that stretched into strands with each bite, occasionally catching on her chin, Margo observed the girl who was dressed as if from a thrift shop: the trendy vintage look. She wore stone-washed jeans, a black V-neck sweater under what must have once been a man's blazer, and short black leather Doc Martin boots with thick rubber soles and squat heels. Her dark, curly hair was cut into short choppy layers in a style popularized by actress Meg Ryan that in real life looks messy. Slim and small-boned, cheap silver bands adorned almost every finger on each of her tanned hands, matched by multiple tiny silver bands along the outer edge of each ear. The worn gray backpack now nestled on her lap and a large plaid flannel bag lay on the floor beneath her feet, bursting at the seams as if all her worldly possessions within. The girl looked up, aware that Margo was watching her, and when Margo smiled, she returned a quick smile, before averting her eyes and slipping a little further in her chair to resume reading.

The girl had neither food nor drink and Margo imagined she might be on a tight budget. She remembered what that was like when she was a schoolgirl.

"Can I buy you a soda? Cup of coffee?"

"Why?" snapped the girl.

Margo smiled. She might have predicted that response, distemper the hallmark of adolescent DNA.

"Because you might enjoy something to drink. Helps pass the time."

"I don't drink much coffee and I never drink soda," she stated flatly.

"No caffeine?"

"Some, sure. One of these days, they'll figure out that caffeine is good for something. Stimulants aren't all bad, you know. Like wine, has its benefits. Caffeine probably is good for the digestion, or respiration, we just don't know what yet. It is natural after all, from a bean, right? Second cousin to a grape."

Margo saw the fire in the girl's hazel eyes, the defiant expression on her bronzed face, like a child who swears she did not commit the crime she surely committed.

"Maybe you're right. I hope so, I drink enough of the stuff."

She took a long swallow, the caffeine leeching into her system and generating the jolt of energy she needed. "School break?"

"I don't go to school anymore."

"Oh, you look like a college girl to me. I guess you're older than you seem."

The girl smiled, clearly pleased with that impression. "Actually, I'm just eighteen, but I've always been mature."

"Eighteen, really? Where you off to?"

"Portland. Had to make a connection here, and now I'm stuck."

"Visiting friends? Family?"

"Moving there. I was going to try San Fran, but it's way too expensive, and Portland is happening, for those in the know."

"Indeed."

"Where are you going?"

"Home. To New York."

The girl eyed Margo's tailored pantsuit. "Here on business?"

"Yes, advertising."

"Ever do anything I know?" the girl asked, as if Margo were a celebrity.

"I don't make commercials. I manage research, strategize, that sort of thing."

"Are you the boss?"

"One of them."

"You like it?"

Margo hadn't stopped to think about whether or not she liked her work in a long time. "Most of the time," she answered.

"You travel a lot?"

"Often enough."

"Go anywhere great?"

"Yes, I've been to many great cities."

"Like where?"

"Well, London, Paris, Barcelona. Hong Kong..."

"Wow!"

"It's not always glamorous. I've spent many nights in hotel rooms in ordinary places, like Houston or Kansas City."

"Ever go to Columbus Ohio?

"Not for business, to visit my family. I grew up there."

The girl sat up straight with a jolt. "Really? Me too."

"Small world."

The girl did not volunteer any more information. She picked up her book to read, hiding her eyes, as if unwilling to be known. Margo moved the salad around on the cardboard plate to drain it a bit of the excess dressing and nibbled just enough to fill up. She was about to pack up and move on to a bar, perhaps a glass of wine might cut the edge, when she took a closer look at the girl. She seemed familiar.

"I'm sorry, but do I know you? I mean, I feel as if I've seen you before."

"Doubtful," the girl answered, as she looked up again to examine Margo's face. "I mean, not everyone in Columbus knows everyone else."

"I grew up in Northland, know that area?"

The girl's eyes grew wide again. "Seriously?"

Margo suddenly recognized the girl's light brown skin, the bright eyes: the elder daughter from the upstairs apartment who had grown into a lovely young woman.

"Aren't you Grace's girl?"

Despite her shocked expression, the girl showed no recognition.

"I'm Margo, Margo Elliott. Do you remember me? I left before you moved in, but we've met now and then when I visit, and my mom talks about you and your brother and sister all the time."

The girl folded down the page of her book and snapped it shut.

"Seriously? Mrs. Elliott's Margo? I should have recognized you. Of course I know you. I'm Becky. The oldest. She talks about you and your brothers and sister all the time. I, I just didn't, I'm sorry, I should have known. She's like a grandmother to me, so that would make us, like, what?"

"Adopted relations, of some sort." Margo chuckled. "Actually, I'm old enough to be your mother." The words stuck in Margo's throat like a chicken bone.

Becky laughed, and wondered what it might have been like to be born to Margo instead of Grace.

"What will you do in Portland?"

"Not sure yet. Maybe I'll get a job in advertising."

Margo smiled. She took the last sip of her soda, sat back and gazed at the scene around them.

"You know, we could make a commercial right here. The frustrated stranded traveler."

"Certainly sell a lot of caffeine. And booze," Becky said, pointing to the bar conveniently located opposite the food court.

"Maybe a B-movie commercial..."

"You mean, like, we wander the airport and end up on a deserted hallway, you know, like Alice in Wonderland or something, and at the end of the hall, there is this great big shiny Pepsi vending machine, all frosty, so you know it's filled with ice-cold sodas, and all we have to do is bang on it, bang, bang, get out the frustration, and with each bang, a can of Pepsi drops out."

"Love it! You've got a talent for advertising," Margo said, applauding.

"Or maybe I just watch too much television," Becky answered. "Why do people want to buy the stuff they see in such stupid ads?"

"Ah, the very essence of advertising," Margo pronounced with a knowing smile. "It's called the willing suspension of disbelief."

Becky digested the words aloud. "Willing suspension of disbelief. What a strange thought. Why? Why are people willing to suspend believing what they know isn't so?"

"It's poetry. Coleridge. 'The willing suspension of disbelief for the moment that constitutes poetic faith.' He said that happiness is made up of minute fractions. Something about soon-forgotten things, like kisses or a smile, a kind look, a compliment... the sorts of things that make us feel good, but only in that moment. A fleeting, feel-good sensation. So, we suspend the disbelief that might contradict the feeling. We let ourselves accept things we know, rationally, are not so, in favor of believing something more pleasing. Or, in the case of advertising, enjoy the fantasy that some thing – a product or service, a place perhaps – will make our lives better. Happier. Those of us in the business, we depend on that moment to make the sale."

"I get it."

Margo smiled. "You're a quick study. My mother always said you were smart. Wait until she hears I ran into you, she will love that. By the way, do you have a cell phone? Want to call home?"

"No, thanks," Becky demurred. "They don't need to know I'm stuck," she added.

Becky sat as stiffly as a mannequin. A young woman who managed adversity without sentiment. Margo imagined she would protect herself well from things that go bump in the night, but what might she forsake along the way?

Becky abruptly stood to go, gathering her bags as if making a hasty getaway. "I need to get to the gate, don't want to miss the connection," she stammered.

"Wait," Margo said, placing her hand on Becky's arm. "Are you all right? Grace knows where you are, right?"

Becky, gripping her bags as if her future depended on them, stared at Margo with a fiercely defiant expression, her shoulders squared, her eyes sharply determined. "Of course my mother knows. She knows I'm heading out of the past, on to the future. Moving on, that's what my life is about right now. I'm eighteen, and my life is finally getting started."

She stood very still, punctuating her belligerence, then, wobbling a bit on her legs, sat back down. Clutching the backpack to her chest, avoiding Margo's gaze, but not moving, she lowered her head and turned away, attempting to hide the tears that had welled in her eyes, like a child who has fallen off her bicycle and wants to appear brave, but cannot sustain the pretense.

"Oh, my. What can I do? Is there something you want to talk about?"

Becky shook her head no.

"I've got time on my hands. I can be a good listener," Margo said. "Ask anyone. And I'm good at keeping secrets."

"I think this is totally beyond someone like you."

Someone like me, Margo thought. What image did she convey? The big city businesswoman? Impervious? Insensitive? The BFE, her older brother nicknamed her: big friggin executive. She knew her mother took pride in that stature, and spoke of Margo often as a mother would speak of a childless daughter, focusing on career achievement.

"Someone like me has heard it all, really. Very little surprises me."

"Okay, try this: I just discovered my father is alive."

"What?"

Becky leaned forward to speak, and Margo leaned in as well, as if they were engaging in gossip.

"My brother found some paperwork my mother had to fill out to officially divorce my father, who has been gone since I was a little girl. Seems he wants to marry again and has to tie up loose ends. Except my mother told us he was dead! Can you imagine lying to us like that? I cried for weeks, months maybe. I felt his absence my whole life. I was barely eight when he disappeared. Gone, like he just evaporated. Whoosh! I mean, what other explanation could there have been? I'm the only one of the three of us who remembers him. All these years, my sweet mother, masquerading as a widow. Hardly ever went anywhere, from home to work and church on Sundays. She lived like a monk. You know my mother, unbelievable, right?"

Margo contemplated her words. "She must have had her reasons."

"Of course she did, that's not the point."

"I understand."

"Maybe you think you do, but there's more."

"Okay, I'm listening."

"You know my father was white, right?"

"Yes."

"And, I feel like, well, without a white father, I mean, it's hard to explain, a father who didn't abandon us, who was really part of us, well, I feel like all I have left is black. Like the color of my skin has suddenly gone dark. I don't want to go backwards. I don't want to be black. I preferred the charade."

Becky stared at Margo, expecting a rebuke, and also with astonishment on her own face, having spoken words she had never said aloud to anyone, not even her siblings.

"Listen, we live in a melting pot culture…"

"Melting pot, my butt. Spare me your big city idealism. You hang out with people who read *Ebony*? Any of them have to poison their scalp to get a comb through their hair? You have no idea what black folks do to fit in. What you're talking about is what they politely call diversity these days. Bullshit. Black and white do not mix, not unless they keep marrying to lighten the line. They've been at that since slavery, you must know that, you're an educated person, even if you don't know everything you should know. Your mother was kind to us, loving, but she's not my grandmother and you are not family."

Margo was momentarily speechless, humbled by the truth. Despite the incredible mix of people in New York City, Nina's husband Barrett was her only African-American friend and only a smattering of lower-level employees at the agency were black or brown. Her assistant, Pam, who had worked with Margo for six years, was the only person of color she saw every day, and while they shared much of their working hours and more than a few confidences, they were socially as separated as their neighborhoods on opposite banks of the East River.

"Are you going to Portland to find your father?"

"Don't be ridiculous. He walked out on us and never looked back. I don't care about him. I don't suppose I blame my mother for wanting to think him dead, but she shouldn't have kept that sort of thing from us. Not forever. Although my brother said he doesn't know what we would have done with the truth, and he might be right. The only thing that man gave us was a whiter look, and for that I'm grateful, but I wouldn't want to know him now."

"And you see yourself as white? Not brown?"

"I'm very light brown, light enough to pass, and that's the litmus test in this country. Lighter than the brown paper bag."

"Who thinks that way now?"

"Oh, please. You really must inhabit an ivory tower." Becky chuckled at her unintentional humor. "Technically, I'm a light-skinned mulatto, the lightest of the bi-racial. My mother was what they used to call quadroon, because she's at least 1/4 white, and I've got a lot more than one white person in my lineage, that's for sure. Most people think I'm tan, maybe Latino, which it's cool to be these days, thanks to JLo. I'm what they used to call a high-yalla. Way up the line. Only my lips are a little bit of a give-away, but thanks to Angelina, thick lips are sexy these days, at least on a white woman."

Margo listened in amazement to a conversation she never imagined she might have, particularly with an adolescent.

"My sister Leah is a shade darker, sort of middle-eastern. Sometimes we pretend we're Turkish or Moroccan or something, put on an accent, a scarf over our heads. People assume we're immigrants and we make-up all kinds of stories. Great posers we are."

Becky stared at Margo like a college professor waiting for a response, but Margo had none, so she went on, happy to educate her.

"I would bet you half the whites living in Columbus have black blood anyway. If they knew, they would die, because even a little bit of blackness, you know, the old one-drop rule, makes them black, at least in this country. What a horrible shock that would be!"

"One drop rule?"

"Never learned that one, huh?"

"Yes, but remind me."

"Not in most history textbooks. They passed a law, just before the Civil War, first in Virginia, land of Jefferson, right? Anyone with even a drop of black blood was officially black. Before that, a child was the race of the father."

"Oh yes, I remember."

"Kind of made it okay for slave owners to procreate without worry their mixed offspring might inherit. Or get ahead."

Margo shook her head in disbelief.

"God bless America," Becky recited, with a heavy dose of sarcasm.

With all the expertise Margo had in consumer psychology, all the understanding of aspiration and affinity groups, she knew nothing of this subject. If not a product to be marketed, she had no real comprehension of the psychology of the minority, and little understanding of anything related to the color line. She was mortified by her ignorance.

"I've heard about color lines, mostly from Spike Lee movies, and there was this other famous movie, many years ago, with Lana Turner, did you see it? *Imitation of Life*. Pretty powerful, but I don't know much more than that. I thought it was old news."

"Hardly," Becky pronounced. "And no one expects you to know. This is something Negroes have been dealing with forever. Our business. Do you even know how many different shades we are?"

Margo opened her mouth to respond, but Becky kept talking.

"Tar, ebony, licorice, alabaster, toffee, chocolate – dark or milk – amber, coffee, café au lait, of course, and mahogany, chestnut, nutmeg, copper, caramel, my personal favorite. Olive, that's my sister. My mother is cinnamon, my grandmother was molasses. We've got a whole set of paint chips, most of them shades of brown. Earth tones, you might say."

"Black Sambo," Margo murmured.

"What?"

"I'm sorry, I was just remembering this book a teacher read to us when I was a little girl: *Black Sambo*. The librarian was furious. She told us we were never to use that term, never to define anyone that way. My mother agreed, she raised us to be color-blind."

"No such thing," Becky said, shaking her head in disgust. "You can hide religion, you can hide politics, you can even hide being a creep, people are real good at that, but you cannot hide from color. Not most folks anyway."

"But that's what you are trying to do, yes?"

"I am who I am, who I've always been. I'm a tan girl, not even brown, tan. Black guys want me because I'm nearly white; white boys like me because tan is sexy. The only people who give me a hard time are darker women, the women who believe black is beautiful, the women who want their men to stay put. I got beat up in high school for being so light, but that's behind me now."

"Maybe you should talk to your father…"

"No way. He is dead to me. He ducked out without a word, although truly I think a white man wasn't tough enough for a resilient black woman like my mother. Sort of like good strong coffee watered down with too much milk. She's better off without him, although she has been lonely too long. Maybe one man was just enough for her. Whatever, this is my life. Black is black, simple as that. Most people would still like to wipe us off the face of the earth."

"No, not any more."

"If you believe that you're a fool. You might call that the racial version of the willing suspension of disbelief. People don't get lynched much down South anymore, not that I know of, but they drop out of school, they don't get good jobs and their kids go to lousy schools, and there are like thousands, maybe a million black men in prison. Take a good look at black models and movie stars, especially those that make it big. All light-skinned. A white version of what looks beautiful prevails. Leah calls them Halle Berry girls. True black women, African-American women, no way."

Margo was speechless. Everything Becky said was true, and she was forced to face the sad reality that she was oblivious to all this. She had worried more about black babies coming into the world diseased or damaged, than the intrinsic obstacles in their path.

"My brother Jake wants to be who he is, he's fine with it, although he's still young and he doesn't know what he's in for. He's not as good a student as Leah and me. He's a good athlete, but not good enough to go pro, so it's likely the Army for him, maybe the best place for a black man, so he can get an education, if he doesn't get killed. I'm nearly as white as you, so that's who I am. My grandmother used to say that every road goes north and south and we choose which way we go. That's the truth and I'm heading north as the girl I have always been."

"Well, it definitely helps to be so certain of yourself."

Becky nodded vigorously in agreement. "You got that right. I am smart. I don't need to go to college, not yet, maybe never. Not going into debt for a piece of paper, that's for sure. I'm going to try on a few things for size. Portland is the place to be, although I might also try Phoenix or Tucson, blend in with the Latinos there." She snickered.

"I must say, please forgive me for this, but Grace must be broken-hearted. Such a gentle soul, she must be terribly sad for you to deny your roots."

"Oh, my mama gets it. Black women get it. She's lived with this thing her whole life. Jake and Leah are still home, for a while, she has company. No offense, Margo, but you're a bright white woman with a big job and a good life in the big city, and your mom is a wonderful woman, but you do not have a clue about my mother, or me!"

Tears unexpectedly spilled again from Becky's eyes. She swiped at them with her sleeve with such force Margo shuddered.

Margo leaned back against the hard seat. She wanted to take Becky in her arms and comfort her, but she knew that was not an option. She marveled at this trick of fate, this poor little runaway. Marginalized. There must be others.

"I think you're very brave."

Becky smiled and nodded, composing herself and moving beyond the conversation with the same alacrity as she hoped to move on from her family history.

"One of these days, you should go to college, make yourself a better life. Education is the best compensation there is and you're too smart to settle for less."

"We'll see," Becky said as she gathered and settled each bag on a shoulder.

She extended her hand to Margo, who clasped it with both of her own. "Nice to see you, Margo. I mean that. Send my love to Mrs. Elliott. Tell her I said she is a darlin.'"

"Safe journey, Becky. And listen, take my card," Margo released Becky's hand and fumbled in her bag to retrieve a business card from a small leather case buried there. "Call me, if you ever land in the big apple, or if you need a friend. Because, well, in a way, we are family."

Becky nodded, took the card and shoved it into a pocket in her jacket and turned, her head high. She walked away without another word and without looking back.

The sky was dark and starless when Margo trudged up the stone steps and the first flight of stairs to the brownstone apartment where Daniel awaited her. He sat on the couch, an iconic white container of Chinese food half-empty before him on the coffee table, and another unopened on the kitchen table. As Margo entered the foyer, he pointed the remote toward the television to turn off the baseball game he had been watching, and rose to greet her. She motioned for him to sit.

"I'll join you," she said.

An open bottle of red wine was on the coffee table with a half-filled glass. As Margo sat, she picked up the glass of wine and drank down the remains in one long gulp.

"You must be beat," Daniel said.

Margo nodded, poured another glass of the wine, and offered it to Daniel, who took a sip and handed it back. She sipped, then placed the wineglass on the table. She nuzzled closer to Daniel and burrowed her body into his in a way she hadn't in a very long time, as if a child in need of protection. A wife desperate for comfort. Daniel wrapped his arms around her and pulled her close, grateful for the simple intimacy that had eluded them for too long.

They held each other in silence for a few moments, neither willing to break the spell, and Daniel knew that whatever it was Margo meant to tell him, she would do in good time.

At last, she sat up to face him. "Daniel, I have to tell you something."

Daniel braced himself for the decision he feared.

"I had an abortion."

"What? When?" Daniel pulled back, stunned by her confession, believing that he had known everything there was to know about her.

"I was nineteen, an innocent nineteen. It was one of those reckless college things. Too much beer. I thought I was safe, on the clock, but, of course, I wasn't. I was such a child. And I knew at once I was pregnant. The body changes so fast, you know, so I went to a clinic, to be sure. I knew it would break my mother's heart, and I knew it would completely change my life. I was terrified. No way was I ready for that."

Daniel sat silent and still for a moment, mulling her words. He heard the anguish in her voice, the fear of repercussion after all these years.

"Why didn't you tell me this before?"

"I never told anyone. Not my sister, not even Nina. I couldn't speak of it. One of those things that happen and you tuck it away, instantly and completely, to convince yourself it never was. I had put it out of my mind, until we decided to have a child. I talked to the doctor about it, and he said I was fine, physically, but, I suppose, when we couldn't get pregnant, I began to think either I had screwed something up, or maybe..." Margo stopped short. She lowered her eyes.

"Maybe what?"

"Maybe I didn't deserve to have one after eliminating the other."

Daniel leaned away just enough to retrieve the napkin on the coffee table, and used an edge to wipe the tears that drifted from Margo's eyes to her pudgy cheeks. She took the napkin from him and held it, as he resettled his arms around her.

"What did you do?"

"I went to Planned Parenthood, then I skipped school one day and went to a tiny room with bright light and steel tools piled on a table, and I was literally vacuumed out, or so it seemed. Then I went home and told my mother that the nurse said I had the flu and needed to rest for a few days. How could I tell her that I gave up a baby after she had lost a child? Children are her whole life. Us. The neighborhood kids. Grace's kids. I never said a word. I stayed home a couple of days and went back to school as if nothing had happened. And now, now I think, I think I lost the chance. And we're too old for babies. I'm not sure I can face the enormity of it. Everything about children is so unpredictable. Every little decision has an impact."

"That's true for all of us. Despite all we know, all we do, very little is predictable, least of all a life."

Margo buried her face once again in Daniel's shoulder. She breathed deeply the scent of soap and soy sauce and the pungency of the wine that clung to Daniel's lips, and she sighed with pleasure that some things, some people, are in fact predictable. In the best possible way.

She sat up again. "Some of us are not meant to have babies, I see that more clearly now. Perhaps better to take in a child who needs a home. A child who feels smaller than a child should feel. No child should feel that way. Maybe, anything can be undone. I think I'm ready to try, if you are."

The smile on Daniel's face was her answer. "Say the word, sweetheart. I'm ready."

"We have to be in this together, Danny. A child needs two parents. For life. Yes?"

"For life, yes."

Daniel sighed with relief and hugged Margo so tightly she thought she might smother in his embrace.

"We can make a difference, I believe that. Just remember, there is no trial run. No testing. We do the due diligence and take what comes, yes?" Daniel said.

"I know."

"And the odds are great the child will be black."

Margo smiled, thoughtfully, knowingly, as if harboring a secret, before she sat back and answered. "More likely a shade of brown."

"Okay," Daniel answered, surprised by the specificity. Margo was not one to dispute visuals, his expertise.

"Perfect," he pronounced with a beaming smile. "An earth tone."

Nina Douglas/2001

But life is long.
And it is the long run that balances the short flare
of interest and passion.
Sylvia Plath

Nina ran as fast as her slim legs would carry her, sprinting through downtown Manhattan streets among throngs of runners, reminiscent of the bulls at Pamplona. Panting, sweating, battling hysteria, they ran from the explosions, from the fierce roar that threatened to swallow them whole, and from the fire and smoke spiraling around them like a tornado, making it hard to see beyond the next layer of runners. They ran from bodies hurtling from the sky and voices screaming like those imagined in hell. They ran from reams of paper swirling around them like heavy snow, all the while hounded by a giant ball of hot ash. They did not know what they were running from, nor why, nor did they have any idea what might happen next, which made the running all the more frantic. They would not know for hours, days, weeks, and might never fully comprehend, why lower Manhattan had exploded like a minefield. In that moment, they knew only they were running for their lives.

Moments earlier, on her way to meet with a client on the 102nd floor of Tower Two at the World Trade Center, Nina called to say she was running late and was confused when no one answered. The phone rang nearly ten times before she gave up, expecting at least a message machine if not a voice, because it was unthinkable so close to the opening bell that no one would answer the phone of a financial firm downtown. Days later, she would discover that her client perished with nearly half of his two hundred employees, and at the time of her call he was issuing commands to his staff to move rapidly down the interior staircase, refusing to exit until everyone else was safely out of the office. She was not surprised. Herman was that sort of man, larger than life, his name still on the door of the firm he founded fifteen years earlier, a firm that quickly, under the steady hand of its surviving lieutenants, relocated and reopened for business within a week, the best tribute they could bestow on their beloved chief executive.

Nina gasped for breath like the terrified animal she was. Sweat dripped from her armpits and encircled her breasts. She was beet red in the face and she trembled uncontrollably, as if she had delirium tremens. She wondered if she too might explode, not certain how long she would be able to continue to run, although transported by the crowd, her legs moving as if of their own accord, propelled as much by momentum as panic.

The sound of explosions had given way to the steady heavy thump of the stampede. The booms had passed, screams diminished by distance, so that now she was able to hear sobbing mixed with the heavy breathing that was in part the result of exertion and in part the assault of the ash. Although her throat burned, she could not breathe through her nose, the acrid smell of smoke and ash neither the comforting fragrance of a wood fire, nor the sweet aroma of meat cooking on the grill; rather an odor more putrid and rank than anything she had ever experienced: the stink of burning flesh and molten steel.

So they all kept running, hoping desperately that soon they might arrive at a place where they could breathe, and where they might no longer be overwhelmed with the hysteria that kept them going, without knowing where they would land.

She was just north of Houston Street, roughly two miles from what would come to be called Ground Zero, when people around her began to collapse at the curb and others lined up at pay-phone booths. Nina too had lost her purse and cell phone, dropped and kicked into oblivion at the start, and she wanted to call her husband, call the school to check on her children, but the lines already snaked down the sidewalks and she knew if she stopped she might be stuck in place indefinitely. In truth, she was more afraid to stop running than to keep running.

The herd had run straight up Broadway; not the great white way known by tourists, punctuated with neon billboards and iconic theaters, all of which would be silent and empty that night, but the broad lower Manhattan thoroughfare, emanating from Wall Street like a ray of light. As they ran north, southbound cars pointed toward them as if an admonishment, and she was increasingly aware of the sirens of fire trucks and police cars that sped down nearby Seventh Avenue, also heading against traffic, as if the city had descended into anarchy.

Traffic had otherwise come to a standstill. Buses and taxis were parked and double-parked, their drivers milled together speaking multiple languages, the modern equivalent of the Tower of Babel. All shapes, sizes, colors and ethnicities, they shared a collective confusion, nothing but hard city streets to ground them.

As Nina slowed down, and the frenzy diminished, she began to think more clearly. Her daughters were safe at their private high school north of the city; she had seen them off on the bus early that morning. Their new school year had started only yesterday. What an awful way to mark an auspicious year: Jennifer, a senior, Emma a freshman. She imagined they must be terrified not to know where their parents were, but she had no way to reach them. She took comfort knowing school officials would keep them on the grounds until safe to return, and the parents' chain of communications would keep them all informed, at least those who were reachable.

Her husband, Barrett, left especially early that morning on his way to his office mid-town, or was he headed elsewhere? She couldn't remember now. He mentioned something about an early meeting, something about not making it to the gym, although she could not recall his exact words. He left as usual with an abbreviated goodbye to his daughters and a kiss on her cheek, on his way to Starbucks for his morning brew: a venti latte with one packet of sugar. Wonderfully predictable. Thank goodness he too was out of the fray. His law firm had relocated uptown just last year, so they were well beyond the chaos, as far as she knew. He would wonder where she was that morning, although she hadn't mentioned her client appointment, so he had no reason to fear she might have been downtown. Her office was only four blocks from his at 51st Street and Madison Avenue, a couple of miles further, if she could make it.

Barrett. Her husband of twenty years. His colleagues, clients and friends, his competitors on the handball and tennis courts, they all called him Barry, but she had been so captivated with his name that the moniker stuck, and she was surprised, and impressed, that the name was derived from his mother's family, distant relatives of

Elizabeth Barrett Browning. She loved his name almost as much as she loved the look of him, a man built like a sturdy tree with long, elegant limbs. Father of her beautiful brown daughters. In their early years, she whispered to him seductively when they were alone together – Barrett, Barrett – rolling the letters on her tongue as if a sexual mantra, and even now, at the thought of his name, she longed to hear his soothing voice, that deep melodious tenor that seemed to match the honey tone of his skin.

They met at a party thrown by a mutual friend. She was working at her first advertising job and attending graduate school at night, and he was completing law school. She resisted at first, knowing she was drawn to a man her family would reject, but she could not stay away. In a matter of months, he took her home to meet his black father, a high school history teacher, and his white mother, a social worker, as if to announce that they were meant to be together forever. An odd move for Barrett, a man who rarely presumed anything of anyone and tread slowly into relationships of all types, but who now and then was clear that he knew exactly what he wanted and nothing else would suffice.

His parents resided in a small house in Mount Vernon, a suburban town, more black than white, and near enough to Manhattan to take the short train ride on weekends to enjoy a museum show or walk through Central Park with their tall brown sons in tow. Sons they raised to resist the discrimination of the color line, who nonetheless lived with first impressions every day of their lives, always believing they had to stand taller, try harder, and commit more intensely to achieve more than what was expected of them.

After a short courtship, they consummated their relationship in a cushy bed at a new boutique hotel in a fancy room that Barrett had reserved for the occasion, enhanced with a bottle of fine champagne and a platter of chocolate-dipped strawberries. The sort of seduction scene he had taken note of in a film, because this was more than consummation to Barrett, Nina understood, this was a melding of cultures and lives and skin. Afterwards, as he slept, she surreptitiously, guiltily, sniffed his skin, because someone she worked with suggested that black skin smelled differently, musty she said, as if the skin of the modern African-American community retained the scent of the cotton fields. As if their true differences might be revealed in scent. It was then that Nina debunked the first of the many myths surrounding her husband: black skin smelled no different than white. Barrett's skin was smooth and warm and his earthy skin tone and lean muscular body made her seem smaller than even her petite frame, a feeling she appreciated only with him. Later in their lives, she would nestle against him in bed and croon to him the theme song from *The Lion King* and he would make a small roar before wrapping his arms around her and clutching her to his body as if they might never be pried apart.

They had a small wedding at the United Nations Chapel, which Nina chose because she saw a picture of it in *The New York Times* and was immediately taken with the intimacy of the space, as well as its ecumenical ideal. They were married in a short ceremony, witnessed by their families and closest friends, presided over by the chapel minister. Nina's parents, and a few aunts and uncles and cousins, claimed the front pews, so that Barrett's family sat behind them, as if relegated to the back of the bus. Nina's mother was heard to grouse that they should have been married in a real church, even if not Catholic, while Barrett's parents remained stoically still and accepting, as they were. Behind the chaplain, a multi-storied white wall served as backdrop, flanked by a large sculptured cross on one side, a star of David on the other, which seemed to Nina a holy antidote to prejudice, a plea for tolerance. She was convinced that day their tenuous marriage would be blessed by all the Gods, and for the most part, it has.

After the ceremony, newlyweds and guests migrated to their first apartment, where Margo set out platters of cold cuts and salads from Zabar's, and they toasted their future with frosty champagne. Everyone was cordial, polite conversation made between munches and sips, and all but Margo and Daniel fled soon after the cake was served, ostensibly leaving the couple to their privacy. They left them more depleted than jubilant, and Nina wearily lamented her family's insensitivity. Barrett replied that his family had faced far worse.

They were idealists then: romantic, bright-eyed young achievers. These days, between the long hours they spend on the job – hers as the Executive Vice President for Account Management at a top-ten advertising agency and his as the Managing Partner of a corporate law firm – and their two adolescent daughters, as well as their pro bono commitments, his daily exercise regimen, her near-daily yoga class, and frequent weekends at their second home in the Hamptons, their lives were in constant motion, never a moment to take stock or consider alternatives, their days slipping away even more rapidly than that morning, as Nina sprinted through downtown Manhattan.

Barrett. She whispered his name. The one and only time in her life she had defied her parents and her culture and stepped out of the good-girl persona. He was the love of her life, and she admired him so. She knew he loved her as well, this man who seemed to have every opportunity – light brown skin, fine sculpted features, great intellect, and loving parents – who nonetheless took his father's admonition to keep his head down and make himself visible only through his accomplishments, ensuring his sustainability and self-respect. And, marry a white woman. His father never said so, not in so many words, but he had done so and Barrett did the same. Nina occasionally wondered if she was a prize or an insurance policy.

She slowed down a bit more, hardly able now to move her legs beyond tiny steps, one after another, as if a marathon runner collapsing at the finish line. She turned the corner at 18th Street, off Broadway, removing herself from the herd that had spread out like cattle spooked by an impending storm. She was so incredibly exhausted she slumped to the curb, her legs rubbery like the hot tar beneath her feet. She sat for a few moments, her breathing slowly returning to normal, as she buried her face on her arms, folded across her knees, trying to still her heart and calm her nerves. She leaned against the base of a meter pole for support.

On any other day, she might have been perceived to be a drunk languishing with a hangover, her body slack, eyes glazed, clothing filthy, and for a moment she felt like the little girl she once was, small and scrawny and always a bit disheveled, to her mother's dismay, growing up in Brooklyn with the migrants of eastern Europe who fled one or another form of fascism. Forging new villages within the city, uncomfortable with English, their children spoke for them, as they struggled to earn a living and understand offspring growing up in a rapidly changing world filled with bizarre music blasting from car radios and forced laughter on television shows that depicted lives unrecognizable to their own. Children who quickly adopted a sense of knowing so much more than their parents that parents cowered in their shadows, even as they attempted to preserve a thread of cultural continuity.

Nina, the only child, what they called in those days a tomboy, perpetually ran around the playground or the park, forever belittled by neighborhood friends because she had to wear glasses by the time she turned eight years old to compensate for a severe case of myopia. The four-eyed girl, she was taunted, despite her delicate features and heart-shaped face. Hidden behind those dark frames and thick glass were crystal-blue eyes that observed everything and absorbed every indignity as if her own. Even when her body grew shapely and a saleswoman at Lord & Taylor taught her how to dress, she never believed she was pretty, until she saw herself reflected in Barrett's eyes.

She had risen from the ashes of a street life to become the first of her family to graduate college, the first to earn a graduate degree, which took her four years part-time at NYU, and the first in the family to earn more than a modest living, much more. The first to own real estate. The first to vacation beyond the east coast. The first to give speeches and win industry awards. The first to marry out of the faith, and out of her skin tone.

Whatever her achievements, Nina's mother and father judged her only on the basis of this transgression. As far as they were concerned, she had betrayed her heritage and her parents' intentions for her to live the American dream. No matter that Barrett was as accomplished as she was, no matter that his parents were educated, middle-class homeowners, and no matter that he had light brown skin.

Nina's father insisted he was not prejudiced. No, he argued, he believed Negroes were entitled to the same freedoms as all Americans. However, he would pronounce as if an officer of the court, his daughter should not marry beneath her. Nina's mother, pained by the rift in the family, but impotent to alter the outcome, visited Nina regularly in Manhattan and, when her granddaughters were born, flouted her husband and welcomed Nina and Barrett and the children back to Brooklyn for holidays. A tenuous peace lasted only a few years, when Nina's mother contracted and died rapidly of stomach cancer, and her father moved to Florida, where he married another woman who also did not take kindly to Barrett, or to Nina's brown daughters.

That morning, running for her life, fearing for the lives of all New Yorkers, she was neither an immigrant girl nor an advertising executive nor the white mother of brown children. They were all the same, every one of them. All members of one immense terrified mob. On that day, and for a short time thereafter, they were one clan with a new enemy, an enemy beyond their comprehension.

One year after the anniversary of this day that would be called 9/11, as the massive labyrinth once known as the Financial Center was still being cleared of debris, mountains of detritus still being sorted and swept away, and reconstruction a concept miles from consensus, Margo would give a speech to the American Management

Association, reprinted in the *Wall Street Journal*, in which she expounded upon the psychographic impact of the bombings, claiming that the lingering effect, beyond high anxiety, was a spike in righteous indignation that propelled cultural consciousness further away from community toward individuality. The headline titled it *The Final Phase of the Me Generation.*

"Following the first days and weeks after the attack, when the global community coalesced behind the United States in an unprecedented embrace, Americans, always motivated by anxiety, remain in the grip of terror. More than ever intent above all on personal protection and determined to exert greater control over their lives and the lives of their loved ones. While many will blame 9/11 for the drastic reduction in trust, attitude research suggests that this has been a steady cultural paradigm shift, emerging like tea leaves at the bottom of a porcelain cup. We are faced with a profoundly altered American persona, one that has evolved from the communal to the demanding individualist. The bombings were merely a final catalyst for what was coming all along. All for one is the new millennium mantra: one for all, long gone."

That day, however, the residents of New York and Washington DC, and all those watching, were intent only on survival, Nina among them. Slumped against a street pole, dazed and disoriented, she felt a gentle poke at the shoulder. She looked up and had to shield her eyes with one hand to bring into focus a man handing a bottle of water toward her.

"You must be thirsty," he said.

She accepted the water gratefully and slugged it down in one long gulp, swiping away the stray droplets that slid down her chin.

"Thank you," she said, looking up to take in her benefactor: a stocky, middle-aged man wearing a white T-shirt under a crisp white apron that stretched from his chest to his knees. Wavy hair straggled into silvered strands at the nape of his neck like thick brush strokes; however, the only signs of age on his face were the gathering of crow's feet behind wire-rimmed glasses and uneven patches of skin scrawled across broad cheekbones. He peered at Nina over the glasses that slipped a bit down an aquiline nose and in that moment, Nina recognized him, not that she knew him personally, but as the kind of boy she once knew in Brooklyn, fellow child of European immigrants. Another grown up street urchin. A member of her tribe. A little paunchy and ragged around the edges now, he likely looked like his father must have looked when he first arrived at Ellis Island.

"Did you run all the way?" he asked.

She heard the trace of an indistinguishable accent, Italian or Austrian, as if he'd landed in America after he learned to speak, or picked up the inflection from parents or grandparents, like so many of the kids with whom she walked to school every day and attended college.

"From just above the plaza."

He shook his head in disbelief.

"I had an appointment, but I never got there," Nina elaborated, relieved to be conversing with a fellow New Yorker.

"Lucky for you."

He sat down on the curb next to her, thoughtfully positioning himself at a western angle, so she would not face the glare of a still-rising sun.

"I keep thinking about those people who work there but had other appointments today," he said. "Or who were up late with a sick kid or something, and just didn't quite get out of bed in time, and got to work late. Definitely blessed."

Nina nodded and blinked back the first round of tears.

"Either it's your time or it's not," he added, shaking his head in sustained disbelief.

"What's going on? Do we know what's happened?" Nina asked.

"Not sure yet. I've watched CNN all morning and I can tell you that after the planes flew into the World Trade Center, the whole thing, every last bit of it, went down in smoke. Did you know that?"

"What do you mean, the whole thing?"

"The whole thing, both buildings, maybe more, not sure, gone, just gone. Those giant towers, pulverized. Whoosh. Like demolitions you see on the news sometimes when they dynamite an old building and it crumbles into a cloud of ash. Know what I mean?"

Nina nodded, unable to speak, the image impossible to process.

"Yeah, that's what it looked like. I've been watching on the TV in the store." He pointed to the bodega on the corner. "You know they also attacked the Pentagon?"

"The Pentagon?" Nina's heart began thrashing beneath her sweaty chest.

"Not much damage, at least that they've told us."

"My God."

"Are you all right? You're not hurt, are you?"

The man peered at her like a physician, his eyes moving from her shoulders to her toes to ascertain the damage.

"I'm, I'm all right. I'm all right," she sputtered. "I just don't know what to do."

"Nothing to do. We wait to see what comes next."

Nina straightened up in alarm.

"Next? Do you think there will be more?"

"Not sure, but I can tell you for sure, this was no accident. One plane, maybe. Two? Three? There's talk there might have been another, in Pennsylvania. No. These planes, flying so low, crashing right through these major buildings? These were strategic targets. These planes were bombs, you can be sure of that."

"Were you in the military?"

He nodded. "Long time ago."

"But who? Who would do a thing like this? Why?"

"Lots of angry people out there. All over the world. Here, everywhere. Some people just got too much and others not enough and there's too much gap between. Too much ignorance. Has always been so, but more so these days. It's that simple, you know. Pretty much about economics. I see it every day, right here in Manhattan, in the great city of New York, filled with the haves and the want-some, and anger is the space between. Not the first time the Trade Center has been bombed. Politics makes things complicated. Religion too."

"But this cannot be political? I mean, that would be war."

Nina leaned back against the pole for support. She felt suddenly terribly vulnerable, a feeling she had not known since she was a girl. The man reached out and placed a thick heavy hand on her upper arm to steady her, and she felt instantly safer, as if she had been catapulted back to her childhood home.

"Everything is political these days," he said, as if in contemplation, and as if they were the only people at that moment on the street. "I don't know about war, haven't heard yet from the President. Not the first time we've had to do battle. The only thing I can tell you for sure, a lot is going to change in this country, and I'm not sure it will be for the good."

"How do you mean?"

"We've been violated. First time since Pearl Harbor. And now they've come to the capitals. New York, Washington. This is serious. We're used to being on the offense. People in this country get nasty when they're on the defense. Real nasty. And a threat to all that we are? Financial district? Pentagon? This is motherhood and apple pie!"

Nina nodded as she processed his thoughts.

"Were you in Vietnam?"

"Yeah, how'd you guess?"

"I had a few friends there."

"So you knew guys like me who screwed around and ended up with a number, doing our time in faraway places doing things we cannot talk about."

Nina nodded.

"War does terrible things to people. We're in for a tough time now," Isaac added sadly.

Nina recognized him for certain now: one of those naïve baby-boomer underachievers, who ended up in the military draft and were dispatched to Vietnam and, those who returned, were never quite the same.

She reached out her hand in greeting and as she did, he grasped both of her hands with his and pulled her with him to standing. Nina wobbled a bit on her feet.

"I'm Isaac, by the way."

"Nina."

"Where you from?"

"Brooklyn born."

Isaac smiled. "Thought so. Brighton Beach."

"Flatbush," she answered.

At that moment, an older man walked toward the store, and when he saw Isaac, he turned toward him.

"Some sort of a day, Isaac," he said.

"I'll say."

"Store open? I'd like to stock up on a few things."

"Sure. Go on in, I'll be right there."

Isaac turned to Nina. "Come into the store. You look like you need something more than water. Maybe juice? Have you had breakfast?"

"Yes. I had breakfast, although seems like ages ago."

Isaac offered Nina his arm and she pressed her hand on it to steady herself. As they walked into the store, she looked back to the street and noticed fewer people, the city beginning its retreat into the aftermath.

The bodega was well lit, filled to the brim with packaged goods, and smelled ever so slightly of everyday dust and fresh paint, a welcome scent from the soot and tar and exhaust fumes outside. A refrigerated case lined the back wall. Narrow passageways meandered between pillars of boxes stacked nearly to her full height, one carton at the top of each column slashed opened to display water bottles, soda bottles and six-packs, cans of tuna, boxes of granola bars and cereals, and crackers and chips of all types. Isaac led her toward a door at the far corner marked by a wooden sign painted with the words *This Door*. He flicked on an overhead bulb that filled the space with a harsh light, and handed her a white hand towel that smelled of a dryer sheet and a small bar of soap still in its wrapper. He closed the door behind her and she locked it with the tiny bolt before she stripped off her pantyhose and tossed it into the trash, then scrubbed the ash from her face and neck and rolled up her sleeves to scrub up to her elbows. She scraped and rinsed her legs, and wiped each limb with the towel until it too was ash gray. She took off her skirt and jacket and shook them out into the bin before replacing them.

She emerged and thanked Isaac as he completed a sale at the counter up front.

"May I use your phone?" she asked.

"Sure," he pointed to a wall phone near the counter. "Cell phones still out."

"Out?"

"Verizon tower down, no cell service. Good ole Ma Bell still works, old reliable."

Nina shook her head in bewilderment.

"Stay as long as you like. Not much in this neighborhood worth bombing. I expect people will be needing stuff, so I have to pull stock from the back, but I'll be around."

"Do you need help?" Nina asked, although she realized as the words came out of her mouth that she did not have the energy to be helpful.

Isaac smiled, revealing a smattering of yellowed teeth and the flicker of silver fillings here and there. His lips were lined and dry as if perpetually parched, but his eyes, she noticed, were the color of a summer sky and his arms tan and strong. She felt relaxed with him, with the natural heart-felt hospitality one finds only with old friends or in the friendliest places.

"Kind of you, but best you take it easy. You've had a hard day, and it's still morning."

No one answered the phone at Barrett's office, so she left a message on his cell phone and another at home to let him know she was stalled for a while downtown but was safe and would get home some time soon. She checked her home phone message machine and listened to a message from Barrett that he was with a client in Stamford, Connecticut, and no trains or cars, no one except emergency personnel were permitted back into the city, so he was borrowing a car and picking up the girls to take them to his parents' house for the night. "Call me there when you can," he said as he hung up. "I need to hear your voice."

She checked in at her office next, and was surprised when her assistant answered.

"Transit at a standstill," she explained. "Office has cleared out, but I'm staying put until the crowds calm down, then I'm going to hoof it to Brooklyn."

"You're going to walk?"

"You have another suggestion? I don't know when they will reopen the subways. Never thought I'd be glad to walk the bridge, but at least I can get home. The kids are already out of school and with a neighbor."

"You can stay at my place if you need to."

"Thanks, Nina, but I need to get home. I need to hug my kids."

"I know what you mean. Just leave me a message at home later, let me know you got there. And stay put, don't come to work until you get the word, okay?"

"Will do."

She called Margo next, who, as she might have expected, never got to her office, turning back as soon as she heard the news to retrieve her daughter Keisha from school, less than half an hour after she had dropped her off.

Keisha, now eleven years old, was adopted when she was six. Every morning, Margo or Daniel escorted her the short walk from their apartment in Brooklyn Heights to school, especially of late, because she was starting to hate school and she had to be cajoled to get to class on time. Keisha had been diagnosed early on with an information processing problem, not severe but sufficient to impact her learning ability, requiring regular intervention. Now, in middle school, reading comprehension was crucial to every subject, making Keisha's life all the more challenging, and, to make matters worse, puberty had set in, with its attendant belligerence and chronic fatigue. Margo and Daniel were sympathetic because they understood their daughter hated being singled out, pulled out of regular class every day to attend a special education class for individualized study.

The only time Keisha seemed happy was at an art class on Saturdays. She had genuine talent, Daniel said, which he recognized the moment she arrived, clutching a stuffed animal so worn there was no filling, only the faded yellow shell of an unidentifiable species, and a journal filled with remarkably sophisticated sketches.

Daniel too had returned to their apartment the moment he heard about the attack, and Margo said the three of them had been glued to CNN all morning. Nina explained where she was and how she got there and she heard Margo's voice sinking further into barely hidden terror.

"Honestly, Nina, I don't know what to make of this. Simply astonishing. They keep playing the footage of the towers going down, and it is incomprehensible. Doesn't seem real. Like a war movie, something you would walk out of because of gratuitous violence. I've just been on the phone with my mother and all the siblings, one after another. They are hysterical in the heartland. Where are Jen and Emma?"

"On their way to the grandparents with Barrett."

"Good. Want to come here?"

"Maybe. Although Lily is at the house and I don't want to leave her alone."

Lily, their Peruvian housekeeper, lived at Nina's apartment through the week, and with her sister in Queens most weekends. She had been their housekeeper and nanny since Jennifer was born eighteen years ago and was like a member of the family. What must Lily be thinking now? Nina wondered. She imagined her watching events unfold on the television in the den or in the kitchen, which Nina knew she kept on throughout the day, stopping now and then to sip one of the seemingly bottomless cups of rich Colombian coffee she drank throughout the day, as if mother's milk, without any semblance of hyperactivity that such consumption would suggest. She was a devotee of soap operas, but also watched several television news programs, which had been the primary source of her English language education, so her conversations were often laced with phrases like "next up" or "stay tuned." Lily was the first to chuckle at her media-peppered vernacular, although her speaking and reading ability were now excellent.

After Nina spoke with Margo, she called Lily and urged her to go downstairs to her fellow housekeeper Adriana's apartment, so she would not be alone. Then she called her in-laws, who were awaiting Barrett's arrival, and let them know she was all right.

After multiple phone conversations, and exhausted as much by trying to fathom the situation as the running, Nina sat on a hard wooden stool behind the narrow counter, where Isaac usually sat. She shifted uncomfortably as she watched the news on the small television perched on an overhead shelf. Her breath was rushed and shallow, as if she were still deprived of oxygen. She would never forget the overwhelming sense of helplessness she felt during the hours she sat there, unable to think about much more than when she might stop shaking and regain equilibrium. When she might shake off a profound sensation of despair.

Isaac moved about the store, rarely a moment at rest, carting boxes, piling goods, stopping often to chat with patrons who wandered in and out, most of whom he seemed to know. Like the proprietor of a small town general store, he fulfilled their basic needs and inquired about their circumstance, occasionally nodding in commiseration or lightly patting a shoulder to offer comfort. She watched him as if watching a video of her childhood, the neighbor's son or the boy in class she once might have known, having graduated to adulthood, but otherwise living a comparable lifestyle and earning a living much as his father and grandfather might have, like the multi-generational career path of police and firemen, the same people rushing at that moment into the disaster at the World Trade Center.

Nina was always impressed with people like Isaac who seemed satisfied with simple lives, as simple as anyone's life appeared on the surface, without the incessant determination to rise above the past or beyond choices that threatened to hold him back.

All the customers that day expressed their collective confusion in muffled somber tones, as if afraid to be heard. Stunned by the attack and its implications. Nina also heard in their voices a determined resignation, typical of New Yorkers, as if all adversity might be overcome merely by time and tenacity and the inherent resilience of the city.

Isaac nodded to her and checked in frequently to make certain she was all right.

"More water? Pepsi? Juice?" he asked, as if she had stopped in for a mid-day refreshment rather than seeking refuge from a man-made storm. "Nice and cold," he said, gesturing to the refrigerated case, packed to the brim with frosty bottles and cans.

"Diet Coke, yes, that would be nice. My vice."

He wiped off the top of a can before handing it to her, and she gulped down the bubbly brew until her throat ached from the cold.

"Thank you."

"Don't mention it," Isaac said as he turned to welcome another customer.

"Glad to see you home safe," he announced to all who entered the store, and she realized that for her, as well as customers seeking asylum at the neighborhood store, Isaac anchored the day, even as they all bobbed in choppy waters. She stayed put, as if to leave might expose her to another storm; as if beyond the border of the bodega she might disappear.

At one point, Isaac vanished for a moment through a doorway along the side of the store, and returned with a sandwich wrapped in foil that might have been packed in a school lunchbox: a large pile of thinly sliced white turkey, topped with lettuce, on dense brown bread that was spread on both sides with Dijon mustard. He presented the lunch to Nina with a napkin and pulled a small bag of Wise potato chips from the stack and another Diet Coke.

She nodded gratefully, her stomach rumbling as she took a large bite of the sandwich, although she ate slowly, her eyes glued to the television news.

Even after she had eaten, wiped the last bit of mustard from her lips and washed it all down with another bottle of water, she didn't have the energy to move, so she sat there as if cemented there, not knowing what she might be waiting for.

As the day wore on, store traffic dwindled and the towers of boxes were steadily diminished, many depleted. Nina had chatted with several customers, each with their own story, their own take on the tragedy, and found these brief personal intimacies reassuring. The comfort of shared experience. She called Barrett at his parents and was able to speak to the girls as well, so she felt calmer, and Barrett urged her to go to Margo's for the night so she would not be alone. She assured him she would.

She was almost never alone in her apartment and she might at any other time have relished the thought. She loved their home. They had traded up from a more modest apartment during the brief housing recession in 1993, and after a thorough renovation, filled the expansive space with English pine furnishings and plush fabrics, and painted each room a progressively lighter shade on a soft color palette, from the taupe of the main rooms to the paint on the walls of the girls' rooms, colors they chose themselves: Emma's buttery yellow, like a chickadee, she said, and Jennifer's lavender, her favorite color.

The apartment was their refuge, far uptown from the mid-town business district, and on the 15th floor. Tall windows faced Park Avenue, where a stillness surrounded them at nightfall as if a blanket, broken only occasionally by a distant siren or a loud drunk. She often sat up late at night, sleep interrupted by an overactive mind, but she cherished the stillness like a museum in which she was the sole visitor. Just last night she had been up for hours, as if an internal alarm warning her that all was not well, although she had no reason to suspect anything specific, certainly nothing of this magnitude. More likely the lingering emotional angst foisted upon her by adolescent daughters.

She had arrived home late for dinner to find the girls sprawled out on the L-shaped sofa in the den, ostensibly doing their homework. Both girls were long and lanky, like their father, and tended to spread out. Jennifer slouched along the length of the couch, while Emma reclined on the chaise extension, the sibling pecking order. Jennifer occasionally thrust out her toe to poke her sister in the arm, which evoked a yelp from Emma once, twice, and on the third thrust, Emma would sit up and yell at Jennifer to stop, and, having achieved the response she sought, Jennifer would make a show of supplication and halt, at least temporarily, depending on her mood.

On the dark floral area rug, backpacks and piles of notebooks were scattered about, and a few textbooks lay on the large, square, glass-topped coffee table. Both were good students, Jennifer better at math and sciences while Emma was an unusually strong humanities student, and both took their education seriously, which was of supreme importance to Nina and Barrett, the living embodiments of rising to higher class status largely because of a good education.

When Nina entered the room, Jennifer barely acknowledged her. Emma, without looking up, scolded her mother. "Mom, Lily is waiting dinner."

Nina meant to get home earlier, but the day had gotten away from her, her boss, founder of the agency, calling a late meeting on a client crisis. There was always something he and many of her colleagues believed to be a crisis when they were, in fact, a snag in the plan, the result of unrealistic expectations. Nina was often the team executive to manage and ameliorate the snag.

Nina noticed the last flicker of light on the television screen and the remote still in Jennifer's hand, but she chose to ignore it, having learned during these adolescent years to choose her battles, a lesson she passed on to Margo as Keisha approached her teens. In truth, Nina was too tired for confrontation, despite the house rule of no television until after homework was completed.

She preferred at that moment only to feel the swell of pride in her daughters. Smart, beautiful, and accomplished, they had their share of struggles by virtue of brown skin and light eyes, and a mixture of their parents' facial features, often confusing to both black and white. Nevertheless, they had weathered their hybrid status with grace. They were more often assumed to be of Mediterranean descent, as there were many children of diplomats at their schools. Although most of their fellow students and friends were white, they tended to take children of color under their wings, as if they might shield them from the prying eyes they had learned to refute.

In the weeks following the World Trade Center attack, both girls, and their brown and black classmates, would become suspect of everyone, even fellow classmates, afraid of anyone that resembled an Arab or Muslim. Anyone with brown skin.

"Mom, can Anna come with us to Sag Harbor next weekend? We are going, right?" Emma asked.

"Yes, of course," Nina said distractedly, browsing through the mail in her hand.

"I'm sleeping at Jessica's Friday night, maybe staying the weekend," Jennifer pronounced.

"The whole weekend?" Nina asked in surprise. "Why is this news to me?"

"Start of the school-year party," Jennifer answered dismissively, as if Nina should know, despite not being informed. "And we have essays to work on. What's the big deal?"

"No big deal, Jen, but I don't see why you have to be there all weekend."

"Her parents are away," Emma muttered, slapping her notebook shut sharply in punctuation, and with a sly grin on her face, having perpetuated a disproportionate response to something her sister must have said or done earlier in the day.

"Shut up!" Jen shouted in a voice so startlingly like Nina's when she was angry that Nina cringed.

"Jen, please. Are her parents away?" Nina asked.

"I don't know," Jen said, examining her shocking pink fingernails as she spoke, avoiding Nina's eyes.

"You can't stay there if they're away, you know that."

Jennifer looked up to face her mother. "Mom, I'm nearly eighteen! We can be trusted."

"Of course you can, but it's not safe."

"That's such a stupid argument. You can trust me but you can't trust anyone else? If you really trust me, then you have to trust me. I mean, for God's sake, they have a doorman in the building. Neighbors. This is not *Law & Order*."

"Jen, if her parents are away, she can stay here."

Nina consciously controlled her voice to remain calm, avoiding the caustic tone that was lying in wait in that conversational bait.

"Do we have to have this discussion again? The rules haven't changed. And, by the way, it's exactly *Law & Order*. Where do you think they get their story lines? Ripped from the headlines, right here in the Big Apple."

"How long are you going to keep this up? Until I'm twenty-five?"

"If you live at home that long, maybe."

Nina smiled, hoping to introduce a bit of levity into the dialogue, but Jennifer's expression had hardened. She tossed her mane of auburn hair and pursed her thick pink lips, overflowing with righteous anger.

"Mom, you are ridiculous."

"Jess can stay here if she likes, although I will be at the Met gala."

"That doesn't make sense."

"As long as her mom knows I'm not home, that's her choice. Lily will be here, and I'll be home, late, but home."

"Lily doesn't leave her room at night, except for a snack; she hardly qualifies as a chaperone."

"Don't be condescending, please. Lily is as trustworthy as they come. She would lay down her life for you, you know that! Jess's mother can trust that, or not. Her choice, not yours."

Jennifer mumbled something unintelligible as she too packed up her things. In the end, there was little conversation at the dinner table and the meal was rushed. Nina felt a troubling sense of foreboding all night, which, in recollection at the bodega, made her shiver. Whatever fears she might have felt for her daughters, in light of the general dangers that lurk in the city, seemed benign compared to what had presented the next morning.

Nina sat on the stool by the register all afternoon, glum and anxious. Despite the slow passing of hours, dusk began to settle over the street, the sunset refracted behind buildings into shifting colors across the sky, as if spotlights with rotating lenses at a Hollywood premiere. The neighborhood descended into an eerie silence. People were no longer visible on the sidewalk. Churches and schools had set up shelters for the downtown displaced. Everyone who could get home was home, shuttered as best as possible against outside forces. Lamplights and televisions flickered images across multiple apartment windows as if stained glass, and many would be saying prayers that night.

Isaac heaved the last boxes into place to replenish what had been sold, pulling several cartons at a time on a rolling cart out of the back room and from basement storage.

"Is this closing time?" Nina asked.

"Usually not until eight or so, but I think people are in for the night."

"I should go," Nina said, although trepidation underscored her words. Still afraid to leave the safety net of the bodega, afraid to walk the same city streets she had called home for so long, and afraid to be home alone.

"I'd be glad to walk you part way," Isaac said.

"That's kind of you, but..." she stammered a moment, uncertain how to ask what she wanted to ask.

Isaac, reading her thoughts, asked, "Would you like to stay a while?"

Nina walked to the front door and peered through the glass to the stillness. She shook her head in disbelief.

"I've never seen anything like this," she said as she turned back to Isaac. "Surely you want to go home?"

"Oh, I am home," he answered and motioned for her to follow him to the side of the store, where he pointed out a staircase tucked behind a doorframe. "I've got a place upstairs."

"All yours?"

"Best way to keep real estate prices under control," he answered with a smile. "Finally paid off the building. You're welcome to stay as long as you like, it's a comfy little place. Not too messy, I hope."

"Any chance I might take a shower, I feel like a slug."

"Sure. Sorry, I should have thought of that."

"No, no, you've been kind enough."

Isaac snapped the deadbolts into place above and below the double glass doors facing Broadway and turned on the outside light. He returned to the doorway where Nina stood waiting, and she looked up to his eyes like a child might beseech a parent for protection. He smiled a smile purposefully reassuring, and led her up narrow, creaking back stairs to his apartment overhead.

Through the doorway at the top of the stairs, Isaac flicked the light switch, which revealed one very large room, with a sleeping alcove separated by a Japanese-style bamboo screen. Overhead track lighting on dimmers cast a soft glow. The space was spotless and serene, the living area and dining area marked by worn kilm rugs in shades of sapphire and burgundy. One wall was filled from floor to ceiling with books and records, one of which Isaac placed on a turntable that sat on a side table like a trophy.

Nina felt oddly safe with this stranger in his hideaway, a stranger who in only a few hours had become a friend.

Isaac had no television. "I watch all day in the store," he explained. "And, I figure, whatever happens overnight can wait till morning. Bad news comes soon enough; good news is worth waiting for. Got an old-fashioned radio, if you like."

Nina shook her head no, grateful at that moment for tranquility.

"Shower's there," Isaac pointed to a door just beyond the kitchen. "Clean towel on the shelf. Use the robe on the door, and we'll find you something to wear."

Nina nodded gratefully, pleased to be told what to do, and anxious to be cleansed of the residue of the day. In the bathroom, as she stripped down, she felt suddenly vulnerable, exposed in a remote place with a strange man, and she thought to move the hook across the door to protect herself, but decided not to, certain that the sound might offend her kind host, and needing at that moment, on a day that challenged faith, to take a leap of faith.

She stepped into the shower and stood in the hot water far longer than she might have otherwise, absorbing the heat as she scrubbed away the last vestiges of ash from skin and scalp. When she at last emerged, wrapped in the oversized terry robe, the aroma of sautéed vegetables and toast greeted her. Isaac had scrambled eggs with onions and tomatoes, topped with a bit of cheddar cheese that he pulled from a small refrigerator below the counter. He warmed in the oven the remains of a baguette, which he smothered in salty butter.

The voices of Crosby, Stills, Nash and Young emanated from the record player, one of their iconic albums, an anthem of their shared history. A bottle of red wine was open and breathing on the counter. When Isaac saw Nina emerge from the shower, he poured the wine into two beveled juice glasses.

"Never understood why wine had to be sipped from stem glasses," he said by way of apology.

"I like this glass," Nina answered.

Isaac clinked his to hers as if a toast, although there was little to celebrate.

She took a long sip of the wine and immediately felt its warmth course through her, complementing the warmth of the shower, the plush robe and cozy space.

Isaac nodded. "Nice to know you, Nina."

"Thank you, for everything, Isaac. And for this lovely meal."

"I appreciate the company."

Over dinner they told each other the abbreviated versions of their life stories and marveled once again at all they had in common, from roots to values. Isaac had spent time in Japan after his military service, married one of the locals and brought her back to the states, to New York, where she had relatives. He had lost her to cancer six years ago. She was a quiet woman, he said, satisfied with small spaces and simple lives, but she was unable to have children and they made peace with that. Now, he added, he has realized that he is not certain the contemporary culture was one he wanted to bequeath to his own offspring. He added that in recent years he had come to appreciate solitude, and Nina answered that solitude was underrated. The conversation came back to the events of the day and they confessed their inability to grapple with the enormity of the situation. They traded thoughts on the import of the attack. They talked about whether New York City would ever be the same and whether or not people might flee. They consumed the bottle of wine.

The city around them was silent and dark. They both felt the fatigue of evening and a penetrating bond of grief.

In the distance, a church bell rang out its last chime. Isaac stood and removed the plates to the kitchen sink. He switched off the record player, which now transmitted the voice of Whitney Huston, reverberating through the small apartment as if she sang only for them. He turned on one small lamp in the main room and extinguished the other lights. He offered her his hand and she grasped it warmly.

He led her to his bed as if they had retired to bed together every night of their lives, and Nina followed, still seeking a safe haven, and fulfilling in that moment a persistent subliminal longing for a life free of complications.

It was a gentle coupling, as natural as anything either had ever experienced. Two people, in the throes of catastrophe, brought together in that moment by the magnetic force of circumstance. A moment that called for spontaneity from people who rarely indulged.

At first, they merely lay together, finding comfort in closeness. They luxuriated in the stillness, the absence of fear. Nina remained wrapped in the robe; Isaac had removed only his shoes and socks, and placed his glasses on a night table. Sleep was not to come any time soon, they knew that, but as there was little to say, they savored this humble affection. The lack of history between them rendered the moment innocent; nearness a precious antidote to the desecration of the day.

At last, Isaac loosened her robe. He respectfully crouched before her, awaiting permission, and when she nodded, he removed his clothes. Nina, without words, tossed the robe to the floor and lay back on the bed with open arms. As he came to her, she saw that their skin was nearly the same color, born of the same heritage, and, try as she might to abolish the thought, she felt protected within their common background. Safer by virtue of similar skin.

They lay entwined for some time, their now naked bodies seamed together. She inhaled his scent, a sweet conglomeration of sweat and wine. At last, the pleasure of the sensory, the willingness to dismiss all other thoughts and feelings in favor of touch, swept over them as if they were the only human beings left in the city and the only man and woman who had experienced the violation that everyone had shared.

When the moment was right, he slid his torso above her and slipped into her. She was ready for him, her body welcoming him, which was as much a surprise as anything that had happened that day. They lay locked together for a few moments, as if they might simply remain enfolded, without friction, clinging to each other like ballast, until, nearly involuntarily, Isaac began a rhythmic penetration, deeper, deeper still, and more and more forcefully, relinquishing himself to the most natural of human impulses. Nina moved with him, thrusting her hips to him as a dance partner, their bodies rocking in sync until first she then he climaxed, flushed and panting, their voices uplifted in one boundless groan that pierced the silence, before collapsing into each other like the towers themselves, reduced merely to embers. Together, they slept.

The first morning light flickered through slats of shutters over the two narrow windows facing the street. Nina, still wrapped in Isaac's arms, took a moment to remember where she was, and why. She briefly returned to their pose, unwilling to face the day. Unwilling to face the guilt of betrayal.

The silence within the apartment echoed the silence that blanketed most of the city that morning, like the inside of a cathedral, solemn and holy.

She had slept peacefully with a stranger, holding him close, as if to recapture her roots. His European accent, his blue eyes, his tanned skin, took her back to her childhood: the cacophony of languages, the blended aromas of goulash and marinara sauce and borscht emanating from apartments all around, down the stairways to the street below, where children, who all looked alike, formed a colony of next generation Americans. Quintessential New Yorkers.

Isaac reluctantly removed himself from bed. He showered and dressed, while Nina lay in his warmth, in wonder at how each human experience is suddenly altered by larger events. One of her clients, the director of a non-profit agency, defines crisis as an opportunity, the Latin word translated as a turning point: a separation between options, as if, in the midst of trauma, one might distinguish truth from interpretation. The client, who ran a shelter for homeless men, said that the indigent are forever in crisis because they do not know how to effect change – they do not recognize their capacity for self-determination, nor can they differentiate paths.

Perhaps, Nina thought, cradled in Isaac's bed, crisis results in change only for the willing. A way of releasing oneself from the shackles of one's own limitations, in order to begin again.

"Stay as long as you like," Isaac said, as he emerged from the bathroom.

He tied a fresh white apron around his waist, over a starched blue shirt and jeans. Ready for another day, as if the day before barely existed.

"I wonder what this day will be like," Nina mused.

Isaac stood before her, pondering the thought for a moment.

"Here's what we know. We're still here, we're alive. The sun is up. I got work to do, so do you, I suppose.

Another day today and another after that, maybe. That's all we can expect."

He leaned down to the bed and tenderly kissed her lips. "Together, we got through the day and through the night. I thank you for that. If our paths cross again, I would be pleased."

Nina smiled. Her savior had taken her in, and just as gently, set her free. No one need ever know.

She dressed and slipped down the stairs and out the door of the bodega while Isaac was in the storage room. She slowly lumbered uptown, acutely aware of the oppressive silence and the blanket of soot that ebbed only as she made her way further north. A bright morning sky followed her as if nothing in the universe had changed.

Lily greeted her with a warm embrace. She had assumed that Nina stayed with Margo, and later Nina would claim she stayed with a colleague downtown. No one questioned her, no reason to. She was not a woman prone to impulsive behavior or disloyalty.

A red light flashing on the phone displayed twelve uncollected messages. She watched the number flicker on and off – 12 12 12 – as if hypnotized, before listening to one voice after another, the voices of friends and colleagues, the voices of her children saying they would be home later in the day, and Barrett, wondering where she was so early in the morning. She shivered at the sound of his voice and waited until Lily handed her a mug of freshly brewed coffee before calling to assure him she was safe.

Emma Douglas/2002

I want to be improbable beautiful and afraid of nothing,
as though I had wings.
Mary Oliver

Nina's daughter Emma began her sophomore year at high school bubbling over with the exhilaration of having moved beyond the lowly status of freshman. The independent secondary school campus perched above the panoramic cliffs of the Palisades along the Hudson River, well north of Manhattan, and she rode the chartered school bus early mornings and late afternoons, parked in the same seat every day among friends with whom she had attended the lower and middle grades at the primary school on the upper eastside of the city. Together they had traveled through American history and struggled with algebra, created science fair projects and memorized the table of elements, perfected their grade-school French and read much of the junior literary canon, and, on the bus and in the cafeteria and in late night hours at sleepover parties, had begun to construct a personal vision of love and sex, and the possibility of who they might become.

Having successfully leaped through the hurdles of elementary school days, at the age of fourteen or fifteen these students were rewarded with a more independent lifestyle on the prestigious high school campus, which resembles the grounds of a small New England college. Sweeping lawns were punctuated with towering oak and maple trees that scattered their red and gold autumn leaves along stone paths between stately gothic buildings, leaves that in late fall swirled in the wind or served as crunchy carpets for largely entitled, high-achieving boys and girls wandering to and from class, until their crumpled faded remains were blown into fragile mountains and vacuumed into huge clear plastic bags for disposal, leaving the grounds once again pristine.

Emma's new best friend, Leslie, greeted her most mornings as the bus arrived. Leslie was dropped off by car, as she lived in a neighboring town. Every morning, her mother waved exuberantly as she drove off, and Leslie nonchalantly raised her hand for a moment, before she turned to Emma with an exaggerated expression of exasperation; a mother's presence at a secondary school campus was intolerable. Leslie had transferred just that year from a nearby public high school, following in the footsteps of her older brother two years earlier. They were members of the school's diversity program, plucked from public schools, high-potential scholarship students who might benefit from a more challenging academic environment. They were among what had come to be referred to as children of color – blacks and browns – all lumped together for the sake of integration. Their numbers were few, thus they stood out among classmates as flagrantly as browned leaves against green grass.

While the handful of scholarship students clustered together during free time, adolescents as tribal as cave dwellers, Emma and Leslie bonded early in the year at pre-season tryouts for the Track & Field Club. Both sprinters, they cackled hysterically when they discovered that they otherwise lacked sports ability and neither liked to work up a sweat; however, running short distances was sufficient to fulfill the school's athletic requirements. In this way, they agreed, they were fellow posturers, bonded by their pretense on the running track.

They also had the same class schedule, so they had become nearly inseparable. They walked together and sat together as if glued together, and could easily have served as a publicity photo from a view book promoting school diversity: Emma, the color of cooled caramel, Leslie mahogany. Both pretty and pert, their long muscular legs peeked out of skirts no longer than the mandated maximum three inches above the knee, capped by soft cable knit sweaters in the shades of the fashion season, and other than on those days when they were required to wear sneakers or ballet flats, they preferred knee-high leather boots in the Mod-style reminiscent of the sixties, an era they had experienced only in music and movies but imagined to have been glamorous. Exactly the same height and nearly the same trim physique, both wore their hair pulled back into ponytails that swayed almost in sync. Emma's lighter brown hair, thick and wavy, held neatly together like bunched wheat, while Leslie's curly mane strained at the band and, when occasionally released, fluffed out into an Afro that she otherwise wore only off school grounds, intent on not calling any more attention to herself than she received by default. Both girls carried matching black backpacks that drooped off their shoulders with the weight of thick textbooks and notebooks meant to underscore a rigorous curriculum. Boys were often seen following them as if a line of ducklings, others observed from a distance and pretended not to notice, all under the watchful eye of teachers and administrators determined to preserve the intellectual ideals of the school and maintain social decorum.

Emma had only recently blossomed from wiry and flat chested to voluptuous, and as such had become just as suddenly attractive to the same boys she had once raced on the playground. As a late bloomer, she was neither as seductive nor as sexually aware as her older sister, Jennifer, or many of her friends. She had more often treated her male classmates as pals and delighted in the silliness of the boys she grew up with, happy to be among them without sexual friction and flattered to be the one they talked to on those rare occasions when they confessed to personal confusion. Now, however, at fifteen, she yearned for romantic affection. She resisted advising her male friends on their liaisons with others, hoping to enhance her own appeal, and she paid closer attention to the boys paying attention to her, having at last come out of the shadow of her charismatic sister, and from the city that had cradled her since birth.

Personal freedom had been elusive to Emma most of her young life. No backyard swing-sets in Manhattan, no country roads to ride bicycles, nor neighborhood packs with whom to cavort without oversight. Her parents were strict and social gatherings were tightly controlled, if for no other reason than apartment building neighbors who had little tolerance for that sort of noise. City living had the benefit of sophistication and culture, and cultivated self-reliance, but Emma felt at the secondary school, far from city streets, and set within tall trees, that she had been sprung into the secret garden of the eponymous book she loved: sensual and lush and ripe with an opportunity to blossom.

From the first day, the sophomore curriculum was more demanding than Emma and friends had ever experienced, and they all recognized they had turned a page toward college. Beyond schoolwork, as if in defense, they focused on the latest hot music video, the next party, the big game, or who might land the lead in the school play, usual pursuits elevated from the banal to the extraordinary in an effort to stay social in an increasingly academic environment.

Emma had been invited to Leslie's sleepover birthday party Saturday night and this was just about all that was on her mind that week. Schoolwork took a back seat. Naturally bright, and a serious student, she was able to slide with minimal effort, at least briefly, while she concerned herself with what to wear to the party and what she might expect there. She had not yet met Leslie's friends, nor was she familiar with the suburban party scene, but she wanted very much to try on her sophomore persona, broaden her horizons, and further cement her friendship to the outsider.

She felt particularly proud to have adopted Leslie as her friend, one of her only African-American friends, as most of her fellow students were white and all comparably affluent. And she was happy to be chosen in return, as if their friendship reconnected her in some way to her father's heritage, and at the same time, promoted her to the status of a human being of true compassion and acceptance. She held her head higher and walked through campus with greater self-assurance, and she was determined to attend Leslie's party, even though the family had planned a weekend visit to Jennifer, who had just settled into her freshman year at Boston University.

Not one as a rule to stand up to her parents, Emma first beseeched her father, thinking he might be more malleable; however she underestimated the importance he had placed on the trip.

"Non-negotiable," Barrett said. "This is important for Jennifer."

"Dad, this is important to me, I'll go next time."

"And besides," he went on, as if Emma had not spoken, "it's never too early for you to look closer at college, start thinking about what type of school might suit you."

She gave up, quick to read her father's position and not one to bang her head against a wall, and approached her mother who, much to her surprise, was sympathetic. Nina seemed to understand that her daughter was making an effort to cement herself as a separate entity at school, not just her big sister's little sister. She was delighted that Emma had befriended the scholarship girl and surprised that Barrett was not as enthusiastic.

"You make plans for the weekend," she told Emma. "Make sure it's all right to stay at Leslie's more than one night, and let me deal with your father."

That night, Nina pleaded with her husband in the privacy of their bedroom, where such conversations were held.

"Barrett, this is a big year for Emma as well, we cannot let everything be about Jen." She raised her palm defensively to deflect what she knew would be Barrett's argument about the critical turning point for the first-born. "Emma is just a sophomore. She doesn't need the pressure of college choices, not just yet, and the odds are she'll be interested in very different schools than Jen. Besides," Nina continued, taking advantage of Barrett's hesitance, "it speaks volumes of our daughter that she has made this new friend. It's hard for the scholarship kids to settle in."

"I thought they go out of their way to integrate them, if you pardon the expression."

"Sure, they assign mentors and watch over them, but it's got to be painfully difficult to be a pack of interlopers in that jungle of white kids. Especially this class, they have known each other forever. It's a virtual blockade. Textbook efforts to facilitate assimilation are more effective in principle than in practice, don't you think?"

"Of course, but we're not talking about Reconstruction; it's a bunch of bright students getting a better chance, yes?"

"Yes, and all the better for Emma to ease the transition for Leslie. They're sports buddies, that's a close bond, you know that. We'll have many more visits with Jen, and Emma was there when we dropped her off at orientation."

"But this is the big weekend, there are all sorts of interesting things going on. She would love to sit in on that lecture by Amy Tan."

"Of course, but there will be other visits, other events. How about we give Emma some time to solidify this friendship."

"We don't even know the parents. Where do they live?"

"New Rochelle. I met her mother at parents' orientation. Indian, maybe Pakistani. You'd like her, very wifey."

"What does that mean, wifey?"

"Oh, you know, the stay-at-home variety. She probably bakes."

Barrett chuckled. "In my next life, I would like one of those."

"Good luck with that," Nina smiled. "The father is a shopkeeper, home furnishings. Perfectly good people."

Barrett shook his head in resignation. "I guess, if you're certain, but I think Emma would love being on the campus," Barrett protested.

"Sure, but on the other hand, I think Jen will appreciate having our full attention. This is her moment to shine. And you know how testy she can get with Emma at such moments."

Barrett frowned and as he did, Nina noticed thick lines forming around his eyes, as if carved into his skin, although the rest of his face was as tight and smooth as always. Black skin ages so well, she was reminded, as if cosmetic compensation.

She pressed her hand to his cheek and he kissed her palm, confirmation he accepted her argument and the conversation was over.

Emma gave both her parents a deeply appreciative hug before they parted Friday morning, promising to be a good guest at the home of her new friend and contact her parents on Sunday to confirm her plans to return to the city.

"Will your brother be around?" Emma coyly asked Leslie as they headed into the cafeteria Friday for their lunch of French fries dipped in vanilla yogurt, a concoction of their own that was spreading among the class as the best new trend in fast food.

Leslie had spent much of her teenage years fielding interest among friends in her handsome brother, Joe, two years older although just one grade ahead in school. Leslie reported to Emma that he had been held back while a toddler. She said the party line in her family was that the decision to retain him was made to ensure Joe's success in school, when in truth he had always been a feisty child and had been tossed out of nursery school even before he got to kindergarten.

Emma was charmed by the thought of the spirited toddler. She had noticed Joe last year, a boy impossible not to notice, but had met him only recently through her friendship with Leslie, and only twice, in the cafeteria, because around school he ignored his sister and generally ignored anyone not in his immediate orbit.

Joe had just turned eighteen and strode across campus like a giraffe, superior by virtue of size and age as well as athletic achievement. Emma thought he had the sexiest smile and most piercingly dark eyes of any boy she had ever known. Mere proximity made her stomach flutter. Six feet three inches tall, buff and broad-shouldered, with dark bristled hair shaved into a buzz cut, and even darker skin, he was prized for his prowess on the soccer and rugby fields, as well as football. According to Leslie, he struggled with his studies and was regularly subjected to academic intervention, not because he wasn't bright, but because he claimed to be disinterested or bored, positioning himself securely as an underachiever. The school administration was committed to ensuring success among scholarship students like Joe and facilitating their placement at good colleges, an outcome they frequently reported with pride during the annual giving campaign. Thus, Joe had access to a plethora of tutorial and counseling services, and the advantage of knowing he was an asset to the school. He would not be permitted to fail.

Leslie stopped short in her tracks when Emma asked about Joe. She turned and leaned in to whisper and Emma leaned closer, expecting a giddy secret.

"Watch out for my brother."

"What do you mean?" Emma responded in surprise.

She stepped back to glean more fully Leslie's reaction, and noticed her expression had turned as reprimanding as a scold.

"Stay away from him. He can be, well, unpredictable. And he doesn't like white girls. Anyway, my mother doesn't want him hanging around my friends."

Emma could not have been more shocked had Leslie slapped her in the face.

"What do you mean, he doesn't like white girls? I'm not a white girl."

"You might as well be." Realizing she might have been offensive, Leslie hastened to keep the peace. "Forget I said that. I mean, you know what I mean."

"I'm not so sure."

"I'm just saying, my brother is dark, in skin and spirit, so watch out, that's all."

"But, I mean, it's fun to hang out with upper classmen, right?"

"Not my brother and his friends."

"I guess you're used to them hanging around."

"My whole life," Leslie pronounced with contempt.

Leslie turned away and headed toward class, leaving Emma to ponder her words. All she had been able to think about for days was Joe. She found herself drawn to him in a way she had never been drawn to a boy. She found his height, his form, his nearly black pearlescent skin, tantalizing. She wanted to touch him and for the first time, she wanted to be touched in places she had never been touched. She dreamed about walking hand-in-hand with Joe across campus and greeting him as he came off the playing field, and she had also begun to picture herself with him at the junior prom. Joe seemed to Emma as important a challenge as acing a paper or placing in a race. At the same time, she felt a visceral connection to him, what she realized was a connection of the clan, as Emma felt a powerful kinship to her black father and grandfather.

When she was a little girl, her grandfather used to tell her she was the descendant of an African princess, and she believed him, although she never spoke of it, not even to Jennifer, who might have mocked her, and she suspected he told her the same. Still, she liked her skin. She believed racism was largely a thing of the past. Her father always said that her light brown skin was special, never to be taken for granted nor scorned, although in summer, her tanned friends were nearly as dark-skinned as she, sometimes darker, but none of them, not even her grandfather, as dark as Joe.

Emma was not one to break rules or disregard an imperative; however, she was not at all certain she would follow Leslie's advice.

She also realized at that moment this might have been a time she would have sought counsel with Jennifer, the more socially adept of the two sisters, if she hadn't become so distant and self-absorbed. Jennifer seemed driven of late to establish a new persona. Bohemian. Alternative. She had always sidled up to the boundaries, never wantonly or recklessly, but close enough to peek over the edge. Unbeknownst to her parents, Jennifer had long frequented rock concerts and downtown jazz clubs using a fake ID she acquired at fifteen that transformed her into a precocious eighteen year-old. She was, however, adept at defraying the attentions of the uninvited, and although far more sexually inquisitive than Emma, she rarely dated, rather traveled in mixed company. Unusually circumspect on the subject of love and sex, Jennifer nonetheless repeatedly warned Emma about unsolicited sexual encounters, beyond the obligatory and repetitive lectures delivered by their mother and teachers the moment they entered puberty, cautioning on everything from safe sex to predators.

Emma had made up her mind independently to save herself, not for marriage, a standing she considered the purview of religious purists and prudes, but for the sheer pleasure of waiting for someone special. However, she was looking forward to experiencing at least something more physical than she had.

Leslie's mother Claire picked them up Friday afternoon in a shiny silver SUV, waving to Joe as he took off with friends in a beat-up Jetta. A woman of small stature and light brown skin, she sat on a cushion to sit taller in the driver's seat and stretched out her short legs to the pedals. She wore a tan skirt and matching sweater with delicate pearl buttons across the bodice, reflecting the strand of pearls around her neck. Claire talked all the way home about a recipe for punch she might serve at the party, a blend of fresh juices and fruits, the special ingredient being kiwi, although she added that she had made the supreme sacrifice of purchasing a case of Diet Pepsi in recognition of the prevailing tastes of sixteen year-olds.

Leslie had previously confided to Emma that her mother was a natural foods fanatic, preparing dishes made only with organic ingredients. Fresh herbs grew in a container garden on the kitchen counter, so the room was consistently scented with mint and thyme, cumin and coriander. Claire alternated traditional curries with Asian cooking and regularly tested new recipes that Leslie reported tasted like most everything else. However Claire preferred to bake more typically American sweets and she announced she had prepared three-dozen vanilla cupcakes for the party, with an abundance of swirled chocolate frosting and sprinkles on top. For dinner the night of the party, she planned both a vegetable casserole and a chicken and rice concoction, catering to a range of tastes as well as dietary concerns.

"Everyone will have something good to eat," she pronounced proudly to Leslie, who grimaced apologetically to Emma in the back seat. Emma smiled in commiseration, but she was delighted at the prospect of an abundance of delicious home-made dishes.

"We would have been fine with popcorn and pizza," Leslie muttered.

"Out of the question!" Claire snapped. "You all eat that stuff quite enough. You have to nourish body and soul. Since you girls will be up late, you ought to at least have a decent dinner. However, as it is your party, I laid in a supply of M&M's, just the regular ones, as some people are allergic to peanuts."

"Right, Mom," Leslie said.

"Tonight I'm making a new recipe for Pad Thai," Claire chirped.

Leslie rolled her eyes. "Did you get the videos I asked for?"

"Yes, most of them. And I told Joey the den belongs to you this weekend."

"Good," Leslie said with a smile.

Emma's heart sank.

They pulled into the driveway of a small white colonial house with glossy black shutters, set back slightly from the sidewalk, similar although smaller than Emma's grandparents' house. To each side of the facade, dense feathery Hemlock trees bordered a white picket fence that served as a boundary between neighboring homes lined up one after the other, with little space between. In the center of a small patch of a neatly sheared front lawn, the ocher leaves of a broad picture-perfect Copper Beech tree announced the fall season.

Claire noticed in the rear-view mirror that Emma stared at the tree, enchanted with its symmetry, and she said with obvious satisfaction, "We planted that lovely tree when we moved in twelve years ago and it has turned out even grander than I hoped."

A distant whir of lawn mowers served as soundtrack and the fragrance of freshly trimmed grass permeated the air. The garage door opened as if by magic, and Claire navigated cautiously into a meticulously organized space. Along the back wall, bikes hung neatly on giant hooks, and aluminum racks were filled with paint cans, oversized bottles of blue window-washing fluid, spray cans of cleansers, tool kits, and an assortment of sponges, rags and implements for tending home and automobile.

The house was as meticulously arranged as a spread in a decorating magazine on how to make the most of small space. Many of Emma's friends had apartments grander and larger in square footage, some on multiple levels, but on the rare occasion when she was in a suburban home, she admired the sense of sturdiness and resilience there, in contrast to stacked urban dwellings or the family's sprawling shingled Sag Harbor beach house so close to the water it might easily be flooded. The center hall was flanked by a small formal dining room, with walls covered with dark green wallpaper in an English pattern of trailing vines, and a colonial-style living room was painted a paler green, the windows fringed with floor-length cream-colored damask draperies. A narrow carpeted staircase connected the main floor to the bedrooms and the dappled shadows of leaves dangling from nearby Elms and Maples reflected through gleaming windows, free of soot on the sills, with curtains pulled back into perfect pleats.

Not one to suffer envy, as a rule, Emma found herself wondering what it would be like to live with a mother who drove her to and from school, who baked and hovered over her children like a mama bear. She wondered what it would be like to live in a two-story house with floral wallpaper and wall-to-wall carpeting, tall trees, a palpable stillness within the breeze, and a handsome older brother.

That evening, the family sat together for dinner in the dining room, what Claire proclaimed their weekend tradition. The table was set with white china with a narrow silver band trimming the edge. Crystal-stemmed water glasses and wine glasses capped the upper right corner of each place setting, bracketed by a spotless silver service, including dessert forks placed above and perfectly parallel to the dinner plates. Emma was seated next to Leslie, across from Joe, and, during dinner, found herself spinning right and left as if at a tennis match to listen to the chatter of Claire and Joseph Senior, who sat at each end and dominated the conversation.

A large platter of Pad Thai was placed at the center of the table: thin browned rice noodles mounded high, topped with finely crushed peanuts and chopped scallions, and surrounded by chunks of browned tofu. A large glass bowl was filled with what Claire called Asian slaw, flanked by two triangular plates of slivered cucumbers and onions in a tart vinegar dressing. A carafe of blood-red wine sat in a coaster in front of Leslie's father, which Joseph poured for himself and for Claire as the food platters made their orbit around the table.

Claire sat upright in her chair, like royalty, while Joseph presided over dinner like a corporate meeting, leaning over his place setting as though perpetually ready to pounce, his elbows pressed against the edges of the table, one hand never relinquishing his fork, the other gripping his knife, which he frequently used as a pointer for emphasis. He was as tall as his son and even broader in the chest. Emma noticed that the family spanned a color continuum from Claire's smooth mocha and Leslie's dark wood, to the darker men, Joe the color of burnt toast, and so much darker than his father that she wondered whether he might have been adopted.

Joe, still in gray sweatpants and T-shirt from a late afternoon run, silently shoveled down a full plate of food. He nodded at the conversation now and then, but said nothing. When his plate was clean, well before anyone else, he declared that he would be going out with his buddies to play pool.

"We have this lovely girl with us tonight," Joseph said, with a nod to Emma. "Why don't you stay home?"

Joe looked at Emma without expression. "I see her at school every day."

Emma nearly burst with joy at the thought that Joe noticed her, every day.

"That's exactly the point," Joseph said. "You're not at school. You can get to know someone better in an intimate setting."

"Dad, can we please not put Emma on the spot," Leslie pleaded.

"I'm not putting anyone on the spot; am I putting you on the spot, Emma?"

Emma shook her head no to be polite.

"Of course not," Joseph said. He dropped his knife on his plate in order to refill his wine glass, the clang momentarily startling.

"Would you like a little wine?" he asked Emma, the carafe poised in his hand.

"Joseph!" Claire barked. "She's underage."

"We're in the privacy of our own home, it's our daughter's sixteenth birthday and her pretty new gal pal is a member of the family tonight, so a little bit of wine won't hurt anyone. As long as no one calls the Department of Children and Families, right Joey?"

He laughed loudly at this, but no one else did, and Emma saw, out of the corner of her eye, that Leslie cringed.

"Joseph, please, let's not go there tonight," Claire said, the expression on her face surprisingly severe.

"Lighten up, honey. I keep telling you, boys will be boys, that's all there is to it, and these bureaucrats make mountains out of mole hills." He turned to Emma. "Boys will be boys, don't you agree, Emma?"

Leslie intervened. "Emma has a sister, she doesn't know about boys being boys."

"A sister, how nice," Joe Senior repeated. "So, a little wine, Emma?"

"No, thank you," Emma said. "I don't think I like wine."

"Well, perhaps you'd like to try a little, you might like it after all."

"Joseph!"

"Jesus, Claire, it's no big deal, really. If we were in Italy, we'd all be drinking a bit of vino. You act like it's moonshine or something. A little alcohol at the end of the day loosens things up a bit. Might make a Friday night more like a Saturday night, if you get my drift."

He winked at his wife who ignored him as she lifted the main dish platter to pass down the table.

"There's plenty, help yourself to seconds."

Only Joe heaped more food on his plate.

"Dad, Emma doesn't drink," Leslie said.

"Ah, a goody-goody? I thought upper eastside kids were precocious. Or was that promiscuous, I always get those words mixed up."

Emma sipped her water and tried to think of an appropriate response.

"That is where you are from, right? Park Avenue I believe Leslie said."

"Yes, sir. We live on Park Avenue and 81st Street."

"Nice. I guess your parents do pretty well to have that address. I came up uptown myself, way uptown, in a little neighborhood called Harlem." He chuckled and sipped his wine. "Now I'm just a small town guy. In your parents' parlance, an entrepreneur. They might call my business the mom and pop variety. Did Leslie tell you we run our own shop? Window coverings – blinds, shutters, shades, drapes, we do it all. And not just neutrals, no, we can match any fabric, any wall color. You will see a sample of our handiwork on every window in this house, the best brands and the best workmanship. Some new things up this year. Claire loves to change out the windows, don't you, honey."

"The price is right," Claire answered, with a flat expression suggesting she had heard his speech once too often.

"Business is pretty good. Real estate is booming. Everyone needs some sort of window covering, especially for the bedrooms. Only werewolves like moonlight, I always say. And some people don't want to be watched."

Joseph winked at Emma, Joe laughed, Claire sipped her wine, and Leslie sunk lower in her chair.

"I think I'll have a beer," Joe said.

"Not if you're driving tonight," Claire said.

Joe stood and raised his full height to glower at his mother, as intimidating as a predator. She stared back at him without flinching, although she seemed to sink a bit in her chair. At last he turned away, without comment, and as he looked up to Joseph, seeking solidarity, his eyes landed on Emma and remained there so long she felt uncomfortable under his scrutiny, although she was sympathetic to him in the trap of parental confrontation. She wished she might say something to express her commiseration, but all she could do was hold his gaze.

"Maybe I'll stay home tonight after all," Joe said, and for the first time, he smiled at Emma.

Leslie winced. "Oh, no. It's girls' night, and the party is tomorrow, and you are not welcome to either one."

"Oh, don't be like that," Joseph said. "I think it's a fine idea for your brother to get to know your new friend. A fellow student, and such a lovely girl. Maybe she'll be a good influence on him, like your mother has been on me."

Joseph chuckled at what appeared to be a family joke, although when Emma glanced across the table at Claire, she was not smiling, rather she sat stone still, with not so much hostility in her eyes but forbearance.

"Of course, as long as she's not a Muslim, you're not Muslim are you? Can't have any terrorists here, no way, not in my house."

Emma was struck dumb, as Joseph and Joe laughed together.

"Dad, please," Leslie implored.

"Please what? I've got the right to be sure about people in my house." He turned to Emma. "I do wonder about the injustice, though, of your father paying through the nose for your education, while my kids get a free ride. Must have something to do with your white mama."

"Mom!" Leslie appealed to her mother.

Joseph threw up his hands and turned to Claire. "We need some dessert, honey, to sweeten your daughter up a bit. Sweeten them both up a little, don't you think? You too. Yes, something sweet, that will do nicely. What ya got? House smells like a bakery. And don't tell me it's for the party, you've been at it all day. Must be plenty."

Claire brightened up. "We've got pecan pie for tonight. Do you love homemade pie, Emma? We do."

"Yes," Emma said, "although my mother doesn't do much baking."

"She's a businesswoman, can't do it all, can we? The pie looks great and I picked up French vanilla ice cream to go with."

She rose from the table and started to pile the plates. Emma stood to help.

"You stay here with us," Joseph said. "Claire will clean up, makes her happy. You're our guest. Leslie, you help Mom while we chat with Emma."

Leslie turned to Emma, as if to speak, and Emma saw the apologetic expression in her eyes, but she silently grabbed plates and platters to pile and carry through the archway to the kitchen. She returned quickly for a second round and then again with dessert plates, which she stacked directly in front of her mother's place.

Joseph pressed Emma further on her pastimes and passions.

"Got a boyfriend yet, Emma?" he said with a wink.

Emma blushed. "No, sir."

"Sir, you don't have to call me sir. I'm just a dad, although it is kind of you to be so respectful to me in my house. Joey, this girl is a good one, you need to get in there before someone else gets to her. And she's a good color."

Emma was shocked by that remark; color was never discussed at her home. Joe had resumed his seat and he stared at Emma with the same sort of scrutiny as his father. Emma felt suddenly as if a bra strap were showing and pulled her sweater closed.

Claire and Leslie returned and as Claire carefully sliced and served a substantial wedge of pie, she passed the plate to Leslie, who dipped a silver-plated scoop into the ice cream container to place a small mound atop the pie, before passing it to her father and brother, then to Emma. A cinnamon scent trailed each plate down the table. The two Joes devoured pie and ice cream without comment, while Claire and the girls ate slowly. Emma was quite full, but to be polite ate all but the crusty edges and the residue of vanilla cream that encircled her plate.

Leslie hurriedly stood to remove plates and forks to the kitchen. "Thanks, Mom, great dinner. We're going to watch movies now."

Leslie nodded to Emma, who stood with plate in hand and, on her way to the kitchen, reached over to take Joe's plate, like a waitress. He acknowledged the gesture with a barely perceptible nod.

"Thank you so much for a wonderful meal," Emma said to Claire as they fled.

"Sweet thing," Joseph was heard to say as the girls disappeared.

"Thank God we're out of there," Leslie whispered. "Let's go."

She placed the plates on the counter, grasped Emma's hand, and pulled her through the foyer, down a hidden stairway to the family room.

A furnished lower level that served as a playroom when Leslie was a child now provided what her mother called "teen space." Centering the room on one wall was a large television screen, attached to video game equipment that was prohibited at Emma's home, opposite which an exceptionally wide and deep, dark brown, U-shaped couch was nearly covered with throw pillows, serving as the flopping place for Leslie and Joe and their friends.

"We will hang here most of the weekend," Leslie said. "My parents make a big show of being around, but they rarely come downstairs, we'll be pretty much on our own. Especially Saturday night." Leslie chuckled. "My parents call it date night, but we know what that means."

Emma was not quite sure what that meant, but she thought it was sweet.

Leslie picked up the pile of videos on a long bench that served as a coffee table and spread them out like cards to be picked. "Good, she got us *Almost Famous,* I loved that movie. And *A Knight's Tale,* Heath Ledger is to die for. And *Trading Places,* I heard that was really funny. Leslie stared at the last box and laughed loudly. "Oh my God, my mother got us *Shrek.* I asked for *Coyote Ugly* and she got us *Shrek.*"

"I love *Shrek,*" Emma said.

"You're not going to watch kids' stuff, are you?" Joe's voice suddenly interrupted

Both girls jumped in their seats.

"You jerk, I hate it when you sneak up like that," Leslie said.

"I didn't sneak, you were preoccupied."

"Bull! Get out, you are not welcome."

"Oh, I think I am," Joe said. "You heard dad. I am instructed to get to know Emma better. He thinks she might be good for me."

He grinned and although Emma heard the sarcasm in his voice, she didn't care. He picked up the pile of videos to peruse. "*Trading Places.* Perfect." He tossed the others to the side without interest.

"Joey, really, this is the first time in a long time I've had a friend over, please don't ruin it for me."

Joe pointedly ignored his sister's remark.

"Do you think you can reform me?" Joe asked Emma.

"You definitely need reforming," Leslie said sharply. "I mean it, get out."

Emma seized the moment. "What exactly do you need reformed?"

"Just about everything, I'm told," Joe said. "I'm sure my sister has warned you about me by now."

Emma shook her head no and avoided Leslie's scowl.

"You are a sweet one," Joe said, sidling closer to Emma on the couch.

"I'm going to get Mom." Leslie cried. "This is not okay and you know it!"

"All right, all right. I'm gone. Goin' out with my boys."

Joe turned once more to Emma, leaned forward slightly toward her, then closer still, as if he might kiss her, and she felt her lips part just slightly, when he abruptly chuckled and stood to leave. "Later, Emma. Have fun with Shrek."

"Not!" Leslie muttered scornfully as she slipped the first video into the player.

All day Saturday, Emma watched for Joe, but he had sporting events and subsequently obeyed instructions to stay away from the lower level party. Disappointed, she resigned herself to seeing him at school or perhaps Sunday, before she returned to Manhattan.

Six neighborhood friends showed up at once for the party and Leslie hastily introduced Emma as they gathered together in a near huddle to chat. They were childhood neighborhood pals, clustered happily like a flock of ducklings. There was only one lighter brown girl, Emma was uncertain if she were black or white, Indian or Latino, and she displayed little interest in Emma, who attempted a few times to connect to the general conversation but had nothing significant to contribute. As the evening wore on, the girls danced to a Michael Jackson album, they watched *Almost Famous* and pranced around the room to the classic rock music. They updated Leslie on who was dating whom at the neighborhood high school. They repeatedly used words and expressions in their own code, meanings established over a lifetime of friendship. Emma felt increasingly invisible among them, as Leslie paid little attention to her.

When Claire descended the stairs with the platter of cupcakes, one of which held a tall white candle, she insisted the girls sing the happy birthday song and urged Leslie to make a wish before blowing out the candle, which she did with a sharp exhalation. Claire remained in attendance and snatched away wrapping paper as Leslie opened her presents: a lacy nightgown from Victoria's Secret, an album by Destiny's Child, perfumed powder, a silk scarf, a couple of gift cards to Barnes & Noble, and Emma's gift of a woolen hoodie from J. Crew that matched one of her own. Leslie exclaimed in delight over every gift, but rushed through the obligatory performance so her mother would leave them to their movies and gossip.

While devouring cupcakes, the girls whined about their weight and bemoaned love handles around what were tiny waists with very little body fat, as most of them were also athletes. They tossed M&Ms at each other, then scooped them up from the couch to gobble by handfuls, swearing to diet come Monday, which caused further riotous laughter. None of the girls had arrived with sleeping bags and when Emma inquired where they would all sleep, Leslie replied that the girls would go home. She whispered that she was not usually permitted to have sleepovers at her house, then turned to scream with laughter at a scene in *Trading Places* where Dan Ackroyd drops his pants standing up to have sex with his uptight and extremely white girlfriend.

When they ran out of punch, Emma offered to bring down more soda from the kitchen, and without waiting for an answer, marched up the stairs.

Joe sat at the kitchen table with a bottle of Heineken beer in front of him.

"How's the party?"

"Fine."

"Do you like Leslie's friends? I've known them all forever. And they know me." He sniggered at this remark in the way people do who harbor unpleasant secrets.

"Sure, they're great. I just, you know, I'm not part of this crowd."

"Does it matter, to be part of the crowd?"

"Not really. I mean, it's good to have forever friends, and, you know, I've hung out with mostly the same kids my whole life too. I guess that's just the way it is. Must be hard for Leslie to start over. Was it hard for you?"

"Well, it's a bit different for us, we had no choice in going to your school. And I'm used to being the odd guy out. Kind of like it. Not one to follow the crowd."

Joe stared at Emma with such intensity that she had to look away. "Could you break with convention, maybe not always do exactly what's expected of you? I mean, what's the point if we all do the same thing and we're all expected to live the same damn life?"

"Good question. You and my sister would get on really well."

"Yeah, where is she?"

"She's at college. Boston."

"Oh, my age. I prefer younger women." He leaned toward Emma. "Sit down, it's just me, I'm not as dangerous as you think."

"I don't think you're dangerous."

Joe raised his beer to his lips and peered at Emma over the neck of the bottle as he drank. "So, you're not afraid of me?"

"No. Why would I be?"

"You're not afraid of the big black boy?"

"My father is black."

"I hear your father is brown."

"No difference to me."

"Big difference to me."

They stared at each other for a moment, Emma unable to turn her eyes away, as if she were being hypnotized.

"Are you afraid of anyone?" he asked.

"Sure. People in the Middle East who want to kill us. The people I see on TV, you know, *CSI, Law & Order.* Hannibal Lector. Psychopaths."

"Would you know a psychopath if you met one?"

"I hope so."

"You think you can trust me?"

"Why not?"

"Trust me enough to hang outside with me right now?"

"I think Leslie would be angry if I left the party."

"She might not even notice."

"I think she will."

"Tell you what, go back downstairs, bring whatever it is you came for, and tell Leslie you're tired and you're going to lie down. It's nearly eleven, the girls will be out of here by midnight, that's curfew around here. No one will know we're gone."

Emma shuddered with the sudden thrill of being alone with Joe and she decided in an instant that she was going to follow his lead.

"I'll be right back," she said, as she grabbed the case of Diet Pepsi to take downstairs.

Joe smiled. "You do that."

Emma returned quickly, as promised and Joe beckoned to her to follow as he opened the sliding door to the backyard and stepped out. The light from within the house illuminated only the immediate periphery, but Joe did not turn on any exterior lights. He moved stealthily into the darkness while Emma took a moment to orient her vision, before following, slowly, reaching out for anything in her path as if suddenly blind. Joe, already out of her frame of vision, turned back and gripped her elbow to guide her across the patio to a trampoline at the edge of the property – a standard issue, full-size trampoline that sat like a lonely creature in the darkness, once beloved and now relegated to a backyard sculpture. Joe hoisted himself up first and reached for Emma's hands to pull her up with him. Emma thrilled to his strength, although he let her go the moment she landed and flopped down on his back, creating ripples on the canvas, so that Emma, on her knees, had to steady herself with outstretched arms, as if she were on a surfboard.

"Lie down. It's a great place to watch the stars."

Emma obeyed his order. They lay side by side in silence, their eyes adjusting to the panorama of sparkling lights against a nearly black sky.

"This might be the only thing I'll miss around here," Joe said.

"Where do you want to go to college?"

"I'm not going to college. Not for me. I'm just going to take off. My father wants me to go into the business, imagine that? He's already taught me the tools of his trade. I can hang a Roman shade perfectly straight and smooth, better than he can, but I cannot imagine anything more boring. The whole idea is dumb. What is the point of being shipped off to a fancy school if I'm going to end up in the same dead-end job as my dad? I mean, the only real fun in life is conquest. Even sports get old."

Emma listened, rapt, thrilled to be having a serious conversation with Joe, and inhaling the romance of close proximity in the dark.

"Where will you go?"

"I don't know. I'm just going to get in my car and go. You know, a roadrunner. Work when I have to, sleep in my car or maybe rent a room now and then. No belongings. No commitments. I can't stand this suburban play by the rules, be a good boy all the time world. We're all just as whitewashed as that picket fence. Makes me want to scream."

"But you'll wait until you graduate, right?"

"I don't know. Not sure I can make it through another year. I feel like I'm busting at the seams. No one gets me."

I get you, Emma thought. Right this moment, I get you.

Joe turned toward her and propped himself up on one arm. In the blackness of night, the difference in their skin color was hardly noticeable, even the coloring of their clothes neutralized by moonlight. Emma barely made out the features of his face, only the sparkling white of his eyes.

"Maybe you get me, what do ya think?"

"Maybe."

Joe took her hand and ran his thumb across her palm, sending tiny shivers through her.

"If there were any light, I could read your palm."

"Really?"

"Yeah. In fact, I don't even need to see the lines. I can tell you will have a long happy life. You will do what is expected of you and settle into the same sort of world you live in now. Happily ever after, yes, that's the way it is for girls like you."

"Is it?" Emma felt surprisingly disappointed by the caricature.

"Yeah, for you. Not for everyone, but for you, yeah."

"What makes you so sure?"

"Nearly white girl from the upper eastside. Rich liberal parents. The best schools. No, no surprises in your future." He dropped her hand suddenly.

"Maybe I would like something different."

"Yeah, sure." Joe returned to a prone position.

Emma lay very still. She wanted something different, but she wasn't sure how to claim it, or even how she might define different. What she wanted at that moment was to feel closer to Joe, truly close, and on a sudden impulse, guided by the ghost of Jane Austen, she shifted her shoulders and upper body nearer to him, stretched her head over his and kissed him.

Joe grabbed her by the waist and pulled her body over his. He grabbed her hair in his fist, and with his other arm, drew her face to him and kissed her with a greater force than expected; a volatile kiss, more desperate than passionate.

"Open your mouth," he growled.

Emma submitted, rounding her lips to receive him, and felt her mouth filled with his probing tongue. Suddenly, as quickly as he had grabbed her, he released her. Emma jolted into reverse and rolled off. Dismissed too soon, she nevertheless felt the momentary thrill of victory, much the way she felt when she won a race.

"You're a sweet one. Better not let too many boys kiss you in dark places. Can be dangerous."

"I don't let anyone kiss me, usually."

"Kissing is overrated anyway."

They lay once again in silence, although Emma thought for certain that Joe might hear the pounding of her heart. After a few minutes, Joe stood, jumped off the far edge of the trampoline, and trudged around to Emma's side. She sat up, reluctant to relinquish the moment, fearing rejection, and uncertain what she might have done to fuel his abrupt departure. Joe reached out his hand for her to help her jump off safely, and let go as soon as she was on the ground, striding briskly ahead of her toward the house as if she weren't there.

When he got to the sliding doors, Joe waited for Emma to enter. Following, he pulled the sliding door shut behind them, and marched directly to his room, ignoring her completely. She trailed him to the staircase and stood at the bottom step awaiting further comment, but Joe turned at the top of the stairs and out of sight. She heard him close his bedroom door behind him, leaving Emma utterly confused as to why he had dismissed her without a word. She trudged upstairs and into Leslie's room, where she pretended to be asleep when she heard Leslie call goodbye to her friends and climb the stairs to her room.

Later that night, as darkness seeped toward dawn, Emma awakened abruptly to find Joe sitting on the edge of her bed. When she startled, he leaned forward and cupped his hand over her mouth to silence her.

"Shush," he whispered. "It's all right, I just wanted to be with you."

Emma was too stunned by the intrusion to react.

"Don't make any noise, you don't want to wake my sister, do you?"

He removed his hand, but left the tips of his fingers hovering over her mouth, grazing her lips in warning.

"Did you, did you want something?" she said, more loudly than she intended.

"Sh. Please whisper. My parents would not be pleased with you. After all, you invited me here, right? That sweet kiss, those lovely lips, you knew I'd come for you."

Emma was too stunned to speak.

"Dad was right, you're a little gem. Maybe we can go out some time."

Emma tried to catch her breath. "Maybe."

"Maybe?"

"Sure. Yes."

Joe ran his fingers along her jawline and down her neck to her collarbone, which he traced with one finger, back and forth, as he spoke in a hushed voice.

"I didn't mean to scare you. I just wanted to see you again. I wanted to make sure you were real."

Emma tried to smile, forcing the corners of her lips to elevate, while swallowing down a scream.

"Better get some sleep now. Before you know it, morning comes. I know because I don't sleep well, I'm a bit of a night owl. I wander a lot. It's wanderlust, that's what they call it, right? Wandering and lust, that's me."

He turned and in one deft movement slipped off the bed onto his feet and disappeared from the room.

Emma pulled the covers up to her neck and lay frozen, trying to steady her shallow rapid breathing.

"I told you to watch out for my brother," Leslie snarled from her bed, and sharply turned to face the wall.

Emma was too confused and frightened to speak. She lay awake until a glimmer of light crept around the tight edges of the window shades. An hour might have passed, but her heart continued to bang in her chest and she felt as if she were burning with fever, or something that felt like fever.

In the morning, Nina called to check in and Emma was happier to hear her mother's voice than she had been in a long time.

"How was the party, honey?"

"Good. Fine. How's my sister?" Emma had to contain a sob in her throat at the thought of her sister, so far away, no longer there to protect her.

"She's great. I think. You know your sister is hard to read sometimes. She likes her roommate, sweet girl from the Mid-west. But, you know, everyone is still in transition. A little uneasy around parents, frankly. We are definitely persona non grata for freshman."

Emma heard Nina take the sort of deep breath she took when struggling with one of her daughters, striving to be the better mother she meant to be; a sigh augmented by the magnification of the cell phone. Emma also knew that Nina would absorb her discomfort and move on, as was her way, so Emma instantly resolved to do the same.

"Jen wanted me to tell you she wants you to come yourself for a weekend. Soon! She promised me she won't throw you to these wolfish college boys." Nina chuckled, although Emma knew her mother was uncomfortable with the thought of her younger daughter being tossed too soon into the sexual melee.

"I wish I were there now. When are you coming home?"

"Big game today, so not until late. Do you want to stay the night and go to school tomorrow with Leslie?"

"No," Emma replied hastily. "I mean, I've got things at home I need."

"What do you need?"

"Just stuff, you know. I didn't bring everything. I can take the train in."

"We'll come and get you, honey, but probably not until, maybe..." Emma heard the fading sound of her mother's voice as she turned to speak elsewhere. "Barrett, what do you think, around nine, to pick up Emma in New Rochelle?"

"Mom, Mom," Emma yelled into the phone, and when Nina returned her attention, she said, "I'll take the train."

"Well, okay, if you'd rather. Lily will be at the apartment this afternoon, she can fix you something to eat. I'll leave her a message. What time?"

"I, I don't know. I'll check the train schedule. Probably after lunch."

"Sounds good."

"Okay," Emma murmured.

Something in Emma's voice suddenly prompted Nina's attention. "Em, is everything all right?"

No, Emma wanted to cry. No, Mom, I'm not all right, she might have said. I'm not sure I'm safe here. Come for me, she wanted to cry. Instead, she said, "Just tired, you know, it was a late night."

"Ah, sleepovers. Well, get your homework done and get some sleep. We'll tiptoe in. Don't wait up."

"Okay," Emma answered, and, afraid she might lose her composure, without saying good-bye, hung up.

Emma and Leslie took a walk before lunch, and Leslie acted as if there had been no disturbance, as if nothing at all unusual had happened, instead serving overtly as tour guide, pointing out to Emma the homes of some of the friends at the party, the path she used to walk to school, the tree she had proudly climbed on her own when she was only six and had fallen, breaking her arm. She pulled up her jacket sleeve to show Emma the tiny half-moon scar from the wound that had been neglected under the cast. She talked most of the time, giving Emma hardly a moment to interact, and when Emma tried to broach the subject, she waved her off.

"You heard my father, boys will be boys," she said dismissively, although she averted her eyes from Emma's plaintiff gaze. Emma was too startled and confused to react and they returned to the house in silence. A platter of turkey and cheese sandwiches, cut into triangles, and a bowl of still-warm potato salad with tiny bits of bacon on top, awaited them on the kitchen counter.

"Emma needs a ride to the train station," Leslie said to her mother, who was scouring the kitchen sink.

"I'll drive her," Joe said, without looking up from the sports page of the local newspaper.

It was the first time Emma had seen him since the previous night, as he had not been at the breakfast table.

"That's a good boy," Claire said, as if speaking to a young child who has agreed to share a toy with a friend. "You don't mind, do you, dear? We've got leaves to get into piles and Leslie has homework.

Emma turned to Leslie who was munching on her sandwich.

"Will you come with us for the ride?" Emma asked.

"Homework," Leslie said, again avoiding eye contact. "It's not far."

Joe tossed Emma's backpack and overnight bag into the back of his dark gray, slightly beat-up sedan, and held the door open for her as she climbed in.

"Buckle up," he said. "I'll give you a real tour. I know the roads around here like the back of my hand, been biking or driving them my whole life."

"I need to catch the 2:15 train," Emma said, noting the time on the car radio.

"There's a train every half hour, you'll get there."

Joe took off and Emma opened the window to let an unusually warm autumn wind blow through her hair. He sped down winding lanes, past larger homes set back from the road, and along a creek where water streamed over rocky layers like miniature falls. The sky was blue, the sun high, and Emma relaxed, convincing herself in the light of day, everything is better. Perhaps she had imagined the menacing tone of the previous night.

"Are you so sure you want to leave this place?" Emma asked, the first time she had spoken since they started the drive.

"Oh, yeah. Totally sure. As sure as I am I want to kiss you again."

A shiver spread through Emma's bones. She looked out the window to see how close they might be to the train station, imagining a farewell worthy of *Casablanca*, but instead of the downtown, or anything resembling a town center, she saw only country roads and a glimmer of houses well beyond tree lines and driveways. At last, Joe approached the end of a dead-end street, where she thought he might turn around; instead, he guided the car onto a leaf-covered trail that led to a clearing amidst a cluster of trees.

The moment Emma realized they were off the road, her heart started pounding in fear. There was not a house in sight. The car came to a sudden halt and Joe turned off the engine, but not the car radio. He turned up the volume just enough to be loud without calling attention to their presence. Emma would remember forever Ben Folds' voice singing from his hit album, *Rockin' the Suburbs*.

Joe sang along as he leaned toward Emma, as he pressed in the mechanism to dislodge her seat belt and pulled back her jacket, as he pushed up her sweater to reach beneath her bra, which he pulled down so hard, it snapped.

"Oops," he said with a laugh as he cupped her breasts, burying his face between them for a moment, biting her nipples, like the sharp nipping bites of a dog, hard enough to leave bruises that would burn in the shower but leave no permanent scars.

"Please," Emma pleaded, but she hardly heard her own voice, trapped as it was in her throat.

Joe sang along with the Folds' tune, sneering at the sentiment. "White boy pain my ass!" he muttered, as he stepped out of the car and came around to open Emma's door. "What the hell does he know?"

"I need to go," Emma cried.

"Yeah, but not yet."

Joe tugged on her arms to pull her from the car. At first, Emma held fast to her seat, her torso and elbows stiff, but he was too strong and quickly extracted her from the car. He left the car door open, so the radio blared its soundtrack into the stillness as he grabbed her around the waist and dragged her to the shade beneath a tall tree, its leaves still dense enough to obscure the sky. There, hidden by low-lying branches, he pressed her down to the ground.

Emma was silent. She offered no resistance, her eyes as glazed as a somnambulist.

He sang loudly now with the music, as if he were doing household chores instead of removing more of Emma's clothes, and it was only when he stopped singing that Emma heard his heavy breathing, like a runner on the last leg of a race.

"Relax," he snarled, but Emma lay as rigid as if she had been embalmed, only the heightened color in her cheeks a sign of life.

"What the hell's the matter with you?" Joe groused, shoving his face into hers to try to bolt her into awareness.

Emma closed her eyes.

"I'm not going to hurt you, pretty little uptown girl. You might learn something here. Get into it with me a little."

He shook her, first gently, then vehemently, but Emma did not budge.

"Damn," Joe muttered. "This is what you wanted, right?"

He stopped and stared at her, recognizing for the first time how placid she had become. "You are there, yes?" When she did not respond, he laughed, shrugged his shoulders, and barked, "Have it your way."

As he unbuckled and pulled down her jeans and her panties simultaneously, to her knees, Emma saw only the darkness behind her eyes. As if she were somewhere else. Someone else. She tried to gather her limbs together, but nothing moved. She tried to scream, but she seemed to be miles away from her mouth, unable to utter a sound. Detached from her body, she imagined herself like silt at the bottom of a pond. Only her own rapid breath reminded her she was still above ground, and her heart pounded so hard she thought it might explode at any moment, and relieve her of the hysteria that coursed through her system like poison, suffocating every natural instinct.

Long after this day, she would wonder why she didn't push him off, pull up her pants and run like the wind. She was certain in hindsight that she might have. In the midst of the assault, however, she could not galvanize any part of her to move. She felt as if she had no skin. No musculature. No name.

Joe climbed over her and prepared to penetrate, but found himself unexpectedly flaccid. Instead of the power of conquest, he experienced for the first time the impotency. Her limpid body, nearly cadaverous, made it impossible for him to continue. As he began to consider that he might have gone too far, he simultaneously experienced a rage even beyond that which accompanied most of his days. He wanted to beat her to smithereens and destroy any evidence of this humiliation. As he raised his fist, Emma's eyes fluttered open. She looked straight at him, and in those gentle eyes he saw no guile, no recrimination, only bewilderment. Still, he had to punish her. Someone had to suffer for this, although he could not bring himself to strike.

He was shocked by the turn of events. Girls always wanted him. As long as he could remember, they invited him, welcomed him, so he believed. He set the bait and they landed. Just as his father had advised him when still a young boy.

"Women," Joseph had said, "will always want a big beautiful black man, even those who pretend they don't."

What would his father think of him now? The fierce magnificent black boy weakened by this brown-skin girl who lay flat and unresponsive, a passive receptor for his anger and despair.

Emma's eyes closed again, her body slumped further to the earth like quicksand. He couldn't go on, but he could not strike her either. He understood there would be repercussions. This girl had parents who would be avenged. Surely he would be punished for this over and above any of the minor infractions he had inflicted on fellow classmates and neighborhood girls in the past. He thought to flee, leave her there to perish in shame, but if he abandoned her now, she might dissolve into the blanket of rotting leaves.

He stood, jerked his pants up and pulled Emma first to a sitting then a shaky standing position. He pulled up her pants, leaned her against his shoulder to guide her back to the car, plopped her into the passenger seat and pushed her legs in front of her before slamming the door hard, hoping she might revive.

Emma remained immobile, her gaze set into nowhere. Joe jumped into his seat, drove fast and reckless to the drop-off spot at the train station, brought the car to a sharp stop, leaped out, and grabbed her bags from the backseat. Emma still didn't move. He cursed her under his breath, looked around to make sure none of his parents' friends or customers were around, then opened her door, as if they were only on a date, and pulled so hard on her arm to force her to step out that the bruise would last for days. He dropped the bags at her feet.

Emma wobbled for a moment like a newborn colt as Joe nudged her out of the way of the car door and slammed it behind her.

"You think you are so much better than me, bitch!" he growled into her ear. "Go home, go home to your fancy life, and don't you ever say a word about this. Never!"

He jumped back into the car and took off.

Emma stood, disheveled and disoriented, as stiff and silent as a tree. She didn't move a muscle until she heard the train rumbling into the station, then, as if slapped into consciousness, she grabbed her coat and bags and followed people stepping out of cars and taxis to make the dash to the city-bound track. The train rumbled in just as she got there and she flinched at the sudden vibration beneath her feet as if an explosion. Once on board, she placed the bags on the seat next to her so no one would sit close. When she paid for her ticket, the conductor peered at her messy clothing and mussed hair with disgust, as if she were drunk or drug-addicted, and she forced herself to breathe steadily to hold back the tears that stung behind her eyes. She leaned her whole body against the armrest and watched as the landscape beyond smudged windows evolved from tall trees and pitched roofs to steel and stone, from the openness of suburban green space to the claustrophobic comfort of the city. With each mile, she began to breathe more evenly, the pounding of her heart against her ribs slowly dissipating to normal.

Soon she would be home, she thought. Soon her parents would be home. And, although she might never feel truly safe again, soon she would be protected.

She would tell no one what happened. Not for years. Neither her mother nor father, despite their queries. Not her sister, who pestered her often to lighten up, until at last she expressed greater concern about what might have happened to dampen her usually genial personality. Emma dismissed all entreaties and asked to be left alone. She answered the same to the guidance counselor, who inquired about what caused her grades to drop her sophomore year, and the school social worker, who contacted Nina when more than one of the teachers suggested that Emma was depressed. She even ignored her father's concerns about why she quit the track team.

She would speak of the event only once, to Leslie. After avoiding each other for three days, Emma pulled Leslie aside, grabbing her arm perhaps too tightly to ensure that she was unable to ignore her any longer.

"Did you know your brother meant to rape me?"

Leslie laughed, a shrill dismissive laughter that Emma would never forget.

"Rape? Is that what you call it? I only remember you flirting like crazy with him all weekend. You've been dying for his attention. And when you found him on your bed, did you scoot him out? No. He's done that before. He tests people. Why do you think I can't have sleepovers? He's been at every girlfriend I ever had." She pulled her arm away angrily. "I told my mother you were different. I thought you were smarter than that, I thought you were my friend." Tears filled Leslie eyes, even as she retained a furious glare. "Maybe you just like hanging out with scholarship kids. Makes you feel like, what, some sort of social worker? Think you are better than we are because you've got a white mama? Because you live on Park Avenue? Maybe you just wanted to see what it might be like to do it with a real black boy. Well, you picked the wrong boy. I warned you, didn't I? Don't say I didn't warn you!"

They never spoke again, snubbing each other throughout the balance of that semester, after which both Joe, following an altercation on the playing field, and Leslie, for reasons unknown, were dispatched to another school.

Years later, when Emma learned more about men and more about herself, she came at last to understand she was not to blame. She had not run because she could not run. She forgave herself, and she also forgave Joe, because they were both products of the same paradigm. She would instead learn from the experience, remembering the child she was then to understand others: a child without cunning, unable to contend with the complicated pathology of an angry black boy and the dynamics of race in America.

Keisha Sherman McGraw/2004

And, no matter how often she came among them,
she still remained someone apart,
a little mysterious and strange, someone to wonder about
and to admire and to pity.
Nella Larsen

Keisha wanted the painting. She had never wanted anything so much; she rarely coveted anything beyond what was given. Abandoned children like Keisha learn early in life that to want is to court disappointment or disaster. But the painting spoke to her, it called to her as if it was meant for her, and she longed to possess it.

Imagine, she whispered to herself as she stared at the painting. To call such a thing your own. To look at it every day, any time of the day, right there in your own home. She imagined she would hang it in her bedroom, opposite the posters of Alicia Keyes and India Arie taped over her bed, so that they too might enjoy the wonder of great art. She would hang it where a framed print by Berthe Morisot hung, an iconic, softly hued impressionist rendering of a woman gazing into the cradle of a sleeping child. Keisha's adopted mother, Margo, placed the print there when Keisha arrived and it had remained in place nearly seven years, almost half of Keisha's life, and every evening, at the tucking hour, she noticed that Margo glanced at the print with an expression of nostalgia. Or was it longing for something that never was? The portrait may have had special meaning to Margo, however Keisha found it too traditional and sentimental, and she imagined with glee the amazing contemporary oil painting in its place. A modern abstract creation that might inspire her to greatness.

She rarely asked for anything, even though she was approaching thirteen and all her seventh grade friends had reached the age of wanting. They had Abercrombie and Fitch clothes, jeans by True Religion, Nike sneakers and iPods. Many of them had televisions in their rooms, and more and more had cell phones. Keisha, for the most part, was grateful to have a room, and to have parents who cared for her, even if they didn't look anything like her and didn't always understand her. She knew they meant well. They provided a safe place with all the creature comforts. They spent a lot of money on tutors to compensate for her learning disabilities, and they seemed willing, when she completed middle school, to spend a small fortune to send her to the private high school on the Hudson River where Nina's daughters attended, and where Margo believed Keisha would get the individualized attention she needed.

Keisha would have preferred to study painting, and she dreamed of attending The High School of Art and Design. Her art teacher suggested to Daniel she might thrive in a school where students were more like her – visual learners who would rather doodle a concept than explain it. High school was nearly two years away, plenty of time to decide, Margo and Daniel said, whenever the subject came up, so she would have to patiently await their decision, and right now, the painting meant more to her than anything to do with schooling. More than anything that lay ahead or came before.

Keisha had never felt such a yearning. Orphaned young, she became adept at acquiescing to circumstance. She had no memory of missing her mother when she was taken from her as an infant, and no sense of loss when, as a toddler, after being shuttled from an uncle to a cousin to a family friend, she finally became a ward of the state. Placed in three different foster homes in three years, she discovered quickly that she had little control over her destiny, and that acceptance of her fate would in some way protect her from the distress that other kids like her suffered, kids who sustained hopefulness for what was long gone. In her adopted mother's parlance, she would have said there was little cause and effect for foster children. No point resisting. She had heard plenty of horror stories about those who attempted to direct their own destiny, and ultimately ended up in terrible places. Their fates were dictated by forces beyond their control. Kids just like Keisha, orphaned by negligent or mentally ill parents, abused by impoverished or drug-addicted relatives, tossed about by the system. Kids who don't learn the way other kids learn.

The social workers assured her each time they moved her to another placement that she had not done anything wrong, and she mostly believed them. The first set of parents decided to adopt a baby and no longer foster school-age children. She was moved the second time when a caseworker had to make room for a sibling placement. The third move was because the foster father, whom she especially liked, decided he wanted to take in black boys only, which he said were in greater need of the sort of discipline and attention he could provide.

She was placed with Margo and Daniel at the tender age of six, a veteran of the child protection system, and by then, all she hoped for was kindness and a nice place to live for as long as that lasted. She never expected to be adopted. In fact, soon after she was placed, when Margo and Daniel were packing to move to a larger apartment, she too packed her belongings, the few personal items she had taken with her from place to place, nothing more, dressed herself as neatly as possible so as to present well, and sat on the couch in the living room with her small backpack, waiting to be picked up by another social worker and placed elsewhere. She sat for over an hour that day before Margo realized she was sitting unusually still, without drawing or watching television, and when Margo inquired, Keisha explained she was expecting the caseworker to come for her to take her to a new home. She shed no tears, and spoke with little evidence of emotion, although she nearly whispered, as if to speak too loudly would be ungrateful.

Margo took Keisha's tiny, dark hand into her large, white hands, and explained that she too was part of their move, that she belonged to them now, she would belong to them forever. Although the concept of forever was foreign to Keisha, she trusted that Margo meant what she said, and that seemed sufficient to make her feel a little less temporary, although the sharp contrast between the colors of their hands seemed anathema to belonging.

When Margo told Daniel about what Keisha said that day, Daniel reminded her of a story about his nephew who, when barely two years old, had scribbled with multiple crayons across the dining room wall, creating a mural matching what he had drawn on the paper. When his mother scolded him, he responded with shocked tear-filled eyes. "But no one told me."

Margo nodded with understanding at the lesson and agreed that they must keep in mind that children don't inherently understand the rules, especially children whose family foundations were fragile, because the worst a parent can do is presume comprehension when confusion is the norm.

They were moving to an apartment in Brooklyn Heights where Margo pictured her daughter riding her bicycle along safe sidewalks and trotting along with friends to the playground along the East River, where skyscrapers smiled across the water and only the gaping hole of Ground Zero disrupted the skyline. Their duplex apartment took up the first floor of a brownstone, with a stairway to bedrooms above. Another family occupied the upper floors, an older couple with grown children who fawned over Keisha whenever they saw her, and whose grandchildren Keisha would one day teach to draw colorful images in chalk on the sidewalk.

Keisha had never seen anything like their new apartment: spacious and bright, with tall ceilings and tall windows that ushered in the light. At first, she felt especially small there, like Alice in Wonderland when she swallowed the potion and shrunk incomprehensively small. Keisha herself was a petite girl, a bit scrawny until she reached puberty, with almond-shaped eyes and a wide nose and thick pink lips that, at the most unexpected moments, exploded into an exuberant grin. She had a sweet face, although not one to attract attention, permitting her to become an astute observer, using everything she witnessed in her artwork.

In those first days and weeks at the new apartment in Brooklyn, she wandered like a tourist, gaping at the spread of space, her fingers gently brushing against curtains and upholstery as she gazed with appreciation at the dark wood tables and chests and the tufted floral fabrics that Margo had placed in every room to complement Daniel's soft pastel wall palette, as if the apartment itself was an impressionist painting, a Renoir or a Monet.

When Keisha at last attended art school, when she began to flex her creative muscle and move beyond the obligatory drawings and sketches of stock characters and still lives, she drafted surrealistic versions of impressionist paintings with multi-racial characters, always set against a background of cloudy skies, contradicting the traditional beauty of the original versions.

From the first, Keisha's white foster parents went out of their way to make things right for her. They hovered around her, sometimes so much so that Keisha felt she needed a bigger sky to breathe. However, every day, when she returned from school, she happily inhaled the pervasive aroma of lemon cleanser and the delicate fragrance of flowers freshened every Friday in a tall glass vase in the foyer, and she listened for the ubiquitous classical music that floated from room to room from the living room radio, as if their personal soundtrack. In the vestibule outside the front door, her bicycle leaned against the wall, and a narrow armoire stored boots and heavy scarves and gloves in winter, and spare sneakers in summer, so every time she arrived at the landing, she was reminded she lived there.

Even with the constant assurance of parents and space, and although she steadily relaxed into the reality that she might not be moved again, she was never entirely certain of her fate. Surely people change their minds. Contracts are broken. So she never asked for much, determined to prove herself a gracious guest.

Margo had quickly embraced the role of a loving disciplinarian, ensuring that Keisha ate well and exercised regularly and completed her schoolwork neatly and fully, and always on time. She read to Keisha, took her to museums and movies and occasionally to her office, where she sat her at her large desk so she might pretend to be in charge.

However, Keisha took a special liking to Daniel, not only because he was a soft-spoken man, with kind eyes and cheerful spirit, but because he was a graphic artist, a person who viewed his surroundings in shapes and colors, as she did. For the first time, Keisha felt the pleasure of attention based not on homelessness or depravation, but talent, a word she had never heard before, but would come to cherish. She began to believe there might be value in the drawings that forever poured from the colored pencils that her first foster mother had given her and which Daniel replaced with a bigger and better set. The happiest moments of her new life were the evenings spent at the kitchen table drawing with Daniel or when they manipulated color and form on the computer, and the afternoons they wandered through the park taking photographs or sketching leaves.

Now and then, Keisha sat in front of her large wooden box of pencils and chunky tinted charcoals studying the color spectrum. She made sure always to replace each one in the proper position so the continuum was sustained, each shade naturally flowing into the next as they were meant to. She had been taught to mix primary colors and understood that base colors might be blended into an infinite variety of tones, as they were at the paint store, where she stopped sometimes with Daniel to study the color chips, lined up as if a swelling rainbow. Few, she came to understand, when it came to color, stood alone. From pencils and charcoals, she graduated to watercolors, watching as flimsy strands of pigment dried into luminous brush strokes, and eventually she learned to work with acrylics, where she began to more assertively combine shades. Just this year, she had started to dabble in oils, learning how to adapt to different brushes, and she was astonished at the richness of images in oil, thicker paint nearly hypnotic in its capacity to illustrate.

The first time she saw the painting at the school library, she was waiting for her reading coach, whom she met with Tuesdays and Thursdays after school. Mondays and Wednesdays, she was tutored in math and science. In addition, once a week, another coach came to her home to help her learn to focus and organize projects and papers, so she was better able to keep up with homework and prepare for high school.

Keisha was not a terrible student. She paid attention in class, most of the time, although her eyes and ears often wandered to the background shapes and sounds in the room, or the way the afternoon sunlight affixed a shadow of her teacher against the blackboard, as if she had been drawn to it. She tended to doodle only when she was especially bored. Unlike some of the other students in the special education program, she liked to read, when she wasn't drawing, although only certain types of reading. She had been taken recently with *The Bluest Eye* and *The Bean Trees*, books that spoke to her the way traditional favorites like *The Secret Garden* or *Anne of Green Gables* had not. While she read, words formed pictures in her mind, and, in this way, novels evolved like storyboards. What she was not able to do easily was glean the key points of factual text, more taken with context than detail, so she scored poorly on comprehension tests.

In math, she had difficulty turning word problems into numbers or equations. Daniel told her she would do better in geometry when she got to high school, so, in preparation, she drew everything she saw as geometric shapes – the school bus as polyhedron, a bicycle tire like the full moon, a slice of cheese as a melting triangle – but more and more she began to prefer abstract art as a way of viewing the world, without linear definition or substance, which more closely matched her view.

Whatever the grades or test scores, Keisha was now old enough and smart enough to know she was smart enough to figure out what she most needed to know, and she could rely on her creative skill to fill in the blanks. She understood this not only inherently, but because Nina's daughter Emma, a surrogate older sister, who was planning to study psychology in college, had spent the previous summer interning at a shelter for adolescents, where she learned a lot about the long-term effects of abuse and neglect. She told Margo there was no greater trauma for a child than to be removed from its mother, even a bad mother, and this often resulted in a form of post-traumatic stress disorder, PTSD, with its lingering anxiety and difficulty with concentration, as well as the more injurious effects of depression and self-destructive behaviors. Margo assured Emma that Keisha had already proven to be resilient, with little tendency to despondency or self-pity, but she acknowledged that her daughter became anxious when expected to spit back information in the classroom and when she had to complete a reading assignment quickly, the words often piled and tangled in her mind like trash at the dump.

What had never occurred to Keisha was that her future might be limited as much by genetics as the incapacity to learn. This concept had only dawned on her recently when she overhead a conversation between Margo and Daniel late one night.

She was supposed to be sleeping, but she often lay awake in those hours between her bedtime and her parents' bedtime, listening to their voices drift up the stairs from the living room below. She rarely construed the words, rather took comfort in the timber of their voices, the gentle modulation that characterized the end-of-the-day intimacy, like a lullaby in which the cradle did not fall and she remained safe in the embrace of the treetops. That night, their cadence was clipped, argumentative, so she crept from her bed to the top of the stairs to better focus on the words, sensing that something of her own future might be at stake.

"She can study at the Art Students League on Saturdays, she can even go to summer classes there, but she will need a first class education if she is to do better in this world," Margo argued.

"Art is going to be her vocation, not her avocation," Daniel answered. "She has real talent, and what a blessing that is. There's a lot more work these days for people with artistic sensibilities. Internet communication is exploding. Website designers are desperate for illustrators. Artists are in huge demand. There's new signage everywhere, new magazines, new packaging, not to mention art direction at ad agencies like yours. A world of possibilities. And let's face it, traditional schooling will be too much of a struggle for her. Why does she have to be put through that?"

"She will get lots of help there, and I would not call that school traditional in any sense of the word. They have a great art program. Nina will get her in, and that's the blessing. Don't you think we would be letting her down to assume that she cannot rise to the challenge?"

"All that so-called challenge will bore her to death. She'll tune out, do you want that? That's the kiss of death. The curriculum is simply too hard, too much she cannot relate to, and, frankly, it won't help to be on that lily-white campus..."

"Come on, there are minority students there."

"Not like Keisha. She won't be one of the diplomat's kids, and she won't be a scholarship kid, she'll be an oddball, socially at least, and that's half of what high school is all about, right? Emma won't be there by then to watch over her. For all the school has to offer, we might be denying her the opportunity to blossom with like kind. And, frankly, I'm not sure she needs to go to college."

Margo stared at Daniel as if he had suggested she drown her own child.

"She absolutely has to go to college. She can study art history or applied art or whatever, but she has to go to college."

"Absolutely? Perhaps she might have a say in this?"

"College is essential, Danny. It's the last thing we can do for her, the last thing she will need to secure a good future. Wasn't that the point?"

"The point was to have a family, to take in a kid who needed a home, and help her thrive, and we're doing that. Don't impose some other priorities on her because, well..."

"Because you think they will reflect better on us. Is that what you think?"

"You said it."

"You think it is inappropriate for me to want the best for my daughter?"

"Our daughter. Our adopted daughter. Margo, after all this time, you still don't get that we adopted a black child, and that set her up for a whole other set of challenges. And, at the same time as you wear blinders on that key point, you personalize the entire civil rights movement on her behalf!"

"Give me a break," Margo snapped.

"I mean it," Daniel went on. "As soon as we accepted that adopting an African-American child was the right thing to do, you took on centuries of guilt. As if we personally perpetuated slavery. Or we organized the Klu Klux Klan. We can only do what we can do for Keisha, not for the entire race. We're white parents with a black child. So be it. She seems happy; she's safe and healthy, that should be sufficient. And all I want is to make sure we do what's right for her, not for us, certainly not to service the race, and definitely not the naysayers, those people who would rather we had not adopted a black child. They are not interested in Keisha's well-being, we are."

"Of course I want what's right for her, but she doesn't process information the way the rest of us do, that's as much a hindrance as her black skin. We have to help her compensate, that's all I'm saying. We have to give her every opportunity."

"Every opportunity to fulfill her own potential, yes, isn't that what parents are supposed to do for their kids?"

"Yes, and the tutoring and coaching, that helps her immensely."

"Not if it's simply to raise the bar. We don't want to set her up for failure."

"We don't even know if she'll get into Art and Design. This is all a bit premature."

Daniel smiled. "Oh, she'll get in. Remember when I taught that class there? Lots of talent, sure, but I can tell you, she's better than most. I showed the principal some of her other drawings and he agreed. She's a lock."

Daniel suddenly looked at Margo with a nostalgic grin on his face. "Remember when we were kids..."

"In the dark ages?"

Daniel chuckled. "Yeah, way back then, at that time when some of us went to college and some of us went to trade schools and we all sort of found our way? This one-size-fits-all thing is not in the best interest of every child, and an art school is where Keisha will blossom. She's already burdened with dark skin, let's not make it any harder than it is."

"Now who is taking on the weight of race?" Margo muttered.

"Practicality, that's all, not self-recrimination. She's not just the sweet little girl we saved from homelessness; she's a black girl in a white world. We have to face that, not for us, for her."

Keisha crept back to bed and tried to process her parents' words. She had previously dismissed from her mind, as much as possible, the difference between the way she looked and the way Margo and Daniel looked. She had accepted the difference, although when she was younger, when they first moved to Brooklyn, she drew sketches of herself with her new family, seated together on the steps leading to their brownstone, all smiling, as if facing a camera, in which she depicted herself as white as they were. She was convinced then that in time she might turn into a white girl, so that she would be just like them, just like the other families around her, and every morning when she woke up, she peeked in the mirror, awaiting the miracle. She peered closely to see if she were even a little bit lighter, perhaps she might evolve into Caucasian a little at a time, like Michael Jackson. Most everyone in her immediate orbit was white or light brown. Friends, neighbors, classmates. So might she not soon be just like them?

That night, still harboring the vestiges of that fantasy, she came at last to the realization that she would live forever in her own dark skin. The next morning, awakening early with her adopted parents' words still clouding her brain, she remembered that she was not only a black girl, she was not smart enough to achieve a white girl's sort of life, but that she might make something of herself with art. So the painting loomed especially large, as if an amulet.

The very next day, the day after the overheard conversation between her parents, Keisha was in the school library when she noticed the large framed painting, laying on its side against the back wall in the reference section, adjacent to a couple of framed black and white photographs, a silver-plated champagne bucket, and a Venetian glass vase, as if in preparation for a garage sale. A trio of chatty fundraising volunteers sat at a table nearby cataloguing items that had been donated for a dinner to raise funds to build a new playground for the middle school.

Keisha bent down as close as possible to the painting and tipped her head sideways to study the image, which was at first glance difficult to discern. Splashes of bold colors bled off the edges, without benefit of matting, and it was framed in a filigreed gold-leaf, contradictory to its modern style, which made it all the more incongruous, nearly confrontational.

Keisha, with Daniel's tutelage, was just learning to categorize artistic movements, and she recognized the painting as a form of abstract impressionism. They had recently seen paintings by Rothko and Motherwell at MOMA, and she was completely taken with overlapping shapes and contrasting tonality. This painting seemed more of a montage, but with the same sort of intensity. Bold and belligerent. On closer scrutiny, brush strokes seemed almost animated, as if the images might bounce out of the frame, yet so thick and startling they could have been applied with a palette knife, rather than a brush, which she had yet to master. When she stood back to take in the full viewing, as she was taught to do, she thought she saw the impression of children at play, children perhaps slightly rambunctious, as if released from school on a summer day, determined to shake out their own cobwebs. She stared at the painting so long that at last the tutor came searching for her and she had to tear herself away. The painting had stirred a profound sensation in the deepest part of her, a sensation of longing previously repressed, suddenly demanding reparation.

There was a typed form scotch-taped to the edge of the picture that indicated a value of $5,000 with a minimum price of $500. Keisha did not understand the workings of silent auctions, thus she was confused by the disparity of prices, and hoped that perhaps her parents might purchase the painting for what she believed was a price tag of $500. Even at that price, Keisha simply had to have that painting.

She felt she deserved to have that painting, as if a rebuttal of the disappointment of her beginnings, the disappointment of her own limitations, as well as an exhortation to test boundaries. She imagined for a moment she might even steal the painting, but she knew that was not possible, so she determined to convince Margo and Daniel to purchase the painting as a birthday gift.

Yes, $500 was a lot of money, but she thought it a small price to pay for such an evocative work of art, and a fine way to usher in adolescence, and that was the case she made to Margo and Daniel. As shocked as they were by the request, they were equally charmed that their young daughter would covet an original oil painting rather than the prototypical adolescent cravings. As Keisha received an allowance of $20 each week in return for the chores she was asked to do at home, beyond keeping her room tidy, she suggested she might repay the purchase price over time, and although she would not have been able to create an algebraic equation to define the pay-out, she understood by the amused expression on Margo's face that this would take much too long.

Having asked for so little up to that point in her life, surely they would comply, she thought. No matter that she had lovely clothes and shoes and a new backpack with a rainbow on the trim, and all the books and notepads and art supplies required for her studies and pastimes. The painting was different. She needed the painting to feel special.

Margo and Daniel always told her she was special, but, in truth, even with everything they had given, she knew she was not, and now she believed that despite Margo and Daniel's commitment, and genuine affection, they were her caretakers, not her parents. She was still an orphan, forever an orphan, and every time she sat with them at dinner, every time they attended museums and movies or open-school nights, even with Nina and Barrett and their girls, even when they spent time with Margo's family in Ohio, none of them were blood relatives and Keisha did not truly belong to them. The evidence was in the mirror, impossible to ignore.

She stared at herself that night in the bathroom mirror as she brushed her teeth. Her face had matured, childhood pudginess giving way to gently sloping cheekbones, but her hair was too thick, her arms and legs too long for her compact torso, and although her hips were narrow, she had a high round butt, so clothes didn't always fit right, and, even when they fit, she never looked anywhere near the same as fellow students wearing the same style. Her ebony skin was so dark that she marveled when she was with Jennifer and Emma, or with her few brown friends, that she was the same race at all.

The painting seemed to reflect all the more to Keisha that she inhabited a narrow space within a broader world, with unassailable boundaries, no matter that her adopted parents were outraged by the injustices of racial discrimination or how hard they attempted to cultivate a color-blind ideal. They would house her and protect her and do their best for her, but, in the end, she was the outsider that Daniel understood her to be.

The evening of the school fundraiser, Keisha was dispatched to Nina's apartment for the night, which she often was, under the watchful eye of their housekeeper, Lily. A light brown immigrant from Peru, Lily fawned over Keisha as she had fawned over Emma and Jennifer since birth, and conversed with Keisha in Spanish to help her with her language study. Although Keisha struggled with the language, the assault of foreign words pummeling her brain into mush, she never felt ashamed with Lily, who spoke her own form of Spanglish.

She especially loved to spend evenings with Emma, who treated her with the affection she might have shown a younger sister. She saw Jennifer only when she returned from college for holidays, and Emma had always been the friendlier of the two, kinder, as if she understood more than such a pretty, nearly white girl of means could possibly understand.

After dinner, Emma finished writing a paper in the den while Keisha watched a new DVD version of *The Lion King*, before she was dispatched to a guest bedroom where she was permitted to keep spare nightclothes in the dresser and her toothbrush in the bathroom. She was certain she was too excited to sleep, as she sat on the bench at the dressing table, brushing her hair 100 strokes, an old-fashioned mannerism passed down from her adopted grandmother, Mrs. Elliott, who read in a fashion magazine that every elegant woman must do. She used a special brush with long, widely spaced prongs, in order to move through her often-tangled thicket of hair.

When, as a child, she had first arrived at her new home, her hair was pulled tightly into high pigtails wrapped with tiny pink bows, so Margo assumed she preferred it that way. Soon after, Nina suggested Keisha might like to wear her hair like Emma, in a low ponytail, and Keisha was thrilled with the look, having already attached herself to Emma, and she was also thrilled to release the tight pull across her scalp which made her feel as if her brain were in a vise. However, throughout the school day, uncontrollable bunches broke free from the band, so by the time she boarded the afternoon school bus, most of her hair had been emancipated into a wild mane. Of late, tentatively displaying adolescent grit, Keisha refused to band her hair, preferring it cut a little shorter and gathered naturally around her head. Margo agreed only if she kept her hair brushed and neat, and she complied.

She slipped onto her knees by the bedside to say her evening prayers, something she rarely did but had seen in movies and thought useful at that moment, clasping her hands together and lowering her eyes, with one and only one thought on her mind.

"Please, Lord. I've done everything I was told to do, and I will do better at school, I will, so please, please, make Margo and Daniel buy me the painting. Amen."

She slept soundly in the end, certain her parents would bring home the prize, if not out of affection, perhaps the guilt Daniel spoke of, or, she hoped, they had been convinced she was deserving of a stunning one-of-a-kind painting that depicted the childhood they would want for her: fearless and lively as broad swaths of color across a canvas.

At the fundraiser that night, Margo and Daniel, accompanied by Nina and Barrett, sauntered around the display tables of silent auction items. They found the painting at once and Margo signed her name on the opening bid for $500.

Daniel perused the painting with a practiced eye. "Not worth much more than a thousand," he pronounced. "Maybe fifteen hundred. I mean, it's good, interesting in that downtown art scene sort of way, but not valuable. The artist is completely unknown, I checked."

"Really?" Margo gazed at the painting to see it through her husband's eyes, and also through Keisha's eyes. "I wonder why it means so much to Keisha."

Nina and Barrett too stepped back for a better viewing.

"It's got a lot of energy, but I'm not sure I see much more," Nina said.

Barrett raised one eyebrow in the non-committal way he had of acknowledging what people had to say, without revealing his opinion. Nina noticed the move, which infuriated her at times, and at other times, such as that moment, was endearing. Barrett, ever the lawyer, was exceptional at holding his tongue, and, when he did speak, spoke in the voice of reason, as if everyone else simply did not have all the facts at their fingertips and missed the point entirely. Married nearly twenty-five years now, her husband was smart and even-tempered and predictable, but also enigmatic. She had once told him she was convinced he took a class in benign indifference at law school, in which they were taught such facial expressions: not so much apathy, rather ambiguity laced with restraint. Barrett had answered that he learned restraint not at law school, but on the streets of Washington DC, during six years at school and apprenticeship, where black men, even light brown men like Barrett, were judged as worthy or unworthy by their veneer.

They strolled the auction display, Nina placing a bid on a pair of earrings she admired, and Margo retreating now and then to check the status of the painting.

"Maybe we should go to $3000," she told Daniel when she checked again on the painting and discovered a bidding war was underway. At Daniel's expression of disbelief, she held up her palm to deflect his argument. "Okay, $2500."

"An awful lot of money for a birthday gift for a thirteen year-old."

"It's a fundraiser, it's a good cause."

"Fine," Daniel nodded, "but that's the cap, yes?"

"Of course," Margo nodded and slipped her arm in his to continue their stroll.

Moments later, when Margo checked again, she returned to the group disappointed that although there were only two bidders left, one of them had already bid $3,000.

Daniel shrugged. "We'll explain what happened. It's an important lesson for Keisha. She absolutely cannot always have what she wants."

"I suspect she knows that," Barrett said, as he turned to Nina. "Shall I check on the earrings for you before we have dinner?" he asked.

"Thanks, honey, yes, but it's not imperative."

"Kids got to have good playground equipment," he said, and kissed her cheek. "I'll meet you at the table."

The next day, the absence of the painting anywhere in the apartment was crushing at first to Keisha, who subsequently consoled herself with the fantasy that the painting was being held for her birthday party the following weekend. She hardly slept at night, awaiting that moment, and had greater difficulty than usual concentrating on her studies, although she tried especially hard, as if to guarantee the outcome.

Daniel and Margo said nothing of it, assuming that because Keisha didn't ask, she hadn't really expected to have the painting, and it might be better left unspoken.

The following Saturday afternoon, after half-dozen friends had feasted on pizza and cake, opened presents and watched *Confessions of a Teenage Drama Queen*, Nina, Barrett and Emma arrived for cake and ice cream, a long-standing custom between the families. Keisha, who had been crushed not to find the painting in her pile of presents, had moped around all afternoon and greeted them without enthusiasm.

"She's brokenhearted about the painting," Margo whispered to Nina as they put out plates and silverware.

Nina nodded. "What did you tell her?"

"Nothing yet, too much going on, but she asked if there were any other gifts and we had to say no, and if you could have seen the look on her face, absolutely awful. We'll talk to her about it later. One of those teachable moments."

Nina nodded and glanced at Barrett, but said nothing.

Once everyone was in the kitchen, Barrett slipped out to the hallway to retrieve the painting, wrapped in brown paper with industrial string. He eased back into the apartment and propped the package against the coffee table in the living room, where Keisha's previously opened gifts were scattered. He had returned to the display table the night of the auction, just before the closing, to place a final bid of $4000, and asked Nina to stay silent, knowing that Margo and Daniel might be displeased with the subterfuge.

They all gathered in the kitchen and after another round of song and another ceremonial extinguishing of candles, Barrett asked Keisha what gifts she had received and which were her favorites. Keisha jumped off her chair to claim the gifts in the adjoining room and when she saw the large wrapped package there, she stopped in her tracks.

"What's this?" she shouted, her heart leaping into her throat, because she knew exactly what it was, although not where it came from.

"Open it," Barrett said.

"You bought the painting?" Margo whispered to Barrett. "Are you crazy?"

Barrett nodded. "Sometimes."

Margo turned to Nina, who shrugged with embarrassment. "I was sworn to secrecy."

"She just needs to know she's special," Barrett added, as if making his case to the jury. "You'll have to forgive me on this one."

"You might have asked," Margo said tartly, offended by Barrett's conceit.

"He did," Daniel answered. "Maybe it's a good investment in the end, not only in an emerging artist, but in our daughter."

The shrieks and hugs that ensued served as validation, and Margo and Daniel hung the painting that night exactly where Keisha envisioned it. Margo took down the print of mother and child, which had moved her at first sight and every time she sat at Keisha's bedside, and hung it in Keisha's bathroom, hoping her daughter might continue to appreciate the sentiment.

"I suppose you might say our little girl is growing up," she said to Daniel, wiping a tear from her eyes.

"I'll say. Her first original oil painting at thirteen, now that's a right of passage. I'll remind her to write an especially thoughtful thank you note to Barrett for such a special gift."

"Indeed!" Margo answered.

Keisha wrote the note with her best fine-point pen, in a script she invented herself, and she added abstracted heart shapes at the corners in bold colors Kandinsky might have used. She never forgot Barrett's kindness, or the sudden sense of supremacy she felt in owning something so extraordinary, and she remembered forever that it was the black man, the man who resembled her reflection in the mirror, who answered her prayer. The black man who made her feel special.

Jennifer Douglas/2005

...none of their children, or any of their ancestors,
or any parts of themselves,
shall be hidden from them.
Alice Walker

Nina's daughter Jennifer curled under the rumpled sheets of a lumpy bed in a dingy room at a Super8 Motel just off the interstate highway south of Los Angeles. She was naked, swathed in a yellow woven cotton blanket she found wrapped in plastic on the top shelf of the closet. Ripples of taught upper arm muscles, earned that summer through a grueling schedule of physical labor, were visible through the thin blanket, punctuated by multiple bruises and minor wounds scattered across her lower arms and hands. Her light brown skin had tanned darker in the sun and thus contrasted more acutely with the pinkish soles of her feet, one of which had popped out of the blanket and dangled off the edge of the bed. A uniquely hotel-style green and gold floral bedspread and bolsters were tossed across the room in a straggly path toward door.

Jennifer's mocha-brown face was flushed with heat, wavy brown hair tousled, and she wore the satisfied smile of the late-night lover. She plumped then propped herself up on two squished pillows and folded her arms behind her neck, listening to Alex hum in the shower, and she chuckled when she recognized the tune: Eric Clapton's *You Look Wonderful Tonight.*

The bathroom door was ajar and Jennifer watched as steam began its foggy march up the mirror, steam she was certain less than an hour earlier hovered over the bed.

They have both been working as crew for the producers of rock musician tours that traveled across the country all summer. Between them, they've contributed to the building and dismantling of gargantuan stages stacked with trap doors and elevated stairways, and presided over the set up and take down of massive lighting, video and recording equipment at a combined sixty-five concert halls and stadiums, ensuring the reliability and quality of sound, proper set elements, and the explosive special effects that have become as essential to the show as the music. Alex was traveling with Billy Joel, Jennifer with Sting, so they had not seen each other in weeks. They shared war stories by phone and occasionally crossed paths, but they had spent little time together since they met last April.

Absence makes the heart grow fonder, it is said, and this was certainly true for these lovers. Their visits have been hypnotically, almost maniacally erotic. More to the point, Jennifer has learned to make love more expertly, and they both know now how to please each other, having experimented whenever they have been together, well beyond their first tentative embraces. They have come to accept how they feel and who they are, Jennifer less willingly, habitually resistant, as this sort of sexuality, which in earlier years hovered only on the periphery of consciousness, has evolved, with Alexandra, into a commanding gravitational pull.

Jennifer was in college the first time she allowed another woman to touch her. Until then, she had engaged in the obligatory sexual life-lessons reserved for affluent well-educated girls who learn first how to flirt and then to submit, discovering much later in life how to make love and, for those with fewer inhibitions, how to engage in erotic sex.

Jennifer had at first followed the same well-worn path of her contemporaries. She allowed middle school boys to press their squirming tongues into her mouth and grope sloppily at her breasts, while huddled in closets or dark corners at loud parties, the threat of discovery spurring speed over the sensory. In high school, she let more aggressive classmates explore all her body parts, disrobed in their childhood beds when their parents weren't home, playing at sex as they had once played marbles or Monopoly. She granted her favors mostly to the boys whom she had known a long time, having recognized at an early age that unknown white boys imagined her to be an easy target and black boys wanted her for more than a good time. Still, despite aggressively participating in exploration as if a treasure hunt, Jennifer never felt anything even remotely approaching the titillation or burst of excitement she had come to expect from the depiction of sexual encounters in movies and books, and from the commentary of friends, even though she was fully cognizant that many, perhaps most, exaggerated their experience.

She had expected to feel a burning in her pelvis. She awaited the yearning deep within. She longed for the moment when she might writhe and moan and explode with pleasure, and the aftermath of sweaty bodies and euphoria. She felt nothing even remotely approaching these expectations, nor, try as she might, did she find herself mooning over any of the boys who entered her orbit, boys equally awkward and inexperienced, but easily satisfied. Consequently, while she continued to play at sex, she resisted fornication, trusting her instincts that she wasn't ready, although never certain why.

By the time she was in high school, she fretted that something wasn't right. She seemed perpetually flat and unresponsive. She feared she might be what she had read in an ancient psychology book she found at the library that referred to women like her as frigid. To explore further, she followed a blueprint to sexuality distributed in a sex education class that promoted abstinence, entitled *How to Have Sex Without Going All the Way*. She let her junior prom date suck on every appendage, right down to her pinky toes, and she returned the favor, bringing him so quickly to ejaculation that she jumped back and laughed at the onslaught, but she felt nothing much more than curiosity, more of an observer than participant.

She had managed at a fairly young age to spend a lot of time at Manhattan music clubs with aspiring songwriters and groupies. She was entranced with music and fascinated by the business, and she also hoped the sheer proximity to alternative lifestyles might help to fulfill her desire to distance herself from what she saw as her family's bourgeois persona. Although she had hoped to be inspired by the downtown scene, she found herself resistant to the hedonistic culture, disinterested in hard drugs or casual sex, so she made it a practice to arrive early and depart early, to stay immune from after-hours seductions, and also avoid the inquisition of her parents.

She became, in effect, a mascot, and she immersed herself happily in the role, using the time to observe the way things worked behind the scenes and on stage. Once, however, when a pretty girl in a mosh pit grabbed her thigh, she repelled the advance with a reactive swipe at the girl's hand, although the moment surfaced frequently in her dreams.

The hardest part was that she had no one to talk to. As progressive as her mother pretended to be, Jennifer was well aware of Nina's inherently conservative nature. And, while her mother worked closely with gay men, she never mentioned lesbian women, and she never mingled with anyone who might have proven a role model. Most of her family's social circle and neighbors were straight, white, urban businesspeople and professionals, and it was hard enough to be brown among them, much less bohemian. Jennifer couldn't imagine having a frank conversation about sexuality with her mother, and a discussion with her father was even farther from the realm of possibility, as both she and her sister Emma were acutely conscious that Barrett worked even harder than Nina to sustain a proper veneer: he tolerated no scratches, no chinks, and definitely nothing that might be perceived as broken parts.

By the time Jennifer graduated high school, she had decided that her mother might have been right about one thing: good sex must be contingent on being in love, which she had never been. During the summer between high school and college, all her friends engaged in nearly frantic sex with the same boys they'd played with in sandboxes or traveled with on school buses, their feigned intimacy serving as a refusal to enter college as virgins, as well as a way of bidding farewell to their childhood selves. Jennifer repelled every advance with a casual remark that she had moved beyond childhood exploratory.

"I'm no longer interested in playthings," she would retort with a perfected patronizing attitude. "I'm ready for a college man."

The first week of her freshman semester at Boston University, Jennifer visited a Planned Parenthood clinic, where a soft-spoken counselor assured her that she was both sane and healthy, and that the right sexual response would come to her in the right moment. She remained doubtful, but took solace in the consolation, hoping she might be merely a late bloomer, and also began to consider the possibility that the problem was with boys still ignorant of the ways of good sex and so selfish as to aim only for their own pleasing.

Inspired by a reading of *Moll Flanders* in freshman English class, she decided to seduce an experienced lover. She targeted graduate student teaching assistants, flirting shamelessly until first one then another happily took her to their beds. She found their caresses pleasant but not stimulating. She experienced no real pleasure in the huffing and puffing, she did not appreciate the coarse stubble of scruffy beards favored by collegiate highbrows, nor overly aggressive spit-laden tongues, and she had little desire for their wooden probing dicks. She never knew exactly what to do with her body and often stiffened in response, which she knew inhibited her own sensuality, but she seemed unable to react otherwise. She wondered if she would recognize an orgasm if she had one.

As much as she craved sexual pleasure, she preferred the cerebral intimacy she found in music clubs and in class, and came to the conclusion that physical intimacy might in some way serve as an obstacle to the scholarly. She read Anais Nin and Susan Sontag, hoping to find meaning in their correlations between passion and intellect, although she failed to grasp the full weight of their words. She resigned herself to the pleasure of music and a few good friends, hoping that might suffice, although, even as she rationalized her choices, she feared she might be passion-impaired. She dismissed the thought as best as possible and buried herself in her studies and at the school radio station, where she cultivated her interest in the behind-the-scenes of the music industry and took her first tentative steps toward a career.

In her sophomore year she met Katharine, a charismatic Irish-American from Chicago who similarly devoured cutting-edge rock music and *Rolling Stone* magazine. Independent-minded and spirited, Katharine appeared equally ambivalent about the boys in her midst. Tall and lean, she wore her curly, shoulder-length, strawberry-blonde hair un-brushed and unruly, as if she had always just emerged from a warm bed. She wore dark eye make-up accentuating sparkling hazel eyes and dangling silver earrings that pointed like arrows to a long, sculpted neck. She lived in tight-fitting jeans and worn hiking boots, and in winter, wrapped her lithe body in thick cardigan sweaters with matching caps and gloves, as warm and cozy as a hearth.

They sat next to each other in biology class and surreptitiously exchanged their doodles of music lyrics that suited the subject of the day. The first time they planned to study together, Katharine slipped one arm through Jennifer's as if they were the oldest of friends, and they strolled first to Starbucks and then to Katharine's tiny studio apartment off campus, where she surprised Jennifer with a lusty embrace.

"This cannot be your first time?" Katharine asked when Jennifer pulled away with a shocked expression.

Jennifer, unwilling to be seen as an innocent, answered, "I don't usually do women, no, but I guess I'm willing to try."

"So, you deny your true self?"

"What makes you so sure this is my true self?" Jennifer asked, horrified by Katharine's presumption.

Katharine answered with a smile. Without words, she took Jennifer's hand and led her to her bed, where she made love to her slowly, tenderly and expertly. Katharine seemed to know exactly where to touch and with just the right pressure and speed. Her grip was tight and forceful, her lips soft and warm, her caresses tantalizing.

Jennifer first allowed herself the experience with the intent of discovery, but quickly found herself aroused to a state of rapture. As delighted as she was stunned, she welcomed the indoctrination to lesbian sex as a learning experience, and when at last she was heaving with desire, Katharine plunged her long fingers deep into what had for the first time been transformed into a hot, moist receptor so craving pleasure that Jennifer immediately came to the sexual climax previously denied to her.

Katharine, who had thoroughly enjoyed the conquest, slipped out of bed, still naked, pulled on a pair of thick knee socks and an oversized sweater and ran on tiptoe to the tiny kitchen at the opposite end of the room, where she poured them both a glass of jug wine. When she hurried back to Jennifer, she found her folded over herself, weeping.

Jennifer wasn't sure at first why she cried, but she sobbed like a child whose favorite toy had been lost. Katharine pulled the blanket over them and wrapped her arms around her. She explained that tears were merely a physical manifestation of repressed sensuality, but Jennifer believed otherwise. She inherently understood that she cried because she had discovered a facet of herself that had been misunderstood and unrealized, and that would set her on a course that society at large would neither comprehend nor condone. The girl who was raised as if she were white, and had accepted that in the larger world she would be treated as brown, recognized painfully that now she would be further set apart from the mainstream, an outsider by virtue of mixed race and sexual preference.

Still, she resisted. She reasoned that she had never felt any special attraction to women before and that the encounter with Katharine might have been an anomaly. She knew a number of heterosexual dorm-mates engaging in lesbian relationships as if scientific experimentation, while others engaged in same-sex liaisons as a place to hide from the doggedness of drunken, testosterone-laden college boys. She too must be in exploratory mode, she reasoned: the true right of a liberated college girl with an acute sense of curiosity. However, try as she might to convince herself that she was merely adventurous, she could not stop thinking about Katharine. She longed for her, but rejected her, choosing instead to re-assert a traditional sexual stance.

She set her sights on four boys in less than two weeks, inviting them to have their way with her and teach her the intricacies of eroticism. All four failed to stimulate true passion; however, two were able to bring her to orgasm using manual or oral stimulation, which at first gave her hope, and quickly deflation, as she recognized the difference between anatomical manipulation and sensuality. Now that she knew what it was to climax, she also realized she could pleasure herself, and that further exacerbated her confusion.

It wasn't long before Jennifer knew the die was cast and although it would be many years before she could make peace with herself, suffering through a prolonged identity crisis, she nonetheless attempted to find some degree of acceptance. However, she was not yet ready to speak aloud her bewilderment and disinclined to tell her parents. She never revealed anything to her sister Emma either, who had become a withdrawn adolescent, terribly shy with boys, so why confuse her, Jennifer reasoned. Neither was she willing to speak of her sexual orientation to her closest friends, although she never minded being different, she had always preferred the persona of the downtown girl.

However sexuality, she had come to understand, like the color of her skin, was determined by DNA, although unlike her skin, she could hide this part of herself. After all, she thought, she didn't look like a lesbian, not in the stereotypical sense. She was a decidedly girlish girl. She wore her wavy hair to her shoulders, she donned skirts when she wasn't wearing jeans, and she sashayed like a runway model when she walked. She knew she had always been attractive to boys, so she took to wearing heavier make-up and lower cut sweaters, promoting the ruse that she was merely a liberated college girl with an extraordinary sexual appetite.

Jennifer was certain she could keep this part of her life private. She argued repeatedly that this was her right, despite the protestations of Katharine and others who followed, all failing to persuade her otherwise.

"What goes on in the privacy of the bedroom is no one's business, right?" she retorted when challenged. "We don't want the government dictating how we live, we don't want them to have dominion over our bodies or sex lives, so why open ourselves up to discovery?"

"Sex, above all things is supposed to be between two people, just two people, at a time, for most of us anyway, so why does that belong in the public domain?"

"Should we all be wearing T-shirts that claim our sexual preferences: Gay, SM, Merely Mission? It's ridiculous. Everyone is into something else, and that's our right, so why do we have to be labeled?"

"Maybe this is just a phase for me. It's quite conceivable that we all have all sorts of sexuality within and we choose in the moment, yes?"

One after another of her companions argued that she protested perhaps too much, and one after another departed, unwilling to enable deception any more than the culture required, despite the more progressive attitudes that had begun to prevail on college campuses and in urban oases like Boston. Most lesbians, Jennifer later discovered, recognized their sexual identity while quite young, and stopped running away from themselves early on. They told Jennifer that she would at some point do the same, in her own good time, and they wished her well.

In the hollow silence of her bedroom late at night, she wondered.

Alexandra was the only lover who was insistent that Jennifer come out. They met at a music studio in Manhattan while interviewing for the summer touring season. Jennifer was just out of college and determined to prove herself. Alexandra was nearly thirty and established in the business, and she had graduated from stage crew to the soundboard, a role typically reserved for men, and a particularly prestigious position, as musicians rely on the board operator to ensure the quality of the sound. Jennifer also aspired to that post.

At first, she imagined that Alexandra might prove to be a mentor, but they connected immediately on a visceral level, like harmonious chords on a guitar. Alexandra was the same height as Jennifer, with a more curvaceous torso, and nearly the same color skin, with crimped espresso-brown hair, dark eyes, a smile like Lena Horne, revealing perfectly straight and startlingly bright white teeth, and a voice so sultry that the very sound over the phone gave Jennifer the shivers. Because Alexandra in summer wore rolled-up jeans and sneakers, in contrast to Jennifer's long skirts and sandals, they might have been likened to an ordinary couple, which Alexandra frequently pointed out.

"We fit, you see. Stop! Look in this window. See our reflection? We match. We are a couple like any other couple. We look good together."

She pulled Jennifer close, their arms looped together, their shoulders touching as they stared into the glass. Jennifer nodded in agreement, although she saw two women reflected there, not the sort of twosome she had envisioned for herself.

"We look like the dearest of friends."

Alexandra pulled away. "Do you hear yourself? You react to everything with schoolgirl denial. You cannot live in hiding. Never has worked, never will. It's demeaning, to both of us. It's really ridiculous, Jen."

Jennifer shook her head. "We're not hiding. We go everywhere together, when we're in the same city, and you said yourself, we look like a couple."

"Let me put it to you this way, sweetie. If we are going to be in a relationship, we need to be whole. I don't do things half way, you know that."

"Why does going public equate to whole? And don't talk about the Gestalt of the thing; I've heard that once too often."

Alexandra smiled. "You've heard it all before, but apparently you need to hear it again. This, this lifestyle or whatever you want to call it..." Alexandra waved her hands in the air as if reaching for words. "It's the same as being brown. It is who you are. That simple. No one can live an honest life without being exactly who they are, no more, no less, and no pretense. For us, especially, we have to take pride in each other. Brown lesbians? The wolves will otherwise swallow us whole."

"This sounds an awful lot like a speech, or should I say preach."

"Preaching the gospel of real life, that's exactly right. Hallelujah! It's about integrity, that's what it is. We have to begin in that place and go from there. Nothing works without that. Nothing! Walk this way, talk this way."

Alexandra swiveled her hips about as her words echoed the Aerosmith tune, and Jennifer ceased arguing in favor of laughter.

They continued the conversation that night while dining at a café in Dallas. Candles flickered on intimate round tables and pink recessed ceiling lights floated above them like clouds. Alexandra took Jennifer's hands in her own and turned them palms up, then back over again, a game she liked to play as if a teenager showing off her tan lines. In response, without thinking, Jennifer looked around to see who might be watching, then shrugged her shoulders in embarrassment when she met Alexandra's eyes.

For a moment, Alexandra was eerily silent. She gently rubbed her thumbs across Jennifer's knuckles and she leaned forward toward her as if to kiss her, but stopped when close enough to command her attention.

"Here's the thing, my girl. Change takes time. After all, fifty years ago, your mama and daddy couldn't have married. Forty plus years feminists have been fighting for equality. Homos fighting a lifetime to stay out of jail. In this country, you have to recognize the hierarchy, and don't be naive, there is a very definite gender hierarchy. White straight men at the top, followed by white straight women, and we won't even get started on the religious breakdown. Next, maybe, white gay men, then black hetero men and black straight women, maybe white lesbians fall in next, then black gay men, and at the bottom of that ladder, that would be us honey, black and brown lesbian women. That's just the way it is."

"That's a powerful argument for laying low. We are not legitimate, Alex. And likely never will be. Worse than being black."

"Only if you choose to hide. Or, you can hold your head up. I don't imagine living more than another fifty years and I cannot devote my life to a movement, so I just want to live. For me. For us."

"Exactly my point. We cannot marry or have kids. We're barely tolerated. Why do we have to wave a flag? Why do we have to make a statement?"

Alexandra shook her head sadly. "The only statement I need to make is that I want to live with you and love you. That's it, just us, one day at a time, in our own way. I want us to walk the walk, hand in hand. But that is not possible until you come out, all the way out, and take my hand without looking over your shoulder. Please, Jen. Please, go with your feelings for once."

Jennifer nodded, but without conviction, even as she felt an aching and formidable grip on her heart, the very feeling that Alexandra urged her to feel, and that she imagined might be love.

Being on tour was a safe place for a lesbian. Musicians and roadies discovered quickly when their advances were unwelcome and moved on to the next target. In the late hours after the show, when a residue of adrenaline pumped through musicians and crew, and despite their collective exhaustion, male members of the team frolicked with the women in their orbit – roadies, groupies, and wives. Some formed deeper attachments, although few lasted longer than the tour. The very essence of life on the road was the brief interlude. Passionate relationships come and go; it has always been so. As there were far more male travelers than female, they sniffed out their options quickly, and when confronted with lesbians, occasionally encouraged the girls to get together for their amusement, a macho fantasy of sex as spectator sport, but nothing more. Now and then, Alexandra tantalized them with the possibility of witness, and most displayed merely locker-room humor, without condemnation. Jennifer, on the other hand, never admitted nor denied her sexuality; she just let them know she was involved, thus unavailable.

This refusal of personal confession had steadily transformed Jennifer from a soul-searching adolescent into a secretive and distrustful young adult, and she tenaciously continued to challenge Alexandra on the subject of sexuality, like a graduate student weighing fact versus theory.

"Why is there a different standard for homosexual men and women? I would rather be called gay, if I have to be labeled at all. Isn't it a much simpler term? Elegant, organic. A Cole Porter word, definitely more acceptable," she asked one night when she and Alexandra were in the same city and had ducked out after their shows for burgers and margaritas.

"They accept the word, not so much the reality," Alexandra answered as she licked a bit of salt off the rim of her frosty glass.

Jennifer watched Alexandra's tongue meet the glass and felt at once a throbbing in her pelvis and a longing that started there and spread through her body like venom. She took a sip of water to compose herself.

"Oh, come on. We're five years into the new millennium. Homosexuality has leaped beyond the gay plague. We're practically mainstream. Look at *Will and Grace.*"

Alexandra leaned forward to swipe burger juice off Jennifer's chin with her napkin. "Window dressing. Good stuff, funny, but homogenized and as white as whole milk. Gay men, always gay men, so cute and funny and hip. Totally Oscar Wilde. Gay women, butch, sexless, if we see them at all, but we come in all shapes and sizes, right? Since the beginning of time. Read the Bible for God's sake. Look at ancient art. Queer has always been here."

"I hate that word," Jennifer muttered.

Alexandra chuckled. "Don't I know it."

A waitress arrived to take their plates and simultaneously presented the dessert that Jennifer had pre-ordered for them to share in honor of Alexandra's birthday.

Jennifer took a forkful of warm molten chocolate cake and let the bittersweet flavor linger on her tongue before swallowing. "Why can't we just live and love, isn't that enough?"

"Now that would be a perfect gift," Alexandra said, and leaned forward to kiss Jennifer who, by instinct, pulled back.

"Your mother would be sympathetic," Alexandra retorted. "Your father, he's a smart guy. Certainly these people understand intolerance, right?"

"I know, I know."

They completed their meal in silence. Alexandra never let up on Jennifer to proudly proclaim her sexuality and cement their relationship, and Jennifer expected this would be especially dramatic in the fall, when the hectic summer touring schedule quieted down and they would determine where they might land for a while.

Alexandra stepped out of the bathroom, wrapped in a towel that barely covered her body. She grabbed the remote from the nightstand and clicked the power button on the television.

"Oh," Jennifer moaned. "You've broken the spell."

Alexandra walked over to the bed and ran her fingers through Jennifer's hair. "I know, but I need to know what's going on down there."

The TV screen sparked to life, brimming with images of Louisiana, where Hurricane Katrina had raged for two days. The devastation was just beginning to sink into the

203

national psyche. Alexandra flipped to CNN, where the silver-haired Anderson Cooper had been broadcasting live commentary nearly round-the-clock.

"I bet he's gay," Alexandra chuckled.

"If he is, he'll never come out. He's on his way to the big time, I don't think he's going to risk losing half his audience, do you?"

"He might gain more than he loses."

"Let's not go there right now, please. And give the guy some credit. At least he's there, he's keeping this madness on the frontline."

"Yeah. Nice white boy paying attention to all those black folk, now there's a novelty."

Alexandra grew up in the rural South, a chestnut-colored girl in the land of dirt-poor black folks. She returned once a year to visit the aunt who raised her, having hitched a ride at sixteen with the lesbian wife of a blues musician, and never looked back. Her hometown of Chalmette was hit hard by the hurricane, the hardest hit parish on the Gulf Coast. The county was hammered not only by the storm, but also the explosion of oil storage tanks that spilled over a million gallons along the shoreline, adding insult to injury.

They watched together in stunned silence as residents of New Orleans, and visitors, were herded into the Superdome like cattle, huddling there as if awaiting slaughter. A multitude of horrifying statistics, embedded in dropout type within a blue banner, scrolled across the bottom of the screen. An estimated twenty thousand people had taken shelter in the stadium, with little or no resources, and more were desperately trying to get there. Houses literally drifted down the river, reminiscent of Dorothy's Kansas home flying through the clouds toward Oz, equally surreal but without expectation of a safe landing. Life-long neighbors of the poorest sections of the city clung to rooftops floating in waters as frenetic as rapids. Dogs, cats, chickens, an occasional goat, were drawn by the current to their death and bloated human bodies intermittently bobbed above the waterline at the edges of the canals.

Alexandra curled up on the bed with Jennifer. She pressed her thighs tightly against the backs of Jennifer's to close any possible gap between them. Droplets from her freshly washed hair drizzled onto Jennifer's shoulders and she shivered, so Alexandra pulled the blanket up over them both as they watched, unable to turn their eyes away.

"It's just beyond belief," Jennifer spit out. "What are they going to do?"

"Go on. These people just go on. Like pebbles on a creek bed, you can toss 'em, displace them for a while, but they ultimately gravitate back to where they belong. Not the first crisis for these folks, surely not the last." She sighed. "I'm going to have to get down there, I should go home. I have to do something."

Jennifer heard the sorrow in Alexandra's voice; she felt her heavy heart. "What can you do?"

"I can be there, that's what I can do. Right after Labor Day, as soon as the last wire is packed away, I'm on the next plane to Baton Rouge."

They continued to watch, taking in horrifying images while holding on to the sense of safety they felt in their motel room, far from the rush of filthy waters.

"The government has to step in, this is as bad as 9/11," Jennifer said.

"Worse. They knew this was going to happen. They knew the levies would not hold. Did you know that

Congress passed the Flood Control Act in 1965? Ten years before I was born! After Hurricane Betsy. My aunt said they thought they would be rebuilt years ago. Still not done. God knows how many hustlers have made money."

Alexandra sat up and shook her head angrily. "Even on a good day, half of N'awlins is under sea level. I think the highest point is something like ten or twelve feet above the water line. Can you imagine?"

"Why didn't more people get out do you think? They were advised to."

"Cooper said a million got out. Maybe more. The rest, I guess they just didn't believe it would be so bad. There have been so many false alarms. Besides, they have work there, families, paychecks; not so easy to leave. Maybe they just don't want to leave. Some people stay put, they stay in one life, they don't abandon their homes or their people. That's the way they are."

"By the time this is over," Alexandra went on, "a whole lot of people will be dead or displaced. Might be worse than 9/11, but no one will care quite so much."

"Because it's not a terrorist attack," Jennifer muttered.

"Because it's not about rich white folks." Alexandra sighed. "A bit like you and me. The Park Avenue girl and the Parish poor. Speaks of many things."

Jennifer held her tongue, uncomfortable with the increasingly antagonistic tenor of recent conversation. She could not fathom why Alexandra would personalize such an enormous tragedy and also had begun to wonder whether or not the divide between them, on so many levels, was too wide to breach.

"Seems wrong somehow to be playing music in the midst of this," Jennifer said, trying to bring their conversation back to more common ground.

"Life goes on. You can bet that more than one musician is going to step up. New Orleans is the spiritual home of every last one of 'em. N'est ce pas?"

Despite the levity in her voice, and her persistently dynamic demeanor, Alexandra was visibly deflated. She pressed so tightly to Jennifer they might not have been pried apart, holding onto each other in that motel bed as if they too had been set afloat on the murky waters of the Mississippi.

Two weeks later, they arrived in Chalmette. What they found there was impossible to describe, well beyond even the most horrific media images. As they scanned the scene, both, without comment, frequently squeezed their eyes shut to dispel the vision of a devastated landscape.

The first night, after they were able to connect with Alexandra's aunt, who had been evacuated twenty miles north, they registered with the Red Cross as volunteers, then slumped into a booth at a make-shift dive, hungry and anxious for a chance to escape their first impressions of the disaster. Little was left of the city, only the slick, oil-coated rubble of a once tight-knit low-country community.

"Let me tell you a little about my hometown," Alexandra said as she sipped and then sipped again at the tip of a room-temperature bottle of beer, refrigeration hard to come by with limited electrical power. "Saint Bernard Parish is named for the saint of de Clairvaux. He was said to be so brilliant and pious, he was revered by popes. Interesting character. A poet, he preached Servum Dei, the predestined man, and he wrote about the relationship between grace and free will. Yet, here is the punch line: he also helped launch the Crusades. Do you believe the contradiction? And not only did this profoundly literary saint turn out to be a zealot, Bernard was French, from Lyon, I think, and this is the home of the Spanish Cajuns." She sighed loudly. "And where the hell is he now?"

"Like walking through the ruins of Pompeii," Jennifer murmured as they gobbled down salty sodden fried shrimp po'boys with charred home fries. The smell alone pleased their taste buds.

"I'm so glad you came," Alexandra said later that night as they huddled in the sleeping bags provided to them at the shelter, where they would stay while they worked. "Means the world to me."

"Where else would I be?"

Harry Connick, Junior had put out the call to the music community to come to New Orleans. Born and raised there, Connick was one of the first to arrive, touring the city by boat and holding the media's attention. He had already made plans to galvanize fellow musicians for a telethon to raise money, and ultimately would establish the Musicians Village to help house roughly 300 of those displaced.

Branford Marsalis, Aaron Neville and Dr. John answered the call; country singers Faith Hill and Tim McGraw arrived quickly, as did New Yorkers Paul Simon, Mariah Carey and Alicia Keys, and gospel-rocker Patti Labelle, among others. From native jazz and swamp rockers to pop singers, musicians of all flavors poured their hearts into music to help heal the city so close to their hearts, the city renowned for trumpets and drumbeats reverberating through the streets of the Latin Quarter, day and night, until silenced by the hurricane.

New Orleans was quickly transformed into a community intent on restoration and rebuilding; however many residents who had evacuated to neighboring Texas and Oklahoma had nothing to return to. The hurricane was a greater disaster for the people than the landscape. Katrina had rendered them refugees, refused even by local communities who might have opened their bridges and homes to their neighbors. Those that remained huddled with family or waited for FEMA shelters that did not arrive soon enough and were inadequate for the throngs.

Alexandra was one of the key members of Connick's touring team the previous year and she responded quickly to his plea for assistance, forwarding his email to another fifty people, who likely forwarded to another fifty, and so went the communications network that attracted a small army of volunteers to the Gulf Coast.

Their first stop was Baton Rouge, where Benny "The Peter" Pete called his Hot 8 Brass Band back together from points north to perform for the evacuees. The word went out that band members had fled with few belongings, so they rocked the crowd playing on instruments donated by Louisiana State University and local high school students. Alexandra and Jennifer were among the team that erected the set and constructed a temporary sound system, and they stayed on-site to provide production support.

Long before President Bush made his speech from Jackson Square, and before Hurricane Rita made landfall two weeks later, just west of the path of Katrina, setting back the recovery effort, a second telethon had already been broadcast on all the major networks, featuring Neil Young and U-2, cementing the music as the heart and soul of the Cajun South. The performance was titled "Shelter from the Storm" but the only shelter to be found was the welcome sanctuary of companionship among volunteers.

Together, day after day, Jennifer and Alexandra labored with a band of friendly strangers to save whatever they could for those who might find their way home. Jennifer often looked up from her labors to see Alexandra thrusting her body into the rubble or massaging her aching shoulders between shovels of debris, and she felt genuine pride in this woman who put herself so completely into whatever she chose to do. Now and then, their eyes met and they smiled the smile of partners who might have been merely catching a glimpse of each other across a crowded bar or from disparate conversations at a party. Although they were just two among many, Jennifer noticed that when they sat together at lunch or left together at the end of the day, others glanced at them with a smile, and she knew that despite whatever cover she attempted to maintain, they had been identified as a couple. She should have been relieved, pleased to be accepted, but she could not shake the lingering shame of that distinction.

Alexandra, on the other hand, seemed especially happy, a satisfied grin on her face at all times, because she was home among what she fondly referred to as kin-folk, and because she began to see herself with Jennifer as others saw them: a couple, working together with a sense of purpose, caring for others as well as themselves.

Jennifer realized that Alexandra would want to remain in New Orleans for an indefinite period, and although she had gladly pitched in to help in the early recovery period, she was already growing anxious to return to a clean place where she might breathe in less odious air and embrace life over death. The upheaval in the South made her all the more apprehensive about her own future, and Alexandra's primitive connection to the landscape, the roots that seemed to sprout the moment she landed, despite so many years gone, had a boomerang effect, making Jennifer want to vanish to somewhere far away.

She loved Alexandra, she had no doubt of this now; however she was not yet ready to settle openly as a lesbian. Still, the thought of their separation made her shudder. Each morning, watching Alexandra in the last throes of sleep, heartache descended like a boom from a crane, nearly crippling. Nevertheless, she knew for certain their days were numbered.

Jennifer had told her family only that she was volunteering with the Katrina cleanup crowd and that she wasn't sure how long she would be there. She cringed at the pride in her mother's voice, absorbing once again the guilt of dishonesty. Just as in the days of her adolescence, when she snuck downtown to listen to the music or to someone's apartment for sexual experimentation, she found it easy to deceive her parents, Nina and Barrett perpetually within their personal orbit, always on track, like racehorses wearing blinders. What was it like, Jennifer often wondered, to have such clarity about your identity? To be so deeply bonded in your commitment?

"What did you tell your parents?" Alexandra asked Jennifer one night as they devoured a generous plate of spicy jambalaya and drank multiple bottles of beer, refrigerated by the grace of generators and served by another team of volunteers.

"I told them I was going to help out in Louisiana."

211

"But of course you didn't tell them with whom."

"Sort of."

"Ah, you told them you were with your friend Alex, right?"

"They didn't ask anything more."

"Don't ask, don't tell."

"Not now, Alex. Please. We're both tired. This is not the time. Or place. Let's just enjoy a little downtime. My bones ache. I don't want to have this conversation right now."

"Fair enough. But we have decisions to make. This is a temporary respite."

Jennifer nodded. "Believe me, I know. You never let me forget."

Alex laughed, the low, throaty, mournful laugh of a woman wearied as much by heartache as hard labor. Weary in body and spirit for family, friends and neighbors gone, her life history nearly erased, and for a future with Jennifer that she had come to see was not to be.

In the weeks since their arrival in Louisiana, they had strained their bodies even more intensely than while on tour. They set up and took down multiple stages, working with builders who created out of old wood and scrap metal the temporary infrastructure needed to put on a show. Between performances, they rolled up their sleeves and did the heavy work that even skilled laborers rarely experience, hauling the remains of homes and personal property out of ditches and drains into giant piles for disposal. They sorted through mounds of detritus to separate reusable elements from rubbish. They raked away debris. Devoting their time to helping others, they avoided the struggle that filled the space between them like the mud and dirt that encrusted their skin and caked under their fingernails, impossible to wash away even when a good shower was available.

They fell onto their cots most nights too tired for conversation or affection, although now and then, as the sun descended into the horizon, Alexandra pulled Jennifer away to a patch of grass only she seemed to know existed, and under the shade of a Cottonwood tree, its branches bent and broken, but its roots still deeply tethered to the earth, they made love, rapidly and with intensity, their lips and fingertips frantic for a soft touch, never knowing when they might have another chance. Less an act of intimacy than distraction, these occasional interludes further depleted what little energy they had left, and while they might have served to bring them closer together, they seemed only to exacerbate the divide.

One night, when the long days of hard labor and exhaustion had taken their toll, Alexandra borrowed a truck and drove them an hour north to a small country inn. They strolled the grounds holding hands and sat on the wide porch sipping creamy Bailey's liqueur on ice, before heading to their room, where Alexandra made love to Jennifer with frightening ferocity. Like a caveman claiming his bride, she stretched Jennifer's legs so far apart she thought she might split. She stroked and invaded every part of her body, probing deeply with fingers and tongue, and she repeatedly brought Jennifer to ecstasy in a tantric sequence, only to withhold the finale and begin again. Their breath and sweat mingled as if one. Jennifer found herself in what might have been an out-of-body experience, had she not felt so acutely, almost painfully, every single touch, fully cognizant of Alexandra's desperation to hold on to her.

At last, Alexandra pushed Jennifer flat on her back. She spread and bent her knees, stopping only for a moment to grab something from her purse. She strapped on a rubber dildo, which they rarely used, their own bodies their preferred equipment. Jennifer was startled by its enormity, and as she was penetrated by mock-masculinity, she cried out, more in anguish than physical pain, as if a violation of spirit beyond the body.

Alexandra pressed her hand over her mouth.

"This is what you want, right? You want to be fucked the old-fashioned way? I can do that. I will do anything for you!"

Jennifer shook her head vigorously and tried to push Alexandra away, but she was pinned down, and as Alexandra began the convulsive thrusting that brought them both to sexual frenzy, she found it hard to breathe. She tried to cry out, passion and pain concurrent and excruciating, until Alexandra at last removed her hand and kissed Jennifer's lips so tenderly that everything that came before seemed to disappear.

Together they climaxed, two voices in one powerful roar; however, in the aftermath, they uttered not a word, hot breath and heavy hearts the only remnants of passion. As deeply wounded as she was by a breach of intimacy that she had not thought Alexandra capable of, Jennifer recognized that her perpetual silence was the greater betrayal.

Jennifer fled a few days later, without a word, without confrontation. She hitched a ride to Houston and caught a bus to Austin, where she took a job as stage manager at Atone's, one of the most revered of the city's downtown blues clubs. She made friends, but avoided intimacy. She took yoga classes. She ran at a rapid clip on the path along the river, in quiet camaraderie with other runners, her eyes focused downward to avoid rocks and ruts, running until the sweat poured down her body and her lungs gave out. She drank too much too often and slept fitfully.

She spent more time on the phone with her sister Emma and made plans for a Thanksgiving reunion in New York. They spoke at length about studies, movies, music and reality television, avoiding deeply personal discourse, keeping secrets for another time, as if their most intimate wounds might infect the other. Both were determined to rise to the promise of their upbringing: the daughters and granddaughters of bi-racial marriages and liberal ideology. Being brown was hard enough, the expectation to be as successful and as mainstream as they could possibly be was their imperative. They owed at least this much to their pioneering parents and grandparents, and all those like them who paved their way. They could do no less.

Leah Brown/2007

...life hurrying past us and running away,
too strong to stop, too sweet to lose.
Willa Cather

Grace's daughter Leah has spent so much time on the couch that the silhouette of her body was etched into the cushions. This, Leah contended, was because the couch had little padding, even less now than when it was purchased at the Salvation Army for fifty dollars one year ago. The sofa was the first major acquisition of her life, a necessity when she moved into her rental cottage, a move she felt compelled to make, despite the expense, to sever noisy, nosey roommates. The faded floral fabric retained a hint of pastel blue and lemon yellow that Leah found cheerful, albeit repressed, and a musty odor emanated from the pillows. Now and then, a feather pushed through the seams, as if to remind Leah of lives that came before.

The night before she moved in, she slipped into the cottage like a cat burglar, using the key the realtor had left for her under the mat. She wandered the house in the dark, guided only by the shadows of a full moon, reaching along the walls for light switches, although not turning them on, preferring the profound sense of privacy within the darkness, stretching her arms out to feel for doorways as if blind, and allowing the texture and scent and sounds of the place to embrace her like a lover and make her its own. The very first place to call her own.

Entry to the tiny house was through a small brick patio at the end of a jagged path, set behind a matching cottage on a narrow parcel of land in Ocean Beach, one of the coastal towns of San Diego. Eucalyptus trees had been trimmed back to usher in as much light as possibly filtered between the steeply pitched rooflines of the surrounding cottages, which made it feel to Leah that she resided in a miniature village. Overgrown red bougainvillea provided the only splash of color and served as home to a host of tiny birds that awakened her at sunrise every day. She never minded. She appreciated the contradiction of their morning mania to her sluggish repose.

"The house was built in 1940," the realtor pronounced to her proudly, as if Leah might appreciate the architectural value, and when she repeated that conversation to her sister, Becky mocked the landlord's words, retorting that nothing in California was truly old, not even old in America much less antique in any other civilization. Leah listened respectfully, as she always listened to her officious big sister, who still bossed her around, and although she never said as much, she preferred the idea of a newer world. A world more focused on future than past.

She took a picture of the front of the little cottage and sent it to her mother, who had moved into a smaller flat just two blocks from where they had all lived together in Columbus, and Grace responded that the house was just about the prettiest thing she'd ever seen. Leah smiled as she listened to her mother's phone message – Grace was always leaving messages because Leah rarely answered her phone – and Grace, having learned to never expect to reach her daughter, was always circumspect with her words, wishing to cheer her daughter, wishing to keep her close in some way, wishing that Leah had stayed nearer to home rather than departing for distant locales like all three of her children, one after the other.

One large room served as living and dining space, flanked by a sleeping alcove enclosed with a beaded curtain that tinkled whenever she passed. Redwood floors made the space feel vigorous despite the paucity of furnishings – the couch and one small table, opposite a television perched on the floor against the wall, an unframed hall mirror, the legacy of the previous tenant, and a pop art poster of Janis Joplin painted in full psychedelic color, over her bed.

In the tiny kitchen at the far end of the living room, she filled a scalloped-edge shelf above the sink with candles and tiny vases from the local thrift shop, items that must have meant something to someone at some time, and now served as passive décor. The little kitchen window was bordered at the top by a white ruffled valance that reminded her of the family home in *Little House on the Prairie* and, embedded on the kitchen wall, was a narrow half-size door that released a mini-ironing board when opened, like a jack-in-the-box. Leah laughed the first time she opened that door, because she had never ironed in her life, not once, and wasn't likely to begin now.

The sound of her laughter was the greater surprise, as it had always been, rare and unexpected.

On top of the old clunky television that she also purchased at the thrift shop was a framed photo of her siblings on the stoop in front of their row house in Columbus, which captured in their expressions each of their personalities, then and now: feisty Becky, fearless Jake, and Leah, the couch potato.

"Why are you always tired?" Becky often asked, intolerant of anything contrary to the life she felt she had to live up to. Becky was presently living near Sacramento and they emailed more often than spoke, their relationship as strained as their differences in outlook, although it was Becky who always made the call, never allowing her little sister to drift too far.

"Just tired," Leah always answered.

Tired of struggling with a melancholy that had been her companion as long as she could remember, from which she emerged only selectively, and which had evolved into more habit than personality disorder.

Now twenty-four years old, Leah had spent her childhood emulating her sister, looking up to her brother, or yearning for her mother's smile. A full-blown lethargy blossomed early in adolescence, in conjunction with puberty and with her sister's sudden departure from home, followed soon after by her brother's preparations for the military. She never blamed Becky for leaving, nor Jake for moving on. Neither did she blame her mother for drifting into her own melancholy. While she could not remember a feeling that might be described as happiness, she often craved what she could not articulate, much like the dog she adopted recently sniffed the air every morning in search of what pleases.

Grace was completely befuddled by Leah's lethargy when she was an adolescent, so consumed with making a living and protecting her children that complications of the psyche were beyond her ken.

"Teenagers are perpetually tired," the pediatrician said, and recommended iron pills.

"She needs a good breakfast," the school nurse said.

"Has she had any trauma?" the school social worker asked, and recommended counseling.

Leah refused therapy, ate as hearty a breakfast as she could swallow, and chose hamburgers over supplements. She immersed herself in schoolwork hoping to secure a scholarship to Ohio State University, but her grades never lived up to her intellect. Instead, as the beneficiary of a grant from the church's women's group, she attended a trade school, where, after eighteen months of intensive study, she earned certification as a medical technician.

Much to her surprise, she liked the work, and was encouraged by the school placement office's refrain that such positions had lasting value in the modern workforce. Although not as lofty a career as nursing, like her mother, or teaching, which had been her childhood aspiration, she believed the vocation to be useful and stable, which seemed sufficient. Useful and stable was what Leah wanted to be.

As soon as the virtual parchment paper was in-hand, Leah bolted to California, tempted by her vagabond sister and drawn to sea breezes and sunshine, nothing left for her in Ohio but cold and disappointment. Leaving was more heartwrenching than she had expected, even though her brother was already serving in Iraq and her sister trying on cities and lifestyles the way shoppers try on shoes.

"Remember your grandmother's words," Grace told Leah as she packed her few belongings. "The road goes north and south, you choose which way you go."

Leah nodded, having heard these words all her life, although never fully appreciating their portent. As far as she was concerned, north and south were markers on a map or compass, nothing more.

Now, after four years in California, Leah returned early evenings after work to her cottage, slipped into baggy sweatpants and second-hand T-shirts, and parked herself on the couch to watch television or listen to recorded books from the library on a portable CD player that her brother sent her years ago as a graduation gift. Her energy revived only occasionally, usually after dark, when she slipped into tight clothes and hung out at local bars, loud soulful music and the company of strangers repressing unnecessary sentiment until the wee hours of morning.

Otherwise, only her dog Hilda got her off the couch. It was Becky who had suggested a companion, and Leah had always wanted a pet, so she began to haunt the local animal pound, wandering frequently through dim passages punctuated by the sad, dark eyes of lonely animals, eyes that reflected back to Leah the longing for contentment that defines domesticated creatures of all types. She noticed Hilda more than once, although the dog was usually curled against the back of the cage in a pose much like Leah's couch position. A German Shepherd and Yellow Lab mix, Hilda had been discovered wild and mangy by Animal Patrol and languished too long at the pound, because adopters were more interested in puppies and cuddly animals. The only reason she was still there was because it was a no-kill shelter, and Leah wondered about her, always in the same spot, always quiet, until at last, Hilda made eye contact, peering out with an expression on her whiskered face that seemed to say, I don't expect much, a sentiment that echoed Leah's own, so she took her home.

Hilda proved to have many expectations. She demanded long walks or she clawed her way out of the cottage, first through window screens and ultimately through door moldings, leaving her paws bloody and scarred. She disappeared for hours at a time, returning home filthy and smug. Her message to Leah was clear: you will walk me or I'm gone. Thus, every morning, and again at day's end, and once more before bedtime, no matter the depth of fatigue nor the insistent pressing of her bones against the couch cushions, Leah rose to exercise Hilda. The morning walk was longer, others only as long as necessary, after which she slumped back on the couch with Hilda perched nearby, awaiting the next opportunity to bolt.

Leah was employed as a technician at the mammography center at the UCSD Medical Center for Women's Health in La Jolla, on the northern edge of the city. She made the nearly thirty minute drive in an aged Honda Civic each morning with rock music blaring and a Peet's coffee cup in one hand, oblivious to the voluptuous topography or the sudden glimpse of craggy coastline and deep blue waters that appeared beyond the bend as she approached campus. At lunch, she sat on a bench surrounded by succulents and sage, nibbling on the sandwich of the day, enjoying solidarity with doctors and nurses, from a distance, admiring of their white jackets and noble intentions.

Throughout the workday, every twenty minutes or so, she repeated to each patient instructions to remove jewelry near the neckline, disrobe to the waist, and tie the pale blue cotton robe loosely, with the opening at the front, before she gently guided each woman, usually middle-aged and older, although she observed an increasing number of younger patients of late, into the awkward placement for the mammogram. She prodded their bodies to wrap around the hard cold machine and, as respectfully as possible, pressed their breasts to the glass, breasts of so many varied shapes, sizes and densities, they came to seem merely an appendage rather than crucial sensual and maternal organs.

Leah herself had large, beautifully shaped breasts and dark, perfectly rounded nipples that responded quickly to the touch. She could not imagine what it would be like to lose one, so she did not think about it, despite the nature of her work. However, after a particularly arduous day, she stripped down to the waist the moment she arrived home, dropped to her knees, curled up against the couch, and cupped her breasts with her hands, as if to comfort them and keep them safe, as she could not do for her patients.

In the years she had been working there, Leah learned that breast cancer was not like any other cancer, even though it was as potentially devastating and too often a death sentence. Most women, she realized, believed their value in the world was tied to their physical form, thus the very possibility of losing a breast could be more terrifying than death. She imagined that many women would sacrifice almost any organ or limb, given the option. Even the bravest and most cavalier betrayed their fear in some way: their hands shook or a tear drifted down their cheek, and Leah pretended not to notice, even while handing them a tissue. She moved them through the procedure with acuity and tenderness, knowing there was little she could do to alleviate their concerns but process them rapidly and release them back to waiting loved ones or private contemplation.

She was required to check the film before she dismissed a patient, to ensure the image was clear, so she was often the first to see what was lurking within their breast tissue: the jarring contrast of white against brown celluloid, the jagged edges of nodules, the ugly amorphous shape of malignancy as gothic an apparition as storm clouds. When she saw that image, she made certain to hug the patient, in a nonchalant manner, as if she concluded every visit just so, offering the little bit of comfort she could. "You're sprung, enjoy the day," she chirped with an especially warm smile, then marked questionable film with a red stick-on flag for more immediate reading by the radiologist.

Leah's patients would never have imagined that she lived constantly with the anxiety that had claimed them in that moment. Her smile was cheerful, her compassion genuine. Women and dogs seemed to nurture what little confidence she had and sustained whatever hope she retained. On the other hand, the men in her life, boys still, were merely an occasional respite.

Like so many young women in southern California, Leah had what appeared to be deeply tanned skin, with a lean, voluptuous body. Thick, curly, brown hair, softened by heavy-duty conditioners, hung down her long neck and grazed her shapely shoulders. She commanded attention, attention she never craved, rather required, like cold water on a hot summer day.

Few ever inquired about race and she never offered clarification. Unlike her sister, she did not hide from her bi-racial roots, but she refused to be classified by color. If anyone had the audacity to ask, she answered, "I'm a mutt, like my dog."

Leah's facial features were proportionate and pleasing to the eye, with large eyes the color of jade, and she was often perceived to be a Latina, a common ethnicity in her line of work. She enjoyed the contrast between her looks and the classic blonde, blue-eyed beach girl, which she believed was in her favor. Males, she knew, were drawn to mystery.

Few lasted long. A nocturnal line-up of surfers tempted her onto their boards. A short skinny waiter tried to convince her to take Jesus as her personal savior. An immigration lawyer suggested cappuccinos. An alcoholic graduate student, mojitos. A sweet Mexican busboy inhaled her light brown skin as if she might remind him of home. A macho mid-western neighbor made minor carpentry repairs in return for listening to his tales of woe, until she bedded him simply to silence his incessant chatter. A fellow lab tech suggested they go to a movie, although there she drew the line, letting him down easily with the caution that one must not swim in the work-pond.

Despite the pleasures of masculine attention, she grew tired of repeated attempts at rehabilitation and bored by boys with nothing more important on their minds than the next wave or the next toke. However, recurring episodes of *Law & Order* grow tedious, and cold sheets, even in a warm climate, are cold.

She met Robert at Tony's, a bar in Ocean Beach where everyone was familiar but otherwise anonymous.

"Not Rob, Bob nor Bobby," he instructed her. "Robert."

She was with her brother Jake at the time, on leave from a recent posting in Iraq. She slipped her arm proudly through his as she showed him the local sights and steered him to the bar for a burger and a beer. When Leah introduced him to a few acquaintances as her brother, it was one of the rare moments that confirmed she was black. Jake was darker than his sisters, proudly so, and had found a home in the military among a plethora of black and brown brothers and sisters, and he had always had a special fondness for his sweet little sister who feigned nothing. Although he admired his sister Becky's pluck, he disdained her determination to pass into a white world, and remarked to Leah that night that Becky never allowed him to visit her wherever she was living, embarrassed to be exposed by her dark-skinned brother.

Leah smiled. "We are who we are, brother Jake."

"We can always do better."

"We can try," Leah answered with a sweet smile, barely there, like her mother's. She planted a kiss on her brother's cheek, sharing the pleasure of the thought that, in truth, they were all doing the best they could with what they had, as their mother had advised them so often to do.

Even though Jake was out of uniform that night, Robert snapped to attention when he entered the bar. Leah suspected it was her brother's shaved scalp, beyond the squared shoulders and military muscle; Robert later confessed that it was Leah who pulled him up short when he first saw her.

A Coast Guard officer recently relocated to San Diego, Robert stood as tall and straight as a flagpole. He wielded his physique like a machine: when he moved, every part of his body shifted in gear. Leah was smitten from the first and surprised to be courted. Most men either presumed or demanded her attention, but Robert took his time. They had brunch; no one had ever taken her to brunch. He called for a second date for dinner, and again with increasing frequency, despite the fact that, on the surface, they had little in common.

"Proof positive that opposites attract," Leah told her neighbor Jane, a shy, cerebral graduate student who lived vicariously through Leah's sexual escapades.

"Maybe," Jane answered, "although you may be more alike than you think."

"What makes you say that?" Leah asked, assuming that Jane imagined all black people were alike.

"He just seems sincere, a little reserved under the surface, like you," Jane answered, and Leah swallowed the guilt of judging her white friend as harshly as she often presumed herself to be judged.

Robert's eyes, like his skin, were nearly coal black, what her mother might have called blue-black. His hair, if not shorn into a military buzz cut, would sprout thick and wiry. He dressed either in uniform or in starched khakis and fresh from the laundry white T-shirts that fit snugly to his muscular frame. Leah, always happy to slip out of her shapeless starched work uniform, preferred tight-fitting tank tops, tucked into jeans stretched onto her body right out of the dryer at the laundromat, where she spent an occasional afternoon only when she ran out of clean clothes.

He was a high energy, bodybuilding military man, and she, a sluggish lab technician. However, Jane turned out to be prescient: they laughed at the same stories, they listened to the same alternative rock bands, they both confessed to an affinity for movies and television series based on Sherlock Holmes stories. They thrived on burgers and pizza, Pepsi and cold beer.

At day's end, when Robert came to claim Leah for the evening, she wrapped her long slender arms tightly around his broad shoulders and stretched her torso upward to nestle her cheek into his chest. Even though she too was tall, she barely reached his chin, and she felt his smile before she peered up to see the bright white of his teeth, like the first sight of the full moon in a dark sky.

Seemingly overnight they were a couple. She introduced him to the classic movie station on television; he took her sailing. They became regulars at neighborhood bars, smiling at fellow regulars before folding into a back booth where their bodies nestled together as if one. He joined her on the walk with Hilda most evenings and began to insist they walk longer – two, sometimes three miles – so when they returned home, Hilda slumped contentedly on her blanket.

Robert was the only man she had ever met who catapulted her out of her preferred inner-sanctum lifestyle. She came quickly to depend on his companionship as if an anchor, and when he left on missions, two or three times a month, a few days at a time, she withdrew to the couch to restore herself until his return.

One day, Robert took her with him to the gym on the Coast Guard base, a state-of-the-art facility ironically restricted to the most able-bodied. Leah thought he was joking the first time he marched her over to the treadmill.

"Can you imagine me at a gym? And this gym, a gym for giants," she told Becky on the phone that night, while soaking her aching muscles in a hot bath. "This could be the deal breaker."

Only two days later, after a Sunday brunch, Robert steered his Jeep through the gates of the base and into the parking lot at the fitness center.

"We've already had a long walk this morning," she reminded him.

"That's different," he said. "You walk the dog, you work out at the gym."

Leah groaned as he escorted her into the expansive gleaming space, nodding here and there to muscular comrades working out at full throttle.

Robert set the dials for her on the dashboard of a treadmill to a prescribed regimen with periodic alterations in speed and inclines. She thought it would be easier than it was and instead found herself, for the first time in her life, in a full-body sweat. She nearly fell off the machine when she completed the routine, dizzy but not daring to quit before she entered the requisite four-minute cool-down. She rejected his demand to lift weights and yelped in exasperation when he pushed her up onto an overhead bar for pull-ups.

"At least ten," he said. "A kid can do ten."

She collapsed after eight and her upper arms ached for two days.

Suddenly, their time together required adherence to a fitness program. Robert prevailed every time and Leah's generally lethargic demeanor morphed into genuine exhaustion. They spent time at the gym, they walked the dog or walked from Leah's cottage to one or another of the local dives, they gobbled down bar food, they made love, and they slept, what Leah began to think of as a regimen rather than relationship.

Yet, after two months of excruciatingly intensive exercise, and despite the tightness in her chest, frequent night sweats and muscle tension, she felt an unfamiliar vigor, as if she had been chemically altered. She slept more soundly. She stood a little taller and engaged more fully with her patients, admiring their haircuts or jewelry, and occasionally conversing with them about their children or grandchildren, or their latest travels to exotic places. Although she often felt a little light-headed after the workout, she found the energy to socialize with Jane and her friends, and when she tried to describe the feeling to Becky, all she could compare it to was when she was a young girl on the swings at the playground, pushing her legs forward to make herself go higher and higher still, or, when no one was looking, simply spinning in the wind under a tall tree, delighting in dizzy exultation.

The only other comparison Leah might have made to this feeling was sex, the one form of exercise she had regularly enjoyed. In this, and only this, Leah took the lead. Years of late-night wandering to neighborhood bars and home again with a companion in tow had tuned her body's sensuality with the same precision as Robert's military muscle, and, much to her surprise, he was less experienced, although loath to admit it.

"Coast Guard men are gentlemen," he argued in his defense, a smattering of unexpected modesty in his downcast eyes.

Robert found Leah's sexual appetite off-putting at first, as if an affront to his masculinity. However, he quickly thrilled to her prowess, succumbing happily to the touch of her fingers in places he had not previously imagined to be erotic, her desire to please, and the complete intimacy and abandon she brought to the sexual act, as if all the energy she withheld from the rest of her life sought release there.

In the first moments of their lovemaking, Leah closed her eyes and let her fingertips trace Robert's body as if Braille. He in turn slowly trailed his large dense hands over her shimmery smooth skin, as if he were sculpting her torso in damp clay. As his hands roamed from collarbone to breastbone, following her centerline like a winding back road on a map, she threw her head back and closed her eyes, a subtle smile waving like a flag, until the moment he rested his palm on the soft pillow between the sharp curves of her hipbones and she reached for him to bring him to her. He especially relished the moment when Leah spread her legs to welcome him, and he couldn't take his eyes off her when she was aroused, unaware she was being observed as her body gently swayed to her inner rhythm.

Leah in turn embraced his remarkable physique, hard and sinewy like a statue carved in black marble, and in this, surprisingly reassuring. The darkness of his skin suggested durability and she thrilled to the contrast of his molasses color against her bronze tone, which might have accentuated their differences, but seemed to Leah natural human striations melded into the patina of the earth: rich, fertile and organic.

The more they learned to please each other, the more their passion grew, rather than diminished, as had been Leah's previous experience, and she relished every moment of intimacy with newfound joy.

Although the pleasure itself was sufficient reward, in submitting to her sexual fervor, Robert required an equal surrender: Leah was expected to commit to muscle building. She yielded, but experienced renewed exhaustion and muscle spasms so severe they jolted her out of bed in the middle of the night. When she refused one day to go to the gym and suggested instead he stop by on his way back, his rebuke was in the voice of a commanding officer.

"You know what they say…"

"No, I don't know what they say, whoever *they* are."

"Pain is weakness leaving the body."

"What a strange expression. Oh, you mean no pain, no gain, right? I've heard that one."

"No, that's not it. That's a cliché. This is a military mantra. Think about it. It's not about gain; it's about releasing weakness from the body, vanquishing what it is that makes you weak to your enemies. Weakness, that's death to us."

"Okay, I get it. Maybe a little dramatic, but I get it."

"I don't think you do."

"We're talking about body building, Robert, not military strategy."

"Everything is strategy. Building muscle is the equivalent of building a fortress or a fleet. Takes time and requires tremendous effort, but every bit of pain is what makes you strong. Don't believe it when they tell you that after a while you won't feel the pain. You always feel the pain. That's the point. We don't run from the pain."

"You think I run away?"

Throughout the conversation Robert had been looking directly into Leah's eyes, his body perfectly parallel in a confrontational pose, stiff and fierce as if she were on trial and he the prosecutor; however, at that moment, he turned slightly away from her, as if she were no longer a person of interest. Leah felt the rebuke as severely as if she'd been punched, reminded of this aspect of his personality most opposite her own – the defender always on the offense.

"When the going gets tough, the tough get going, that's what you're saying," she muttered with a sigh. "Robert, I'm not strong like you. I need a break now and then."

"You still don't get it. You need to build strength, you can't give up, especially not on yourself. Not ever."

He raised one arm with his fist clenched in a black power salute, which she considered, at that moment, to be bordering on ridiculous.

"Robert, this is not war, this is exercise. I mean, sometimes, acceptance is a powerful weapon as well, don't you think? We cannot all be driven, what kind of world would that be?"

"Maybe a world where there would be less pain?"

Leah gave up. She was unable to refute this sort of thinking and Robert always won the argument, as deep down she knew she was firmly in his grip. She understood that perhaps the weakness he spoke of was as real for him as for her, demanding to be expunged, and this tug-of-war between strength and weakness was crucial to their personal engagement.

She had learned much by watching her mother over the years, patiently dealing with the difficulties placed in her path, without complaint, and never expecting more than she believed within reach, although she too collapsed most nights on the couch from the exhaustion of merely living.

"I wonder," Leah said to Jane one evening. "I wonder if the reason breast cancer so often goes undetected is that there is no pain. You know, the pain comes later."

"Yes, that's what they say."

"That disgusting, ugly malignancy festers, without notice."

"Awful."

"And, I mean…"

"What?"

"If what Robert says is true, well, it makes me wonder if weakness is the source of the cancer. Like, well, we have to purge our own weakness, before it is too late."

Leah and Robert began to spend more hours together at the gym than anywhere else. On the days he was at sea, he ordered her to continue the training, and reproached her on his return when she struggled through the workout, claiming she was falling behind.

"This is not a race," she exclaimed.

"Yes, it is, it is exactly a race, a race with yourself, the best kind."

They should have been able to find common ground, and Leah worked diligently at her workouts, but they began quarreling regularly. They bickered over every little thing, even where there had once been accord, as lovers who have become disenchanted argue their way out of a relationship. She saw it for what it was, but held on, unwilling to relinquish what they had, so by the time Robert proclaimed they needed a break, Leah felt especially let down. The first liaison that mattered had suddenly slipped away.

She walked Hilda near his apartment in hopes of running into him and occasionally drove to the gym and tried to convince the guard that he was expecting her, but she never got past security. She returned to the couch and hoped he might reconsider. Becky consoled her that she would never have been able to be a military wife, not the type of woman able to move from place to place and live with so much uncertainty. She was right. Leah knew a long-term relationship would never have worked, and, perhaps more to the point, as Becky reminded her, Robert was the kind of man who needed a companion willing to be commanded, which Leah had only just discovered she was not willing to be.

"He never quits, you know, never, but he doesn't seem to delight in anything," Leah told Jane one evening as they sat on the couch munching a double batch of microwave popcorn while watching *Mad About You* re-runs they had seen countless times.

"Not even the sex?"

"Even that, it's like just something else he has to master. Honestly, he's absolutely driven. Obsessive. What do you call that?"

"Monotonous," Jane answered, and they laughed so hard their bodies smacked into each other, the bowl of popcorn spilling onto the floor, where Hilda gobbled up a good many salty clusters before Leah swiped them up, affectionately scratched the dog behind her ear and nudged her back to her blanket.

On her own again, Leah became bored by repetitive television. She drifted more often outdoors, as if a new planting reaching for the sun. She took Hilda for sunset walks to Dog Beach, a strip of sand along the bay carved out for animals of all types and sizes to work out their aggression and enjoy each other's company, much like their owners. She inhaled salty sea breezes as if the scent of a new lover. She stayed home most nights, resistant for the moment to anyone who might demand anything more of her than casual conversation. She awakened earlier for longer walks before work, and again at day's end, without the fatigue of long nights with an arrogant graduate student or stoned surfer.

Becky, on a rare weekend visit, coerced Leah onto a boogie board. They spent all afternoon happily flopping around in the waves. A few days later, she bought a used board and went back to the beach, where Hilda raced through the waves by her side. From then on, Leah and Hilda walked in the mornings and boarded at sunset. Her brown hair took on the highlights of the sun and her skin turned darker. She felt for the first time that her life was completely her own and that she was doing more than her best, she was doing better.

One evening at the library, where she used the computer, she encountered a link to a website called Couchto5K that offered a training program for walkers to become runners. The site was designed for beginners and Leah suddenly believed she might begin again, challenge herself to do something one step beyond herself, without any thought of where that might lead, and without instruction or oversight. The next morning she embarked on the program, taking each day as directed, one step at a time, scrupulously obeying the regimen as if in military training.

"It's like baby steps. Really, one minute the first day, for three days, and then two minutes the next day," she told Grace during a surprise phone call and Grace almost did not recognize her daughter's cheerful voice.

"It's a really slow progression, and that's a good way to get used to it, I guess," Leah added, hoping to delight her mother with this new version of herself.

"Baby steps, that's how you learn," Grace said, offering encouragement without demanding any more of her youngest daughter than she might be able to achieve.

"Exactly," Leah said. "I walk nineteen minutes and run one. For a few days. Then eighteen and two. See the pattern? Takes months, but one of these days I should be able to run a mile."

"How do you feel when you run?" Grace asked. "Do you feel sometimes like you're leaping on clouds?"

Leah had no recollection of the time, long ago, when the thrill of the run vibrated through her mother's tired bones, yet Grace's plaintive voice made her want to weep.

"The truth is, Mama, it's nothing like that. I know I'm supposed to feel that sort of thing. That's what the runners' websites talk about. Serotonin uptake, exhilaration, that sort of stuff, but I don't feel any of that. Running is hard for me. I'm in pain when I run. Sometimes it's just boring. It's really kind of the opposite of doing what feels good. I guess, I don't know, my friend Jane, she's studying to be a social worker, she says it's more than a challenge to the self; it's doing something really hard without looking for a way out. The only time I feel good is when I don't have cramps and when I'm still moving and I can breathe steadily. Maybe that's the point. It's not supposed to be easy. It's never going to be easy, I know that now. Does that make any sense?"

"Makes perfect sense," Grace answered, somberly, having come to believe late in life that one should run toward something for the running to mean something.

"Why don't you ask Mom about running?" Becky asked Leah during a subsequent phone call.

"Why?"

"She was a runner."

"When? She didn't mention that on the phone the other night. Are you sure? Mama?"

"Oh yes, I'm sure. She ran like three times a week. After work. Mrs. Elliott told me she also ran in high school. I guess you were too young to remember."

"Why did she stop?"

"Don't know. She just stopped."

"I wonder why," Leah mused. "Now that I think of it, she seemed nostalgic about it when we spoke. Actually, sort of sad."

"I asked her once and she said she just didn't have time for it anymore. I remember it seemed kind of sudden to me, but she never said anything more than that. She must have been exhausted most of the time, she worked those horribly long hours, like sixteen hours straight some days, remember? I guess it was all too much."

"I only remember Mom working or cleaning or cooking, I don't remember much of anything else, I mean, not without us."

Silence filled the space between them for a moment as they contemplated their mother's life, a life they had rarely considered beyond her extension to their own. Leah tried to remember a time when Grace was a runner. She couldn't imagine it, so contrary to her mother's quiet methodical manner. How could she not remember?

"Everything changed, you know, all of a sudden. Everything," Becky murmured. "I mean, he was gone a long time by then, but, I don't know, something changed in her."

Becky never quite got over their father's betrayal, nor their mother's deception, while Leah considered the existence of their father merely an aberration, his memory so dim he might as well have been dead. Once the three children got over the shock that he was alive and had abandoned them, they dismissed him from their histories as permanently as Grace had before them.

That night, as Leah prepared for sleep, she thought back on her childhood when she played happily under the watchful eye of their loving neighbor, Mrs. Elliott, while Grace worked at the hospital. She remembered her mother's gentility. She remembered her constancy. And she remembered her as a woman who went on, day after day, steadfast but disheartened, as if delight and optimism had been deleted from her genetic code. She had no recollection of her running.

Leah lost weight, but her calf muscles grew taut and her thighs thicker. At the urging of a friendly representative at the local organic market, she took potassium and magnesium to treat leg cramps. She ate smaller meals more frequently and twice a day she drank fruit smoothies with yogurt and hemp protein powder. She added Omega supplements to her regimen and snacked on almonds and figs. She carried a large thermos of ionic water at all times. She took on Saturday morning shifts to pay for better running shoes. Jake and Becky chipped in to buy her an iPhone, so she might better track her progress and have music to accompany her on her runs.

Although the weather in San Diego is generally warm and sunny, wintry days are as short as everywhere else, so she joined 24-Hour Fitness for the winter months. She despised the tedium of running in place on a treadmill, enclosed in space surrounded by sweaty high-achievers like Robert, so by mid-March, she once again rushed home from work, jumped into sweatpants and running shoes, and took a long run with Hilda by her side. She ran faster every day, down tree-dappled residential streets leading to the beach, and ultimately across the causeway to a path along Mission Bay where she enjoyed silent communion with other runners, escorted by gently rippling waters.

"Do you think you'll get him back?" Becky asked one night on what were now weekly phone calls.

"Who?"

"Robert, of course. Isn't that what this is all about?"

"No," Leah said, shaking her head vehemently. "This is not about him."

"Sure," Becky said.

"Really!"

"I get it, I do."

Clearly, she was not convinced, nor was Leah entirely.

Jane asked the same question and Leah wondered: was this the motive? She answered herself by running one mile in ten minutes time, her personal best.

Six months later, she ran a 5K and signed up for a half-marathon. She trained in the evenings, cooler air easier to breathe, the run a way of taking stock of the day. She also enrolled in a Pilates class to strengthen her core muscles and gain flexibility.

Some nights, after an evening run, she caught up with friends at the bar. She had discovered that the pungency of her sweat dissipated to a sweet scent she liked. She rarely drank alcohol any more, too dehydrating. The bartender at Tony's knew her routine and poured her a sparkling water with cranberry juice when she walked in, before she was even seated on a stool, and when he asked her out, she told him she was in training, for a while. He said he would wait.

Six thousand runners were at Balboa Park in downtown San Diego the day Leah participated in her first half-marathon. She was overjoyed by the buoyancy of camaraderie and good will, and although at the back of the pack, she was not the last, and after struggling toward the final mile, she bolted into the last leg with vigor. Becky snapped a photo as Leah came across the finish line: an iconic image of an exhausted runner with an ecstatic expression on her face, exactly what self-satisfaction looks like. She sent the photo to Grace with a note that read: *The couch potato runs.*

A few weeks later, Leah ran into Robert on the late day jog. He ran at a smooth steady pace with his head down, his eyes on the pavement beneath his feet, so he did not notice her. She trailed after him for five minutes before she called out to him.

"Slow down, officer."

Robert smiled when he turned to her, the smile that had captured her heart; however, the smile disappeared instantly. Robert was not himself. They ran in tandem, but he didn't speak. She hoped he would be impressed, or at the very least acknowledge that she was able to sustain a brisk stride, but he seemed lost in thought.

After the run, they cooled down with a walk around the bay. Robert confided that he had just returned from a mission off the waters of the downtown skyline. Two pleasure boats had collided and although the Coast Guard team was anchored nearby and rushed to their aid, pulling most of the passengers from choppy waters, they had not arrived soon enough to save them all. Two men drowned. Robert admitted he felt as if he personally had failed them, all the supercilious manifestations of his military might humbled in the face of one failure.

They strolled to Tony's. They sat adjacent to each other at a high-top table, oblivious to the crowd. Robert sipped his beer and continued in a low steady voice to chronicle the tragedy, describing every detail in an effort to make sense of his failings. Leah nudged her stool a bit closer to his and wrapped one arm around his shoulder, hoping her touch would provide comfort. He kept talking. She bought him another beer, and another, before she enticed him back to her cottage and back to her bed, physical intimacy the only form of solace she had left to offer.

For one hour, they rekindled their romance. They spoke not a word. A ferocious charge surged between them, like bolts of lightning in an otherwise clear sky. Robert expressed neither delight nor desire, only desperation to bury himself in her body, and Leah understood that as he burrowed into her flesh, he laid to rest the vision of the dead and the reflection of weakness he was dedicated to exorcising. Much the way she had once buried herself in her couch pillows.

Afterwards, he fell immediately into a deep sleep and she watched him, recognizing in the shadows of starlight the act for what it was: she had conquered him as he had conquered her. That was all there ever was between them. One conquest after another, their bodies their weapons. Like adding mileage to a run or pacing toward the finish line.

Leah had taken advantage of this rare moment of frailty, although perhaps Robert had taken advantage of hers from the first, and, realizing this truth, while he slept, she sobbed. Hefty, long-withheld tears of a woman who has accepted the ending as a beginning. The starting line as imperative, perhaps even more so, than the finish.

Pain is weakness leaving the body.

Becky Brown/2008

Light, bright and damn near white.
Your daddy's black and your mommy's white.
Southern Playground Chant

Two years in any one place had become routine for Grace's daughter Becky, as if a warranty ran out after twenty-four months, the parts worn and irreplaceable. Over the course of multiple two-year stints, she had grown increasingly existential, luxuriating in an incessant theoretical inquisition with colleagues or a friend, which made her an interesting conversationalist, albeit repetitive to the point of tiresome. Someone who often made other people shift uncomfortably in their own skin.

The first two years after she fled Columbus were spent in Portland, Oregon, where she rented a room on the upper floor of an imposing Victorian home that had been transformed into a modern-day boarding house. The allure of the room was the one large window that looked down on an inner courtyard, where determined wildflowers popped up between cobblestones, a scene reminiscent of a Parisian image depicted in a picture book presented by the Northland librarian long ago, an image wedged in Becky's memory as if she had resided there. The view was shaded in early fall by overgrown crepe myrtle that spread dark pink blossoms just beyond the window like flocked wallpaper, so that after a long day at work, and again each morning, Becky felt as if she resided in an enchanted garden.

That residence was on a street of similar vintage homes near the Hawthorne Bridge, the oldest of the eight bridges that cross the Willamette River. Once, despite a map, she had to ask directions on her way to an interview, and a passerby prompted her to walk south three bridges and turn left. Becky was charmed, and reminded of her grandmother's directive, believed she was on the right path.

Portland was the first time she purchased a city map that folded neatly into her purse, visually marking every one of those bridges, and in every place that followed, she started with a map, and took great pride in subsequently mastering the grid of her adopted towns.

After Portland, she spent two years in Seattle, Washington, where she found the incessant precipitation soothing, perpetually moist air like silk against her skin. She felt there as if she had landed inside a rain forest and spent many Saturdays hiking Mount Rainier, which she found ironically serene in contrast to its potentially explosive nature. She moved from Seattle to Eugene, Oregon, where local artists filled the streets with color and music, and where she enjoyed a drawing class despite immediate confirmation that she lacked artistic talent.

She settled next in Sacramento, California, although she left shy of the usual timeframe, having found for the first time that she could not pay her way. At the time, she was working the late shift as a cashier at a midtown restaurant, where the manager, a sloppy little man with a receding hairline and a perpetual sneer, approached her late one night, after the last of the wait staff had departed, only a solitary dishwasher still in the kitchen with iPod earphones blocking sound, and he groped her with a sense of entitlement that riled Becky so severely she shoved her knee into his groin with a force she was certain must have caused him permanent damage. While he writhed on the floor, groaning and cursing, she opened the cash register and counted out the four days' pay due to her, not a penny more, returned to her rented room, packed her suitcase and backpack with her few personal treasures, and fled, trembling nearly uncontrollably and fearing repercussions. As much as she would have liked to hold him responsible for his actions, without witness, she painfully recognized her culpability.

As she had pre-paid the rent for the month and was unable to retrieve her security deposit for two weeks, she slept at an overnight shelter on the south side, where she was befriended by an aged drunk who sang to her the complete repertoire of Ray Charles, mimicking his gravelly voice to perfection, and without missing a word, despite the frequent slur. In his lucid moments, following morning coffee with a beer chaser, he recited an extended rant on the righteous way to live, advising her repeatedly to do as he says, not as he does, because, he whispered, leaning in to ensure he was heard, and lowering his eyes in shame, "Some of us just don't seem to know how to live, so the rest of you need to balance things out."

Becky found it nearly impossible to sleep those nights amidst the phlegm-filled snores of the drunk and despairing, and the indecipherable ramblings of insomniacs, all lined up like cadavers on cots in a prefabricated building on an undeveloped parcel of city-owned land near the highway. She tossed and turned in the darkness, clutching her precious belongings to her chest, dozing only an hour or so at a time, fleeing at the first crack of sunlight each morning, her suitcase tucked into a locked storage cubicle provided by the shelter, and returning reluctantly at dusk for another sleepless restless night.

She vowed then to always have an extra month's rent in her pocket should she have to take off in a hurry. Once homeless, one forgets neither the humiliation nor the horror, motivation enough for Becky to seek more reliable work, no matter how boring or repetitive or thankless, as long as she was not in harm's way. Nomadic, yes, that was a lifestyle, but homeless, no, that, Becky believed, was simply bad planning.

From Sacramento she tried on Lake Tahoe, Nevada, where she tried skiing, although the sport was too expensive to possibly sustain, and subsequently landed in the woods between Grass Valley and Nevada City, back in California, because she liked the idea of living near the site of the original gold rush. There, where trees were tall and riverbeds still sparkling, she bonded with the spirit of pioneers who had come west seeking adventure and discovered instead the challenges of transience.

From Grass Valley, she migrated down to Santa Cruz to try on a coastal community, because a drifter like herself said it was a place where one can be oneself and still be one among many. She imagined the proximity to college students and aged hippies might elevate her intellect by osmosis. She learned to surf and thoroughly enjoyed the daily parade of Jerry Garcia lookalikes as well as the sweet scent of marijuana that blew on the breeze like waves flowing from shore to sea.

From place to place, Becky tried most everything, once, but rarely took on habits, because habits smacked of predictability, a persona she steadfastly refused to adopt.

From the day Becky had run away from her midwest roots, she delighted in moving around. She imagined herself a modern-day migrant. A natural nomad. However, in each place, there was a pattern: first, a palpable sense of displacement, laced with the thrill of discovery – plotting city streets and hiking trails, foraging for food at the cheapest happy hours, finding in the least expected place a Dickensian bookshop, a friendly face – followed before long by the sameness of days marked by menial jobs and the resulting oppressive boredom, familiarity breeding both contempt and claustrophobia. Thus, every time, within a similar period of time, without reason to stay, she felt once again the desire to flee.

In each location, she lived in small furnished rooms or studio apartments in the best neighborhoods she could afford, inhabiting someone else's effects, space sparse and tidy, personalized only by an unframed wall poster of a pitcher of sunflowers painted by Van Gogh and a portrait by Modigliani of a long-necked, light-brown woman who reminded her of her mother. All flats were walk-ups in a stately home or row house, where she lived without television, without technology other than a cell phone, and where she relished quietude after a day of work or wandering. Most evenings, she dressed up a pot of rice with steamed frozen vegetables or a chunky soup from the salad bar at a nearby supermarket, in sufficient quantity to enjoy a second day as if the first.

Living a minimalist life, Becky had convinced herself that she needed little beyond her independence, her spirit of adventure, and the daily imperative to be the person she saw in the mirror: a nearly white girl determined to permanently sever all ties to her bi-racial heritage.

However, in each place, draped across a bed or sofa, she held onto one precious belonging: a pastel patchwork quilt Grace had given her to dress up her life and keep her closer to her roots. On cold nights, she wrapped herself in that quilt and listened to rock or rap music on a beat-up but working radio she found in a trash can, the volume turned high to obliterate uncertainties.

Employment was rarely hard to find and sufficient to subsidize her meager expenses, at least until the recession, and even then, jobs were generally available to a girl with a bright smile and a congenial personality, especially an articulate and attractive girl like Becky, with smoldering hazel eyes and pleasingly bronze skin. A girl who was willing to do almost anything asked of her. She was never afraid of hard work; in fact, she embraced it, as if penitence for an itinerant lifestyle. She knew she had neither particular talent nor special skills, neither the personality of an entrepreneur nor the tenacity or passion to set herself on one particular course, which, she rationalized, was for the best, as she was less likely to be disappointed and less likely to be stuck in place. She accepted her modest prospects, determined only to surprise her colleagues and supervisors with quick mastery of whatever was required of her, and deflect undue attention to herself.

In a country filled with perky girls with limited education and expectations, Becky rose to the surface largely because she was adept at engaging the people around her without giving much in return. This quality also made her especially appealing to men, those she occasionally allowed into her tightly controlled sanctum, all drawn to her by the same aloofness that would ultimately repel them. She never permitted any true depth of connection, as if anyone too close might hold her back, or sanction dependency, polar opposition to the high-minded woman Becky meant to be.

Every job, no matter how menial, presented an opportunity to learn, and this, as well as the books she read incessantly, nurtured Becky's intellect. In Portland, she worked as a receptionist at Nike, although she was rarely invited to share a night out with the pert self-impressed college grads overflowing cubicles in their collective quest to perpetuate an icon. She trained as a barista at Starbucks in Seattle, and was subsequently able to secure employment at one or another Starbucks in almost every American city. In these busy storefronts, she enjoyed glimpses of life among the urban upwardly mobile, who sat in their coffee-scented hovels for hours and days, conversations as heated as their cappuccinos, shoulder to shoulder with the homeless and the disenchanted who also made Starbucks their daily dens. She eavesdropped often as she wiped crumbs and smudges off composite tables, and smiled knowingly at the pretense that hovered over them, all of them, the haves and have-nots, each with their own truths clouded like foam in their lattes.

Easy to judge, of course, when one is a perpetual outsider. Becky understood this because she believed she understood herself far more than others, and this frequently became the basis of banter with a cohort.

"True maturity is defined by self-awareness, that's what it's all about," she contended. "Do you know what I mean?"

She was chatting at the time with a short, stocky, Southern blonde who had migrated to Seattle to shed her conservative skin. Studying for an MBA at the university at night and working by day at Starbucks, Jeannie believed she would achieve a more in-depth business education, better able to balance the theoretical with the experiential.

"How exactly do you define self-awareness, that's the question," Jeannie asked. "We talk about that in marketing class all the time. How do people really see themselves? Very important question."

"Either they allow themselves to be defined by others or, the smarter ones, create themselves. They determine who they are in their own minds and that is who they become." Becky spoke as if composing an essay for a sociology exam. "A little nature, a little nurture, but in the end, we can mold our own clay. We evolve into who we wish to be. I mean, people have to know what makes them tick, and accept that, to some extent, but always try to be better. I know we are who are we are, sort of, but if we're not growing, what's the point? And if you get that, that's the moment you mature. We all grow up, so to speak, but how many of us actually *grow up*?"

Jeannie, wide-eyed, listened to Becky as if a modern-day philosopher in a smoky downtown club, instead of a fellow barista-in-training at one of the ubiquitous Starbucks.

"Okay, I get all that, but, you know, some people are grown-ups before they're grown," Jeannie said. "Like my sister, she just has a kind of axis running through her, like a double yellow line on the highway. Total clarity. That girl just knows who she is, what she wants and how to get it."

"Lucky girl, although, what she wants, does that fit with who she is? Lots of people don't reach far enough, and others are always over-reaching, don't you think? I know this big-shot advertising executive who got out of Columbus and got herself a big job and a perfect husband, and she is very successful, but I can tell you she doesn't have a damn clue what real life is all about."

"How do you know?"

"It's a type. Accomplished and self-assured, but in a vacuum. And not nearly as open-minded as she imagines herself to be. Most of these people here are the same. I mean, look at them."

Becky extended her arm with her palm pointed outward, as if presenting an exhibit to a social science class. Jeannie listened attentively, a star student, even as her eyes flickered briefly to an attractive young man in the corner nursing an iced-coffee and reading a thick paperback with scribbles up and down the margins.

"Reading the paper, working on the Internet, writing," Becky went on, fully immersed in her diatribe. "They are all aiming for something more than what they have. End game is all that matters. No sense of the journey."

"That's the American way."

"For sure."

"And the heart of the business world. That's what it's all about, you know: aspirations. Businesses market to aspirations and aspirations require stuff. The very essence of capitalism."

"I thought it had something to do with the willing suspension of disbelief."

Jeannie nodded affirmatively, impressed that Becky had command of business lingo. "That's the advertising technique, but that's also about stuff."

"Stuff? Stuff equals capitalism? Never quite thought about it that way," Becky said.

"Yeah. That's it in a nutshell. The day we all stop being interested in the next new thing and the nicest stuff, instead of the things that really matter, you know, like healthy forests and pure food and peace of mind... When we stop wanting stuff, the economy is going to collapse."

"Scary thought."

"Yep. This country needs a whole new identity. We definitely need to get along better with the rest of the planet."

"Isn't stuff just as important in other places?"

"Only because of the westernization of the world. You talk about self-awareness; we could use a little national self-awareness. We don't even know who we are anymore, as a country I mean."

"Well, who do you think we are?"

"Stuff."

They laughed boisterously as they prepared themselves two black Americanos for their afternoon break. Jeannie sprinkled a packet of brown sugar into her cup; Becky took it straight.

"Seriously, it's stuff that's going to bring China and India into the modern world," Jeannie went on. "More and more of those people work to make our stuff, or service our stuff, so they make more money, and then they want their own stuff. Happening everywhere. Globalization is basically about stuff."

Becky mulled her words. "This sounds like political science to me, why are you a business major?"

"If you can't fight 'em, might as well join 'em. Who knows, maybe I can make a difference. Or maybe I can get rich, I have a lot of student loans to pay off."

"That's a load."

"Ya think?"

Becky continued the conversation the next night at happy hour at a local pub with her neighbor, Joni, an aspiring yoga teacher who worked as a nanny to pay her way. Joni was tall and lean, with hair to match; however, dressed in a long skirt and clogs, with strands of beads around her neck, she looked more like a sixties folksinger than a yogi, as if she should have a guitar slung across her shoulder instead of a yoga mat.

"Do you think self-awareness is the essence of adulthood?" Becky asked, and without waiting for an answer added, "and, do you think that self-awareness is the basis for the American economy?"

Joni sat back in her chair and stared at Becky. She was used to these slightly convoluted conversations, but sometimes was confounded by Becky's dogged quest to understand more than most, and more than even her own fellow new-age practitioners, archetypal students of the mysteries of the universe.

"I have no clue what that means," Joni answered.

"Well, I believe most people never really get themselves, or they get themselves and settle too easily for less, which means they never fully mature."

"Like that AA mantra."

"What?"

"You know, the serenity prayer they call it. Grant me the serenity to accept or change, or know the difference. That's the short form."

"Right, I've heard it. Maybe self-awareness is serenity. Or, serenity is self-awareness." Becky chuckled at her metaphysical humor.

"You sound a little like a Buddhist."

"I'm working on that," Becky said with a smile, proud to be considered part of that movement.

"Ah, but you will have to forsake all attachments and accept that life is a struggle from day one and we must

254

accept our destiny and merely minimize our misery. You know, 'pain is everywhere, suffering is optional.'" Joni laughed. "OMG, that's the most horribly simplistic definition of Buddhism ever. Shame on me. The Dalai Lama would be appalled."

"I think he has the most beautiful smile of any man on earth."

"That's because he has released all attachments and made peace with the universe. Not to mention the fact that he's adorable."

"The attachment part, that's easy," Becky said. "I don't do attachment. And I know life is hard, that's a given. But following some predetermined path? Not sure that will work for me. I like to choose my way."

"You cannot control the outcome," Joni said.

"Maybe not, but you can plot the course."

"I do love the idea of serenity though," Joni said as she drained the last of her beer. "That's what we aim for in yoga, although in truth, lately, I'm not sure there's much of that to be had in this crazy world."

"I think you're on to something. Serenity is the key."

"Inner peace."

"Does anyone have inner peace? Truly? Anyone other than a monk."

"A monk. Or people without a conscience. And maybe that naturalist writer, Thoreau?"

Becky made a mental note to read Thoreau. "Americans are not big on acceptance. We're all about change. Jeannie thinks the essence of American life is never accepting anything for too long, always replacing or replenishing in some way."

Joni nodded. "I see that. Actually, that's a really good thought. We replenish, we don't restore. There is a difference."

"Yes."

"It's always the next new gadget, the next boyfriend, the next pair of designer jeans. That's what we're about. So, maybe serenity, or self-awareness, is impossible when you're constantly in flux. Maybe Americans are destined to be always in motion. And you simply cannot find peace if you cannot be still."

Becky considered the comment, briefly, before embellishing the thought.

"Change has to be more than change, it has to be evolution. Change, just for change, goes nowhere."

"Too true. If we are going to evolve, the human race that is, and that's what this is really about, humans evolving to a higher plane, then we can never truly stay put. Yoga is all about that; even the poses are transitional. Every session is different and every session different for each person. We never land, we never master anything, we simply sustain the practice. Does that make sense?"

Becky took a long slug of beer and slumped back in her chair, reminiscent at that moment of her sister, Leah, at the end of a race, depleted by the very audacity of the quest.

"If we were drunk, it would make more sense, but we're not, and I don't have the money to get drunk, so I say we get a pizza and call it a night."

The next time Becky had this discussion was some time later with Leah, whom, she realized, had cultivated a highly developed sense of self-awareness. Their bonds were deep, and in recent years, the friction derived by their differences had dissipated, despite their dissimilar lifestyles. Leah was content to stay in one place, on one path, devoted to a few friends and her work, and recently happily settled in a steady relationship, while Becky was already thinking about where she might go next and what else she might like to do.

"You must understand what I'm saying, right?" Becky asked Leah during one of their marathon phone conversations, made possible by free nights and weekend cell phone plans.

"I'm never sure."

"Self-awareness, you know all about that. You know who you are."

"Maybe, maybe not," Leah answered. "Some of us just settle on one path sooner than others, and if we're lucky, if the path seems right, we have no reason to go off track."

"Yeah, maybe that's all it is: to each our own."

As she spoke, Becky crunched the phone between her shoulder and ear, so she could use both hands to rub off old toenail polish, obliterating a dark pink in preparation for a fresh coat of a deep blue color called Midnight. The polish was a cheap mood elevator and, as she looked at the bottle, she smiled at the thought that she too succumbed now and then to stuff.

"Everyone is motivated by something else," Leah said, as she leaned forward to stretch first one leg and then the other, both stiff after a long run.

"Is it really motivation? I think some of us are just grounded and some of us are restless."

"Is that why you move around so much?"

"I get bored, I thought you understood that. Restless. And I don't want to be predictable. I don't want anyone to count on me. The thing is, I know this about myself. I know who I am. It's not so much that I don't fit, I just don't stick. Sort of like that round peg settling into a square hole. I mean, you can squeeze something round into a square, right? But that doesn't mean it was meant to be there."

"Very deep," Leah said.

"You dare to mock your big sister?" Becky said with feigned irritation, although she could not restrain a chuckle.

"I wouldn't dare. Besides, truly, I think you're much more interesting than people like me who run in a straight line."

Becky sighed. "Don't second guess yourself. It works for you, that's all that matters. Besides, it's some sort of personal mission that propels us, both of us. Live, learn and move on. You know, north or south."

Leah smiled as she pondered the family motto. "I think I know what you mean, as sure as I am of what anything means."

No matter how fascinated or impassioned Becky was about the meaning of life, she was well aware there were no simple answers. Still, she aspired to figure it all out and she thoroughly enjoyed the existential journey, especially on long bus rides, her preferred form of transportation. Peering out of windows into blurred lights and unfamiliar pathways, she imagined other lives as the lives she read about in books, lives that seemed steadfast on the surface, devoid of deeper truths, or forever in flux, without solid ground, like quicksand. No, Becky would not succumb to easy pleasures, nor would she settle for less than what she believed she deserved. Nothing less than the person she chose to be. From the edgy adolescent she was when she first left Ohio, she had grown into a thoughtful student of human nature, and she consistently came to one conclusion: humans can do better. She believed this to be particularly so in matters of race.

However nomadic, she was also practical, and while she had no expectation of a career, per se, and she appreciated the constancy of Starbucks, she sought something that would earn a decent wage and also allow her to work evening hours, better to savor the pleasures of daylight and minimize the loneliness of dark nights.

She saved for two years the paltry remains of paychecks to afford a bartending course and, armed with a diploma when she arrived at the Sierra Nevada mountain towns, she secured a position as an assistant bartender at the Golden Gate Saloon in the historic Holbrook Hotel in Grass Valley. There she poured all flavors and varieties of alcohol, beer, and wine, and she learned to master mixed drinks and talk about the cocktail menu in such a way that regular patrons began to seek out her recommendations.

At her little apartment just outside of town, well into the wee hours of night, she avidly read back issues of trade journals and scanned every page of distributor catalogues. On workdays, she arrived early to sit in on buyer meetings, sipping samples until satisfied to determine the right tastes for patrons, at the best possible prices. When the senior bartender moved on, the owner gave Becky an opportunity to be the buyer as well.

"On probation, of course," he said.

Becky nodded with gratitude and determination. "You won't be disappointed."

The Holbrook Hotel was built in 1851 and rebuilt after a fire destroyed most of the town. Standing proudly on Main Street, as if a remnant from a movie set, the hotel at one time played host to four presidents, including Ulysses S. Grant, as well as writers Mark Twain and Bret Harte. The saloon itself, built with a mahogany and mirrored inlay barback imported from Italy, was said to be the oldest continually operating saloon west of the Mississippi; legend had it that not even Prohibition shut it down. Glass doors flanked Main Street on one end, and on the other, the hotel lobby, giving the saloon an exaggerated sense of greatness, like a drawing room at Versailles. Although there had been several owners over the years, several renovations and restorations, the saloon had retained its historical stature while serving as a modern-day meeting place.

Becky often felt there the ghosts of visitors past and she took to quoting Twain whenever possible, as if channeling his spirit. At the same time, she thoroughly enjoyed the juxtaposition of historical artifact and the contemporary drinks she concocted: pink cosmopolitans or green apple martinis. Not exactly the shot glasses lined up on the bar one might see in old western films, although she served those as well.

Five nights a week, from 5:00 PM to midnight, or later, Becky presided over the bar. On arrival, she made certain that exposed bottles were wiped clean and shelved in their proper place, an adequate quantity of lemons and limes cut and piled for squeezing or for shots, full bottles of Rose's lime juice and grenadine for mixed drinks, as well as margarita and mojito mixes prepared for blending, sufficient rock salt and sugar for dusting rims, and maraschino cherries, cocktail onions and olives handy for flourish. She checked that the most popular choices were in the liquor well and in the temperature controlled wine cooler, local beers by the bottle chilled and ready, and a full supply on tap.

Throughout the night, she glided the length of the long bar, cleaning-up repeatedly with one of the white cloths triple-folded to hang neatly from loops on a canvas apron. She always wore clean jeans and colorful, slim-fitting shirts, and she chatted amiably with customers, flashing to all her best smile and earning more in tips than she had imagined possible. At the end of each evening, she made certain everything was in its proper place before she hobbled home, guided by starlight, and slid into her still rumpled bed to sleep contentedly until late morning the following day.

It is true what they say about bartenders. They are counselor and confessor, parent, sibling or lover, to the lonely who line the bar, night after night: those who need a buffer between their workday and home, or need to unwind without the obligation of a gym or yoga class. Others simply need a place to feel less alone, aided and abetted by alcohol and congeniality, and the anonymity of dim lighting. In this role, Becky shined, waxing philosophically to whoever might listen or lending an ear to their woes, compassionate and kind and always forgiving because, as she often said, there but for the grace of something or someone, we all go.

Most nights, Becky mixed a vodka martini for Doctor Phillips the moment he charged through the door, precisely at six o'clock, before he was firmly secured on his regular stool, after which he bid farewell and headed home for the dinner his dutiful wife kept warm for his arrival. She chilled a bottle of cheap white zinfandel for the three shop girls from the handicrafts store down the street, who stopped in Wednesday nights and again on Fridays to share their tales, all the while keeping their eyes peeled for an attractive male who might have wandered into their orbit. She happily read off the list of beers to newcomers, even though they were always posted on the chalkboard above the bar, and she promptly filled orders from waiters providing table service.

She also tended attentively to the local drunks, shutting them off when they became loopy or agitated, taking hold of their car keys when necessary and calling a taxi, for which the only acknowledgement was a larger tip the next time they showed up. For these, the drinkers who denied their addiction, or those who moved in and out of recovery, always vowing to do better, she had come to feel particular affection, as if bonded to them in some way, even though she saw herself as the antithesis to the alcoholic, addicted neither to substances, people nor place. She pictured the drinkers who lined the bar night after night as the grown-ups who never quite grew up: lost boys and girls, lacking in self-awareness, hiding themselves to themselves, only occasionally glancing into their psychic mirrors and never liking what they saw. What had they suffered, she wondered, somewhere, someplace, long ago, that made them drown themselves in drink, only to find the despair darker and more desperate there?

Even as she asked herself those questions, she also recognized that she resided comfortably among them because she moved from place to place as if barstool to barstool. If she were one to succumb to that sort of dependency, she might have been exactly like them. As Becky knew them, they too knew her, and they understood the motivations of a perpetual outsider perhaps better than she understood her own.

It was in Grass Valley that Becky found herself settling more than any place since Columbus. She had begun to allow the small town to embrace her as a local and she imagined the ghosts of residents past beckoning to her to stay.

Most mornings, the moment she walked into Starbucks, the counter staff greeted her by name and prepared her favorite blend without need to order. She took classes in river rafting and joined a hiking group, exploring voluptuous mountain terrain. She stopped at the public library every Friday to select her next book and sought out the counsel of a librarian there who took to saving in her desk drawer a new work of history or a memoir she thought Becky might want to read. She accepted an occasional invitation to her landlord's home for dinner, not only to keep the peace, but because the landlord was Irish and prepared big pots of stews and large round loaves of soda bread that reminded Becky of childhood dinners at Mrs. Elliott's apartment.

She had long ago stopped keeping a town map in her purse, having learned all the byways and shortcuts, aware when a street lamp was out or a house had been painted a different shade, because these were the streets she walked every day and she knew them the way those who have lived in one house for a long time can reach for light switches in the dark and always find them.

She spoke to Leah regularly, keeping watch from a distance, and counseling with her sister on her incessant quest for greater meaning. During one of those conversations, Leah urged Becky to make good on a long-promised visit to San Diego.

"Margo's daughter Keisha just moved out here, you know, trying on the southern coast, so why don't you take a weekend off and we'll show her a good time?"

"How old is she now?"

"Eighteen."

"Seriously?"

"She just graduated high school. She's a wonderful artist, got a job as a web designer, for now. Margo is beside herself that she is moving so far away, and I'm not sure she doesn't blame me."

"Why you?"

"When they came out on holiday last year, I showed Keisha around and she fell in love with the beach towns."

"Got it."

"She said she felt the pull of the surf, so she's here. Living in a little place in Mission Beach with two roommates she found on Craigslist, one white, one Latina."

"Nice mix," Becky murmured, although she was only half-listening as she scanned an issue of *Beverage Digest*.

"I suppose, but she's not sure she likes either one of them. I invited her to sleep on the couch at my place whenever she needs to, but I doubt she'll take me up on it. She's a tough-it-out sort."

"Good trait."

"Let's show our support. She's Mrs. Elliott's granddaughter, practically family."

"Sure, but it's such a long ride down there. Damn bus makes so many stops. Why don't you drive up here? Easier for you."

Leah was startled, as her sister rarely invited her to visit, but she had to decline.

"I can't get away right now and she just started the job. Another time, yes, ask me again, but for now, get on the bus, grab some sunshine."

"You know I stay out of the sun, I'm as brown as I want to be."

"Oh Becky, still hiding?"

"And you don't?"

"No, I don't, you know that. I am just a woman of many faces, depends entirely on who is looking."

"And your new boy?"

"Color of licorice and just as sweet."

"And he likes brown girls."

"He likes me."

Leah, who had waited a while after Robert to engage with another man, was more than a little enamored of her new companion, and, although she could not express her feelings, certainly not to Becky, she preferred his dark skin, as she had with Robert, as if she were safer in some way. As if a brown woman and black man belonged together in the same bed. While she never resented her mother for marrying a white man, and she refrained as often as possible from reproaching her sister for her determination to pass, she preferred the history she shared with African-Americans and might pass on to children someday, whatever the intrinsic challenges they will face.

Two weeks later, Becky arrived in San Diego on a Friday afternoon and the three girls head out to celebrate their reunion at Jimmy's, a harbor-side restaurant with a bustling bar scene. A dense throng overflowed inside and out, all young and tan, hair long or shaggy, many well into the happy hour buzz. The girls waited for a table on the patio, then ordered a pitcher of beer and nachos. In the softer shadows of dusk, they might have been seen as fellow students or secretaries, the only difference between them their representation on the color line from nearly black to brown to nearly white.

Becky, slim and shapely, had developed an air of elegance in maturity, exactly the confident self-awareness for which she had strived for more than a decade. Her dark hair was shorn into a layered cut, similar to the day she ran away, minus the garish highlights, her waves softened by an intensive texturizer, and she wore only a hint of a coral blush on her cheeks, with matching lipstick. Leah's curly hair still tumbled halfway down her back and her pale eyes and spotless burnished skin shimmered against a wide silver cuff bracelet on one arm, a gift from her beau. Keisha, the youngest, was the most effervescent. She wore dangling glass earrings and an African print scarf wrapped along the crest of her forehead, and a large peace sign made of stone hung from black rope around her neck. They all dressed in tight-fitting jeans, with skimpy T-shirts from Old Navy or Target, and they chatted exuberantly, and loudly, to be heard over the commotion of the crowd.

Inevitably, Becky steered the conversation to self-awareness, holding court on the subject until Keisha decided to pull her own weight.

"Speaking of self-awareness, aren't you excited about Obama?" Keisha asked. "My first presidential election and I get to vote for a black man!"

"I wouldn't get too excited, he cannot win," Becky said dismissively.

"Why do you say that?" Keisha asked with obvious dismay.

"Honey, he's a black man. Light-skinned, sure. Smart, sure, really smart, I'll give you that, but I repeat, he's a black man. Never gonna happen."

"I think it can, and I think if anyone can make it, he will," Leah chimed in.

Becky snickered.

"You can laugh, but read the polls. He's got a real shot."

"Your boyfriend tell you that?"

Leah smiled. "He reads the newspaper, yes, every day, and he fills me in on what I missed, yes. Doesn't hurt to know what's going on. Self-awareness is all well and good, but we live in a great big world. Awareness needs perspective."

"Well said, little sister, but let's say for a moment, Obama does win. What difference does it make, really?"

"Are you kidding?" Keisha asked. "This will be life altering, for millions."

"How so?"

"Becky, Obama will make everything better for us," Leah said.

Becky refilled her glass, licking the edge of the rim to take in the froth, and motioned to the waitress for another pitcher. She munched a few nacho chips, allowing the cheese to melt in her mouth, and stared at her little sisters before she went on, leaning closer to be heard.

"Listen girls, optimism, that's a lovely thing, but don't be delusional. Seriously. Even if Obama gets there, they will find a way to crucify him. A political lynching."

"Why?" the girls asked in unison.

"Because, at the end of the day, he will be seen as an uppity nigger, even in the White House. Maybe especially there."

"I can't believe you would say such a thing!" Keisha cried.

"I speak truth. Plenty of folks are nearly hysterical about the possibility and likely already making plans to rid themselves of the big house nigger. You should hear the talk at the bar. It's madness."

"Times have changed, Becky," Leah said sternly. "And please don't use the N word."

"Some things do not change," Becky said, anger seeping into her voice. "And things definitely don't change just because some people think it's the right time. Or because one exception wants to make it change. It doesn't work that way. Not for us, especially not for us. At best, things change very slowly. In stages. Baby steps, like that runner's training program you were on, my sister. A little bit at a time. That's the best we can hope for. Has always been. Any more than that, we cause a ruckus. We press too many buttons. Upset, you know, what do they call that?"

"The status quo," Keisha stated solemnly, the truth of Becky's words settling in.

"Yes, the status quo. The backlash could set us back years. And besides..." Becky paused for a moment.

"Besides what?" Keisha asked.

"I prefer to fly under the radar."

"What does that mean?" Keisha asked.

"That means she pretends to be a tan white girl, rather than a light-skinned sister," Leah retorted.

"Really?" Keisha stared at Becky in astonishment, having not known her predilection to stay as high up the color line as possible. "So, how does that fit into this self-awareness you preach?"

"This is exactly self-awareness. I have defined myself well."

"By pretense?"

"No, this is my tribe. The moment my black mother married a white man, I got to choose which way to go."

"Well, seems to me," Keisha pondered aloud, "seems to me I heard your white daddy ran out on you, so why on earth would you want to choose that side of the family?"

"Wait a minute!" Becky snapped. "You have a lot of nerve talking about parents who run out on you. Your black family dumped you as I recall, right? And who was it took you in? Not your kin, no; the white folks. Well off white folks. You were one lucky girl."

Leah put her hand on each of the girls' arms to mediate before the conversation got out of hand.

"Stop, we're family. We have histories, and we've all made the best of it, yes?"

Becky and Keisha nodded, properly admonished, although the glare in their eyes smoldered.

"And, my sister," Leah added, "we are brown, mulatto maybe, or bi-racial, whatever the word, but not white, can we agree on that, at least in principle."

"We are all posers, one way or another," Becky muttered.

"No way, I don't pretend anything," Keisha said.

"Well, no offense, little one, but you cannot."

Becky moved her arm closer to Keisha's to display the contrast between Keisha's dark skin and her own muted tone.

"Oh, so now you're telling me that because your daddy was white, you are better than me?" Keisha sputtered.

"Not better, just different."

"Separate but equal?" Leah posed.

"Oh, yeah, that worked out well," Keisha sniggered.

"Well, you might say I'm sort of more white than you are. I mean, both my parents are white, and I was raised in a white way, so, there you go."

"Dream on, girl, you will never be anything but black. Skin tells it all. It's the only thing that shows."

"Becky, you cannot straddle clans. You're black or white, and that's it," Leah argued.

"In truth, we're all some shade of brown, and Caucasian is not even white, not really," Keisha said.

"There you go, the artist speaks. So when are you going to get real? You are not white!" Leah proclaimed.

"Well, you're not black," Becky answered.

"OMG! Color semantics. Black, brown... it is absurd to keep playing the color game, we should be beyond this by now," Leah cried.

"You're not a hypocrite? You've switched who you are with the boy you're with like a mood ring!" Becky fired back at her sister.

"No, I just accept all for who they are, not what color they are, as long as they accept me for who I am. Not a hypocrite, I am a chameleon!"

After a stunned moment of silence, they all laughed together so hard tears slipped from their eyes. However, even as Keisha laughed, she felt terribly saddened.

"These days," Leah said, a warm remnant of a smile on her face. "I prefer to stick with my people."

"That's called segregation," Becky said.

"No, that's called self-awareness," Leah pronounced, and Keisha chuckled.

"Black or brown," Becky said, "We're all a little bit in hiding, and if Obama gets into office, we're outed. Back in the spotlight, and I tell you, that can't be good."

"I won't believe that. I think his candidacy is amazing, and says a whole lot about how far we've come. And I think he will open a lot of doors," Keisha insisted.

Becky smiled. "You sound like your parents."

"So? My parents went out on a limb for me, and although sometimes I wish I hadn't been split like Solomon's baby, it's been mostly a gift. I'm thankful and you disrespect your mother by swatting her DNA like a fly."

Becky sat back as if she too had been swatted. Her lips pursed into an angry line and she was about to snap when she stopped herself, knowing this challenge was hard to defend. She had in fact dismissed her mother's lineage, although she meant no disrespect; in fact, isn't this exactly what her mother had in mind when she married a white man? When she moved them to a mixed neighborhood and taught them to live as one with the rest of the community?

"Well, we'll see what happens," Becky said, breaking the angry silence. "As for me, I'll go on contemplating the mysteries of the universe and moving around, whoever is president."

"Whatever works," Keisha said.

"Yes, my little sister," Becky said with a smile and a friendly pat on Keisha's arm. "Whatever works. Let's drink to that."

They clinked their glasses together and chugged a bit of beer to soften their edges. Leah placed one hand on top of

Keisha's hand as she turned to Becky. "We'll see how the people speak in November."

The conversation ended there. Leah believed to her very core that her sister's self-awareness was self-deception. A brown woman moving through white worlds, one after the other, never belonged to anyone or any place. She was equally enthusiastic that the change Obama promised would happen and the country would be a better place. She told Becky as much when she escorted her back to the bus station early Monday morning, and on the long bus ride, Becky gazed out across valleys and fertile farmlands and pondered the possibilities of a life without color-laden segmentation. No matter how deeply she wanted to share her sister's optimism, she thought she knew better.

In Grass Valley, five nights a week, at exactly eight o'clock, a dark-haired, pale-skinned, lanky boy in his early twenties, always wearing faded jeans with a slightly rumpled shirt, as if just out of the dryer, made his way to Becky's bar for a beer. Perpetually shifting in his seat, Andrew sat with his eyes focused on an invisible distant point, slightly beyond and off-center to the face of the person he spoke to, and one of the few people he spoke to was Becky. He rarely smiled. He often seemed lost in thought. His hands were usually folded and glued to his lap, like a kindergarten child reprimanded to sit still.

Andrew worked the night shift at the hotel front desk, a shift that rarely put him into contact with clientele beyond the occasional late arrival, which suited his antisocial personality. He had been taught to nod to guests as they moved through the lobby on their way to their rooms, his eyes otherwise on the pages of a worn paperback book he carried in his back pocket, usually of a scientific nature. A seeker of knowledge, he was nevertheless a college dropout, having spent only one year at a community college in his hometown of Santa Clara. He moved north, he said, for fresher air and open space, and spent his daylight hours hiking the nearby riverbed, studying rock formations or staring at ripples of water cascading over shallow outcroppings. He spent his nights behind the reception desk until dawn. Although he never smiled at Becky, he ambled up to the bar with as much familiarity as he accorded anyone.

"What are you reading these days, Andrew?" Becky asked, as she slowly poured Andrew's favorite drink, Black River Stout, an especially rich smooth micro-beer, dark as night, into a tall frosty glass.

As they conversed, Becky scrubbed the stainless steel sink until it sparkled, and rarely looked up to Andrew, which, she believed, took the pressure off him to engage.

"Oliver Sacks," Andrew answered as he sipped the creamy head of the beer and smacked his lips in a show of satisfaction, as if the first time every time.

Becky, approaching the end of her two years in Grass Valley, had begun to think that if she left, she might miss Andrew, even though their time together was restricted to these brief interactions. Andrew was another among the roster of friendly misfits who filled her nights and ground her to place. And, every night, when she left the bar at the end of her shift, Andrew jumped up from his seat behind the desk to open the front door as if she were a guest, then stood there, leaning as far as possible from the doorway to watch until she was completely out of sight. She was never certain if he watched as admirer or protector, or because the slow steady sound of her footsteps was soothing to him in some way.

"I don't think I've read Oliver Sacks, should I?" Becky asked.

"Yes. Yes, read Oliver Sacks. Amazing man. A doctor. Anthropologist. No, that's not right. A neurologist. Highly credentialed. He practices medicine. Psychology, maybe. He writes. Teaches. A most amazing man."

When Andrew spoke of people whose writings or achievements he found especially extraordinary, his whole body straightened up as if called to attention, and although his eyes remained vacant, they sparkled. Becky was aware that when he wasn't interested, his body gently swayed, as if to an inner rhythm meant to comfort or contain, and as if no one else was there.

"What's the name of the book?" Becky asked.

"*An Anthropologist on Mars.*"

"Science fiction?"

"No. No. Essays. Like, scientific phenomena. No, medical. Medicine. Medical phenomena. He writes a lot about that."

"For example?"

"For example. Yes. An example. There was this man, a doctor. He had Tourette's syndrome. Do you know what that is?"

"I think so."

"No tics. No symptoms, I mean, when he operates. A surgeon! Like, like, he's a different person in the operating room."

"Fascinating."

Andrew nodded and sipped his beer, glancing at his watch to make certain he wasn't yet required at the front desk, and up again a moment later to double check the time on the clock over the bar. He sat silently, because Andrew never spoke until spoken to.

"Can you give me another example?"

"Yes. Another example. My favorite. A girl, an amazing girl, who does amazing things. She has autism." He leaned slightly forward toward Becky and whispered, almost conspiratorially. "Do you know what that is?"

"Sure, I know about autism. They keep finding more and more people have it. Something to do with vaccinations, right?"

"Unconfirmed," Andrew said. "There is more than one type. Some people are very sick with autism. Some not so bad."

"So I hear. What's the story about? Why is this girl so special?"

"Special, yes, special. Accomplished. Extremely accomplished. There should be another word for someone like her. Like, a genius. No, different. Like an extraterrestrial!"

Becky smiled. "She must have had a lot of help."

Andrew nodded. "Smart mom. Good mom. Good science teacher."

"And Oliver Sacks?"

"He wrote the story."

"Well, maybe telling her story will inspire someone else, right?"

Becky saw a rare glimmer of a smile flicker in Andrew's eyes. "Yes. Correct." He looked up again at the clock. "Time to go to work."

He sipped the last of the dark brew at the bottom of the glass and licked the last cloud of foam off the rim, another ritual of his evening visit.

"See ya," Becky said, but he had already turned toward the door, and Andrew never looked back.

A few nights later, just after Andrew had made his nightly trek to and from the bar, a burly, lightly bearded, brown man, aged roughly thirty, entered the bar. He wore the brown uniform of a UPS driver, slightly rumpled after a long day. Muscular arms protruded from short sleeves and a bit of chest hair peeked out. A metallic nametag pinned to his shirt pocket introduced him as JARED. He plopped down at the bar and wedged his long legs under the stool. It was a Friday night and the bar was overflowing with regulars, but rather than scan the room, he locked in immediately on Becky, as if attracted by an invisible beacon.

"Tell me," he said when Becky stood before him, his deep brown eyes focused on her, his full lips slightly parted between words, molding the next thought. "I'm new to these parts, what beer have you got on tap? Anything especially delicious for a thirsty hardworking man?"

He spoke with a southern drawl tempered with a hint of a twang, perhaps earned in Texas or Oklahoma. Becky had become quite adept with American accents, and she was certain his was an amalgam. He smiled broadly after he delivered his question, eyes glimmering with irony like a professor enticing an earnest student, as he waited patiently for Becky to respond.

Becky smiled her best bartender smile, friendly but without any hint of intimacy, revealing white teeth against the dark pink lipstick she reapplied regularly to brighten her smile and soften her skin tone.

"We are humble folks here, just Bud and Bud Lite on tap."

"Well, I prefer my beer and my women dark," he said loudly.

There was a sudden audible hush among the customers and Becky felt an unaccustomed blush run up her neck to her cheeks.

"I only serve beer," she answered.

The same patrons chuckled and Becky enjoyed a moment of victory, having won the first round.

"I do have a nice dark stout by the bottle," she added. "Local favorite. Will that do?"

Jared nodded just once. He stared at Becky, without expression, neither benign nor threatening, although the intensity of his gaze was unsettling.

As attractive as Becky was, others might have wondered what he saw in her that fascinated him. Becky recognized at once the instant connection of modern mulatto children. Simultaneously, although she would have denied it, she felt a sexual charge spread from her pelvis up through her breastbone and to the very tips of her fingers. A longing that comes from loneliness and from that instantaneous, inexplicable chemistry that often happens at a bar, under the influence of not only drink, but want.

She took her time to retrieve the beer, needing to make him wait, to release herself from the hold he had momentarily placed on her and that she had just as instantly determined to resist.

When she returned, she gripped the bottleneck tightly against the slippery frost and grabbed with her other hand the bottle opener that hung from her jeans belt loop. Her hands shook ever so slightly as she snapped the bottle cap from its snug closure and began to pour the brew on a perfect angle into a tall glass. Jared leaned forward on his bar stool, reached one thick arm out and, with a firm grip on her wrist, steadied her hand as she poured, her eyes never leaving the bottle, his eyes never leaving her face. When the glass was filled to the brim and the dark liquid crowned by a pearlescent froth, she pulled her hand away and tossed the bottle into the recycling barrel with such force that the clang served to call to attention everyone at the bar.

For a moment, they all stared at her, as if she meant to make an announcement, and when she smiled sheepishly and turned to ring up the bill for the beer, conversation resumed once again, the din music to Becky's ears. She moved to the other end of the counter to tend to her regulars, and leave as much space as possible between herself and Jared, although she was painfully aware of his scrutiny, a penetrating stare, and a moment later, she saw in her peripheral vision that he wore a wide grin, his upper lip dusted with foam.

"Good call," he said loudly. "You have good taste."

Becky nodded, but did not answer him. Nor did she allow her eyes to meet his during the two hours he sat watching the last of the baseball playoff game on the large wall-mounted television screen. He had ordered another beer, then another, and a plate of sliders as filler, sitting patiently at the bar until closing.

A few stragglers finally settled their bills and at last the bar was empty, the chatter of patrons resounding from the street, their footsteps steadily fading to silence. Jared watched Becky move about as she set the last glasses and dishes into a large bin for the dishwasher, packaged the remains of olives and cherries for refrigeration, checked that the opened wine bottles in the cooler were tightly corked, and gave the dark wood bar one last thorough wipe to obliterate smudges and restore its shine. She was aware that he watched, but she ignored him, humming to herself as she worked, as if any other night, although her skin felt as if she had baked in the sun all day.

What Becky hated most was the presumption that she might be known. She despised the sort of familiarity that some people establish immediately, without invitation, violating personal boundaries. Her defenses were on high alert and she suppressed whatever attraction she might have felt for the handsome stranger in favor of autonomy.

She surveyed the bar one last time and turned to Jared, her shoulders solidly squared and her head erect, ready for battle.

"We're closing, in case you hadn't noticed."

"I'll walk you home," Jared said.

"No need."

"No problem."

"No thanks," Becky said tersely, meeting his eyes with a hostile glare.

Jared raised both arms, his palms facing Becky as if in surrender. "I'm harmless. Really. It's just that, we're the same, you know that."

"You don't know me. We are not the same."

"Sure we are. You and me, we come from the same stock. Not too many of us around these parts. So, I just thought we should get to know each other."

Becky felt a sudden and crushing sense of panic. Nearly two years at the bar and as far as she knew, her race had never been in question. What friends and neighbors might have imagined, if at all, they kept to themselves, which was the norm in almost all the places she had lived on the west coast, places she chose to a large extent because of a limited black population. Rather than standing out, such places provided neutrality, a greater likeliness of being perceived as a darker-toned white girl. Member of no particular tribe. To perpetuate and preserve that image, she rarely went barefoot, she washed and conditioned her hair daily, she wore a liquid foundation on her face a shade lighter than her skin, but not too light to be noticeable along the jawline, and in the evening at the bar, she enjoyed the cover of soft lighting.

Every day, Becky looked in the mirror and was reminded of roots she remained determined to ignore, and over time had begun to believe her own ruse. In her mind's eye, she was just another American girl. She had no interest in being seen as like kind with a black man.

"Actually, I hang around with my guy at the desk for a while after work, so you don't fit in any way to my schedule."

Jared peered beyond the glass doors to Andrew, who sat on the staircase adjacent to the reception desk, a favorite seating place, head bowed, eyes buried in a book.

"Perhaps another time," Jared said. "I meant no offense. I don't know too many people around here. I thought..." He turned to look at Andrew again. "Another time," he said with a knowing smile.

Becky realized that he saw through her deception, too astute to envision an outgoing and attractive bartender in a relationship with a likely autistic night manager.

"I'm not going to be around here much longer," she said, and at the moment she spoke those words, she knew the time had come to move on.

"Sorry to hear that, I could have used a friend."

It was then that Becky saw in Jared's eyes the intrinsic loneliness of the outsider. The thought occurred to her it was that bond that had attracted him to her, beyond race, and in this, they were indeed like kind.

Jared slowly peeled himself off the barstool.

"It's a nice town," Becky called to him. "You'll find friends."

"Ah, but will I find a compatriot?" He turned to face her again.

"That depends on who you identify with."

"Is it that simple for you?"

Becky nodded. "Absolutely."

"A mere matter of choice?"

"Exactly."

Jared stared at Becky for a moment before turning again to leave. He shook his head in an expression of disapproval. "Here I thought I might have found a brown friend in this land of white folk," he remarked over his shoulder, before turning to face her again. "And instead, I find myself an old-fashioned poser."

Becky took a sharp intake of breath, stunned by his condemnation, which she finally let out in a blunt stream before she answered.

"You are incredibly presumptuous."

"Presumption, my ass. You need to grow up, girl."

"You need to get out of my bar!"

"Get over yourself. Face it, you are a light-skinned sister. Half the black women in this country would trade a lot of something for that."

"I mean it, you need to go."

"I'm going, but you should be proud to be a brownskin. And it's gonna be even better for us some time soon, because we'll have a man in the White House. And, I happen to know, contrary to conventional wisdom, you can run and yes, you can hide, for a time, but not forever."

Becky stood very still, unwilling to respond further for fear of collapsing into her shaky knees. She looked beyond Jared through the glass doors to where Andrew sat. He had looked up when he heard argumentative voices and watched them now, expecting her to emerge, perhaps aware that something was amiss but uncertain of what that might be or what he might do about it.

Jared stared at Becky a moment longer, as if hoping she might reconsider her response. Her silent intractable stance was his answer. He left the bar, sauntering through the lobby to the hotel's front door. Andrew watched him leave, relieved, without knowing why.

Becky stopped shaking, reclaimed her courage, and shrugged off what she would try to think of as just an encounter at the bar, although Jared's rebuke had shaken her and would stay with her, a psychic pebble in her shoe.

She glanced around one last time to ensure that everything at the bar was as it should be, grabbed her bag and sweater, and lifted a bar stool in one hand, which she carried with her into the hotel lobby. She placed the stool to the side of the reception desk, opposite Andrew, and sat, still calming her breathing and gathering her thoughts.

They sat for a few moments in silence and in those moments, a rare experience for Andrew, he felt something akin to compassion. Becky's shallow breathing slowly settled to an even rhythm and the erratic pounding of her heart resumed a normal pace. At last, she took a deep sigh, once again in control of her emotions and her intentions.

"Andrew, what do you think matters most in the world?"

"I don't understand."

"Do you think it is better to recognize who you are and accept who you are? Or to be always striving to be better than you are?"

"Not sure."

"What would Oliver Sacks think?"

"I think, I think he would say we should be both. Not sure."

Becky smiled. "Accept what you can change, and what you cannot, right?"

"Yes. Yes. That sounds good."

"And know the difference."

Andrew perked up a little in his chair. "Confirmed. Know the difference. That's right. That's the hard part."

"Definitely the hard part. And who are you? What can you do or not do?"

"I am Andrew. I read a lot."

Becky nodded. "You are a smart boy, Andrew. I'm glad to know you."

"I'm glad to know you."

"In fact, you may be the most mature person I know."

"Confirmed," Andrew responded.

Becky chuckled and stepped forward to give Andrew a hug, but he recoiled, throwing his hands up in front of his face in a powerful natural instinct to protect himself from physical intimacy, even someone known to him. Becky understood too well.

"Sorry," Becky said as she withdrew. "Sorry," she repeated, as she lifted her bar stool to return to its place. "Sorry," she muttered as she locked the door of the bar behind her, knowing that perhaps Andrew might miss his only friend. "Sorry," she said over and over again as she walked home to plan her next move.

Andrew watched her go as he had watched Jared go, illuminated by a star-filled night sky, back to her tiny studio apartment tucked into treetops off a back road. Back to the disenchantment they all shared.

Three weeks later, Becky migrated south to Santa Cruz, a town anchored by a university set on a ranch and a rocky Pacific shoreline, frequently concealed like buried treasure by morning fog. A good place to hide.

Soon afterwards, when Barack Obama was elected, when he stood at Grant Park in Chicago and exhorted all Americans to look forward, Becky stood behind another bar watching among a packed crowd on large overhead television screens. She moved around the bar, ensuring her customers all had another round at the moment needed, keeping tabs current, while she observed them, predominantly white faces, faces that alternated between rapt silence and rowdy exultation.

Whether stunned or victorious, they all seemed humbled by Obama's triumph, by the sheer implausibility of that moment, and Becky began to wonder if cultural change might be possible after all. If the nation's self-awareness might converge with her own, blinded at last to the color line.

Nevertheless, she was unconvinced. She listened to the president-elect's speech as if he spoke to others, not to her. Although she experienced an unexpected thrill at his ascendancy and was in awe of his poise, she could not shake the nagging belief that even Barack Obama was yet another pretender in a long line of pretenders, with perhaps the sole distinction of a highly developed sense of self and a vision for the future she found impossible to imagine.

Grace and Mrs. Elliott/2010

Still waters run deep.
Proverb

"My mother used to say I was born to run," Grace mused aloud as she lit a squat white candle in a saucer on the side table next to the sofa. With a tiny hiss, the wick took the flame, revealing melted wax that had settled into the dish like day-old snow. Even though the room was suffused with late afternoon light, a cool light that produced gentle shadows, Grace preferred the warmth of candlelight, its flickering an antidote to gray skies, and something she has taken to often in recent years, in effect cursing the darkness. She inhaled the vanilla scent that wafted with the smoke through the room, hoping the scented candle might trigger memories associated with an oven full of cookies.

Grace lit the candle every afternoon when she arrived at Mrs. Elliott's apartment, and turned on the nearly ancient radio, a carved wooden box with burnished edges, to a classical station playing at that moment a faintly familiar piano sonata. This daily ritual, candlelight and music, brightened an otherwise somber space, offering as much comfort for her as she hoped for Mrs. Elliott. She hummed quietly with the tune, although she could never match the composer to the music as her mother had. Beethoven, Mozart, Chopin, they all jumbled in her mind, but soothed her spirits equally. Other private duty nurses played livelier music for their patients, and her daughter Leah argued that a smidgeon of Sade or Michael Franti might better boost a person's mood, but Grace fancied the simplicity and elegance of a sonata.

"Seems so far away to me now," Grace murmured, her words drifting into the room on the sweet-scented smoke.

She placed her hands on Mrs. Elliott's shoulders to guide her to the sofa and nudged her back against the cushions. Mrs. Elliott, smaller and rounder than her younger self, was dressed in one of her favorite outfits: a dark green skirt, what they used to call hunter green, with a matching cardigan sweater buttoned up to the neck, the triangular collar of a crisp white cotton blouse peeking out, nearly matching short, white, wispy hair combed tightly to her head and tucked behind her ears.

Grace insisted that Mrs. Elliott dress every day as she has always dressed, eat meals at the kitchen table, take a short walk in the sun, and spend the late afternoon on the living room sofa or seated in her tufted reading chair. No reclining in bed past the morning light, and no immobility in any one spot too long, so that her routine was as consistent and active as possible, not only for her general health, but so the remembrances associated with daily life might be encouraged to surface now and then.

As she sat, Mrs. Elliott's skeletal hands gripped the edges of the sofa cushion, as if clinging to a life preserver. Her body was slack now, without the hardiness that for most of her years draped over her like shimmery fabric; however, even in this repose, she exuded the dignity that Grace has admired the many years of their friendship.

"Sorry I was late today. I was at a service, a funeral service, for my old friend. Delia. You've heard me speak of her, I'm sure, although not for some time."

A sob caught in Grace's throat, which she swallowed instantly. Anyone other than Mrs. Elliott might have noticed that her shoulders were hunched today, and her chin drooped toward her bony chest in a posture of regret. Rather than her usual nursing uniform, she wore a black knit dress, with tiny black buttons at the cuff, that clung to her slim silhouette, and her brown skin seemed surprisingly darker in contrast, darker even than against her nursing whites and against the pale of Mrs. Elliott's nearly translucent skin.

Now fifty-six years old, Grace remained limber, sturdy, her shoulders only slightly rounded and her ankles occasionally swollen, signs of age largely in the light dusting of gray in her softly curled short hair, eyes ringed with a darker shade of brown, and the occasional shuffle of those who harbor sadness too long.

She sat on the couch, the pressure of her body creating a ripple in the cushion, like a gentle wave, which Mrs. Elliott rode without notice or comment.

"They say her heart gave out." Grace muttered. "Her heart gave out ages ago."

Grace has never spoken of Delia, or the day Josiah died. She has lived with his memory like an arthritic joint. When she thought of him, or when she thought about his mother, who grieved for twenty years, she quickly banished the memory, as she did once again today, in favor of keeping spirits uplifted in Mrs. Elliott's presence. Another pretense in a lifetime of pretense, all in the name of good intentions.

What irony, she thought, as she has often thought of late, that dear Mrs. Elliott has lost her memories, lost her connection to her past and her loved ones, while Grace fights to forget. She has spent twenty years trying to obliterate the lingering memory of her husband's abandonment and the recurrent vision of her betrayal of Delia's son, and, subsequently, Delia.

Now, she also tries to forget that her son Jake is gone. Buried. A month past and she still hasn't spoken of it, not a word, not to anyone except Mrs. Elliott. Otherwise she cannot bear to say the words aloud. Even at his memorial service she said nothing, allowing her daughters to eulogize their brother, and his wife to read a poem on his behalf, as Grace kept herself erect and held tightly as possible to her composure to resist imploding, or exploding, she was certain one or the other would result that day. Mrs. Elliott was there as well, without knowing where she was. For the best, Grace thought at the time, as Jake was like a grandson. Margo had come to escort her mother, and to show her respect. A few others attended, hardly known, and after the brief service, the women walked together, arm in arm, to the gravesite and stood silently to claim the American flag presented to them in gratitude for Jake's service.

Grace withheld her tears, as if to shed them would force her to say good-bye, which she has yet to do. She has been unable to accept his death, pretending he is only on assignment again, another tour of duty overseas, and he will return to her as he has so many times before.

Today, sitting with Delia's mourners, she tried once again to distance herself from her memories, to bury her own grief, and shame, with Delia.

Grace shook herself from her thoughts and willed herself to focus on the task at hand. She stood and shuffled into the kitchen, returning with a fresh pot of tea, a caffeine-free Irish breakfast tea that always seemed to please. She dropped a sugar cube into one cup, and two into her own, and watched as they turned brown and dissolved under the assault of the steamy brew. She stirred just once to ensure that sweetness was swirled through every sip.

"My mother used to dip the moistened rim of a tea cup into granulated sugar and sip the tea through it, but I never liked the rough edges of sugar crystals on my lips," she said as she placed the tea service on the table.

"She was something else, my mother. Eleanor. Ellie. What haven't I told you about her?"

Grace weighed her own words, recognizing that Mrs. Elliott would not remember anything she had told her before, so she might repeat any of her stories, any talk that would shutter thoughts too close to the grief that today especially threatens to consume her.

"My grandmother said Ellie thought from the first she had a say in how her life played out. That her destiny was of her own choosing, mostly. Imagine that! Becky takes after her in this way, in the way she believes she deserves better than her lot in life. She is audacious that one."

The thought of her feisty nomadic daughter perpetuated a fluttering of anxiety that Becky might never find peace, although Grace simultaneously harbored pride in such independent spirit.

"Hard to believe that my mother, born right at the start of the Great Depression, a little girl the color of tilled soil, might have felt special in any sort of way. I mean, those were really hard times, as you well know. Of course, every generation has them. My mother told me once she didn't know she was dirt poor. When everyone around you is the same, you don't notice such things, right? Not sure she knew what it meant to be black either, although she figured that out soon enough."

"Somehow, along the way, she realized she was far more certain of herself than most. But she was just a child, wasn't she? Had her first baby at seventeen." Grace shook her head side to side as if to refute truth. "Just wise before her time, I suppose. I always thought you and she would have been great friends."

Mrs. Elliott sat in the same pose, hardly moving a muscle, never seeming to notice whether Grace spoke, or not, although Grace believed that the sound of her voice, if not the content of her words, were engaging for dear Mrs. Elliott. More than white noise.

"A different sort of innocence in those days. Innocent of expectations, you might say. You know, I do believe it is only expectations that disappoint. Otherwise, well, life would just play out. One way or another."

She brought a teacup to her lips to test the temperature, decided it was still too hot and replaced it carefully on the saucer. She sighed so heavily her shoulders lifted and deflated all at once, like a balloon that doesn't quite capture the air.

"I think about my mother often these days, although she's been gone so long now. Sometimes I stare at her photo as if she were a stranger. A photo is just so flat. No scent, no voice. I miss her voice, still."

She reached into her pocket and withdrew a photograph of Jake on his first leave from training camp – his head freshly shaved military-style, his smile exactly the same as when he was a boy, taunting his sisters, delighting in the smallest of treasures he found at the playground: a perfectly round stone marked by squiggly striations, she still had that one, or a lost GI Joe doll, she remembered his joy when he found it and asked to keep it and Mrs. Elliott said yes. "Finders keepers, losers weepers," she told him. Jake repeated that expression throughout his life, always with delight.

Finders keepers, losers weepers. Well, if that were completely true, Grace would be doing a lot of weeping, and this she never does. A matter of pride, still, to hold back her tears.

"Every time you attend another funeral, well, all the people you've loved, the ones who are lost, they all sit with you, in the pew behind you or right next to you. Did you ever feel that? I swear it felt that way today. I felt, I felt as if Jake was there…"

Grace again swallowed a sob that threatened to seep from her throat, and which she knew she must emancipate, sometime, but not yet. As if one good cry might release a tsunami of sorrow that would devour her. No, not yet.

She picked up a cookie from a plate that had been set on the table before she arrived and gobbled it all in two bites. She had taken the day off from her day job for the service and has hardly eaten a thing, opting not to attend the gathering at Delia's brother's place, following the burial. Instead, after the service, she quickly made her way uptown to Mrs. Elliott's.

Every afternoon, Grace scaled the same outside stairs to the apartment building that she had climbed for nearly twenty years before she moved into a smaller apartment. The eponymous mall is gone, but the neighborhood shopping area has been rejuvenated, as if a village main street, attracting younger families aspiring to fresher lives. A white family lived on the third floor, but she rarely encountered the parents, and only occasionally noticed surly teenagers barreling down the stairs; they ignored her as if she were invisible. Two female graduate students had lived in the second floor apartment the last couple of years and they were kind enough to shop for Mrs. Elliott once a week when they did their own grocery shopping, but otherwise kept to themselves. Grace imagined some of the neighbors scoffed at them, murmuring that they were more than roommates, and if Mrs. Elliott were able, she would have told them all to mind their business. Oh, how Grace missed Mrs. Elliott's proclamations.

"My mother was a quiet girl, like Leah in that way, but she spoke her mind when she felt it was called for," Grace went on. "Mostly she was a good listener. Must have been all that music she listened to, night and day. All kinds of music, although she loved the women most of all: Billie Holiday, Anita O'Day, Ella, oh how she loved Ella. I could hear the radio blaring from half a block away on my way home from school."

Grace smiled. Yes, some memories were sweet.

"Seems to me, listening so well to the stories in the music, that might be how she grew so wise. My Uncle Henry, the youngest of my mother's brothers, told me once that she just seemed to understand the way men and women get on with each other. Or don't. She was not a woman of many words, but when she spoke, she knew the right thing to say. Like you."

Grace took another sip of the tea and, satisfied that the temperature was suitable for drinking, lifted the other cup to Mrs. Elliott's lips. She sipped only because the rim pressed against her mouth, slurped a little, and licked her lips with satisfaction, although only Grace might have known that, having learned to interpret her expressions, even the grunts and groans, better than anyone else.

Grace wiped Mrs. Elliott's chin with one of the cloth napkins she kept on hand to dress up their afternoon tea.

"There were things I would have liked to talk to my mother about, especially after I moved here, but she was gone so soon. Way too young. And, well, maybe that was best, because I would not have wanted to disappoint her. She would have hated to see me give up on anything, certainly not my marriage, although she might have been the first to dismiss my husband as unworthy. Good riddance to rubbish, she would have said. She had no patience for certain things, that's for sure. I wish I had inherited that trait. I know she would have been surprised that I gave up on running. Gave up on God..."

Grace's words drifted off, thoughts she never spoke aloud, although these days she talked about most everything to Mrs. Elliott, here in the quiet safety net of the apartment that felt like home. No one else to hear, no one to repeat anything she might say, no one to judge, words dissipating into the air with the candle smoke.

"I'm so glad Leah runs," she said, sitting up a bit straighter to fortify her thoughts. "Marathons, imagine that? Who'd have thought that couch potato would be such a good runner? Wish Becky would find her footing." Grace took another sip of the tea. "And she's a hospice nurse now, did I tell you that? Finally doing what she wanted to do. That quiet little girl has turned out to be tenacious, in her way. Gets what she wants, and she does not look back, no mam. Not our little Leah. Not any of my children in fact, they don't look back. Good thing, mostly."

Mrs. Elliott smiled, a tiny smile, hardly there, but Grace noticed at once. Even this little bit of a grin was important, as the neurologist told Margo the smile was said to be the last thing to go. Unfathomable. How hard that must have been for Margo to hear. Something as basic as a smile, such an important natural instinct we take for granted, always at the ready. Everyone is born with a smile, and Grace believed they should die with it, take it to heaven to be reborn.

Mrs. Elliott hardly spoke anymore, not even the gibberish she uttered boisterously for a while. She used to laugh loudly at the noises that came out of her own mouth, as if a private joke. These days, she chuckled now and then, less and less often, and for no apparent reason, but otherwise rarely made a sound. An occasional "no" slipped out, which Grace sometimes interpreted as "I know" based on the context, and something that sounded like "nothing" which might also be "not a thing." Grace was never completely convinced, but she reacted as if she were, and she frequently interpreted conversations for Margo so Margo might feel a little more connected to her mother, and might believe her mother was still present.

The other day, Mrs. Elliott said "darlins," which Grace was certain referred to her own children, and her heart warmed with the memory of those many evenings when she returned from her long shift at the hospital and there were Becky, Jake and Leah, safely tucked into Mrs. Elliott's apron, as if they were her own grandchildren. Only a color photograph might have suggested otherwise.

Grace gently rested Mrs. Elliott's hands atop her own for a moment, a reflex, without intent. She examined the dotted blueprint of age and the pronounced purple veins beneath the pallid membrane, a stark contrast to her own still smooth, cinnamon-brown skin.

She looked forward every day to talking to Mrs. Elliott, saying whatever was on her mind without fear of repercussion or humiliation or exposure. The Elliott family believed that Grace had given them a great gift by tending to the Alzheimer's patient four hours a day. Grace, of course, believed that the freedom to speak her mind, tell her stories, confess her sins, this was the greater gift.

"What was I talking about? Oh yes, Eleanor. She did well in school, my mama, although I'm told she was impatient with studies. She would rather have listened to music. I guess she never imagined for a moment she might have had a career in music, she wasn't much for ambition. She knew her place, even if she thought herself superior in some way, well, not exactly superior, rather, well, I can't say exactly, just her own person. I don't imagine anyone encouraged her to consider a career. Women were not expected to do much more than they were expected to do. And there it is again, expectations." Grace nodded, agreeing with herself.

"She did her chores without complaint, she smiled sweetly at all her cousins and aunts and uncles, there were lots of them in the neighborhood, most of them living together in a few houses, and went to work as a maid when she was twelve. All her friends came to her for advice. She had good old-fashioned common sense. Yes, that's what she had. And good instincts."

"And she had something else," Grace added, an afterthought. "She had sex appeal."

She chuckled at the vision of her mother, even at fifty, before she became ill, exuding what seemed the epitome of femininity. An animal magnetism that stretched like an invisible string from her mane of curly hair to her red-polished toes.

From the first, Eleanor liked men. She liked the way she felt when she was around them and she liked the way she could make them feel. By the time she was sixteen, she knew how to touch a man and move beneath him to bring him to a kind of ecstasy that would draw him to her again and again. And she never asked for much, which sealed the deal, because most women wanted something in return. Not Eleanor. And, in not asking, she received from those men kindness and a degree of respect others might never have had, so those women gossiped about her. She dismissed their talk, and took umbrage at any suggestion from neighbors or family members that she might be a loose woman, because, although she accepted the tenets of the church as a devoted follower, when it came to sexual relations, she remained skeptical.

"The Lord would not have created the pleasures of the flesh were his people not expected to delight in them," she insisted. For that matter, she did not believe in original sin. "No," she said. "No sin, only reaching out for more. And I think the Lord meant for us all to reach out, maybe not for more than we've earned, but for what good there is for the taking."

When Eleanor sang with the choir from the makeshift stage behind the church pulpit, she felt as if she was reaching out to Jesus, and he would bless her even as she soothed the souls of her men. However, Eleanor was choosey, and she made her choices known, preferring large men, quiet men, lonely men; the men those other women overlooked. Men of every shade on the color line, although never white. In this she understood her place. Still, each of her children was a different shade of brown. Eleanor used to call them colors of the wheel. From daylight to darkness. Grace, the lightest, her father the man Eleanor fondly referred to as her brown sugar man.

Eleanor never said much about Grace's husband Ray, her white son-in-law, whom she knew only a short time. She never judged other women's choices, not even her daughter's. She smiled contentedly when he was presented to the family. Times had changed, some, and she was proud, without saying so, that Grace had attracted a white man. Alternately pleased and concerned with her first grandchild, so high on the color line, so light she was nearly white, like that playground rhyme Eleanor remembered from her own childhood. A color that might suggest reaching too far.

"Black men back in those days liked women with meat on their bones," Grace recollected. "What was that ditty she used to sing?" Grace hummed for a moment before breaking out in song.

"I want a big fat mama, a big fat mama. A big fat mama with meat hanging off her bones... something like that."

She laughed so shrilly that Mrs. Elliott startled.

"Sorry, dear," Grace said, but Mrs. Elliott had already resumed her quietude, and Grace felt suddenly ashamed, as if she had demeaned the memory of her loved ones in frivolity, but she simply had to recall happier memories, or she would surely succumb to despair.

She sat up taller again, as if constantly pulling her own spine out of her seat in order to stay upright.

"Nothing angular or hard about Ellie. She had five children by the time she was twenty-five. A colored woman with big rounded breasts and wide hips, and plump lips thick with pink lipstick. Everything was soft about her, a gentle slope of skin all around, like a great big mama bear. Made it all the more awful when she just withered away. So young. So fast. Nearly nothing left of her when she passed."

Grace shook her head side to side to shake out the reverie. She offered Mrs. Elliott another sip of tea, but Mrs. Elliott turned her head away, toward the window, staring out to the buildings beyond as if watching for evening to fall. Grace placed the cup and saucer back on the coffee table.

"Always one step ahead, Ellie was, although she held some with destiny. Remember that saying? I know I've said this many times: the road goes north and south, we choose which way we go. My kids repeat that now. Still makes good sense, if you keep your eyes ahead."

Mrs. Elliott turned back toward Grace and her lips parted, as though she might speak, as if she had something suddenly essential to contribute to the conversation, but she only stared at Grace in that way she had of staring now, a penetrating stare without focus, like the blind, although Grace always saw the smile behind those blank eyes.

"Dear friend, do you hear me rambling all afternoon? Does anything make sense? My Lord, I've told you my whole life story these last few months. More than once. You know just about everything there is to know about me, as if you didn't before. More than anyone else."

Mrs. Elliott turned her eyes back to the window. Grace picked up a white bottle from the coffee table and pumped a bit of creamy lotion into her palm. The scent of gardenia flew out of the bottle and dissipated just as quickly, leaving only the barest residue, like the fragrance of a sophisticated woman that lingers long after she has left the room. Grace would have liked to live in a garden full of scented flowers, like gardenia, a place where life renews year after year, hibernating only to restore itself. Never really gone, if properly tended.

She reached for Mrs. Elliott's hand and massaged the cream into her fingers, one after another, her thumbs gently pressing around swollen knuckles and tiny cuticles, stroking the underside of each finger and pushing into pressure points on the palm to soothe the stress that she was convinced, despite Mrs. Elliott's passive demeanor, lingered just beneath her skin, as just beneath her psyche. Mrs. Elliott allowed her hand to be manipulated, but remained expressionless.

Mrs. Elliott was eighty years old now, but well into her seventies she was as vivacious and active as she had always been, and only as forgetful as age demands. Soon after she buried Mr. Elliott, Margo noticed a constant mumbling of meaningless words. Her siblings explained this away as a reflex of sorts, as an elderly wife transitions into living alone, conversations with loved ones like a phantom limb. However, it was soon obvious that the nattering, the vague expression so often in her eyes, the meandering from room to room, and into the hallway or to the street below without purpose or recognition, required medical attention. The diagnosis was swift and severe, and the medication prescribed barely slowed the progress, as if a giant boulder poised on the edge of a steep hill, gravity pausing only briefly before taking hold.

Her children deliberated placement in a specialized nursing facility, but Margo sought Grace's advice, and she suggested that Mrs. Elliott might be cared for just as well, perhaps better, at home. The siblings were grateful for that option and all made generous payments into an account that supported nursing care in two ten-hour shifts. Grace coordinated the nurses' hire, and kept an eye on them, as well as covering the four hours in the afternoons, between shifts, refusing to allow the family to compensate her.

Margo visited most often and Grace understood it was hardest on the elder daughter to sit with a mother who no longer recognized her. Harder every time. Very soon, they would all arrive to sit with her again at Thanksgiving dinner, without her cognition, which seemed yet another cruelty, but they owed their mother the honor of placing her once again at the head of the table.

Grace had counseled with doctors and read everything she could on this increasingly ubiquitous disease, despairing that she could do no more than watch her friend disappear. Perhaps this was worse than death. To be unknown, unrecognized, by a loved one. Especially hard for her children to lose the attention of the matriarch. A crucial presence. Who are we if we are not known by those we love most?

Late afternoon gray began its descent through the picture window into the living room. A chill passed through Grace's bones and she shuddered ever so slightly, wrapping her arms around herself for warmth. At this time of day, just before the sight of the moon, before stars filled the sky, she felt the sadness most acutely. The ending of every day another day without loved ones.

She unwrapped herself and took Mrs. Elliott's hands, layering one atop the other, then stood, flexing her spine like a cat after a long nap. She crept across the room, clicked on a floor lamp and turned up the thermostat. Within moments, the familiar clang of pipes echoed from the basement furnace and the musty scent of the first rush of heat emanated from the radiator. A smell and sound that had greeted her for many years. Such comfort in the familiar. Another good reason for Mrs. Elliott to spend her last days in the apartment where she raised her children and ladled out stew and watched over her neighbors. The place where memories were made and stored.

Memories, beyond DNA, define us. Grace suddenly remembered those words, the words of a physician who lectured at her nursing school class, hoping nurses might consider the whole person – mind, body and spirit. Words she took to heart.

She flipped the stations on the radio to shut down the talk show that had replaced the music and shattered their serenity. She detested the incessant chatter that has permeated radio and television, all day long, the same loud chatter that emanated from televisions to fill long empty days for hospital patients. She scanned channels and stopped when she heard *The Waltz of the Sugar Plum Fairy*. It was mid-November, before Thanksgiving, but all the trappings of Christmas were in full sway. She remembered a time when the orange and black of Halloween gave way first to images of pilgrims and then at last to the bright colors of Christmas. Now they all seem to blend together, as if color no longer mattered, although, of course, Grace knew, color mattered.

The shopping district was decorated in poinsettias and sparkling lights in a matter of moments after Halloween, and neighbors, day by day, added their shiny ornaments, silver tinsel and flickering lights. Always a festive time, Grace's favorite time of year when the children were young, although the days from holiday to holiday slipped away so quickly, like that steam gushing through heating pipes, from the last warmth of early autumn until year-end and on through the long days of frost, the days of waiting for spring.

Grace was so captured at that moment by the charm of the music that she raised her arms over her head and pirouetted across the living room rug. Mrs. Elliott laughed loudly and clapped her hands. Grace stopped in her tracks. She stepped toward Mrs. Elliott, who stared straight at her, as if staring through her. Grace imagined that the song triggered a holiday memory, one of those recollections that flickered across Mrs. Elliott's face now and then like candlelight. Perhaps, once upon a time, Margo and her sister Patrice twirled around and around to holiday music on this very carpet. Likely Leah and Becky as well, and Keisha when she was here for the holidays. Perhaps the boys shot mock rifles as if toy soldiers while the sisters danced. Jake might have pranced around the room like the nutcracker prince, he so loved the tale, taken with the very idea that one might alter identity so dramatically, magically, although that was the one thing he could never do.

So many happy times infused in this apartment, memory enduring, albeit diminished, like the faded wallpaper.

The laughter lasted only a few seconds, but a tiny smile remained on Mrs. Elliott's lips, and then, just as abruptly, disappeared. Grace watched for it each day. When the smile goes, the course of the disease would accelerate. A little like a run: one last sprint, one last adrenaline rush before the finish line. After all, once even the tiniest smile is gone, when the heart no longer flutters with joy, surely there is no life to be lived.

Grace has memory, but few smiles. Perhaps some time soon she too will lose her smile altogether. She stopped running long ago because she no longer deserved joy, punishing herself all these years for her failure to save Delia's son. Failure to speak truth. Pleasure denied, contentment withheld, unresponsive even to the delight of her children, as if nothing could heal her aching heart.

Now, her son too, gone. An eye for an eye, a son for a son.

"Becky has moved to Oakland," Grace said, resisting the melancholy, forging ahead with her monologue. "She says she's outgrown that sweet little surf town. Remember the place, pretty town on the coast? She almost made two years there before she bolted. Again. Just as she has outgrown every place she has lived. She said she would have gone to Berkeley, but she feels too much a minority there. Can you imagine that? All those students, all sorts of shades of brown, I hear, but not for Becky. I suppose it's more because she never got to college. I think maybe that's been on her mind. Either way, she's nearly white, she can fit in anywhere, and she does, and still she imagines people see her as brown if she stays put too long. The very thing she has been running from her whole life."

She sighed deeply as if to echo her daughter's discontent. "There's just so much we can do for our children. You'd be the first to remind me of that. I mean, you could never protect Margo from her disappointment, but it all turned out well in the end. Imagine, Keisha on a fellowship to that art college. A grown girl, on her way, like all the others. It's true what they say: where one door closes, another opens. But Becky, she leaves every door ajar, just goes whistling through one after another; never keeps a key. How much longer can she do that?"

"When I was a girl, I thought color was what kept the world vibrant. You know what I mean? I guess I still believe that, deep down. I need to believe that. Why would there be so many shades anyway, like flowers, if not for the sheer beauty of the garden? All different shapes and sizes, and colors. Without flowers, without color, this world is just plain drab. I know that, you know that, most people must know that, deep down."

"As self-reliant as Becky is, I worry about that girl. She takes care of herself, and she sure is fearless, but nothing flowers without roots."

Grace paused to go to the kitchen to pour them each a glass of water. When she returned, Mrs. Elliott turned away from the glass Grace brought to her lips. Grace took no mind. She placed that glass on the coffee table and drank her own to empty with an audible gulp, wiping her lips before going on.

"Did I tell you Leah ran another marathon? Came across that finish line with her arms spread wide like a caramel-colored peacock. Becky was there, she snapped a picture of her with her phone and sent it to me straight away, almost as if I was there too. That was the day before we got the word about Jake…"

She stopped speaking and took another deep breath, deep into her lungs, swallowing her thoughts momentarily.

"Three times in Iraq, twice in Afghanistan. I cannot even imagine what terrible things he saw in those places. Before he left, this last time, he said we would be out of there soon. Obama is getting us out of there, he said. Not soon enough. Not for my boy. Too many boys. Then again, there will always be some place else, some place in the world that demands our military muscle. Dorene and the babies are still at Camp Pendleton. She has friends there. She didn't re-up, no reason to now. Better to be a civilian. She's looking for a job and a new place..."

The phone rang and Mrs. Elliott turned her head to the sound, but did not react.

Grace stood and quickly made her way to the table in the entry where the landline phone had been as long as she could remember. "Elliotts," she answered.

"Grace, hi, it's Margo, how are you?"

"Margo, good to hear your voice."

She turned to Mrs. Elliott and said loudly, "Margo is on the phone, dear."

"How is she doing today?" Margo asked.

"Just fine. We're having our afternoon tea."

"I'm looking forward to seeing you next week."

"Yes. Will be nice for everyone to be together. Well, almost everyone..."

"Oh Grace, how are you doing?"

"Looking forward to Thanksgiving, dear."

"Yes. Yes, everyone is. I ordered dishes and silverware and glasses, and an extra table, to be delivered to the house Tuesday afternoon."

"I'll make a note of that."

"The best part is after the dinner, all we have to do is rinse everything and replace in the crates, they will pick up Friday. So much easier that way."

"I'll say."

"I get there Tuesday afternoon as well, maybe we can have tea together when I arrive, yes? Before the gang descends."

"Quite a crowd this year. Well, I guess the more the merrier. Certainly will be nice for your mom to have so much company."

"You think she will notice?"

"Oh, yes, dear. I think she notices much more than we realize. And just the sense of the crowd might be a comfort."

"I hope so."

"Yes."

"And Keisha will fly home with Becky and Jen. You remember Jennifer, Nina's girl?"

"Of course. Is she living in Oakland now?"

"She's in Berkeley. Same airport. And she told me that she and Becky had coffee recently, so perhaps they too will be friends."

"Lovely."

"Emma, Nina's youngest, is the only one still on the east coast, she loves Philadelphia. She's going to drive here, meet her parents at the airport, she said."

"How nice that Nina and Barrett will come as well. Such lovely friends."

"Yes, they're practically family and their parents are gone now, and Barrett's brother lives in London these days, so they will feast with us. The more the merrier, I agree."

"I've always wanted to go to Philadelphia," Grace mused. "So much history there."

"Go. Emma has a tiny apartment but I'm sure she would be glad to put you up."

"I'm a good couch sleeper," Grace murmured.

Margo chuckled. "I would imagine Emma would give you the bed."

"Well, some time, perhaps. Too much to do here now."

"Yes, thank you a million times over, Grace."

"No need Margo. No need. And what school is it where Keisha will be attending?"

"The San Francisco Art Institute. Great school. Great for her to spend all her time with fellow artists. She will get an excellent grounding for an artistic life. She is already tired of website work, and didn't want to work for Daniel's firm, said too close to home, so this is good."

"You must be proud."

"No more than you are of your daughters."

"Yes, thank you."

"I do worry. The arts, that's such a hard road. Keisha may always need a day job. And you know, we had nothing to do with this talent; it's in her DNA. When a child is not born to you, you realize how little influence you have. They come with their own destiny."

"They all do, whoever the parents."

"I guess I'd like to think we gave Keisha what she needed to grow into herself."

"Truth is, in the end, all we give our children is the color of their skin and a few body parts. Love and comfort goes a long way, of course, but the rest, out of our hands. The Lord giveth..."

"The Lord taketh away," Mrs. Elliott proclaimed loudly, as if a responsive reading in church, and Grace turned to her in surprise. Mrs. Elliott was staring straight into space, as if she hadn't spoken at all.

"Your mother just chimed into the conversation."

"She did?"

"Yes, sometimes she does, I guess when something strikes her worth saying."

Margo was silent and Grace imagined a tear drifting down her cheek.

"The Lord needs to give more," Grace muttered, surprising herself, and Margo.

"You sound tired today, Grace. Are you feeling all right?"

"Sorry dear. An old friend of mine was buried today. A fellow nurse."

"I am so sorry. Was she ill long?"

"You might say."

"Makes Thanksgiving all the more thankful, yes?"

"Yes." Grace answered loudly, to convince herself.

"Seems like ages since we all visited. Your grandkids will have grown, even in just this month."

"Yes, I'll be glad to see them," Grace whispered, slipping into the chair by the phone to take the weight off her wobbly legs.

"We have much to be grateful for."

"Yes."

"Tell Mom I'll be there soon."

"She knows you're coming, dear, I'm sure of it."

"Thank you, Grace. I don't know how we could have done this without you."

"I don't know how I could have managed my life without Mrs. Elliott."

Grace hung up the phone and returned to the couch. The two women sat silently for a few moments. Holiday music still filled the room. Grace knew some time soon she would grow tired of the incessant repetition of *Silent Night* and the *Nutcracker*, but at the moment, familiar melodies soothed.

"Should be snowing," Grace murmured. "I mean, the music ought to match the weather." She sighed. "Well, it's getting colder, and snow comes soon enough."

She reached for her sweater that was folded over a chair, pulled it around her body and buttoned up to the top button. She munched another cookie. She stopped talking for a few moments, exhausted by the sound of her own voice, and the heft of sorrow. At that moment, as so many moments during the last twenty years, she wished she might take a run, restore herself in some way, but that time had long passed.

Grace glanced at a magazine on the coffee table, a copy of *Real Simple* that Margo had long ago subscribed to for her mother and which made Grace cringe, as if life might be simplified by a smidgeon of this or a little less of that.

"My mother wanted to be cremated and my brothers were furious," she went on with her memories of Eleanor. "Not our way, you know, but it was her choice, was it not? I told them so and of course they argued with me, but since I ended up in charge… always the daughter in charge of such things, right? So I took care of it and we had a memorial service. Lots of people wanted to be there to say good-bye, we were all struck by how much she meant to so many people. But no coffin. Becky, even so young, was curious, fascinated in some way, as she tends to be, perhaps even then taken with the possibilities of impermanence."

"I kept the urn, you know. For a time. Right on the mantel. Never told my brothers, never told a soul. And then, for no special reason, I woke up one Saturday morning and took the ashes to the lake to shake them loose, let them roam free, as my mother would have liked. And when I shook them out, those ashes were picked up on the breeze, and drifted up toward the hillside, and then up again, toward the sky, as if the Lord Himself reached out from heaven and gathered them in his hands. That's what it felt like. I suppose that was a sign that my mother was forgiven her trespasses, such as they were. Some of the ashes settled on the rocks on the edge of the lake and for all I know they remain there still. As good a final resting place as any, although better to be able to visit, someplace, some spot, like the one I found for Jake."

Grace realized she was gasping for breath and she felt a flush rising through her chest into her cheeks like a fever. Her heart was pounding as if she were running rather than sitting utterly still.

"They sent his body in a bag, you know. A brown body bag," she whispered. "I had seen them at the hospital, a couple of times, but not... not my own. Not like this. I don't know how Dorene goes on. So young, with babies. All on her own. The military will help her transition. Small compensation, but something. I mean, I was young, I had three children when Ray left, but they were a bit older, and it was... different. Not death, although he might as well have been."

"Time heals," Grace murmured. "For some. Lord, I have to pull myself together for Thanksgiving. Focus on thanks."

Grace tried to catch her breath, her speech now as erratic as her breathing.

"Every time he went to the Middle East, I was terrified. The last time especially, I guess I knew his luck had run out. I knew the Lord would take him. I knew I had no right to keep my son. But, he was such a good boy. Even Delia would have spared him."

Grace had watched Delia disappear in place, her life dimmed day after day by despondency. In effect, Delia's life had been pummeled out of her as her son's had, and Grace held her tongue, in guilty silence, as Delia continued nursing, tending to patients as needed, but rarely smiling, as if to do so might bury the anguish, and with it, the tether to her precious boy, his memory discolored by the sight of him on the coroner's table that night. A vision Delia clung to, unwilling, or unable, to let it go, and refusing to accept the police explanation, certain her son had not participated in any wrongdoings. Certain he was an innocent victim, trapped by the wrong people, with no one to speak up for him.

"Perhaps time heals only those capable of healing," Grace mumbled.

Grace had convinced herself she could not help Delia, hypocrisy a further disgrace. She distanced herself, avoiding connection to the one human being she could not face, abandoning Delia as she believed she had abandoned Josiah.

Grace suddenly felt like a doll that has to be re-wound to prevent stalling in place. Her shift was coming to an end. When she left Mrs. Elliott's apartment, she would slowly make her way to her little place, warm a bit of leftover soup and put her feet up to watch some mindless television show, because she that's what she did most nights, until she fell asleep on the couch, until the next morning when she rose with the sun to begin again.

312

"Did I ever tell you I used to play Dodgeball?" Grace asked, trying one more time to revive. "I was just a girl, nine or ten, maybe eleven, and into middle school. Know that game? Kids run, running inside an invisible boundary, running in circles, trying to avoid the ball thrown by the other team. Dodge the ball, that's what I used to repeat under my breath, all the time I was running, so I wouldn't be hit. Dodge the ball, dodge the ball. Because, if you got hit, you were weak. You'd be tossed out of the game."

"And that's the way it feels these days. As if I've been tossed out of the game. Maybe never in the game at all. Always dodging the ball. Then again, I guess I took myself out of the game, didn't I? When I stopped living, stopped hoping for more. Never demanding more."

"Jake is dead because of me, because I lost the game," Grace whimpered.

Mrs. Elliott, who sat quietly staring into space, abruptly turned to Grace as if she had only just noticed she was there. She smiled the same broad smile she always had for her friends and neighbors.

"No!" The word came out harshly, even through smiling lips.

"No what?" Grace asked.

Mrs. Elliott stared directly at her, her eyes for the moment less vacant, beseeching Grace to speak the truth.

Silently commanded, Grace slowly recounted, for the first and only time, the description of Josiah's death. She spoke in a subdued voice, as if seated in a confessional, loud enough only to be heard by Mrs. Elliott, wavering now and then as she described the brutal assault on Delia's son. Tears streamed down her cheeks, unwilling to be held at bay any longer. She confessed to hiding behind the tree, withholding herself for fear of exposure, running home, hiding further in shame, abandoning her friend in her time of need only to protect herself, and never speaking the truth.

As she completed her narrative, Grace gave herself over to the sobs, her whole body convulsing as the words that had been stuck in her throat for so long escaped like prisoners from an inhumane confinement.

Mrs. Elliott, the instinct to comfort still within, wrapped her arms around Grace's shoulders and held her tightly, their bodies swaying in sync for several minutes, as Grace wept, her heart so weary, so many tears to be shed, she could hardly breathe.

"I know," Mrs. Elliott stated clearly.

Grace bolted from their embrace and extracted herself just enough from Mrs. Elliott's grip to face her. She sniveled her tears back and stared at Mrs. Elliott as they sat together with their hands clasped to each other's arms. Grace recognized in that split second, by the look in Mrs. Elliott's eyes, that she must have known all along. She would have read the local newspaper report and put together Grace's bloodied clothes and dazed demeanor with the horrible news, knowing that Grace often ran near the factory where Josiah's body was found. She knew too that terrible things happened to black boys, things that were rarely spoken of in a seemingly integrated community, words that would blight a collective sense of optimism and tarnish a mother's hope. She knew and she never said a word: a priest protecting Grace's secrets, and offering, without words, absolution.

"Oh, my," Grace cried. "I have forsaken the golden rule. I was a healer, not a killer. How could I stay silent?

And now, my boy is gone. My punishment through him. Why not me?"

She will never be able to resolve for herself why she, or her children for that matter, were more worthy of life than Josiah. She will never to her satisfaction answer that question or make peace with her penance. Yet, having spoken the words aloud, having at last voiced the truth, Grace surrendered to the healing power of Mrs. Elliott's smile.

Darkness had overtaken the apartment, the last of candlelight flickering wildly as Grace turned on table lamps, so the room was now infused with light from every corner, and, as she generated light, she regained her composure. She was nurse, not patient, she admonished herself. If there was comfort to be given, it was her job to do so.

She returned to her seat on the couch next to Mrs. Elliott, who was once again staring into the room without cognition.

"It will indeed be fine when the families are here for Thanksgiving," Grace said as she took Mrs. Elliott's hands again into her own. "We need to take time to be thankful, I know. No point belaboring the past. No point."

She paused a moment. "I thought more would change, you know? Because of the President. A fine black man in the White House. A dream come true. But the divides are just as great. Maybe greater. Just enough has changed since I was a girl, I suppose, to make it all seem, oh, what's the word? Acceptable? Palatable? As if a little better is good enough. Yes, that's it, good enough. But it's not really, is it? Not good enough at all."

Grace had ceased speaking to Mrs. Elliott; she spoke now to herself.

"We don't talk about these things until something terrible happens. A riot. Another election. Too many body bags. After the fact, they all tear it apart and dissect it on the radio and television, day and night, day and night, until nothing makes sense anymore, and we just go back to where we were."

She sighed deeply. "I want more," she whispered, as if testing her own voice. "I want more," she repeated, a little louder. "I want my children to be more than safe. I want them to have a real chance. To be truly equal. That's what I want for my children. For all the children."

Grace heard the key in the lock. Her watch was coming to an end. She took a deep breath.

"Perhaps the Lord will forgive me my trespasses," she pondered as she gathered the remaining glassware and dishes to take to the kitchen, then abruptly replaced them on the coffee table with a clang and sat down again to face Mrs. Elliott squarely.

"What I want for them, what I want for my children, is, for them…" She stumbled on her words. "What I want for them is to have the same rights as you have. You and your children, and grandchildren. The lily white children."

Her chest spread out before her with indignation, as if the spirit of her mother Eleanor had risen to inspire her.

"They should have the right to be truly free. No limitations. To know their rights, never question their rights. To be safe and sound. That's what I want for them, Ida," she cried loudly. "Is that too much to ask? Do I even have the right to ask?"

"Well, here with you, yes, I will ask. Being thankful for what we have, all well and good. We must always be grateful. But it's not enough. Not yet. Oh no, not enough. Not for Eleanor's grandchildren. Nor mine. Or yours. We must do better!"

Grace took a deep breath, squared her shoulders, and stood to greet the night nurse. She pressed down her dress and reclaimed the dishware. On the way to the kitchen, she turned off the radio and blew out the candle, and with it, her own words, buried in the last wisps of smoke curling into the air.

Mrs. Elliott sat motionless, as still as the silence. No response, no smile.

Keisha/2013

At fifteen, life had taught me undeniably that surrender,
in its place, was as honorable as resistance,
especially if one had no choice.
Maya Angelou

The courtroom is as still as a tomb. Moments pass so slowly one can hear the proverbial pin drop, barely a shuffle or cough now and then to break the tyrannical silence.

The last time they were all together was one year ago, at Mrs. Elliott's funeral, and before that, Leah's wedding, and before that, Thanksgiving, the previous year, only weeks after they had come together for the memorial service for Jake. A nearly annual assembly of this makeshift clan, bonded over time, despite their disparate legacies and skin tones, and, as extended and adopted family members separated by geography, they will continue to congregate mostly at holidays and celebrations, and funerals, not typically in a court of law, but here they are.

Mrs. Elliott might have been happy to see them together, whatever the circumstance, and in some way, Keisha feels the same. In any other family, she might sense only the shame of imposing this calamity upon them, but they all believe in her innocence, she knows this, and would rather be with her than anywhere else, she knows this too. Even after all the years since her adoption, she marvels at her circumstance, and wonders what might have become of her had she been left in foster care or taken in by another family. Or, perhaps it is true that all roads lead to the same place.

Keisha sits facing forward, avoiding eye contact, remaining stalwart for benefit of the watchers in the courtroom. She can imagine her family's embrace, without word or nod, and this has sustained her. As if a newly stitched quilt, with just one square left to be bound, they are thematically attached, even as they sit silently in their own seats, alone with private thoughts, lifetimes of regrets and misgivings weighing heavily on their hearts.

Barrett's hands are clasped together over his black leather-bound notepad, staring at the empty bench in the front of the room as if he might will the judge to appear and render the proper ruling. Free them from the shackles of this charade. He reaches one hand down to pat Keisha's hands, which rest together in her lap as if she is again the dutiful little girl, awaiting another caseworker to extract her for another placement. His touch momentarily ruffles her bearing: her fingers flinch, a tiny shudder reverberates through her. She is less stoical than when she was a child, hard as she tries, because she has become accustomed to the comfort of belonging, and such comfort ironically renders a person more vulnerable. More easily wounded.

Still, her expression remains impassive, unwavering. Barrett has admired Keisha's resilience since the day she arrived at Margo and Daniel's apartment with her bright eyes and worn sketchbook and her determination to always do better, and this alone deserves vindication, if not by the court, by whatever spiritual entity watches over her.

Barrett has been watching over her from the first, resolved from the moment she was adopted to ensure she had an advocate, someone who shared her cultural history. Someone closer to the color of her skin. And Keisha has always known Barrett was in her corner, a message first conveyed with the purchase of the painting that hangs prominently in her apartment in Oakland, his dedication fortified by constant presence at birthdays and graduations and art shows, or as a voice on the phone when private counsel was required. Her honorary Uncle understood best, despite Margo and Daniel's noble intentions, that this little black girl needed a counterweight to white parents and whitewashed neighborhoods and peach-toned schoolmates and the menacing media images associated with black culture, and this he has provided.

He never, however, anticipated having to sit beside his honorary ward in a court of law and Barrett wells with repressed rage at the persistent insidious racial divide in America, a divide his parents did their best to nullify and his marriage largely ignored. If he has learned anything during these proceedings, he has learned, rather confirmed, that the color line remains intact. Despite the dual elections of a black president, despite civil rights legislations and affirmative action, and despite his own achievements and the achievements of people like him, a psychic segregation prevails. Earth tones or hybrids they remain, clustered together on the color wheel by virtue of even a tiny drop of black blood, all but the purest of the pure whites are, if not legally, or even in principle, in reality, second class.

He has always intended to believe and behave differently, and his wife, Nina, despite the narrow-mindedness of her upbringing, fervently needs to believe differently, and they have transmitted their beliefs to their daughters, who in their own way have nearly dismissed the concept of the color line. However, truth has descended on them all over the years, one way or another, and now with the force of a tornado.

Emma, Barrett's younger daughter, who assiduously obliterated the memory of the assault by her friend's brother, banished shame long ago in favor of forgiveness. She has learned to pursue comprehension and compassion, without judgment, as hard as that is in moments like these, and this makes her an exemplary psychotherapist. She has juggled her growing client list in order to travel across country from Philadelphia to be with Keisha, her little sister in practice if not by blood, and, despite the horror of the situation, she swells with pride that Keisha did not allow herself to be violated. Proud that this once shy creature did not cave to the ferocity of racism, nor did she remain silent for fear of offense: she stood up for herself, she struck back, and in this, she is deserving of praise not condemnation.

Jennifer, her arm looped through sister Emma's, taking comfort as she also means to provide it, feels similar admiration, because Keisha refused to hide, she has faced both her attacker and those who will judge her with dignity.

Becky, the elder of Keisha's honorary sisters, has been uncharacteristically somber of late, less swift to anger than usual, more distressed, disheartened, that this sweet girl's dark skin-tone has make her a target for political rage. She sees Keisha's situation as merely another in a long line of assaults throughout history and throughout the world, as if the annihilation of one person, one woman, or any one race, might restore the rights of the others.

Sister Leah, joined in the pew by her husband, a black man who has known his share of skirmishes, and who also has taken time off from work to unite with the family, empathizes for everyone involved – mostly for Keisha, of course, but also for the parents of the boy who paid a terrible price for venting his hatred. No one wins, no matter the crime, and in this case, the consequence was especially severe: a boy dead, and a girl whose life will be forever altered for standing her ground.

Grace, who also sits in quiet contemplation, remembers Josiah, also destroyed by anger, a boy too young to know better, yet old enough to believe he had few options. A boy, she understands in hindsight, who must have meant to take more than he was given, stealing from those who steal from others seemingly less a crime. Josiah stood alone against his adversaries and paid for his error in judgment with his life, while Keisha fought back. During the testimony, Grace was chilled to the core as the police described the altercation and as the medical examiner expounded on the consequences of the assault. Even as the details came into focus, and she more than most understood what had happened to the boy's body, she too felt, unexpectedly, the same pride that everyone felt for Keisha, a girl who might have succumbed to the danger. The odds were not in her favor, but she fought back, driven by an unassailable disposition for self-preservation. However, no matter the outcome, Grace knows Keisha will live with the memory forever. Memory unfaltering in its censure.

Keisha absorbs everyone's good will, nevertheless she wonders if she will become a poster child for yet another exhibition of racism. Or, will she fade from public consciousness as merely another glitch on the cultural radar? Neither conclusion will make a difference. They all know this, and that may be the most disheartening reality of all. No matter the determination of the court, people believe what they choose to believe. Little will change.

That day last fall, the day of the 2012 presidential election, Keisha bolted from her drawing class in downtown San Francisco the moment the instructor announced dismissal, in order to make her way to a voting booth near her apartment across the bay. She sat on the BART train, her heart pounding with excitement, and she listened to animated conversation around her speculating on the possibilities, as she had listened for weeks to classmates and teachers argue whether or not President Obama might be elected to a second term. She had spoken on the subject often by phone and Skype to her parents, Margo uncharacteristically uncertain, Daniel cautiously optimistic but unwilling to predict, as if he might taint the outcome, and they regaled her with some of the crazy phone conversations they had been having with the undecided during calls made from Brooklyn Democratic campaign headquarters, where they patiently answered lingering questions and offered a dose of sanity to counter the manic harangue of the media.

In the weeks and even days before the election, handicappers and statisticians had flooded news outlets with prophecies of all sorts, but despite Keisha's concern that President Obama, her president, the first ballot she had cast, the first president to reflect her family history, might fail to secure a second term, she suspended her anxiety in favor of optimism.

A few days before the election, in need of reassurance, Keisha stopped at Becky's apartment in Oakland, not far from her own, which Becky shared with her boyfriend, a similarly vociferous and existential assistant professor named Lee. Keisha had grown increasingly fond of Becky's quirky personality and incessant quest for enlightenment, and Becky, now thirty-four years old, arrogance tempered by age and permanence, and a year-long relationship with the UC Berkeley philosopher, took her responsibility to Mrs. Elliott's granddaughter seriously. However they met infrequently because their schedules rarely matched. Becky bartended at night and took classes on-line during the day in preparation for college, while Keisha worked mornings at the art supply center at the Institute and took classes in the afternoons, often into the early evening, before retiring to the library or her studio apartment to study or draw.

Keisha also preferred to spend time with Jennifer, who lived in a section of Berkeley on the border of Oakland, and who felt more like a true sister. Jennifer had completed a course of study to become a music engineer and recently entered into a business partnership with another former stage manager to establish a recording studio in Oakland. She regularly made time to meet Keisha for coffee or a meal, and Keisha was often invited to dinner at the iconic craftsman cottage off College Avenue that Jennifer shared with her partner, Mary, a music professor at Mills College. That day, just before the election, Jennifer was busy with work, and Keisha, unwilling to confront her anxiety alone, made her way to Becky's apartment.

"Lee has advisory session, and I'm crazed with this paper I have to write, never my strong suit, you know, so you are a good excuse for a break," Becky said by way of greeting at the door, ushering Keisha into the kitchen. She poured them both cups of steaming coffee from a French press, which Becky had recently acquired and proclaimed the one true method of coffee making.

They sat at a round, glass-topped dining table, nestled into the bay window at the far end of the main room of the apartment, a space large enough to carve out an eating area and study and a proper living room, with the bedroom off to the side. Keisha noticed the desk was covered with Lee's papers and books, while Becky's laptop and notebooks were scattered across an oversized rumpled couch, matching pillows tossed to the floor.

Becky, reading Keisha's thoughts, as she often and disturbingly seemed able to do, commented she preferred to study on the couch.

"I'm not the sit-at-the-desk sort of student. I prefer cozy. And that way, sometimes, Lee can do his thing and I can do mine, as if separate but equal." She chuckled, always one to enjoy her own brand of humor.

"How goes it?" Keisha asked, reaching for a sugar cube in the crystal container on the table that Grace had sent to Becky when she at last settled in one place.

"Well, you know, I'm a student of life, so to speak, but better to have a degree, maybe I'll be able to get a day job in a few years, once this damn recession is over. Although there's no recession at the bar, that's for sure. But I'm sort of done with the night thing. Lee and I hardly have time together. So, study I must to get into college, not Berkeley, mind you, not even close to possible, even with Lee there, but plenty of good schools around for social work."

"Social work," Keisha murmured and shook her head with admiration and dismay. "You're going to see some nasty shit, you know."

"Yes, I know, but I can handle that. Nobody is going to mess with me." Becky laughed and Keisha laughed with her. "And you? How's the budding Rembrandt?"

"Ha! My portfolio will take all year, but it's been great to have that work to concentrate on, because I am crazy nervous about this election," Keisha answered.

"You should be. They are determined to dispatch him to oblivion. The house slave must be returned to the cotton fields."

"Do you really believe that? My father said that even if he loses, which he does not believe he will, it would not be a romp."

"The count won't matter in the end, as long as they rid themselves of the pretender to the throne, in their eyes."

"So you support him now?" Keisha asked coyly, challenging Becky to admit her previous resistance.

"Of course, he is our president," Becky answered. "And I sure don't want to see him take a political whipping."

Rather than assurance, Becky made Keisha more anxious, so she clung to the voices of others who believed he would win, as if the communal opinion of her extended family was the only statistic that mattered. Her parents believed he would win, Barrett and Nina believed he would win, and most of her sisters believed he would win.

"He will win," she repeated under her breath over and over until the election, like a prayer or a mantra, something that might have served her well during the court proceedings, if she had been able to believe as vehemently in her own future.

There had been a palpable static electricity in the air the day of the election. Not as profound as the landmark vote of 2008, but for many, equally significant: another opportunity for Americans to make a statement on national identity. The stunning rise of conservative politics in Washington was never more evident than on television news in the final days and hours. Pundits on all sides railed against one another, although more moderate commentators did their best to suggest that regardless of the winner, all signs pointed to sustained disappointment in a speedy economic revival, and even if voters were ripe for change, the prevailing pattern of roadblocks and verbal assaults and potential government shut downs had sobered them nearly to the point of apathy.

Keisha believed her family's prognostications and she believed the high-profile pollsters and statisticians who claimed in the final days before the election that Obama would win, yet her stomach fluttered as she made her way to the voting booth that day, the same sort of butterflies zooming in and out that she often felt as a child, and even now, whenever she had to present a project at school. She could barely eat a bite that morning and she found herself rushing to the train and rushing from the train, even though the voting booths were open late, and she knew that all she could do was cast her vote and hope for the best, add her voice to the prayers that collective wisdom might prevail.

By midnight, half the country was celebrant, half confounded, and Keisha had killed a white boy.

"So let's make sure we make this clear. Did you kill Bill Wallace?" the defending attorney asked when all the expert testimony had been given and Keisha was called to confirm the details, to speak her own truth.

"Yes," Keisha answered, looking him squarely in the eye, not with defiance, with certainty, although she thought the judge, peering toward her with a severe expression, might have heard her knees knocking.

"Did you mean to kill him?"

"No."

"Did you know you killed him?"

"No, not at first."

"How many times did you kick him?"

"Twice, I think."

"You're not certain?"

"It all happened so fast, no, I am not certain."

"And you had a minor concussion from being knocked off your bicycle to the ground."

"Yes, but I didn't know that, I was just terrified."

"But you know that now."

"Yes, I know that now."

After she had cast her vote, and unable to quell the anxiety, Keisha spent the late afternoon at Joaquin Miller Park, where she often perched on the grass to sketch the giant redwood trees. She drew them as if gargantuan mythological creatures, in garish colors, their multiple branches like long arms extended to the sky, plucking birds to their fingers as if preparing to lick their tips after a satisfying meal. She had become known at school for her surrealistic landscapes, harkening back to the painting she first called her own, and hoped some time soon to have a sufficient body of work to entice gallery interest.

That day, the drawing was more therapy than creative endeavor, and the time passed slowly until nearly dusk, when she packed her supplies into her backpack and climbed back onto her bicycle to race to Becky's bar to join the crowd watching the returns. Jennifer and Mary awaited her there, and Lee, and an assortment of their friends, and a few neighbors Keisha recognized, most hoping to celebrate victory rather than convene a wake.

The crowd was boisterous and buzzed when she arrived. The sheer exuberance of the young racially mixed throng was invigorating, as spirited as a Sunday football crowd. Becky had turned the volume as high as possible on the multiple LCD screens perched over the bar, yet hardly a spoken word was heard. Banners floating across the screens reported what they most needed to know, and computer simulated state maps shifted color now and then to announce projections.

Every table seat was taken and patrons were lined up three deep at the long bar. Lee waved to Keisha from the far end and she made her way toward them. Jennifer greeted Keisha with a hug and offered her seat, squeezing onto a barstool with Mary, and as she sat, Mary wrapped her arms around her to keep her from slipping off. Becky, with a nod and a smile, handed Keisha a bottle of light beer, then turned to serve others. Keisha noticed that the vast majority of customers were wearing blue or purple, those in red favoring other bars.

Returns from the east coast were coming in, without surprises, and everyone knew, as the commentators continued to remind them, that the election would come down to the so-called swing states, among them Ohio, Becky's pedigree, and Virginia, Mary's home state.

California would surely vote Democratic, although nothing was certain, and even as the analysts attempted to predict nearly to the precinct level, the Romney campaign was in full celebratory swing, confusing those watching and providing additional fodder for commentators.

The crowd alternately cheered or groaned as state returns came in, one by one, with a bit of mostly good-natured grumbling here and there, and Keisha began to relax into the prospect of victory. "He will win," she repeatedly to herself, again and again. Another four years, she allowed herself to believe, of Barack Obama's face on the television screen, Michelle Obama's graceful presence, and an occasional sighting of their beautiful dark-skinned children. Even with the sinister call among the most venomous voices to bring the white back to the White House, Keisha began to believe that Obama might be the face of the country for another four years.

By early evening, predictions of high-profile statisticians like Nate Silver seemed to be assured and a jubilant atmosphere reigned. Keisha had a splitting headache by then and she was exhausted as much by relief as the prolonged anxiety leading up to the finale. She excused herself to throw cold water on her face in the ladies room and, as she stood at the sink, she stared at herself in the mirror, wondering suddenly what she might look like as an older woman. She had never imagined herself elegant, nor graceful, like Michelle Obama, but she might be a woman of distinction, a woman who held her head high and whom art students like herself might someday admire. She smiled at the visage of her older self before returning to the bar to say goodbye to the group and return home, where she hoped to nap briefly before Obama's acceptance speech.

"How many times did you kick him?" the attorney had asked in the first interview, and she was asked again each time she was prodded to recount the incident, first to Becky, subsequently to the police, to Margo and Daniel and Barrett, the attorneys and the prosecutors.

Becky's instinct that night was to contain the situation. She believed that without eyewitness, no one would know what happened, and the greater danger would be for Keisha's version of the assault to be challenged.

"Keisha will be punished because there was no witness," she whispered to Lee as Keisha sat with her head bent over folded arms on the bar, too shaken to speak. "No one to speak up for her, no matter the physical evidence," Becky argued. "A black girl killed a white boy, it's that simple."

Keisha lifted her head. "Call Barrett, please," she whimpered, and Becky made the call.

Barrett advised Keisha to do the right thing and go to the police, and she never questioned his direction, despite the terror, because she knew, as he knew, she could not live with silence. More to the point, she had stood her ground against hatred and she felt an obligation to continue to stand her ground in her own defense. Barrett would be her ally and her parents as well. They would stand up for her, she knew, even against their own.

Each time she recounted the events of that night, she cemented the facts in her own mind, because the first couple of days her memory was a bit blurry. Over time, she was able to recall the incident clearly, in the same way each time, and in the same words, recollection gelling in her memory in order to make sense of it. Although she was not always certain that her memory of the event matched the truth.

When she left the bar, she guided her bike along the back alley behind buildings because the streets were already overflowing with people and honking cars. Keisha often preferred the alley route, peeking into rear windows behind shops and houses, back doors the entry for friends and family and thus a welcoming place. She never minded the putrid whiff of rotting garbage in trash barrels scattered along the way, what she considered the organic odor of a bustling city, like the loamy scent of soil freshly turned and mulched for planting. From the alley that night, she glimpsed residents cooking at the stove or enjoying a late meal, the flickering of televisions brighter than usual, while other windows were totally dark because so many people were on the streets or at bars or with friends on this important night.

As she glided into an extended alley, only one block from her apartment, two young men, barely out of adolescence, suddenly blocked her path. She thought nothing of it at first, assuming them to be woozy drunks making their way home, but as she attempted to skim to the side, the taller of the two reached out and pushed her off the bicycle. She landed first on her hip, the bicycle on top of her, and her skull hit the pavement hard, leaving her briefly dazed. When she looked up again, through slightly blurred vision, the bike had been shunted aside, she was on her back, and one of the boys was poised above her with a fist coming toward her face; however, the other, the one who had first knocked her down, had grabbed his compatriot's arm to hold him back.

She shook her head to try to clear her vision and felt a searing pain shoot down her neck and jaw and into her back. The boy hovered over her, with his other hand pressed hard against her chest, holding her down, and she knew at once she was in grave danger by the barrage of racial slurs being hurled at her and the sickening smell of alcohol on his breath. She would discover his name much later: Bill, the boy who would be labeled the victim, the fatality, the casualty of a confrontation in an alley.

Having consumed multiple shots with beer chasers during the long evening, the two boys, both white, both trainers at a local gym, had sullenly watched the election returns at another bar, commiserating with other drunks that the country was going to the dogs. There was angry talk that they would have to take matters into their own hands. Bill's friend, Jamie Edwards, contended that conversation was hypothetical. He suggested they might join an opposition group, maybe sign up to distribute flyers or sit at folding tables outside supermarkets and convince passers-by that Obama is the new Hitler.

Jamie had come to his senses when he saw how hard Keisha fell to the ground and realized the dire intentions of his friend. Sobered suddenly by the severity of their behavior, he did not wish to see Bill do physical harm to the girl. Jamie's mother relied in part on his income and his sisters still lived at home, and even though he was known to taunt women, literally flex his masculine muscle, he was not violent and he certainly did not want to end up in prison.

"We have to do something, we have to show these people once and for all that the country has gone mad. America is white, god damn it! These people have to be put back in their place," Bill yelled, his eyes wild, as Jamie attempted to pull his arm away.

"She's just a girl, Billy," Jamie pleaded.

"Don't be a pussy, I'm not gonna kill her. I'm gonna teach her a lesson."

"You're on your own then," Jamie snarled, as he turned to leave.

As Bill shouted at Jamie to stay, Keisha seized the opportunity to thrust her knee into his groin, and he fell back, grabbing at Keisha's leg to restrain her from further offense. Keisha kicked at him again to free herself from his grip. Bill may have meant to stand, or he twisted on an angle to avoid the full force of the kick, so the last kick knocked him down hard, momentarily winded, or so it seemed. Keisha seized that moment to stand.

"How many times did you kick him?"
Each time she answered the same.
"Twice, I think."
"You're not certain?"
"It all happened so fast, I don't remember for sure."

The medical examiner explained that the number of kicks was inconsequential. Once would have been enough because the autopsy revealed a latent genetic frailty that made his carotid artery susceptible to instant death. One blow was all it would take. Martial arts experts know of this possibility so they teach students to avoid blows to the neck. Keisha's attorney argued that because a strike to the neck or throat might cause death, the legal litmus test is that such a strike is the deliberate application of deadly force, justified only when in fear of one's life or imminent danger.

Keisha knew none of this then, no one knew until the findings were released and even then, testimony was taken. Jamie had been found and interrogated and reported only that he fled as it was happening, before he had any idea that his friend was killed.

Once Bill was down on the ground and momentarily defused, Keisha stood, and, wobbly as she was, she kicked at Bill one more time, as if a reflex, to make sure he would stay down. She glared at him, prepared to defend herself again, when suddenly she lifted her foot and stomped on his neck once more, as if to stomp out his very existence.

By then he lay lifeless, a blank expression in his open eyes and blood streaming from his lips. Keisha stood over his body, unsteady on her feet, gasping for breath, and when she looked around for assistance, she saw no one. No one to help, no one to witness. Jamie seemed to have vanished. Keisha was alone, as if an orphan all over again.

She jumped on her bike and raced back to the bar, despite blurry vision and the searing pain reverberating through her skull. She prayed that her sisters were still there. They would know what to do.

Now the facts had been heard. There was no question she had acted in self-defense, but Bill's parents wanted legal action. At the very least, a hearing was required because a boy was dead. A black girl had killed a white boy and this could not be ignored.

Bill's parents, and members of the community, believed there would be justice for him, that he was belligerent and unruly, but not a vigilante. The media had a field day and his parents had expected more sympathy from the court. A white boy, drunk, sure, behaving badly, yes, but murderous? Lethal intention? No, there had to be more. They believed in their own righteousness and they approached the court with the superiority of a white family facing the family of a black girl.

They had not reckoned with Keisha having white parents. They had not imagined the high level of defense she would secure. They had not expected Jamie's testimony to vilify their son. They were advised that the circumstances of his death might not warrant an inquiry much less further litigation, yet they hoped for better. They hoped to clear their son's name. They hoped for retribution. They sat quietly in the court, angry and impotent, awaiting a decision from the judge.

Jamie was the only person who knew exactly how many times Keisha kicked at Bill, but he would never say. He would never speak of the killing. He had meant to flee the scene, believing that beating up a helpless black girl was a bad idea, no matter how angry they were at Obama. And although he would think of Keisha, and speak of her, as that black bitch who killed Billy, he privately, grudgingly, respected her for standing up to her attackers. What he had taught his sisters to do. Even if Bill meant only to hurt her, to shake her up a bit, Jamie knew that such things have a way of getting out of hand.

A lot of people had seen them at the bar. They heard Jamie yell that Obama may be president again, but he was not his president, he would never be his president, and they heard Bill shouting they needed to rid the country of black folks – all the colored people and immigrants, all who do not belong. These had been their last cries before they stormed out the back door toward the alley and began their drunken march home.

Failing to convince Bill not to hurt the girl, Jamie sprinted down the alley, intending to make his way home and pretend he wasn't even there. Was it fear for his future or for the girl that made him stop and look back? Perhaps an innate sense of fairness? He would never be sure.

He stopped in his tracks and watched from behind the corner of a building, where he could see but not be seen. Where he could be certain the girl would only be shaken up, nothing more.

By then, Bill was flat on the ground, and Jamie saw Keisha kick at his lifeless body. He was stunned by her aggression, but believed there was nothing to be done. Surely Bill would only be badly bruised. Embarrassed.

He turned and ran home. He never described how his buddy was killed. What would they think of him? Abandoning his friend that way. Proving to be a coward as well as a racist.

When the police identified Jamie as an accomplice, and took his statement, he told the truth about how it started and what happened before he left the scene, but with this one crucial omission. He claimed he never turned back. He never saw Keisha kick his friend to his death.

He agonized at first about what to say, but he could not bring himself to speak the truth, and once he had made his statement, he could not renege. No, he could not go to jail. His mother needed him. And how would he ever be able to look his sisters in the eye?

Even Jamie understood that Keisha would be treated differently because she had skin the color of tar. But she was also a girl, so the court might be lenient, he thought, as if the two things might cancel each other out. He also knew a whole lot of people had something at stake and he wasn't even sure how he would have cast his vote, because even though Keisha was guilty, she was also innocent. And, at court, she was innocent until proven guilty and only he could prove her so, but not without divulging his complicity.

He would never confess to deserting his friend. It was not his place to decide guilt or innocence, only to live with regret. The decision was up to the court, and Jamie consoled himself with the belief that, in truth, they were all guilty and all innocent.

A rear door opens and the bailiff calls for all to rise as the judge enters, and then calls again for all to be seated. Keisha remains standing. She has seen in movies and on television that the accused must stand while a verdict is rendered, but this is not a trial, and Barrett nudges her arm and whispers to her that she can sit. Still, Keisha remains standing. She squares her shoulders to face the judge. She remains standing as if once again standing her ground.

The judge says nothing, rather gazes head on at Keisha. Her fate is in his hands and he appreciates her respect. He can see that she is terrified. Barrett, seeing the judge's expression as a tacit endorsement, stands with her. He is followed by chief counsel, and, one by one, Keisha's assembly of family and friends. Becky first, Grace and Leah, Margo and Daniel, Nina, Jennifer and Emma. Husbands and partners stand with them. Friends. Supporters. They all stand, the scrape of their chairs creating sufficient disturbance for the bailiff to step forward, intending to instruct them to sit, but the judge motions to him to stay in place.

Confused, but unwilling to defy the court, the observers stand as well, until at last, the only people not standing are Bill's family, seated with Jamie and his mother and sisters. Perplexed, realizing they are the only exceptions, they are the last to stand.

Keisha briefly turns to face all the people who are standing. With a grateful smile, she returns her gaze to the judge, who has watched with interest as his courtroom filled like a standing ovation at the theater. A silent appreciative audience. He understands they wish to align themselves with the defendant, as well as the principles of fairness, and, in that moment, he is struck with the realization, not the first time in his long tenure, that although justice is meant to be blind, and he has always done his best to fulfill the creed of the court, true justice may be out of his hands.

END

For my wonderful compassionate daughters: Dana & Julie.

Readers
Chris, Robyn, Leslie, MK, Liz, Carole,
Deborah, Elizabeth, Deana, Marianna.

Cheerleaders
Carol G, Laura, Ginger & Joe, Byron, CQ, Carol F, Edie,
Andrea, Hollie, Joy, Dan, Christine, Amy, Barbara DeMB.

Special thanks to History and Women's Studies Professor,
Elizabeth Hohl, PhD.
And to Marianna for a piercing red pen.

Inspiration
Maya Angelou, James Baldwin, Michael Franti, Marita
Golden, Herbie Hancock, Billie Holiday, Langston Hughes,
Janis Joplin, Nella Larsen, Joni Mitchell, Toni Morrison,
Tillie Olsen, Wallace Thurman, Alice Walker,
Isabel Wilkerson, Richard Wright.
Big Fat Mama lyrics by Tommy Johnson.

Hugs to the bookies at
Diane's Books of Greenwich and *Laguna Beach Books.*

Thanks for writing space and iced-tea
Pain du Monde, Dana Point, CA. *Zinc,* Corona del Mar, CA.
Montage, Laguna Beach, CA. *Café Contento,* San Miguel de
Allende, MX. *Le Pain Quotidian*, NYC and Greenwich, CT.

Cover Design
Lindsay Wiley Designs

Colors of the Wheel

A Reader's Guide

1. Grace is emotionally paralyzed when Josiah is killed – why is her impotence a tragedy? Who suffers most?

2. The concept of the willing suspension of disbelief plays an integral role in Margo and Nina's way of thinking – is it liberal ideology or ignorance?

3. What does Ray represent? Why did he leave?

4. Keisha, the one black character, is the one who ends up fighting for her life and for her future – why is she so important to everyone else?

5. Both elder daughters are gutsy, however Becky is outspoken and Jennifer holds her tongue – what is their common ground?

6. Younger sisters Emma and Leah view their circumstance and their skin color with greater equanimity – why? What does this bode for the future?

7. Nina sought safety in a way that betrayed her values – why?

8. Silence is a common theme throughout. Why? What is the significance of Mrs. Elliott's silence?

9. What does Eleanor represent and why does her shadow cross generations?

10. Grace silently witnessed the murder of a black boy and 22 years later, a white boy stays silent on the murder of his white friend – was there any difference?

11. Keisha is both innocent and guilty – is that possible?

12. What does the judge mean when he hypothesizes that justice is out of his hands?

Recommended Readings

A short list of good books on race and the color line.

Color Complex:
The Politics of Skin Color Among African Americans
Kathy Russell, Midge Wilson, Ronald Hall

Don't Play in the Sun:
One Woman's Journey Through the Color Complex
Marita Golden

The Sweeter the Juice: A Family Memoir in Black and White
Shirlee Taylor Haizlip

The Blacker the Berry
Wallace Thurman

Women on the Color Line: Evolving Stereotypes and the Writings
of George Washington Cable, Grace King, Kate Chopin
Anna Shannon Elfenbein

Silences
Tillie Olsen

The Souls of Black Folk: Essays and Sketches
W. E. B. Du Bois

Anything and everything by
Maya Angelou
James Baldwin
Langston Hughes
Nella Larsen
Toni Morrison
Alice Walker
Richard Wright

www.randykraftwriter.com

randykraftwriter.blogspot.com

@ocbookblogger